A WORD, ONLY A WORD,
Complete

By

Georg Ebers

Translated from the German by
Mary J. Safford

Published by Left of Brain Books

Copyright © 2023 Left of Brain Books

ISBN 978-1-396-32386-7

First Edition

PUBLISHER'S PREFACE

About the Book

A Word, Only a Word is a novel by Georg Moritz Ebers.

About the Author

Georg Moritz Ebers (1837 - 1898)

"Georg Moritz Ebers (Berlin, March 1, 1837 - Tutzing, Bavaria, August 7, 1898), German Egyptologist and novelist, discovered the Egyptian medical papyrus, of ca 1550 BCE, named for him (see Ebers papyrus) at Luxor (Thebes) in the winter of 1873-74. Now in the library of the University of Leipzig, the Ebers papyrus is among the most important ancient Egyptian medical papyri. It is one of two of the oldest preserved medical documents anywhere, the other main source being the Edwin Smith papyrus (c. 1600 BCE).

At Gottingen he studied jurisprudence, and at Berlin Oriental languages and archaeology. Having made a special study of Egyptology, he became in 1865 Dozent in Egyptian language and antiquities at Jena, and in 1870 he was appointed professor in these subjects at Leipzig. He had made two scientific journeys to Egypt, and his first work of importance, Agypten und die BÃ¼cher Moses, appeared in 1867-1868. In 1874 he edited the celebrated medical papyrus (Papyrus Ebers) which he had discovered in Thebes (translation by H. Joachim, 1890)."

(Quote from wikipedia.org)

CONTENTS

VOLUME 1

CHAPTER I.

"A word, only a word!" cried a fresh, boyish voice, then two hands were loudly clapped and a gay laugh echoed through the forest. Hitherto silence had reigned under the boughs of the pines and tops of the beeches, but now a wood-pigeon joined in the lad's laugh, and a jay, startled by the clapping of hands, spread its brown wings, delicately flecked with blue, and soared from one pine to another.

Spring had entered the Black Forest a few weeks before. May was just over, yet the weather was as sultry as in midsummer and clouds were gathering in denser and denser masses. The sun was still some distance above the horizon, but the valley was so narrow that the day star had disappeared, before making its majestic entry into the portals of night.

When it set in a clear sky, it only gilded the border of pine trees on the crest of the lofty western heights; to-day it was invisible, and the occasional, quickly interrupted twittering of the birds seemed more in harmony with the threatening clouds and sultry atmosphere than the lad's gay laughter.

Every living creature seemed to be holding its breath in anxious suspense, but Ulrich once more laughed joyously, then bracing his bare knee against a bundle of faggots, cried:

"Give me that stick, Ruth, that I may tie it up. How dry the stuff is, and how it snaps! A word! To sit over books all day long for one stupid word--that's just nonsense!"

"But all words are not alike," replied the girl.

"Piff is paff, and paff is puff!" laughed Ulrich. "When I snap the twigs, you always hear them say 'knack, knack,' and 'knack' is a word too. The juggler Caspar's magpie, can say twenty."

"But father said so," replied Ruth, arranging the dry sticks. "He toils hard, but not for gold and gain, to find the right words. You are always wanting to know what he is looking for in his big books, so I plucked up courage to ask him, and now I know. I suppose he saw I was astonished, for he smiled just as he does when you have asked some foolish question at lessons, and added that a word was no trifling thing and should not be despised, for God had made the world out of one single word."

Ulrich shook his head, and after pondering a few minutes, replied.

"Do you believe that?"

"Father said so," was the little girl's only answer. Her words expressed the firm, immovable security of childish confidence, and the same feeling sparkled in her eyes. She was probably about nine years old, and in every respect a perfect contrast to her companion, her senior by several summers, for the latter was strongly built, and from beneath his beautiful fair locks a pair of big blue eyes flashed defiance at the world, while Ruth was a delicate little creature, with slender limbs, pale cheeks, and coal-black hair.

The little girl wore a fashionably-made, though shabby dress, shoes and stockings--the boy was barefoot, and his grey doublet looked scarcely less worn than the short leather breeches, which hardly reached his knees; yet he must have had some regard for his outer man, for a red knot of real silk was fastened on his shoulder. He could scarcely be the child of a peasant or woodland laborer--the brow was too high, the nose and red lips were too delicately moulded, the bearing was too proud and free.

Ruth's last words had given him food for thought, but he left them unanswered until the last bundle of sticks was tied up. Then he said hesitatingly:

"My mother--you know.... I dare not speak of her before father, he goes into such a rage; my mother is said to be very wicked--but she never was so to me, and I long for her day after day, very, very much, as I long for nothing else. When I was so high, my mother told me a great many things, such queer things! About a man, who wanted treasures, and before whom mountains opened at a word he knew. Of course it's for such a word your father is seeking."

"I don't know," replied the little girl. "But the word out of which God made the whole earth and sky and all the stars must have been a very great one."

Ulrich nodded, then raising his eyes boldly, exclaimed:

"Ah, if he should find it, and would not keep it to himself, but let you tell me! I should know what I wanted."

Ruth looked at him enquiringly, but he cried laughingly: "I shan't tell. But what would you ask?"

"I? I should ask to have my mother able to speak again like other people. But you would wish...."

"You can't know what I would wish."

"Yes, yes. You would bring your mother back home again."

"No, I wasn't thinking of that," replied Ulrich, flushing scarlet and fixing his eyes on the ground.

"What, then? Tell me; I won't repeat it."

"I should like to be one of the count's squires, and always ride with him when he goes hunting."

"Oh!" cried Ruth. "That would be the very thing, if I were a boy like you. A squire! But if the word can do everything, it will make you lord of the castle and a powerful count. You can have real velvet clothes, with gay slashes, and a silk bed."

"And I'll ride the black stallion, and the forest, with all its stags and deer, will belong to me; as to the people down in the village, I'll show them!"

Raising his clenched fist and his eyes in menace as he uttered the words, he saw that heavy rain-drops were beginning to fall, and a thunder-shower was rising.

Hastily and skilfully loading himself with several bundles of faggots, he laid some on the little girl's shoulders, and went down with her towards the valley, paying no heed to the pouring rain, thunder or lightning; but Ruth trembled in every limb.

At the edge of the narrow pass leading to the city they stood still. The moisture was trickling down its steep sides and had gathered into a reddish torrent on the rocky bottom.

"Come!" cried Ulrich, stepping on to the edge of the ravine, where stones and sand, loosened by the wet, were now rattling down.

"I'm afraid," answered the little girl trembling. "There's another flash of lightning! Oh! dear, oh, dear! how it blazes!--oh! oh! that clap of thund-er!"

She stooped as if the lightning had struck her, covered her face with her little hands, and fell on her knees, the bundle of faggots slipping to the ground. Filled with terror, she murmured as if she could command the mighty word: "Oh, Word, Word, get me home!"

Ulrich stamped impatiently, glanced at her with mingled anger and contempt, and muttering reproaches, threw her bundle and his own into the ravine, then roughly seized her hand and dragged her to the edge of the cliff.

Half-walking, half-slipping, with many an unkind word, though he was always careful to support her, the boy scrambled down the steep slope with his companion, and when they were at last standing in the water at the bottom of the gully, picked up the dripping fagots and walked silently on, carrying her burden as well as his own.

After a short walk through the running water and mass of earth and stones, slowly sliding towards the valley, several shingled roofs appeared, and the little girl uttered a sigh of relief; for in the row of shabby houses, each standing by itself, that extended from the forest to the level end of the ravine, was her own home and the forge belonging to her companion's father.

It was still raining, but the thunder-storm had passed as quickly as it rose, and twilight was already gathering over the mist-veiled houses and spires of the little city, from which the street ran to the ravine. The stillness of the evening was only interrupted by a few scattered notes of bells, the finale of the mighty peal by which the warder had just been trying to disperse the storm.

The safety of the town in the narrow forest-valley was well secured, a wall and ditch enclosed it; only the houses on the edge of the ravine were unprotected. True, the mouth of the pass was covered by the field pieces on the city wall, and the strong tower beside the gate, but it was not incumbent on the citizens to provide for the safety of the row of houses up there. It was called the Richtberg and nobody lived there except the rabble, executioners, and poor folk who were not granted the rights of citizenship. Adam, the smith, had forfeited his, and Ruth's father, Doctor Costa, was a Jew, who ought to be thankful that he was tolerated in the old forester's house.

The street was perfectly still. A few children were jumping over the mud-puddles, and an old washerwoman was putting a wooden vessel under the gutter, to collect the rain-water.

Ruth breathed more freely when once again in the street and among human beings, and soon, clinging to the hand of her father, who had come to meet her, she entered the house with him and Ulrich.

CHAPTER II.

WHILE the boy flung the damp bundles of brushwood on the floor beside the hearth in the doctor's kitchen, a servant from the monastery was leading three horses under the rude shed in front of the smith Adam's work-shop The stately grey-haired monk, who had ridden the strong cream-colored steed, was already standing beside the embers of the fire, pressing his hands upon the warm chimney.

The forge stood open, but spite of knocking and shouting, neither the master of the place, nor any other living soul appeared. Adam had gone out, but could not be far away, for the door leading from the shop into the sitting-room, was also unlocked.

The time was growing long to Father Benedict, so for occupation he tried to lift the heavy hammer. It was a difficult task, though he was no weakling, yet it was not hard for Adam's arm to swing and guide the burden. If only the man had understood how to govern his life as well as he managed his ponderous tool!

He did not belong to Richtberg. What would his father have said, had he lived to see his son dwell here?

The monk had known the old smith well, and he also knew many things about the son and his destiny, yet no more than rumor entrusts to one person concerning another's life. Even this was enough to explain why Adam had become so reserved, misanthropic and silent a man, though even in his youth lie certainly had not been what is termed a gay fellow.

The forge where he grew up, was still standing in the market-place of the little city below; it had belonged to his grandfather and great- grandfather. There had never been any lack of custom, to the annoyance of the wise magistrates, whose discussions were disturbed by the hammering that rang across the ill-paved square to the windows of the council-chamber; but, on the other hand, the idle hours of the watchmen under the arches of the ground-floor of the town-hall were sweetened by the bustle before the smithy.

How Adam had come from the market-place to the Richtberg, is a story speedily told.

He was the only child of his dead parents, and early learned his father's trade. When his mother died, the old man gave his son and partner his blessing, and some florins to pay his expenses, and sent him away. He went directly to Nuremberg, which the old man praised as the high-school of the smith's art, and there remained twelve years. When, at the end of that time, news came to Adam that his father was dead, and he had inherited the forge on the market-place, he wondered to find that he was thirty years old, and had gone no farther than Nuremberg. True, everything that the rest of the world could do in the art of forging might be learned there.

He was a large, heavy man, and from childhood had moved slowly and reluctantly from the place where he chanced to be.

If work was pressing, he could not be induced to leave the anvil, even when evening had closed in; if it was pleasant to sit over the beer, he remained till after the last man had gone. While working, he was as mute as the dead to everything that was passing around him; in the tavern he rarely spoke, and then said only a few words, yet the young artists, sculptors, workers in gold and students liked to see the stout drinker and good listener at the table, and the members of his guild only marvelled how the sensible fellow, who joined in no foolish pranks, and worked in such good earnest, held aloof from them to keep company with these hairbrained folk, and remained a Papist.

He might have taken possession of the shop on the market-place directly after his father's death, but could not arrange his departure so quickly, and it was fully eight months before he left Nuremberg.

On the high-road before Schwabach a wagon, occupied by some strolling performers, overtook the traveller. They belonged to the better class, for they appeared before counts and princes, and were seven in number. The father and four sons played the violin, viola and reboc, and the two daughters sang to the lute and harp. The old man invited Adam to take the eighth place in the vehicle, so he counted his pennies, and room was made for him opposite Flora, called by her family Florette. The musicians were going to the fair at Nordlingen, and the smith enjoyed himself so well with them, that he remained several days after reaching the goal of the journey. When he at last went away Florette wept, but he walked straight on until noon, without looking back. Then he lay down under a blossoming apple-tree, to rest and eat some lunch, but the lunch did not taste well; and when he shut his eyes he could not sleep, for he thought constantly of Florette. Of course! He had parted from her far too soon, and an eager longing seized upon him for the young girl, with her red lips and luxuriant hair. This hair was a perfect golden-yellow; he knew it well, for she had often combed and braided it in the tavern-room beside the straw where they all slept.

He yearned to hear her laugh too, and would have liked to see her weep again.

Then he remembered the desolate smithy in the narrow market-place and the dreary home, recollected that he was thirty years old, and still had no wife.

A little wife of his own! A wife like Florette! Seventeen years old, a complexion like milk and blood, a creature full of gayety and joyous life! True, he was no light-hearted lad, but, lying under the apple-tree in the month of May, he saw himself in imagination living happily and merrily in the smithy by the market-place, with the fair-haired girl who had already shed tears for him. At last he started up, and because he had determined to go still farther on this day, did so, though for no other reason than to carry out the plan formed the day before. The next morning, before sunrise, he was again marching along the highway, this time not forward towards the Black Forest, but back to Nordlingen.

That very evening Florette became his betrothed bride, and the following Tuesday his wife.

The wedding was celebrated in the midst of the turmoil of the fair. Strolling players, jugglers and buffoons were the witnesses, and there was no lack of music and tinsel.

A quieter ceremony would have been more agreeable to the plain citizen and sensible blacksmith, but this purgatory had to be passed to reach Paradise.

On Wednesday he went off in a fair wagon with his young wife, and in Stuttgart bought with a portion of his savings many articles of household furniture, less to stop the gossips' tongues, of which he took no heed, than to do her honor in his own eyes. These things, piled high in a wagon of his own, he had sent into his native town as Florette's dowry, for her whole outfit consisted of one pink and one grass-green gown, a lute and a little white dog.

A delightful life now began in the smithy for Adam. The gossips avoided his wife, but they stared at her in church, and among them she seemed to him, not unjustly, like a rose amid vegetables. The marriage he had made was an abomination to respectable citizens, but Adam did not heed them, and Flora appeared to feel equally happy with him. When, before the close of the first twelvemonth after their wedding, Ulrich was born, the smith reached the summit of happiness and remained there for a whole year.

When, during that time, he stood in the bow-window amid the fresh balsam, auricular and yellow wallflowers holding his boy on his shoulder, while his wife leaned on his arm, and the pungent odor of scorched hoofs reached his nostrils, and he saw his journeyman and apprentice shoeing a horse below, he often thought how pleasant it had been pursuing the finer branches of his craft in Nuremberg, and that he should like to forge a flower again; but the blacksmith's trade was not to be despised either, and surely life with one's wife and child was best.

In the evening he drank his beer at the Lamb, and once, when the surgeon Siedler called life a miserable vale of tears, he laughed in his face and answered: "To him who knows how to take it right, it is a delightful garden."

Florette was kind to her husband, and devoted herself to her child, so long as he was an infant, with the most self-sacrificing love. Adam often spoke of a little daughter, who must look exactly like its mother; but it did not come.

When little Ulrich at last began to run about in the street, the mother's nomadic blood stirred, and she was constantly dinning it into her husband's ears that he ought to leave this miserable place and go to Augsburg or Cologne, where it would be pleasant; but he remained firm, and though her power over him was great, she could not move his resolute will.

Often she would not cease her entreaties and representations, and when she even complained that she was dying of solitude and weariness, his veins swelled with wrath, and then she was frightened, fled to her room and wept. If she happened to have a bold day, she threatened to go away and seek her own relatives. This displeased him, and he made her feel it bitterly, for he was steadfast in everything, even anger, and when he bore ill-will it was not for hours, but months, nor at such times could he be conciliated by coaxing or tears.

By degrees Florette learned to meet his discontent with a shrug of her shoulders, and to arrange her life in her own way. Ulrich was her comfort, pride and plaything, but sporting with him did not satisfy her.

While Adam was standing behind the anvil, she sat among the flowers in the bow-window, and the watchmen now looked higher up than the forge, the worthy magistrates no longer cast unfriendly glances at the smith's house, for Florette grew more and more beautiful in the quiet life she now enjoyed, and many a neighboring noble brought his horse to Adam to be shod, merely to look into the eyes of the artisan's beautiful wife.

Count von Frohlingen came most frequently of all, and Florette soon learned to distinguish the hoof-beats of his horse from those of the other steeds, and when he entered the shop, willingly found some pretext for going there too. In the afternoons she often went with her child outside the gate, and then always chose the road leading to the count's castle. There was no lack of careful friends, who warned Adam, but he answered them angrily, so they learned to be silent.

Florette had now grown gay again, and sometimes sang like a joyous bird.

Seven years elapsed, and during the summer of the eighth a scattered troop of soldiers came to the city and obtained admission. They were quartered under the arches of the town-hall, but many also lay in the smithy, for their helmets, breast-plates and other pieces of armor required plenty of mending. The ensign, a handsome, proud young fellow, with a dainty moustache, was Adam's most constant customer, and played very kindly with Ulrich, when Florette appeared with him. At last the young soldier departed, and the very same day Adam was summoned to the monastery, to mend something in the grating before the treasury.

When he returned, Florette had vanished; "run after the ensign," people said, and they were right. Adam did not attempt to wrest her from the seducer; but a great love cannot be torn from the heart like a staff that is thrust into the ground; it is intertwined with a thousand fibres, and to destroy it utterly is to destroy the heart in which it has taken root, and with it life itself. When he secretly cursed her and called her a viper, he doubtless remembered how innocent, dear and joyous she had been, and then the roots of the destroyed affection put forth new shoots, and he saw before his mental vision ensnaring images, of which he felt ashamed as soon as they had vanished.

Lightning and hail had entered the "delightful garden" of Adam's life also, and he had been thrust forth from the little circle of the happy into the great army of the wretched.

Purifying powers dwell in undeserved suffering, but no one is made better by unmerited disgrace, least of all a man like Adam. He had done what seemed to him his duty, without looking to the right or the left, but now the stainless man felt himself dishonored, and with morbid sensitiveness referred everything he saw and heard to his own disgrace, while the inhabitants of the little town made him feel that he had been ill- advised, when he ventured to make a fiddler's daughter a citizen.

When he went out, it seemed to him--and usually unjustly--as if people were nudging each other; hands, pointing out-stretched fingers at him, appeared to grow from every eye. At home he found nothing but desolation, vacuity, sorrow, and a child, who constantly tore open the burning, gnawing wounds in his heart. Ulrich must forget "the viper," and he sternly forbade him to speak of his mother; but not a day passed on which he would not fain have done so himself.

The smith did not stay long in the house on the market-place. He wished to go to Freiburg or Ulm, any place where he had not been with her. A purchaser for the dwelling, with its lucrative business, was speedily found, the furniture was packed, and the new owner was to move in on Wednesday, when on Monday Bolz, the jockey, came to Adam's workshop from Richtberg. The man had been a good customer for years, and bought hundreds of shoes, which he put on the horses at his own forge, for he knew something about the trade. He came to say farewell; he had his own nest to feather, and could do a more profitable business in the lowlands than up here in the forest. Finally he offered Adam his property at a very low price.

The smith had smiled at the jockey's proposal, still he went to the Richtberg the very next day to see the place. There stood the executioner's house, from which the whole street was probably named. One wretched hovel succeeded another. Yonder before a door, Wilhelm the idiot, on whom the city boys played their pranks, smiled into vacancy just as foolishly as he had done twenty years ago, here lodged Kathrin, with the big goitre, who swept the gutters; in the three grey huts, from which hung numerous articles of ragged clothing, lived two families of charcoal-burners, and Caspar, the juggler, a strange man, whom as a boy he had seen in the pillory, with his deformed daughters, who in winter washed laces and in summer went with him to the fairs.

In the hovels, before which numerous children were playing, lived honest, but poor foresters. It was the home of want and misery. Only the jockey's house and one other would have been allowed to exist in the city. The latter was occupied by the Jew, Costa, who ten years before had come from a distant country to the city with his aged father and a dumb wife, and remained there, for a little daughter was born and the old man was afterwards seized with a fatal illness. But the inhabitants would tolerate no Jews among them, so the stranger moved into the forester's house on the Richtberg which had stood empty because a better one had been built deeper in the woods. The city treasury could use the rent and tax exacted from Jews and demanded of the stranger. The Jew consented to the magistrate's requirement, but as it soon became known that he pored over huge volumes all day long and pursued no business, yet paid for everything in good money, he was believed to be an alchemist and sorcerer.

All who lived here were miserable or despised, and when Adam had left the Richtberg he told himself that he no longer belonged among the proud and unblemished and since he felt dishonored and took disgrace in the same dogged earnest, that he did everything else, he believed the people in the

Richtberg were just the right neighbors for him. All knew what it is to be wretched, and many had still heavier disgrace to bear. And then! If want drove his miserable wife back to him, this was the right place for her and those of her stamp.

So he bought the jockey's house and well-supplied forge. There would be customers enough for all he could do there in obscurity.

He had no cause to repent his bargain.

The old nurse remained with him and took care of Ulrich, who throve admirably. His own heart too grew lighter while engaged in designing or executing many an artistic piece of work. He sometimes went to the city to buy iron or coals, but usually avoided any intercourse with the citizens, who shrugged their shoulders or pointed to their foreheads, when they spoke of him.

About a year after his removal he had occasion to speak to the file-cutter, and sought him at the Lamb, where a number of Count Frolinger's retainers were sitting. Adam took no notice of them, but they began to jeer and mock at him. For a time he succeeded in controlling himself, but when red-haired Valentine went too far, a sudden fit of rage overpowered him and he felled him to the floor. The others now attacked him and dragged him to their master's castle, where he lay imprisoned for six months. At last he was brought before the count, who restored him to liberty "for the sake of Florette's beautiful eyes."

Years had passed since then, during which Adam had lived a quiet, industrious life in the Richtberg with his son. He associated with no one, except Doctor Costa, in whom he found the first and only real friend fate had ever bestowed upon him.

CHAPTER III.

FATHER Benedict had last seen the smith soon after his return from imprisonment, in the confessional of the monastery. As the monk in his youth had served in a troop of the imperial cavalry, he now, spite of his ecclesiastical dignity, managed the stables of the wealthy monastery, and had formerly come to the smithy in the market-place with many a horse, but since the monks had become involved in a quarrel with the city, Benedict ordered the animals to be shod elsewhere.

A difficult case reminded him of the skilful, half-forgotten artisan; and when the latter came out of the shed with a sack of coal, Benedict greeted him with sincere warmth. Adam, too, showed that he was glad to see the unexpected visitor, and placed his skill at the disposal of the monastery.

"It has grown late, Adam," said the monk, loosening the belt he was accustomed to wear when riding, which had become damp. "The storm overtook us on the way. The rolling and flashing overhead made the sorrel horse almost tear Gotz's hands off the wrists. Three steps sideways and one forward--so it has grown late, and you can't shoe the rascal in the dark."

"Do you mean the sorrel horse?" asked Adam, in a deep, musical voice, thrusting a blazing pine torch into the iron ring on the forge.

"Yes, Master Adam. He won't bear shoeing, yet he's very valuable. We have nothing to equal him. None of us can control him, but you formerly zounds!....you haven't grown younger in the last few years either, Adam! Put on your cap; you've lost your hair. Your forehead reaches down to your neck, but your vigor has remained. Do you remember how you cleft the anvil at Rodebach?"

"Let that pass," replied Adam--not angrily, but firmly. "I'll shoe the horse early to-morrow; it's too late to-day."

"I thought so!" cried the other, clasping his hands excitedly. "You know how we stand towards the citizens on account of the tolls on the bridges. I'd rather lie on thorns than enter the miserable hole. The stable down below is large enough! Haven't you a heap of straw for a poor brother in Christ? I need nothing more; I've brought food with me."

The smith lowered his eyes in embarrassment. He was not hospitable. No stranger had rested under his roof, and everything that disturbed his seclusion was repugnant to him. Yet he could not refuse; so he answered coldly: "I live alone here with my boy, but if you wish, room can be made."

The monk accepted as eagerly, as if he had been cordially invited; and after the horses and groom were supplied with shelter, followed his host into the sitting-room next the shop, and placed his saddle-bags on the table.

"This is all right," he said, laughing, as he produced a roast fowl and some white bread. "But how about the wine? I need something warm inside after my wet ride. Haven't you a drop in the cellar?"

"No, Father!" replied the smith. But directly after a second thought occurred to him, and he added: "Yes, I can serve you."

So saying, he opened the cupboard, and when, a short time after, the monk emptied the first goblet, he uttered a long drawn "Ah!" following the course of the fiery potion with his hand, till it rested content near his stomach. His lips quivered a little in the enjoyment of the flavor; then he looked benignantly with his unusually round eyes at Adam, saying cunningly:

"If such grapes grow on your pine-trees, I wish the good Lord had given Father Noah a pine-tree instead of a vine. By the saints! The archbishop has no better wine in his cellar! Give me one little sip more, and tell me from whom you received the noble gift?"

"Costa gave me the wine."

"The sorcerer---the Jew?" asked the monk, pushing the goblet away. "But, of course," he continued, in a half-earnest, half-jesting tone, "when one considers--the wine at the first holy communion, and at the marriage of

Cana, and the juice of the grapes King David enjoyed, once lay in Jewish cellars!"

Benedict had doubtless expected a smile or approving word from his host, but the smith's bearded face remained motionless, as if he were dead.

The monk looked less cheerful, as he began again "You ought not to grudge yourself a goblet either. Wine moderately enjoyed makes the heart glad; and you don't look like a contented man. Everything in life has not gone according to your wishes, but each has his own cross to bear; and as for you, your name is Adam, and your trials also come from Eve!"

At these words the smith moved his hand from his beard, and began to push the round leather cap to and fro on his bald head. A harsh answer was already on his lips, when he saw Ulrich, who had paused on the threshold in bewilderment. The boy had never beheld any guest at his father's table except the doctor, but hastily collecting his thoughts he kissed the monk's hand. The priest took the handsome lad by the chin, bent his head back, looked Adam also in the face, and exclaimed:

"His mouth, nose and eyes he has inherited from your wife, but the shape of the brow and head is exactly like yours."

A faint flush suffused Adam's cheeks, and turning quickly to the boy as if he had heard enough, he cried:

"You are late. Where have you been so long?"

"In the forest with Ruth. We were gathering faggots for Dr. Costa."

"Until now?"

"Rahel had baked some dumplings, so the doctor told me to stay."

"Then go to bed now. But first take some food to the groom in the stable, and put fresh linen on my bed. Be in the workshop early to-morrow morning, there is a horse to be shod."

The boy looked up thoughtfully and replied: "Yes, but the doctor has changed the hours; to-morrow the lesson will begin just after sunrise, father."

"Very well, we'll do without you. Good-night then."

The monk followed this conversation with interest and increasing disapproval, his face assuming a totally different expression, for the muscles between his nose and mouth drew farther back, forming with the underlip an angle turning inward. Thus he gazed with mute reproach at the smith for some time, then pushed the goblet far away, exclaiming with sincere indignation:

"What doings are these, friend Adam? I'll let the Jew's wine pass, and the dumplings too for aught I care, though it doesn't make a Christian child more pleasing in the sight of God, to eat from the same dish with those on whom the Saviour's innocent blood rests. But that you, a believing Christian, should permit an accursed Jew to lead a foolish lad. . . ."

"Let that pass," said the smith, interrupting the excited monk; but the latter would not be restrained, and only continued still more loudly and firmly: "I won't be stopped. Was such a thing ever heard of? A baptized Christian, who sends his own son to be taught by the infidel soul- destroyer!"

"Hear me, Father!"

"No indeed. It's for you to hear--you! What was I saying? For you, you who seek for your poor child a soul-destroying infidel as teacher. Do you know what that is? A sin against the Holy Ghost--the worst of all crimes. Such an abomination! You will have a heavy penance imposed upon you in the confessional."

"It's no sin--no abomination!" replied the smith defiantly.

The angry blood mounted into the monk's cheeks, and he cried: threateningly: "Oho! The chapter will teach you better to your sorrow. Keep the boy away from the Jew, or ......"

"Or?" repeated the smith, looking Father Benedict steadily in the face.

The latter's lips curled still more deeply, as after a pause, he replied: "Or excommunication and a fitting punishment will fall upon you and the vagabond doctor. Tit for tat. We have grown tender-hearted, and it is long since a Jew has been burned for an example to many."

These words did not fail to produce an effect, for though Adam was a brave man, the monk threatened him with things, against which he felt as powerless as when confronted with the might of the tempest and the lightning flashing from the clouds. His features now expressed deep mental anguish, and stretching out his hands repellently towards his guest, he cried anxiously "No, no! Nothing more can happen to me. No excommunication, no punishment, can make my present suffering harder to bear, but if you harm the doctor, I shall curse the hour I invited you to cross my threshold."

The monk looked at the other in surprise and answered in a more gentle tone: "You have always walked in your own way, Adam; but whither are you going now? Has the Jew bewitched you, or what binds you to him, that you look, on his account, as if a thunderbolt had struck you? No one shall have cause to curse the hour he invited Benedict to be his guest. See your way clearly once more, and when you have come to your senses--why, we monks have two eyes, that we may be able to close one when occasion requires. Have you any special cause for gratitude to Costa?"

"Many, Father, many!" cried the smith, his voice still trembling with only too well founded anxiety for his friend. "Listen, and when you know what he has done for me, and are disposed to judge leniently, do not carry what reaches your ears here before the chapter no, Father--I beseech you--do not. For if it should be I, by whom the doctor came to ruin, I--I...." The man's voice failed, and his chest heaved so violently with his gasping breath, that his stout leathern apron rose and fell.

"Be calm, Adam, be calm," said the monk, soothingly answering his companion's broken words. "All shall be well, all shall be well. Sit down, man, and trust me. What is the terrible debt of gratitude you owe the doctor?"

Spite of the other's invitation, the smith remained standing and with downcast eyes, began:

"I am not good at talking. You know how I was thrown into a dungeon on Valentine's account, but no one can understand my feelings during that time. Ulrich was left alone here among this miserable rabble with nobody to care for him, for our old maid-servant was seventy. I had buried my money in a safe place and there was nothing in the house except a loaf of bread and a few small coins, barely enough to last three days. The child was always before my eyes; I saw him ragged, begging, starving. But my anxiety tortured me most, after they had released me and I was going back to my house from the castle. It was a walk of two hours, but each one seemed as long as St. John's day. Should I find Ulrich or not? What had become of him? It was already dark, when I at last stood before the house. Everything was as silent as the grave, and the door was locked. Yet I must get in, so I rapped with my fingers, and then pounded with my fist on the door and shutters, but all in vain. Finally Spittellorle--[A nickname; literally: "Hospital Loura."]--came out of the red house next mine, and I heard all. The old woman had become idiotic, and was in the stocks. Ulrich was at the point of death, and Doctor Costa had taken him home. When I heard this, I felt the same as you did just now; anger seized upon me, and I was as much ashamed as if I were standing in the pillory. My child with the Jew! There was not much time for reflection, and I set off at full speed for the doctor's house. A light was shining through the window. It was high above the street, but as it stood open and I am tall, I could look in and see over the whole room. At the right side, next the wall, was a bed, where amid the white pillows lay my boy. The doctor sat by his side, holding the child's hand in his. Little Ruth nestled to him, asking: 'Well, father?' The man smiled. Do you know him, Pater? He is about thirty years old, and has a pale, calm face. He smiled and said so gratefully, so-so joyously, as if Ulrich were his own son: 'Thank God, he will be spared to us!' The little girl ran to her dumb mother, who was sitting by the stove, winding yarn, exclaiming:

'Mother, he'll get well again. I have prayed for him every day.' The Jew bent over my child and pressed his lips upon the boy's brow--and I, I--I no longer clenched my fist, and was so overwhelmed with emotion, that I could not help weeping, as if I were still a child myself, and since then, Pater Benedictus, since...." He paused; the monk rose, laid his hand on the smith's shoulder, and said:

"It has grown late, Adam. Show me to my couch. Another day will come early to-morrow morning, and we should sleep over important matters.

But one thing is settled, and must remain so-under all circumstances: the boy is no longer to be taught by the Jew. He must help you shoe the horses to-morrow. You will be reasonable!"

The smith made no reply, but lighted the monk to the room where he and his son usually slept. His own couch was covered with fresh linen for the guest--Ulrich already lay in his bed, apparently asleep.

"We have no other room to give you," said Adam, pointing to the boy; but the monk was content with his sleeping companions, and after his host had left him, gazed earnestly at Ulrich's fresh, handsome face.

The smith's story had moved him, and he did not go to rest at once, but paced thoughtfully up and down the room, stepping lightly, that he might not disturb the child's slumber.

Adam had reason to be grateful to the man, and why should there not be good Jews?

He thought of the patriarchs, Moses, Solomon, and the prophets, and had not the Saviour himself, and John and Paul, whom he loved above all the apostles, been the children of Jewish mothers, and grown up among Jews? And Adam! the poor fellow had had more than his share of trouble, and he who believes himself deserted by God, easily turns to the devil. He was warned now, and the mischief to his son must be stopped once for all. What might not the child hear from the Jew, in these times, when heresy wandered about like a roaring lion, and sat by all the roads like a siren. Only by a miracle had this secluded valley been spared the evil teachings, but the peasants had already shown that they grudged the nobles the power, the cities the rich gains, and the priesthood the authority and earthly possessions, bestowed on them by God. He was disposed to let mildness rule, and spare the Jew this time--but only on one condition.

When he took off his cowl, he looked for a hook on which to hang it, and while so doing, perceived on the shelf a row of boards. Taking one down, he found a sketch of an artistic design for the enclosure of a fountain, done by the smith's hand, and directly opposite his bed a linden-wood panel, on which a portrait was drawn with charcoal. This roused his curiosity, and, throwing the light of the torch upon it, he started back, for it was a rudely executed, but wonderfully life-like head of Costa, the Jew. He remembered him perfectly, for he had met him more than once.

The monk shook his head angrily, but lifted the picture from the shelf and examined more closely the doctor's delicately-cut nose, and the noble arch of the brow. While so doing, he muttered unintelligible words, and when at last, with little show of care, he restored the modest work of art to its old place, Ulrich awoke, and, with a touch of pride, exclaimed:

"I drew that myself, Father!"

"Indeed!" replied the monk. "I know of better models for a pious lad. You must go to sleep now, and to-morrow get up early and help your father. Do you understand?"

So saying, with no gentle hand he turned the boy's head towards the wall. The mildness awakened by Adam's story had all vanished to the winds.

Adam allowed his son to practise idolatry with the Jew, and make pictures of him. This was too much. He threw himself angrily on his couch, and began to consider what was to be done in this difficult matter, but sleep soon brought his reflections to an end.

Ulrich rose very early, and when Benedict saw him again in the light of the young day, and once more looked at the Jew's portrait, drawn by the handsome boy, a thought came to him as if inspired by the saints themselves--the thought of persuading the smith to give his son to the monastery.

CHAPTER IV.

THIS morning Pater Benedictus was a totally different person from the man, who had sat over the wine the night before. Coldly and formally he evaded the smith's questions, until the latter had sent his son away.

Ulrich, without making any objection, had helped his father shoe the sorrel horse, and in a few minutes, by means of a little stroking over the eyes and nose, slight caresses, and soothing words, rendered the refractory stallion as docile as a lamb. No horse had ever resisted the lad, from the time he was a little child, the smith said, though for what reason he did not know. These words pleased the monk, for he was only too familiar with two fillies, that were perfect fiends for refractoriness, and the fair-haired boy could show his gratitude for the schooling he received, by making himself useful in the stable.

Ulrich must go to the monastery, so Benedictus curtly declared with the utmost positiveness, after the smith had finished his work. At midsummer a place would be vacant in the school, and this should be reserved for the boy. A great favor! What a prospect--to be reared there with aristocratic companions, and instructed in the art of painting. Whether he should become a priest, or follow some worldly pursuit, could be determined later. In a few years the boy could choose without restraint.

This plan would settle everything in the best possible way. The Jew need not be injured, and the smith's imperiled son would be saved. The monk would hear no objections. Either the accusation against the doctor should be laid before the chapter, or Ulrich must go to the school.

In four weeks, on St. John's Day, so Benedictus declared, the smith and his son might announce their names to the porter. Adam must have saved many florins, and there would be time enough to get the lad shoes and clothes, that he might hold his own in dress with the other scholars.

During this whole transaction the smith felt like a wild animal in the hunter's toils, and could say neither "yes" nor "no." The monk did not insist upon a promise, but, as he rode away, flattered himself that he had snatched a soul from the claws of Satan, and gained a prize for the monastery-school and his stable--a reflection that made him very cheerful.

Adam retrained alone beside the fire. Often, when his heart was heavy, he had seized his huge hammer and deadened his sorrow by hard work; but to-day he let the tool lie, for the consciousness of weakness and lack of will paralyzed his lusty vigor, and he stood with drooping head, as if utterly crushed. The thoughts that moved him could not be exactly expressed in words, but doubtless a vision of the desolate forge, where he would stand alone by the fire without Ulrich, rose before his mind. Once the idea of closing his house, taking the boy by the hand, and wandering out into the world with him, flitted through his brain. But then, what would become of the Jew, and how could he leave this place? Where would his miserable wife, the accursed, lovely sinner, find him, when she sought him again? Ulrich had run out of doors long ago. Had he gone to study his lessons with the Jew? He started in terror at the thought. Passing his hands over his eyes, like a dreamer roused from sleep, he went into his chamber, threw off his apron, cleansed his face and hands from the soot of the forge, put on his burgher dress, which he only wore when he went to church or visited the doctor, and entered the street.

The thunder-storm had cleared the air, and the sun shone pleasantly on the shingled roofs of the miserable houses of the Richtberg. Its rays were reflected from the little round window-panes, and flickered over the tree-tops on the edge of the ravine.

The light-green hue of the fresh young foliage on the beeches glittered as brightly against the dark pines, as if Spring had made them a token of her mastery over the grave companions of Winter; yet even the pines were not passed by, and where her finger had touched the tips of the branches in benediction, appeared tender young shoots, fresh as the grass by the brook, and green as chrysophase and emerald.

The stillness of morning reigned within the forest, yet it was full of life, rich in singing, chirping and twittering. Light streamed from the blue sky through the tree-tops, and the golden sunbeams shimmered and danced over the branches, trunks and ground, as if they had been prisoned in the woods and could never find their way out. The shadows of the tall trunks lay in transparent bars on the underbrush, luxuriant moss, and ferns, and the dew clung to the weeds and grass.

Nature had celebrated her festival of resurrection at Easter, and the day after the morrow joyous Whitsuntide would begin. Fresh green life was springing from the stump of every dead tree; even the rocks afforded sustenance to a hundred roots, a mossy covering and network of thorny tendrils clung closely to them. The wild vine twined boldly up many a trunk, fruit was already forming on the bilberry bushes, though it still glimmered with a faint pink hue amid the green of May. A thousand blossoms, white, red, blue and yellow, swayed on their slender stalks, opened their calixes to the bees, unfolded their stars to deck the woodland carpet, or proudly stretched themselves up as straight as candles. Grey fungi had shot up after the refreshing rain, and gathered round the red-capped giants among the mushrooms. Under, over and around all this luxuriant vegetation hopped, crawled, flew, fluttered, buzzed and chirped millions of tiny, short-lived creatures. But who heeds them on a sunny Spring morning in the forest, when the birds are singing, twittering, trilling, pecking, cooing and calling so joyously? Murmuring and plashing, the forest stream dashed down its steep bed over rocks and amid moss-covered stones and smooth pebbles to the valley. The hurrying water lived, and in it dwelt its gay inhabitants, fresh plants grew along the banks from source to mouth, while over and around it a third species of living creatures sunned themselves, fluttered, buzzed and spun delicate silk threads.

In the midst of a circular clearing, surrounded by dense woods, smoked a charcoal kiln. It was less easy to breathe here, than down in the forest below. Where Nature herself rules, she knows how to guard beauty and purity, but where man touches her, the former is impaired and the latter sullied.

It seemed as if the morning sunlight strove to check the smoke from the smouldering wood, in order to mount freely into the blue sky. Little clouds floated over the damp, grassy earth, rotting tree-trunks, piles of wood and heaps of twigs that surrounded the kiln. A moss-grown but stood at the edge of the forest, and before it sat Ulrich, talking with the coal-burner. People called this man "Hangemarx," and in truth he looked in his black rags, like one of those for whom it is a pity that Nature should deck herself in her Spring garb. He had a broad, peasant face, his mouth was awry, and his thick yellowish-red hair, which in many places looked washed out or faded, hung so low over his narrow forehead, that it wholly concealed it, and touched his bushy, snow-white brows. The eyes under them needed to be taken on trust, they were so well concealed, but when they peered through the narrow chink between the rows of lashes, not even a mote escaped them. Ulrich was shaping an arrow, and meantime asking the coal-burner numerous questions, and when the latter prepared to answer, the boy laughed heartily, for before Hangemarx could speak, he was obliged to straighten his crooked mouth by three jerking motions, in which his nose and cheeks shared.

An important matter was being discussed between the two strangely dissimilar companions.

After it grew dark, Ulrich was to come to the charcoal-burner again. Marx knew where a fine buck couched, and was to drive it towards the boy, that he might shoot it. The host of the Lamb down in the town needed game, for his Gretel was to be married on Tuesday. True, Marx could kill the animal himself, but Ulrich had learned to shoot too, and if the place whence the game came should be noised abroad, the charcoal-burner, without any scruples of conscience, could swear that he did not shoot the buck, but found it with the arrow in its heart.

People called the charcoal-burner a poacher, and he owed his ill-name of "Hangemarx" to the circumstance that once, though long ago, he had adorned a gallows. Yet he was not a dishonest man, only he remembered too faithfully the bold motto, which, when a boy, one peasant wood-cutter or charcoal-burner whispered to another:

"Forest, stream and meadow are free."

His dead father had joined the Bundschuh,--[A peasants' league which derived its name from the shoe, of peculiar shape, worn by its members.]-- adopted this motto, and clung fast to it and with it, to the belief that every living thing in the forest belonged to him, as much as to the city, the nobles, or the monastery. For this faith he had undergone much suffering, and owed to it his crooked mouth and ill name, for just as his beard was beginning to grow, the father of the reigning count came upon him, just after he had killed a fawn in the "free" forest. The legs of the heavy animal were tied together with ropes, and Marx was obliged to take the ends of the knot between his teeth like a bridle, and drag the carcass to the castle. While so doing his cheeks were torn open, and the evil deed neither pleased him nor specially strengthened his love for the count. When, a short time after, the rebellion broke out in Stuhlingen, and he heard that everywhere the peasants were rising against the monks and nobles, he, too, followed the black, red and yellow banner, first serving with Hans Muller of Bulgenbach, then with Jacklein Rohrbach of Bockingen, and participating with the multitude in the overthrow of the city and castle of Neuenstein. At Weinsberg he saw Count Helfenstein rush upon the spears, and when the noble countess was driven past him to Heilbronn in the dung-cart, he tossed his cap in the air with the rest.

The peasant was to be lord now; the yoke of centuries was to be broken; unjust imposts, taxes, tithes and villenage would be forever abolished, while the fourth of the twelve articles he had heard read aloud more than once, remained firmly fixed in his memory "Game, birds and fish every one is free to catch." Moreover, many a verse from the Gospel, unfavorable to the rich, but promising the kingdom of heaven to the poor, and that the last shall be first, had reached his ears. Doubtless many of the leaders glowed with lofty enthusiasm for the liberation of the poor people from unendurable serfdom and oppression; but when Marx, and men like him, left wife and children and risked their lives, they remembered only the past, and the injustice they had suffered, and were full of a fierce yearning to trample the dainty, torturing demons under their heavy peasant feet.

The charcoal-burner had never lighted such bright fires, never tasted such delicious meat and spicy wine, as during that period of his life, while vengeance had a still sweeter savor than all the rest. When the castle fell, and its noble mistress begged for mercy, he enjoyed a foretaste of the promised paradise. Satan has also his Eden of fiery roses, but they do not last long, and when they wither, put forth sharp thorns. The peasants felt them soon enough, for at Sindelfingen they found their master in Captain Georg Truchsess of Waldberg.

Marx fell into his troopers' hands and was hung on the gallows, but only in mockery and as a warning to others; for before he and his companions perished, the men took them down, cut their oath-fingers from their hands, and drove them back into their old servitude. When he at last returned home, his house had been taken from his family, whom he found in extreme poverty. The father of Adam, the smith, to whom he had formerly sold charcoal, redeemed the house, gave him work, and once, when a band of horsemen came to the city searching for rebellious peasants, the old man did not forbid him to hide three whole days in his barn.

Since that time everything had been quiet in Swabia, and neither in forest, stream nor meadow had any freedom existed.

Marx had only himself to provide for; his wife was dead, and his sons were raftsmen, who took pine logs to Mayence and Cologne, sometimes even as far as Holland. He owed gratitude to no one but Adam, and showed in his way that he was conscious of it, for he taught Ulrich all sorts of things which were of no advantage to a boy, except to give him pleasure, though even in so doing he did not forget his own profit. Ulrich was now fifteen, and could manage a cross-bow and hit the mark like a skilful hunter, and as the lad did not lack a love for the chase, Marx afforded him the pleasure. All he had heard about the equal rights of men he engrafted into the boy's soul, and when to-day, for the hundredth time, Ulrich expressed a doubt whether it was not stealing to kill game that belonged to the count, the charcoal-burner straightened his mouth, and said:

"Forest, stream and meadow are free. Surely you know that."

The boy gazed thoughtfully at the ground for a time, and then asked:

"The fields too?"

"The fields?" repeated Marx, in surprise. "The fields? The fields are a different matter." He glanced as he spoke, at the field of oats he had sown in the autumn, and which now bore blades a finger long. "The fields are man's work and belong to him who tills them, but the forest, stream and meadow were made by God. Do you understand? What God created for Adam and Eve is everybody's property."

As the sun rose higher, and the cuckoo began to raise its voice, Ulrich's name was shouted loudly several times in rapid succession through the forest. The arrow he had been shaping flew into a corner, and with a hasty "When it grows dusk, Marxle!" Ulrich dashed into the woods, and soon joined his playmate Ruth.

The pair strolled slowly through the forest by the side of the stream, enjoying the glorious morning, and gathering flowers to carry a bouquet to the little girl's mother. Ruth culled the blossoms daintily with the tips of her fingers; Ulrich wanted to help, and tore the slender stalks in tufts from the roots by the handful. Meantime their tongues were not idle. Ulrich boastfully told her that Pater Benedictus had seen his picture of her father, recognized it instantly, and muttered something over it. His mother's blood was strong in him; his imaginary world was a very different one from that of the narrow-minded boys of the Richtberg.

His father had told him much, and the doctor still more, about the wide, wide world-kings, artists and great heroes. From Hangemarx he learned, that he possessed the same rights and dignity as all other men, and Ruth's wonderful power of imagination peopled his fancy with the strangest shapes and figures. She made royal crowns of wreaths, transformed the little hut, the lad had built of boughs, behind the doctor's house, into a glittering imperial palace, converted round pebbles into ducats and golden zechins--bread and apples into princely banquets; and when she had placed two stools before the wooden bench on which she sat with Ulrich her fancy instantly transformed them into a silver coronation coach with milk-white steeds. When she was a fairy, Ulrich was obliged to be a magician; if she was the queen, he was king.

When, to give vent to his animal spirits, Ulrich played with the Richtberg boys, he always led them, but allowed himself to be guided by little Ruth. He knew that the doctor was a despised Jew, that she was a Jewish child; but his father honored the Hebrew, and the foreign atmosphere, the aristocratic, secluded repose that pervaded the solitary scholar's house, exerted a strange influence over him.

When he entered it, a thrill ran through his frame; it seemed as if he were penetrating into some forbidden sanctuary. He was the only one of all his playfellows, who was permitted to cross this threshold, and he felt it as a distinction, for, in spite of his youth, he realized that the quiet doctor, who knew everything that existed in heaven and on earth, and yet was as mild and gentle as a child, stood far, far above the miserable drudges, who struggled with sinewy hands for mere existence on the Richtberg. He expected everything from him, and Ruth also seemed a very unusual creature, a delicate work of art, with whom he, and he only, was allowed to play.

It might have happened, that when irritated he would upbraid her with being a wretched Jewess, but it would scarcely have surprised him, if she had suddenly stood before his eyes as a princess or a phoenix.

When the Richtberg lay close beneath them, Ruth sat down on a stone, placing her flowers in her lap. Ulrich threw his in too, and, as the bouquet grew, she held it towards him, and he thought it very pretty; but she said, sighing:

"I wish roses grew in the forest; not common hedgeroses, but like those in Portugal--full, red, and with the real perfume. There is nothing that smells sweeter."

So it always was with the pair. Ruth far outstripped Ulrich in her desires and wants, thus luring him to follow her.

"A rose!" repeated Ulrich. "How astonished you look!"

Her wish reminded him of the magic word she had mentioned the day before, and they talked about it all the way home, Ulrich saying that he had waked three times in the night on account of it. Ruth eagerly interrupted him, exclaiming:

"I thought of it again too, and if any one would tell the what it was, I should know what to wish now. I would not have a single human being in the world except you and me, and my father and mother."

"And my little mother!" added Ulrich, earnestly.

"And your father, too!"

"Why, of course, he, too!" said the boy, as if to make hasty atonement for his neglect.

CHAPTER V.

THE sun was shining brightly on the little windows of the Israelite's sitting-room, which were half open to admit the Spring air, though lightly shaded with green curtains, for Costa liked a subdued light, and was always careful to protect his apartment from the eyes of passers-by.

There was nothing remarkable to be seen, for the walls were whitewashed, and their only ornament was a garland of lavender leaves, whose perfume Ruth's mother liked to inhale. The whole furniture consisted of a chest, several stools, a bench covered with cushions, a table, and two plain wooden arm-chairs.

One of the latter had long been the scene of Adam's happiest hours, for he used to sit in it when he played chess with Costa.

He had sometimes looked on at the noble game while in Nuremberg; but the doctor understood it thoroughly, and had initiated him into all its rules.

For the first two years Costa had remained far in advance of his pupil, then he was compelled to defend himself in good earnest, and now it not unfrequently happened that the smith vanquished the scholar. True, the latter was much quicker than the former, who if the situation became critical, pondered over it an unconscionably long time.

Two hands more unlike had rarely met over a chess-board; one suggested a strong, dark ploug-ox, the other a light, slender-limbed palfrey. The Israelite's figure looked small in contrast with the smith's gigantic frame. How coarse-grained, how heavy with thought the German's big, fair head appeared, how delicately moulded and intellectual the Portuguese Jew's.

To-day the two men had again sat down to the game, but instead of playing, had been talking very, very earnestly. In the course of the conversation the doctor had left his place and was pacing restlessly to and fro. Adam retained his seat.

His friend's arguments had convinced him. Ulrich was to be sent to the monastery-school. Costa had also been informed of the danger that threatened his own person, and was deeply agitated. The peril was great, very great, yet it was hard, cruelly hard, to quit this peaceful nook. The smith understood what was passing in his mind, and said:

"It is hard for you to go. What binds you here to the Richtberg?"

"Peace, peace!" cried the other. "And then," he added more calmly, "I have gained land here."

"You?"

"The large and small graves behind the executioner's house, they are my estates."

"It is hard, hard to leave them," said the smith, with drooping head. "All this comes upon you on account of the kindness you have shown my boy; you have had a poor reward from us."

"Reward?" asked the other, a subtle smile hovering around his lips. "I expect none, neither from you nor fate. I belong to a poor sect, that does not consider whether its deeds will be repaid or not. We love goodness, set a high value on it, and practise it, so far as our power extends, because it is so beautiful. What have men called good? Only that which keeps the soul calm. And what is evil? That which fills it with disquiet. I tell you, that the hearts of those who pursue virtue, though they are driven from their homes, hunted and tortured like noxious beasts, are more tranquil than those of their powerful persecutors, who practise evil. He who seeks any other reward for virtue, than virtue itself, will not lack disappointment. It is neither you nor Ulrich, who drives me hence, but the mysterious ancient curse, that pursues my people when they seek to rest; it is, it is.... Another time, to-morrow. This is enough for to-day."

When the doctor was alone, he pressed his hand to his brow and groaned aloud. His whole life passed before his mind, and he found in it, besides terrible suffering, great and noble joys, and not an hour in which his desire for virtue was weakened. He had spent happy years here in the peace of his simple home, and now must again set forth and wander on and on, with nothing before his eyes save an uncertain goal, at the end of a long, toilsome road. What had hitherto been his happiness, increased his misery in this hour. It was hard, unspeakably hard, to drag his wife and child through want and sorrow, and could Elizabeth, his wife, bear it again?

He found her in the tiny garden behind the horse, kneeling before a flower-bed to weed it. As he greeted her pleasantly, she rose and beckoned to him.

"Let us sit down," he said, leading her to the bench before the hedge, that separated the garden from the forest. There he meant to tell her, that they must again shake the dust from their feet.

She had lost the power of speech on the rack in Portugal, and could only falter a few unintelligible words, when greatly excited, but her hearing had remained, and her husband understood how to read the expression of her eyes. A great sorrow had drawn a deep line in the high, pure brow, and this also was eloquent; for when she felt happy and at peace it was scarcely perceptible, but if an anxious or sorrowful mood existed, the furrow contracted and deepened. To-day it seemed to have entirely disappeared. Her fair hair was drawn plainly and smoothly, over her temples, and the slender, slightly stooping figure, resembled a young tree, which the storm has bowed and deprived of strength and will to raise itself.

"Beautiful!" she exclaimed in a smothered tone, with much effort, but her bright glance clearly expressed the joy that filled her soul, as she pointed to the green foliage around her and the blue sky over their heads.

"Delicious-delicious!" he answered, cordially. "The June day is reflected in your dear face. You have learned to be contented here?"

Elizabeth nodded eagerly, pressing both hands upon her heart, while her eloquent glance told him how well, how grateful and happy, she felt here; and when in reply to his timid question, whether it would be hard for her to leave this place and seek another, a safer home, she gazed at first in surprise, then anxiously into his face, and then, with an eager gesture of refusal, gasped "Not go--not go!" He answered, soothingly:

"No, no; we are still safe here to-day!"

Elizabeth knew her husband, and had keen eyes; a presentiment of approaching danger seized upon her. Her features assumed an expression of terrified expectation and deep grief. The furrow in her brow deepened, and questioning glances and gestures united with the "What?--what?" trembling on her lips.

"Do not fear!" he replied, tenderly." We must not spoil the present, because the future might bring something that is not agreeable to us."

As he uttered the words, she pressed closely to him, clutching his arm with both hands, but he felt the rapid throbbing of her heart, and perceived by the violent agitation expressed in every feature, what deep, unconquerable horror was inspired by the thought of being compelled to go out into the world again, hunted from country to country, from town to town. All that she had suffered for his sake, came back to his memory, and he clasped her trembling hands in his with passionate fervor. It seemed as if it would be very, very easy, to die with her, but wholly impossible to thrust her forth again into a foreign land and to an uncertain fate; so, kissing her on her eyes, which were dilated with horrible fear, he exclaimed, as if no peril, but merely a foolish wish had suggested the desire to roam:

"Yes, child, it is best here. Let us be content with what we have. We will stay!--yes, we will stay!" Elizabeth drew a long breath, as if relieved from an incubus, her brow became smooth, and it seemed as if the dumb mouth joined the large upraised eyes in uttering an "Amen," that came from the inmost depths of the heart.

Costa's soul was saddened and sorely troubled, when he returned to the house and his writing-table. The old maid-servant, who had accompanied him from Portugal, entered at the same time, and watched his preparations, shaking her head. She was a small, crippled Jewess, a grey-haired woman, with youthful, bright, dark eyes, and restless hands, that fluttered about her face with rapid, convulsive gestures, while she talked.

She had grown old in Portugal, and contracted rheumatism in the unusual cold of the North, so even in Spring she wrapped her head in all the gay kerchiefs she owned. She kept the house scrupulously neat, understood how to prepare tempting dishes from very simple materials, and bought everything she needed for the kitchen. This was no trifling matter for her, since, though she had lived more than nine years in the black Forest, she had learned few German words. Even these the neighbors mistook for Portuguese, though they thought the language bore some distant resemblance to German. Her gestures they understood perfectly.

She had voluntarily followed the doctor's father, yet she could not forgive the dead man, for having brought her out of the warm South into this horrible country. Having been her present master's nurse, she took many liberties with him, insisting upon knowing everything that went on in the household, of which she felt herself the oldest, and therefore the most distinguished member; and it was strange how quickly she could hear when she chose, spite of her muffled ears!

To-day she had been listening again, and as her master was preparing to take his seat at the table and sharpen his goose-quill, she glanced around to see that they were entirely alone; then approached, saying in Portuguese:

"Don't begin that, Lopez. You must listen to me first."

"Must I?" he asked, kindly.

"If you don't choose to do it, I can go!" she answered, angrily. "To be sure, sitting still is more comfortable than running."

"What do you mean by that?"

"Do you suppose yonder books are the walls of Zion? Do you feel inclined to make the monks' acquaintance once more?"

"Fie, fie, Rahel, listening again? Go into the kitchen!"

"Directly! Directly! But I will speak first. You pretend, that you are only staying here to please your wife, but it's no such thing. It's yonder writing that keeps you. I know life, but you and your wife are just like two children. Evil is forgotten in the twinkling of an eye, and blessing is to come straight from Heaven, like quails and manna. What sort of a creature have your books made you, since you came with the doctor's hat from Coimbra? Then everybody said: 'Lopez, Senor Lopez. Heavenly Father, what a shining light he'll be!' And now! The Lord have mercy on us! You work, work, and what does it bring you? Not an egg; not a rush! Go to your uncle in the

Netherlands. He'll forget the curse, if you submit! How many of the zechins, your father saved, are still left?"

Here the doctor interrupted the old woman's torrent of speech with a stern "enough!" but she would not allow herself to be checked, and continued with increasing volubility.

"Enough, you say? I fret over perversity enough in silence. May my tongue wither, if I remain mute to-day. Good God! child, are you out of your senses? Everything has been crammed into your poor head, but to be sure it isn't written in the books, that when people find out what happened in Porto, and that you married a baptized child, a Gentile, a Christian girl......"

At these words the doctor rose, laid his hands on the servant's shoulder, and said with grave, quiet earnestness.

"Whoever speaks of that, may betray it; may betray it. Do you understand me, Rahel? I know your good intentions, and therefore tell you: my wife is content here, and danger is still far away. We shall stay. And besides: since Elizabeth became mine, the Jews avoid me as an accursed, the Christians as a condemned man. The former close the doors, the latter would fain open them; the gates of a prison, I mean. No Portuguese will come here, but in the Netherlands there is more than one monk and one Jew from Porto, and if any of them recognize me and find Elizabeth with me, it will involve no less trifle than her life and mine. I shall stay here; you now know why, and can go to your kitchen."

Old Rahel reluctantly obeyed, yet the doctor did not resume his seat at the writing-table, but for a long time paced up and down among his books more rapidly than usual.

CHAPTER VI.

ST. John's day was close at hand. Ulrich was to go to the monastery the following morning. Hitherto Father Benedict had been satisfied, and no one molested the doctor. Yet the tranquillity, which formerly exerted so beneficial an effect, had departed, and the measures of precaution he now felt compelled to adopt, like everything else that brought him into connection with the world, interrupted the progress of his work.

The smith was obliged to provide Ulrich with clothing, and for this purpose went with the lad and a well-filled purse, not to his native place, but to the nearest large city.

There many a handsome suit of garments hung in the draper's windows, and the barefooted boy blushed crimson with delight, when he stood before this splendid show. As he was left free to choose, he instantly selected the clothes a nobleman had ordered for his son, and which, from head to foot, were blue on one side and yellow on the other. But Adam pushed them angrily aside. Ulrich's pleasure in the gay stuff reminded him of his wife's outfit, the pink and green gowns.

So he bought two dark suits, which fitted the lad's erect figure as if moulded upon him, and when the latter stood before him in the inn, neatly dressed, with shoes on his feet, and a student's cap on his head, Adam could not help gazing at him almost idolatrously.

The tavern-keeper whispered to the smith, that it was long since he had seen so handsome a young fellow, and the hostess, after bringing the beer, stroked the boy's curls with her wet hand.

On reaching home, Adam permitted his son to go to the doctor's in his new clothes; Ruth screamed with joy when she saw him, walked round and round him, and curiously felt the woollen stuff of the doublet and its blue slashes, ever and anon clapping her hands in delight.

Her parents had expected that the parting would excite her most painfully, but she smiled joyously into her playmate's face, when he bade her farewell, for she took the matter in her usual way, not as it really was, but as she imagined it to be. Instead of the awkward Ulrich of the present, the fairy-prince he was now to become stood before her; he was to return without fail at Christmas, and then how delightful it would be to play with him again. Of late they had been together even more than usual, continually seeking for the word, and planning a thousand delightful things he was to conjure up for her, and she for him and others.

It was the Sabbath, and on this day old Rahel always dressed the child in a little yellow silk frock, while on Sunday her mother did the same. The gown particularly pleased Ulrich's eye, and when she wore it, he always became more yielding and obeyed her every wish. So Ruth rejoiced that it chanced to be the Sabbath, and while she passed her hand over his doublet, he stroked her silk dress.

They had not much to say to each other, for their tongues always faltered in the presence of others. The doctor gave Ulrich many an admonitory word, his wife kissed him, and as a parting remembrance hung a small gold ring, with a glittering stone, about his neck, and old Rahel gave him a kerchief full of freshly-baked cakes to eat on his way.

At noon on St. John's day, Ulrich and his father stood before the gate of the monastery. Servants and mettled steeds were waiting there, and the porter, pointing to them, said: "Count Frohlinger is within."

Adam turned pale, pressed his son so convulsively to his breast that he groaned with pain, sent a laybrother to call Father Benedict, confided his child to him, and walked towards home with drooping head.

Hitherto Ulrich had not known whether to enjoy or dread the thought of going to the monastery-school. The preparations had been pleasant enough, and the prospect of sharing the same bench with the sons of noblemen and aristocratic citizens, flattered his unity; but when he saw his father depart, his heart melted and his eyes grew wet. The monk; noticing this, drew him towards him, patted his shoulder, and said: "Keep up your courage! You will see that it is far pleasanter with us, than down in the Richtberg."

This gave Ulrich food for thought, and he did not glance around as the Father led him up the steep stairs to the landing-place, and past the refectory into the court-yard.

Monks were pacing silently up and down the corridors that surrounded it, and one after another raised his shaven head higher over his white cowl, to cast a look at the new pupil.

Behind the court-yard stood the stately, gable-roofed building containing the guest-rooms, and between it and the church lay the school-garden, a meadow planted with fruit trees, separated from the highway by a wall.

Benedictus opened the wooden gate, and pushed Ulrich into the play-ground.

The noise there had been loud enough, but at his entrance the game stopped, and his future companions nudged each other, scanning him with scrutinizing glances.

The monk beckoned to several of the pupils, and made them acquainted with the smith's son, then stroking Ulrich's curls again, left him alone with the others.

On St. John's day the boys were given their liberty and allowed to play to their hearts' content.

They took no special notice of Ulrich, and after having stared sufficiently and exchanged a few words with him, continued their interrupted game of trying to throw stones over the church roof.

Meantime Ulrich looked at his comrades.

There were large and small, fair and dark lads among them, but not one with whom he could not have coped. To this point his scrutiny was first directed.

At last he turned his attention to the game. Many of the stones, that had been thrown, struck the slates on the roof; not one had passed over the church. The longer the unsuccessful efforts lasted, the more evident became the superior smile on Ulrich's lips, the faster his heart throbbed.

His eyes searched the grass, and when he had discovered a flat, sharp-edged stone, he hurriedly stooped, pressed silently into the ranks of the players, and bending the upper part of his body far back, summoned all his strength, and hurled the stone in a beautiful curve high into the air.

Forty sparkling eyes followed it, and a loud shout of joy rang out as it vanished behind the church roof. One alone, a tall, thin, black-haired lad, remained silent, and while the others were begging Ulrich to throw again, searched for a stone, exerted all his power to equal the 11 "greenhorn," and almost succeeded. Ulrich now sent a second stone after the first, and, again the cast was successful. Dark-browed Xaver instantly seized a new missile, and the contest that now followed so engrossed the attention of all, that they saw and heard nothing until a deep voice, in a firm, though not unkind tone, called: "Stop, boys! No games must be played with the church."

At these words the younger boys hastily dropped the stones they had gathered, for the man who had shouted, was no less a personage than the Lord Abbot himself.

Soon the lads approached to kiss the ecclesiastic's hand or sleeve, and the stately priest, who understood how to guide those subject to him by a glance of his dark eyes, graciously and kindly accepted the salutation.

"Grave in office, and gay in sport" was his device. Count von Frohlinger, who had entered the garden with him, looked like one whose motto runs: "Never grave and always gay."

The nobleman had not grown younger since Ulrich's mother fled into the world, but his eyes still sparkled joyously and the brick-red hue that tinged his handsome face between his thick white moustache and his eyes, announced that he was no less friendly to wine than to fair women. How well his satin clothes and velvet cloak became him, how beautifully the white puffs were relieved against the deep blue of his dress! How proudly the white and yellow plumes arched over his cap, and how delicate were the laces on his collar and cuffs! His son, the very image of the handsome father, stood beside him, and the count had laid his hand familiarly on his shoulder, as if he were not his child, but a friend and comrade.

"A devil of a fellow!" whispered the count to the abbot. "Did you see the fair-haired lad's throw? From what house does the young noble come?"

The prelate shrugged his shoulders, and answered smiling:

"From the smithy at Richtberg."

"Does he belong to Adam?" laughed the other. "Zounds! I had a bitter hour in the confessional on his mother's account. He has inherited the beautiful Florette's hair and eyes; otherwise he looks like his father. With your permission, my Lord Abbot, I'll call the boy."

"Afterwards, afterwards," replied the superior of the monastery in a tone of friendly denial, which permitted no contradiction. "First tell the boys, what we have decided?"

Count Frohlinger bowed respectfully, then drew his son closer to his side, and waited for the boys, to whom the abbot beckoned.

As soon as they had gathered in a group before him, the nobleman exclaimed:

"You have just bid this good-for-nothing farewell. What should you say, if I left him among you till Christmas? The Lord Abbot will keep him, and you, you...."

But he had no time to finish the sentence. The pupils rushed upon him, shouting:

"Stay here, Philipp! Count Lips must stay!"

One little flaxen-headed fellow nestled closely to his regained protector, another kissed the count's hand, and two larger boys seized Philipp by the arm and tried to drag him away from his father, back into their circle.

The abbot looked on at the tumult kindly, and bright tear-drops ran down into the old count's beard, for his heart was easily touched. When he recovered his composure, he exclaimed:

"Lips shall stay, you rogues; he shall stay! And the Lord Abbot has given you permission, to come with me to-day to my hunting-box and light a St. John's fire. There shall be no lack of cakes and wine."

"Hurrah! hurrah! Long live the count!" shouted the pupils, and all who had caps tossed them into the air. Ulrich was carried away by the enthusiasm of the others; and all the evil words his father had so lavishly heaped on the handsome, merry gentleman--all Hangemarx's abuse of knights and nobles were forgotten.

The abbot and his companion withdrew, but as soon as the boys knew that they were unobserved, Count Lips cried:

"You fellow yonder, you greenhorn, threw the stone over the roof. I saw it. Come here. Over the roof? That should be my right. Whoever breaks the first window in the steeple, shall be victor."

The smith's son felt embarrassed, for he shrank from the mischief and feared his father and the abbot. But when the young count held out his closed hands, saying: "If you choose the red stone, you shall throw first," he pointed to his companion's right hand, and, as it concealed the red pebble, began the contest. He threw the stone, and struck the window. Amid loud shouts of exultation from the boys, more than one round pane of glass, loosened from the leaden casing, rattled in broken fragments on the church roof, and from thence fell silently on the grass. Count Lips laughed aloud in his delight, and was preparing to follow Ulrich's example, but the wooden gate was pushed violently open, and Brother Hieronymus, the most severe of all the monks, appeared in the playground. The zealous priest's cheeks glowed with anger, terrible were the threats he uttered, and declaring that the festival of St. John should not be celebrated, unless the shameless wretch, who had blasphemously shattered the steeple window, confessed his fault, he scanned the pupils with rolling eyes.

Young Count Lips stepped boldly forward, saying beseechingly:

"I did it, Father--unintentionally! Forgive me!"

"You?" asked the monk, his voice growing lower and more gentle, as he continued: "Folly and wantonness without end! When will you learn discretion, Count Philipp? But as you did it unintentionally, I will let it pass for to-day."

With these words, the monk left the court-yard; and as soon as the gate had closed behind him, Ulrich approached his generous companion, and said in a tone that only he could hear, yet grateful to the inmost depths of his heart:

"I will repay you some day."

"Nonsense!" laughed the young count, throwing his arm over the shoulder of the artisan's son. "If the glass wouldn't rattle, I would throw now; but there's another day coming to-morrow."

CHAPTER VII.

AUTUMN had come. The yellow leaves were fluttering about the school play-ground, the starlings were gathering in flocks on the church roof to take their departure, and Ulrich would fain have gone with them, no matter where. He could not feel at home in the monastery and among his companions. Always first in Richtberg, he was rarely so here, most seldom of all in school, for his father had forbidden the doctor to teach him Latin, so in that study he was last of all.

Often, when every one was asleep, the poor lad sat studying by the ever-burning lamp in the lobby, but in vain. He could not come up with the others, and the unpleasant feeling of remaining behind, in spite of the most honest effort, spoiled his life and made him irritable.

His comrades did not spare him, and when they called him "horse-boy," because he was often obliged to help Pater Benedictus in bringing refractory horses to reason, he flew into a rage and used his superior strength.

He stood on the worst terms of all with black-haired Xaver, to whom he owed the nickname.

This boy's father was the chief magistrate of the little city, and was allowed to take his son home with him at Michaelmas.

When the black-haired lad returned, he had many things to tell, gathered from half-understood rumor, about Ulrich's parents. Words were now uttered, that brought the blood to Ulrich's cheeks, yet he intentionally pretended not to hear them, because he dared not contradict tales that might be true. He well knew who had brought all these stories to the others, and answered Xaver's malicious spite with open enmity.

Count Lips did not trouble himself about any of these things, but remained Ulrich's most intimate friend, and was fond of going with him to see the horses. His vivacious intellect joyously sympathized with the smith's son, when he told him about Ruth's imaginary visions, and often in the play-ground he went apart with Ulrich from their companions; but this very circumstance was a thing that many, who had formerly been on more intimate terms with the aristocratic boy, were not disposed to forgive the new-comer.

Xaver had never been friendly to the count's son, and succeeded in irritating many against their former favorite, because he fancied himself better than they, and still more against Ulrich, who was half a servant, yet presumed to play the master and offer them violence.

The monks employed in the school soon noticed the ill terms, on which the new pupil stood with his companions, and did not lack reasons for shaking their heads over him.

Benedictus had not been able to conceal, who had been Ulrich's teacher in Richtberg; and the seeds the Jew had planted in the boy, seemed to be bearing strange and vexatious fruit.

Father Hieronymus, who instructed the pupils in religion, fairly raged, when he spoke of the destructive doctrines, that haunted the new scholar's head.

When, soon after Ulrich's reception into the school, he had spoken of Christ's work of redemption, and asked the boy: "From what is the world to be delivered by the Saviour's suffering?" the answer was: "From the arrogance of the rich and great." Hieronymus had spoken of the holy sacraments, and put the question: "By what means can the Christian surely obtain mercy, unless he bolts the door against it--that is, commits a mortal sin?" and Ulrich's answer was: "By doing unto others, what you would have others do unto you."

Such strange words might be heard by dozens from the boy's lips. Some were repeated from Hangemarx's sayings, others from the doctor's; and when asked where he obtained them, he quoted only the latter, for the monks were not to be allowed to know anything about his intercourse with the poacher.

Sharp reproofs and severe penances were now bestowed, for many a word that he had thought beautiful and pleasing in the sight of God; and the poor, tortured young soul often knew no help in its need.

He could not turn to the dear God and the Saviour, whom he was said to have blasphemed, for he feared them; but when he could no longer bear his grief, discouragement, and yearning, he prayed to the Madonna for help.

The image of the unhappy woman, about whom he had heard nothing but ill words, who had deserted him, and whose faithlessness gave the other boys a right to jeer at him, floated before his eyes, with that of the pure, holy Virgin in the church, brought by Father Lukas from Italy.

In spite of all the complaints about him, which were carried to the abbot, the latter thought him a misguided, but good and promising boy, an opinion strengthened by the music-teacher and the artist Lukas, whose best pupil Ulrich was; but they also were enraged against the Jew, who had lured this nobly-gifted child along the road of destruction; and often urged the abbot, who was anything but a zealot, to subject him to an examination by torture.

In November, the chief magistrate was summoned, and informed of the heresies with which the Hebrew had imperiled the soul of a Christian child.

The wise abbot wished to avoid anything, that would cause excitement, during this time of rebellion against the power of the Church, but the magistrate claimed the right to commence proceedings against the doctor. Of course, he said, sufficient proof must be brought against the accused. Father Hieronymus might note down the blasphemous tenets he heard from the boy's lips before witnesses, and at the Advent season the smith and his son would be examined.

The abbot, who liked to linger over his books, was glad to know that the matter was in the hands of the civil authorities, and enjoined Hieronymus to pay strict attention.

On the third Sunday in Advent, the magistrate again came to the monastery. His horses had worked their way with the sleigh through the deep snow in the ravine with much difficulty, and, half-frozen, he went directly to the refectory and there asked for his son.

The latter was lying with a bandaged eye in the cold dormitory, and when his father sought him, he heard that Ulrich had wounded him.

It would not have needed Xaver's bitter complaints, to rouse his father to furious rage against the boy who had committed this violence, and he was by no means satisfied, when he learned that the culprit had been excluded for three weeks from the others' sports, and placed on a very frugal diet. He went furiously to the abbot.

The day before (Saturday), Ulrich had gone at noon, without the young count, who was in confinement for some offence, to the snow-covered play-ground, where he was attacked by Xaver and a dozen of his comrades, pushed into a snow-bank, and almost suffocated. The conspirators had stuffed icicles and snow under his clothes next his skin, taken off his shoes and filled them with snow, and meantime Xaver jumped upon his back, pressing his face into the snow till Ulrich lost his breath, and believed his last hour had come.

Exerting the last remnant of his strength, he had succeeded in throwing off and seizing his tormentor. While the others fled, he wreaked his rage on the magistrate's son to his heart's content, first with his fists, and then with the heavy shoe that lay beside him. Meantime, snowballs had rained upon his body and head from all directions, increasing his fury; and as soon as Xaver no longer struggled he started up, exclaiming with glowing cheeks and upraised fists:

"Wait, wait, you wicked fellows! The doctor in Richtberg knows a word, by which he shall turn you all into toads and rats, you miserable rascals!"

Xaver had remembered this speech, which he repeated to his father, cleverly enlarged with many a false word. The abbot listened to the magistrate's complaint very quietly.

The angry father was no sufficient witness for him, yet the matter seemed important enough to send for and question Ulrich, though the meal-time had already begun. The Jew had really spoken to his daughter about the magic word, and the pupil of the monastery had threatened his companions with it. So the investigation might begin.

Ulrich was led back to the prison-chamber, where some thin soup and bread awaited him, but he touched neither. Food and drink disgusted him, and he could neither work nor sit still.

The little bell, which, summoned all the occupants of the monastery, was heard at an unusual hour, and about vespers the sound of sleigh-bells attracted him to the window. The abbot and Father Hieronymus were talking in undertones to the magistrate, who was just preparing to enter his sleigh.

They were speaking of him and the doctor, and the pupils had just been summoned to bear witness against him. No one had told him so, but he knew it, and was seized with such anxiety about the doctor, that drops of perspiration stood on his brow.

He was clearly aware that he had mingled his teacher's words with the poacher's blasphemous sayings, and also that he had put the latter into the mouth of Ruth's father.

He was a traitor, a liar, a miserable scoundrel!

He wished to go to the abbot and confess all, yet dared not, and so the hours stole away until the time for the evening mass.

While in church he strove to pray, not only for himself but for the doctor, but in vain, he could think of nothing but the trial, and while kneeling with his hands over his eyes, saw the Jew in fetters before him, and he himself at the trial in the town-hall.

At last the mass ended.

Ulrich rose. Just before him hung the large crucifix, and the Saviour on the cross, who with his head bowed on one side, usually gazed so gently and mournfully upon the ground, to-day seemed to look at him with mingled reproach and accusation.

In the dormitory, his companions avoided him as if he had the plague, but he scarcely noticed it.

The moonlight and the reflection from the snow shone brightly through the little window, but Ulrich longed for darkness, and buried his face in the pillows. The clock in the steeple struck ten.

He raised himself and listened to the deep breathing of the sleepers on his right and left, and the gnawing of a mouse under the bed.

His heart throbbed faster and more anxiously, but suddenly seemed to stand still, for a low voice had called his name.

"Ulrich!" it whispered again, and the young count, who lay beside him, rose in bed and bent towards him. Ulrich had told him about the word, and often indulged in wishes with him, as he had formerly done with Ruth. Philipp now whispered:

"They are going to attack the doctor. The abbot and magistrate questioned us, as if it were a matter of life and death. I kept what I know about the word to myself, for I'm sorry for the Jew, but Xaver, spiteful fellow, made it appear as if you really possessed the spell, and just now he came to me and said his father would seize the Jew early to-morrow morning, and then he would be tortured. Whether they will hang or burn him is the question. His life is forfeited, his father said--and the black-visaged rascal rejoiced over it."

"Sileutium, turbatores!" cried the sleepy voice of the monk in charge, and the boys hastily drew back into the feathers and were silent.

The young count soon fell asleep again, but Ulrich buried his head still deeper among the pillows; it seemed as if he saw the mild, thoughtful face of the man, from whom he had received so much affection, gazing reproachfully at him; then the dumb wife appeared before his mind, and he fancied her soft hand was lovingly stroking his cheeks as usual. Ruth also appeared, not in the yellow silk dress, but clad in rags of a beggar, and she wept, hiding her face in her mother's lap.

He groaned aloud. The clock struck eleven. He rose and listened. Nothing stirred, and slipping on his clothes, he took his shoes in his hand and tried to open the window at the head of his bed. It had stood open during the day, but the frost fastened it firmly to the frame. Ulrich braced his foot against the wall and pulled with all his strength, but it resisted one jerk after another; at last it suddenly yielded and flew open, making a slight creaking and rattling, but the monk on guard did not wake, only murmured softly in his sleep.

The boy stood motionless for a time, holding his breath, then swung himself upon the parapet and looked out. The dormitory was in the second story of the monastery, above the rampart, but a huge bank of snow rose beside the wall, and this strengthened his courage.

With hurrying fingers he made the sign of the cross, a low: "Mary, pray for me," rose from his lips, then he shut his eyes and risked the leap.

There was a buzzing, roaring sound in his ears, his mother's image blended in strange distortion with the Jew's, then an icy sea swallowed him, and it seemed as if body and soul were frozen. But this sensation overpowered him only a few minutes, then working his way out of the mass of snow, he drew on his shoes, and dashed as if pursued by a pack of wolves, down the mountain, through the ravine, across the heights, and finally along the river to the city and the Richtberg.

VOLUME 2

CHAPTER VIII.

THE magistrate's horses did not reach the city gate, from the monastery, more quickly than Ulrich.

As soon as the smith was roused from sleep by the boy's knock and recognized his voice, he knew what was coming, and silently listened to the lad's confessions, while he himself hurriedly yet carefully took out his hidden hoard, filled a bag with the most necessary articles, thrust his lightest hammer into his belt, and poured water on the glimmering coals. Then, locking the door, he sent Ulrich to Hangemarx, with whom he had already settled many things; for Caspar, the juggler, who learned more through his daughters than any other man, had come to him the day before, to tell him that something was being plotted against the Jew.

Adam found the latter still awake and at work. He was prepared for the danger that threatened him, and ready to fly. No word of complaint, not even a hasty gesture betrayed the mental anguish of the persecuted man, and the smith's heart melted, as he heard the doctor rouse his wife and child from their sleep.

The terrified moans of the startled wife, and Ruth's loud weeping and curious questions, were soon drowned by the lamentations of old Rahel, who wrapped in even more kerchiefs than usual, rushed into the sitting-room, and while lamenting and scolding in a foreign tongue, gathered together everything that lay at hand. She had dragged a large chest after her, and now threw in candlesticks, jugs, and even the chessmen and Ruth's old doll with a broken head.

When the third hour after midnight came, the doctor was ready for departure.

Marx's charcoal sledge, with its little horse, stopped before the door.

This was a strange animal, no larger than a calf, as thin as a goat, and in some places woolly, in others as bare as a scraped poodle.

The smith helped the dumb woman into the sleigh, the doctor put Ruth in her lap, Ulrich consoled the child, who asked him all sorts of questions, but the old woman would not part from the chest, and could scarcely be induced to enter the vehicle.

"You know, across the mountains into the Rhine valley--no matter where," Costa whispered to the poacher.

Hangemarx urged on his little horse, and answered, not turning to the Israelite, who had addressed him, but to Adam, who he thought would understand him better than the bookworm: "It won't do to go up the ravine, without making any circuit. The count's hounds will track us, if they follow. We'll go first up the high road by the Lautenhof. To-morrow will be a fair-day. People will come early from the villages and tread down the snow, so the dogs will lose the scent. If it would only snow."

Before the smithy, the doctor held out his hand to Adam, saying: "We part here, friend."

"We'll go with you, if agreeable to you."

"Consider," the other began warningly, but Adam interrupted him, saying:

"I have considered everything; lost is lost. Ulrich, take the doctor's sack from his shoulder."

For a long time nothing more was said.

The night was clear and cold; the men's footsteps fell noiselessly on the soft snow, nothing was heard except the creaking of the sledge, and ever and anon Elizabeth's low moaning, or a louder word in the old woman's soliloquy. Ruth had fallen asleep on her mother's lap, and was breathing heavily.

At Lautenhof a narrow path led through the mountains deep into the forest.

As it grew steeper, the snow became knee-deep, and the men helped the little horse, which often coughed, tossing its thick head up and down, as if working a churn. Once, when the poor creature met with a very heavy fall,

Marx pointed to the green woollen scarf on the animal's neck, and whispered to the smith "Twenty years old, and has the glanders besides."

The little beast nodded slowly and mournfully, as if to say: "Life is hard; this will probably be the last time I draw a sleigh."

The broad, heavy-laden pine-boughs drooped wearily by the roadside, the gleaming surface of the snow stretched in a monotonous sheet of white between the trunks of the trees, the tops of the dark rocks beside the way bore smooth white caps of loose snow, the forest stream was frozen along the edges, only in the centre did the water trickle through snow- crystals and sharp icicles to the valley.

So long as the moon shone, flickering rays danced and sparkled on the ice and snow, but afterwards only the tedious glimmer of the universal snow- pall lighted the traveller's way.

"If it would only snow!" repeated the charcoal-burner.

The higher they went, the deeper grew the snow, the more wearisome the wading and climbing.

Often, on the doctor's account, the smith called in a low voice, "Halt!" and then Costa approached the sleigh and asked: "How do you feel?" or said: "We are getting on bravely."

Rahel screamed whenever a fox barked in the distance, a wolf howled, or an owl flew through the treetops, brushing the snow from the branches with its wings; but the others also started. Marx alone walked quietly and undisturbed beside his little horse's thick head; he was familiar with all the voices of the forest.

It grew colder towards morning. Ruth woke and cried, and her father, panting for breath, asked: "When shall we rest?"

"Behind the height; ten arrow-shots farther," replied the charcoal-burner.

"Courage," whispered the smith. "Get on the sledge, doctor; we'll push."

But Costa shook his head, pointed to the panting horse, and dragged himself onward.

The poacher must have sent his arrows in a strange curve, for one quarter of an hour after another slipped by, and the top was not yet gained. Meantime it grew lighter and lighter, and the charcoal-burner, with increasing anxiety, ever and anon raised his head, and glanced aside. The sky was covered with clouds-the light overhead grey, dim, and blended with mist. The snow was still dazzling, though it no longer sparkled and glittered, but covered every object with the dull whiteness of chalk.

Ulrich kept beside the sledge to push it. When Ruth heard him groan, she stroked the hand that grasped the edges, this pleased him; and he smiled.

When they again stopped, this time on the crest of the ridge, Ulrich noticed that the charcoal-burner was sniffing the air like a hound, and asked:

"What is it, Marxle?"

The poacher grinned, as he answered: "It's going to snow; I smell it."

The road now led down towards the valley, and, after a short walk, the charcoal-burner said:

"We shall find shelter below with Jorg, and a warm fire too, you poor women."

These were cheering words, and came just at the right time, for large snow-flakes began to fill the air, and a light breeze drove them into the travellers' faces. "There!" cried Ulrich, pointing to the snow covered roof of a wooden hut, that stood close before them in a clearing on the edge of the forest.

Every face brightened, but Marx shook his head doubtfully, muttering:

"No smoke, no barking; the place is empty. Jorg has gone. At Whitsuntide--how many years ago is it?--the boys left to act as raftsmen, but then he stayed here."

Reckoning time was not the charcoal-burner's strong point; and the empty hut, the dreary open window-casements in the mouldering wooden walls, the holes in the roof, through which a quantity of snow had drifted into the only room in the deserted house, indicated that no human being had sought shelter here for many a winter.

Old Rahel uttered a fresh wail of grief, when she saw this shelter; but after the men had removed the snow as well as they could, and covered the holes in the roof with pine-branches; when Adam had lighted a fire, and the sacks and coverlets were brought in from the sledge, and laid on a dry spot to furnish seats for the women, fresh courage entered their hearts, and Rahel, unasked, dragged herself to the hearth, and set the snow-filled pot on the fire.

"The nag must have two hours' rest," Marx said, "then they could push on and reach the miller in the ravine before night. There they would find kind friends, for Jacklein had been with him among the 'peasants.'" The snow-water boiled, the doctor and his wife rested, Ulrich and Ruth brought wood, which the smith had split, to the fire to dry, when suddenly a terrible cry of grief rang outside of the hut.

Costa hastily rose, the children followed, and old Rahel, whimpering, drew the upper kerchief on her head over her face.

The little horse, its tiny legs stretched far apart, was lying in the snow by the sledge. Beside it knelt Marx, holding the clumsy head on his knee, and blowing with his crooked mouth into the animal's nostrils. The creature showed its yellow teeth, and put out its bluish tongue as if it wanted to lick him; then the heavy head fell, the dying animal's eyes started from their sockets, its legs grew perfectly stiff, and this time the horse was really dead, while the shafts of the sledge vainly thrust themselves into the air, like the gaping mouth of a deserted bird.

No farther progress was possible. The women sat trembling in the hut, roasting before the fire, and shivering when a draught touched them.... Ruth wept for the poor little horse, and Marx sat as if utterly crushed beside his old friend's stiffening body, heeding nothing, least of all the snow, which was making him whiter than the miller, with whom he had expected to rest that evening. The doctor gazed in mute despair at his dumb wife, who, with clasped hands, was praying fervently; the smith pressed his hand upon his brow, vainly pondering over what was to be done now, until his head ached; while, from the distance, echoed the howl of a hungry wolf, and a pair of ravens alighted on a white bough beside the little horse, gazing greedily at the corpse lying in the snow.

Meantime, the abbot was sitting in his pleasantly-warmed study, which was pervaded by a faint, agreeable perfume, gazing now at the logs burning in the beautiful marble mantel-piece, and then at the magistrate, who had brought him strange tidings.

The prelate's white woollen morning-robe clung closely around his stately figure. Beside him lay, side by side, for comparison, two manuscript copies of his favorite book, the idyls of Theocritus, which, for his amusement, and to excel the translation of Coban Hesse, he was turning into Latin verse, as the duties of his office gave him leisure.

The magistrate was standing by the fire-side. He was a thick-set man of middle height, with a large head, and clever but coarse features, as rudely moulded as if they had been carved from wood. He was one of the best informed lawyers in the country, and his words flowed as smoothly and clearly from his strong lips, as if every thought in his keen brain was born fully matured and beautifully finished.

In the farthest corner of the room, awaiting a sign from his master, stood the magistrate's clerk, a little man with a round head, and legs like the sickle of the waxing or waning moon. He carried under his short arms two portfolios, filled with important papers.

"He comes from Portugal, and has lived under an assumed name?" So the abbot repeated, what he had just heard.

"His name is Lopez, not Costa," replied the other; "these papers prove it. Give me the portfolio, man! The diploma is in the brown one."

He handed a parchment to the prelate, who, after reading it, said firmly:

"This Jew is a more important person than we supposed. They are not lavish with such praise in Coimbra. Are you taking good care of the doctor's books Herr Conrad? I will look at them to-morrow."

"They are at your disposal. These papers. . . ."

"Leave them, leave them."

"There will be more than enough for the complaint without them," said the magistrate. "Our town-clerk, who though no student is, as you know, a man of much experience, shares my opinion." Then he continued pathetically: "Only he who has cause to fear the law hides his name, only he, who feels guilty, flees the judge."

A subtle smile, that was not wholly free from bitterness, hovered around the abbot's lips, for he thought of the painful trial and the torture- chamber in the town hall, and no longer saw in the doctor merely the Jew, but the humanist and companion in study.

His glance again fell on the diploma, and while the other continued his representations, the prelate stretched himself more comfortably in his arm-chair and gazed thoughtfully at the ground. Then, as if an idea had suddenly occurred to him, he touched his high forehead with the tips of his fingers, and suddenly interrupting the eager speaker, said:

"Father Anselm came to us from Porto five years ago, and when there knew every one who understood Greek. Go, Gutbub, and tell the librarian to come." The monk soon appeared.

Tidings of Ulrich's disappearance and the Jew's flight had spread rapidly through the monastery; the news was discussed in the choir, the school, the stable and the kitchen; Father Anselm alone had heard nothing of the matter, though he had been busy in the library before daybreak, and the vexatious incident had been eagerly talked of there.

It was evident, that the elderly man cared little for anything that happened in the world, outside of his manuscripts and printing. His long, narrow head rested on a thin neck, which did not stand erect, but grew out between the shoulders like a branch from the stem. His face was grey and lined with wrinkles, like pumice-stone, but large bright eyes lent meaning and attraction to the withered countenance.

At first he listened indifferently to the abbot's story, but as soon as the Jew's name was mentioned, and he had read the diploma, as swiftly as if he possessed the gift of gathering the whole contents of ten lines at a single comprehensive glance, he said eagerly:

"Lopez, Doctor Lopez was here! And we did not know it, and have not consulted with him! Where is he? What are people planning against him?"

After he had learned that the Jew had fled, and the abbot requested him to tell all he knew about the doctor, he collected his thoughts and sorrowfully began:

"To be sure, to be sure; the man committed a great offence. He is a great sinner in God's eyes. You know his guilt?"

"We know everything," cried the magistrate, with a meaning glance at the prelate. Then, as if he sincerely pitied the criminal, he continued with well-feigned sympathy: "How did the learned man commit such a misdeed?"

The abbot understood the stratagem, but Anselm's words could not be recalled, and as he himself desired to learn more of the doctor's history, he asked the monk to tell what he knew.

The librarian, in his curt, dry manner, yet with a warmth unusual to him, described the doctor's great learning and brilliant intellect, saying that his father, though a Jew, had been in his way an aristocratic man, allied with many a noble family, for until the reign of King Emanuel, who persecuted the Hebrews, they had enjoyed great distinction in Portugal. In those days it had been hard to distinguish Jews from Christians. At the time of the expulsion a few favored Israelites had been allowed to stay, among them the worthy Rodrigo, the doctor's father, who had been the king's physician and was held in high esteem by the sovereign. Lopez obtained the highest honors at Coimbra, but instead of following medicine, like his father, devoted himself to the humanities.

"There was no need to earn his living--to earn his living," continued the monk, speaking slowly and carefully, and repeating the conclusion of his sentence, as if he were in the act of collating two manuscripts, "for Rodrigo was one of the wealthiest men in Portugal. His son Lopez was rich, very rich in friends, and among them were numbered all to whom knowledge was dear. Even among the Christians he had many friends. Among us--I mean in our library--he also obtained great respect. I owe him many a hint, much aid; I mean in referring me to rare books, and explaining obscure passages. When he no longer visited us, I missed him sorely. I am not curious; or do you think I am? I am not curious, but I could not help inquiring about him, and then I heard very bad things. Women are to blame for everything; of course it was a woman again. A merchant from Flanders--a Christian--had settled in Porto. The doctor's father visited his house; but you probably know all this?"

"Of course! of course!" cried the magistrate. "But go on with your story."

"Old Doctor Rodrigo was the Netherlander's physician, and closed his eyes on the death-bed. An orphan was left, a girl, who had not a single relative in Porto. They said--I mean the young doctors and students who had seen her--that she was pleasing, very pleasing to the eye. But it was not on that account, but because she was orphaned and desolate, that the physician took the child--I mean the girl."

"And reared her as a Jewess?" interrupted the magistrate, with a questioning glance.

"As a Jewess?" replied the monk, excitedly. "Who says so? He did nothing of the sort. A Christian widow educated her in the physician's country-house, not in the city. When the young doctor returned from Coimbra, he saw her there more than once--more than once; certainly, more often than was good for him. The devil had a finger in the matter. I know, too, how they were married. Before one Jew and two Christian witnesses, they plighted their troth to each other, and exchanged rings--rings as if it were a Christian ceremony, though he remained a Jew and she a Christian. He intended to go to the Netherlands with her, but one of the witnesses betrayed them--denounced them to the Holy Inquisition.This soon interposed of course, for there it interferes with everything, and in this case it was necessary; nay more--a Christian duty. The young wife was seized in the street with her attendant and thrown into prison; on the rack she entirely lost the power of speech. The old physician and the doctor were warned in time, and kept closely concealed. Through Chamberlain de Sa, her uncle--or was it only her cousin?--through de Sa the wife regained her liberty, and then I believe all three fled to France--the father, son and wife. But no, they must have come here...."

"There you have it!" cried the magistrate, interrupting the monk, and glancing triumphantly at the prelate. "An old practitioner scents crime, as a tree frog smells rain. Now, for the first time, I can say with certainty: We have him, and the worst punishment is too little for his deserts. There shall be an unparalleled execution, something wonderful, magnificent, grand! You have given me important information, and I thank you, Father."

"Then you knew nothing?" faltered the librarian; and, raising his neck higher than usual, the vein in the centre of his forehead swelled with wrath.

"No, Anselme!" said the abbot. "But it was your duty to speak, as, unfortunately, it was mine to listen. Come to me again, by and bye; I have something to say to you."

The librarian bowed silently, coldly and proudly, and without vouchsafing the magistrate a single glance, went back, not to his books, but to his cell, where he paced up and down a long time, sorrowfully murmuring Lopez's name, striking himself on the mouth, pressing his clenched hand to his brow, and at last throwing himself on his knees to pray for the Jew, before the image of the crucified Redeemer.

As soon as the monk had left the room, the magistrate exclaimed:

"What unexpected aid! What series of sins lie before us! First the small ones. He had never worn the Jews' badge, and allowed himself to be served by Christians, for Caspar's daughters were often at the House to help in sewing. A sword was found in his dwelling, and the Jew, who carries weapons, renounces, since he uses self-protection, the aid of the authorities. Finally, we know that Lopez used an assumed name. Now we come to the great offences. They are divided into four parts. He has practised magic spells; he has sought to corrupt a Christian's son by heresies; he has led a Christian woman into a marriage; and he has--I close with the worst--he has reared the daughter of a Christian woman, I mean his wife, a Jewess!"

"Reared his child a Jewess? Do you know that positively?" asked the abbot.

"She bears the Jewish name of Ruth. What I have taken the liberty to make prominent are well chosen, clearly-proved crimes, worthy of death. Your learning is great, Reverend Abbot, but I know the old writers, too. The Emperor Constantius made marriages between Jews and Christians punishable with death. I can show you the passage."

The abbot felt that the crime of which the Jew was accused was a heavy and unpardonable one, but he regarded only the sin, and it vexed him to see how the magistrate's zeal was exclusively turned against the unhappy criminal. So he rose, saying with cold hauteur:

"Then do your duty."

"Rely upon it. We shall capture him and his family to-morrow. The town-clerk is full of zeal too. We shall not be able to harm the child, but it must be taken from the Jew and receive a Christian education. It would be our right to do this, even if both parents were Hebrews. You know the Freiburg case. No less a personage than the great Ulrich Zasius has decided, that Jewish children might be baptized without their father's knowledge. I beg you to send Father Anselm to the town-hall on Saturday as a witness."

"Very well," replied the prelate, but he spoke with so little eagerness, that it justly surprised the magistrate. "Well then, catch the Jew; but take him alive. And one thing more! I wish to see and speak to the doctor, before you torture him."

"I will bring him to you day after to-morrow." The Nurembergers! the Nurembergers!...." replied the abbot, shrugging his shoulders.

"What do you mean?"

"They don't hang any one till they catch him." The magistrate regarded these words as a challenge to put forth every effort for the Jew's capture, so he answered eagerly: "We shall have him, Your Reverence, we shall surely have him. They are trapped in the snow. The sergeants are searching the roads; I shall summon your foresters and mine, and put them under Count Frohlinger's command. It is his duty to aid us. What they cannot find with their attendants, squires, beaters and hounds, is not hidden in the forest. Your blessing, Holy Father, there is no time to lose."

The abbot was alone.

He gazed thoughtfully at the coals in the fireplace, recalling everything he had just seen and heard, while his vivid power of imagination showed him the learned, unassuming man, who had spent long years in quiet seclusion, industriously devoting himself to the pursuit of knowledge. A slight feeling of envy stole into his heart; how rarely he himself was permitted to pursue undisturbed, and without interruption, the scientific subjects, in which alone he found pleasure.

He was vexed with himself, that he could feel so little anger against a criminal, whose guilt was deserving of death, and reproached himself for lukewarmness. Then he remembered that the Jew had sinned for love, and that to him who has loved much, much should be forgiven. Finally, it seemed a great boon, that he was soon to be permitted to make the acquaintance of the worthy doctor from Coimbra. Never had the zealous magistrate appeared so repulsive as to-day, and when he remembered how the crafty man had outwitted poor Father Anselm in his presence, he felt as if he had himself committed an unworthy deed. And yet, yet--the Jew could not be saved, and had deserved what threatened him.

A monk summoned him, but the abbot did not wish to be disturbed, and ordered that he should be left an hour alone.

He now took in his hand a volume he called the mirror of his soul, and in which he noted many things "for the confession," that he desired to determine to his own satisfaction. To-day he wrote:

"It would be a duty to hate a Jew and criminal, zealously to persecute what Holy Church has condemned. Yet I cannot do so. Who is the magistrate, and what are Father Anselm and this learned doctor! The one narrow-minded, only familiar with the little world he knows and in which he lives, the others divinely-gifted, full of knowledge, rulers in the wide domain of thought. And the former outwits the latter, who show themselves children in comparison with him. How Anselm stood before him! The deceived child was great, the clever man small. What men call cleverness is only small-minded persons' skill in life; simplicity is peculiar to the truly great man, because petty affairs are too small for him, and his eye does not count the grains of dust, but looks upward, and has a share in the infinitude stretching before us. Jesus Christ was gentle as a child and loved children, he was the Son of God, yet voluntarily yielded himself into the hands of men. The greatest of great men did not belong to the ranks of the clever. Blessed are the meek, He said. I understand those words. He is meek, whose soul is open, clear and pure as a mirror, and the greatest philosophers, the noblest minds I have met in life and history were also meek. The brute is clever; wisdom is the cleverness of the noble-minded. We must all follow the Saviour, and he among us, who unites wisdom to meekness, will come nearest to the Redeemer."

CHAPTER IX.

MARX had gone out to reconnoitre in a more cheerful mood, for the doctor had made good the loss sustained in the death of his old nag, and he returned at noon with good news.

A wood-carrier, whom he met on the high-road, had told him where Jorg, the charcoal-burner, lived.

The fugitives could reach his hut before night, and in so doing approach nearer the Rhine valley. Everything was ready for departure, but old Rahel objected to travelling further. She was sitting on a stone before the hut, for the smoke in the narrow room oppressed her breathing, and it seemed as if terror had robbed her of her senses. Gazing into vacancy with wild eyes and chattering teeth, she tried to make cakes and mould dumplings out of the snow, which she probably took for flour. She neither heard the doctor's call nor saw his wife beckon, and when the former grasped her to compel her to rise, uttered a loud shriek. At last the smith succeeded in persuading her to sit down on the sledge, and the party moved forward.

Adam had harnessed himself to the front of the vehicle. Marx went to and fro, pushing when necessary. The dumb woman waded through the snow by her husband's side. "Poor wife!" he said once; but she pressed his arm closer, looking up into his eyes as if she wished to say: "Surely I shall lack nothing, if only you are spared to me!"

She enjoyed his presence as if it were a favor granted by destiny, but only at chance moments, for she could not banish her fear for him, and of the pursuers--her dread of uncertainty and wandering.

If snow rattled from a pine-tree, if she noticed Lopez turn his head, or if old Rahel uttered a moan, she shuddered; and this was not unperceived by her husband, who told himself that she had every reason to look forward to the next few hours with grave anxiety. Each moment might bring imprison-ment to him and all, and if they discovered--if it were disclosed who he, who Elizabeth was. . . .

Ulrich and Ruth brought up the rear, saying little to each other.

At first the path ascended again, then led down to the valley. It had stopped snowing long before, and the farther they went the lighter the drifts became.

They had journeyed in this way for two hours, when Ruth's strength failed, and she stood still with tearful, imploring eyes. The charcoal- burner saw it, and growled:

"Come here, little girl; I'll carry you to the sleigh."

"No, let me," Ulrich eagerly interposed. And Ruth exclaimed:

"Yes, you, you shall carry me."

Marx grasped her around the waist, lifted her high into the air, and placed her in the boy's arms. She clasped her hands around his neck, and as he walked on pressed her fresh, cool cheek to his. It pleased him, and the thought entered his mind that he had been parted from her a long time, and it was delightful to have her again.

His heart swelled more and more; he felt that he would rather have Ruth than everything else in the world, and he drew her towards him as closely as if an invisible hand were already out-stretched to take her from him.

To-day her dear, delicate little face was not pale, but glowed crimson after the long walk through the frosty, winter air. She was glad to have Ulrich clasp her so firmly, so she pressed her cheek closer to his, loosened her fingers from his neck, caressingly stroked his face with her cold hand, and murmured:

"You are kind, Ulrich, and I love you!"

It sounded so tender and loving, that Ulrich's heart melted, for no one had spoken to him so since his mother went away.

He felt strong and joyous, Ruth did not seem at all heavy, and when she again clasped her hands around his neck, he said: "I should like to carry you so always."

Ruth only nodded, as if the wish pleased her, but he continued:

"In the monastery I had no one, who was very kind to me, for even Lips, well, he was a count--everybody is kind to you. You don't know what it is, to be all alone, and have to struggle against every one. When I was in the monastery, I often wished that I was lying under the earth; now I don't want to die, and we will stay with you--father told me so--and everything will be just as it was, and I shall learn no more Latin, but become a painter, or smith-artificer, or anything else, for aught I care, if I'm only not obliged to leave you again."

He felt Ruth raise her little head, and press her soft lips on his forehead just over his eyes; then he lowered the arms in which she rested, kissed her mouth, and said: "Now it seems as if I had my mother back again!"

"Does it?" she asked, with sparkling eyes. "Now put me down. I am well again, and want to run."

So saying, she slipped to the ground, and he did not detain her.

Ruth now walked stoutly on beside the lad, and made him tell her about the bad boys in the monastery, Count Lips, the pictures, the monks, and his own flight, until, just as it grew dark, they reached the goal of their walk.

Jorg, the charcoal-burner, received them, and opened his hut, but only to go away himself, for though willing to give the fugitives shelter and act against the authorities, he did not wish to be present, if the refugees should be caught. Caught with them, hung with them! He knew the proverb, and went down to the village, with the florins Adam gave him.

There was a hearth for cooking in the hut, and two rooms, one large and one small, for in summer the charcoal-burners' wives and children live with them. The travellers needed rest and refreshment, and might have found both here, had not fear embittered the food and driven sleep from their weary eyes.

Jorg was to return early the next morning with a team of horses. This was a great consolation. Old Rahel, too, had regained her self-control, and was sound asleep.

The children followed her example, and at midnight Elizabeth slept too.

Marx lay beside the hearth, and from his crooked mouth came a strange, snoring noise, that sounded like the last note of an organ-pipe, from which the air is expiring.

Hours after all the others were asleep, Adam and the doctor still sat on a sack of straw, engaged in earnest conversation.

Lopez had told his friend the story of his happiness and sorrow, closing with the words:

"So you know who we are, and why we left our home. You are giving me your future, together with many other things; no gift can repay you; but first of all, it was due you that you should know my past."

Then, holding out his hand to the smith, he asked: "You are a Christian; will you still cleave to me, after what you have heard?"

Adam silently pressed the Jew's right hand, and after remaining lost in thought for a time, said in a hollow tone:

"If they catch you, and--Holy Virgin--if they discover.....Ruth....She is not really a Jew's child.....have you reared her as a Jewess?"

"No; only as a good human child."

"Is she baptized?"

Lopez answered this question also in the negative. The smith shook his head disapprovingly, but the doctor said: "She knows more about Jesus, than many a Christian child of her age. When she is grown up, she will be free to follow either her mother or her father."

"Why have you not become a Christian yourself? Forgive the question. Surely you are one at heart."

"That, that....you see, there are things....Suppose that every male scion of your family, from generation to generation, for many hundred years, had been a smith, and now a boy should grow up, who said: I--I despise your trade?'"

"If Ulrich should say: 'I-I wish to be an artist;' it would be agreeable to me."

"Even if smiths were persecuted like us Jews, and he ran from your guild to another out of fear?"

"No--that would be base, and can scarcely be compared with your case; for see--you are acquainted with everything, even what is called Christianity; nay, the Saviour is dear to you; you have already told me so. Well then! Suppose you were a foundling and were shown our faith and yours, and asked for which you would decide, which would you choose?"

"We pray for life and peace, and where peace exists, love cannot be lacking, and yet! Perhaps I might decide for yours."

"There you have it."

"No, no! We have not done with this question so speedily. See, I do not grudge you your faith, nor do I wish to disturb it. The child must believe, that all its parents do and require of him is right, but the stranger sees with different, keener eyes, than the son and daughter. You occupy a filial relation towards your Church--I do not. I know the doctrine of Jesus Christ, and if I had lived in Palestine in his time, should have been one of the first to follow the Master, but since, from those days to the present, much human work has mingled with his sublime teachings. This too must be dear to you, for it belongs to your parents--but it repels me. I have lived, labored and watched all night for the truth, and were I now to come before the baptismal font and say 'yes' to everything the priests ask, I should be a liar."

"They have caused you bitter suffering; tortured your wife, driven you and your family from your home....."

"I have borne all that patiently," cried the doctor, deeply moved. "But there are many other sins now committed against me and mine, for which there is no forgiveness. I know the great Pagans and their works. Their need of love extends only to the nation, to which they belong, not to humanity. Unselfish justice, is to them the last thing man owes his fellow-man. Christ extended love to all nations, His heart was large enough to love all mankind. Human love, the purest and fairest of virtues, is the sublime gift, the noble heritage, he left behind to his brothers in sorrow. My heart, the poor heart under this black doublet, this heart was created for human love, this soul thirsted, with all its powers, to help its neighbors and lighten their sorrows. To exercise human love is to be good, but they no longer know it, and what is worse, a thousand times worse, they constantly destroy in me and mine the desire to be good, good in the sense of their own Master. Wordly wealth is trash--to be rich the poorest happiness. Yet the Jew is not forbidden to strive for this, they take scarcely half his gains;--nor can they deny him the pursuit of the pleasures of the intellect--pure knowledge--for our minds are not feebler or more idle, and soar no less boldly than theirs. The prophets came from the East! But the happiness of the soul --the right to exercise charity is denied to us. It is a part of charity for each man to regard his neighbor as himself--to feel for him, as it were, with his own heart--to lighten his burdens, minister unto him in his sorrows, and to gladden his happiness. This the Christian denies the Jew. Your love ceases when you meet me and mine, and if I sought to put myself on an equality with the Christian, from the pure desire to satisfy his Master's most beautiful lesson, what would be my fate? The Jew is not permitted to be good. Not to be good! Whoever imposes that upon his brother, commits a sin for which I know no forgiveness. And if Jesus Christ should return to earth and see the pack that hunts us, surely He, who was human love incarnate, would open His arms wide, wide to us, and ask: 'Who are these apostles of hate? I know them not!'"

The doctor paused, for the door had opened, and he rose with flushed face to look into the adjoining room; but the smith held him back, saying:

"Stay, stay! Marx went out into the open air. Ah, Sir! no doubt your words are true, but were they Jews who crucified the Saviour?"

"And this crime is daily avenged," replied Lopez. "How many wicked, how many low souls, who basely squander divine gifts to obtain worthless pelf, there are among my people! More than half of them are stripped of honor and dignity on your altar of vengeance, and thrust into the arms of repulsive avarice. And this, all this....But enough of these things! They rouse my inmost soul to wrath, and I have other matters to discuss with you."

The scholar now began to speak to the smith, like a dying man, about the future of his family, told him where he had concealed his small property, and did not hide the fact, that his marriage had not only drawn upon him the persecution of the Christians, but the curse of his co-religionists. He took it upon himself to provide for Ulrich, as if he were his own child, should any misfortune befall the smith; and Adam promised, if he remained alive and at liberty, to do the same for the doctor's wife and daughter.

Meantime, a conversation of a very different nature was held before the hut.

The poacher was sitting by the fire, when the door opened, and his name was called. He turned in alarm, but soon regained his composure, for it was Jorg who beckoned, and then drew him into the forest.

Marx expected no good news, yet he started when his companion said:

"I know now, who the man is you have brought. He's a Jew. Don't try to humbug me. The constable from the city has come to the village. The man, who captures the Israelite, will get fifteen florins. Fifteen florins, good money. The magistrate will count it, all on one board, and the vicar says...."

"I don't care much for your priests," replied Marx. "I am from Weinsberg, and have found the Jew a worthy man. No one shall touch him."

"A Jew, and a good man!" cried Jurg, laughing. "If you won't help, so much the worse for you. You'll risk your neck, and the fifteen florins. ....Will you go shares? Yes or no?"

"Heaven's thunder!" murmured the poacher, his crooked mouth watering." How much is half of fifteen florins?"

"About seven, I should say."

"A calf and a pig."

"A swine for the Jew, that will suit. You'll keep him here in the trap."

"I can't, Jorg; by my soul, I can't! Let me alone!"

"Very well, for aught I care; but the legal gentlemen. The gallows has waited for you long enough!"

"I can't; I can't. I've been an honest man all my life, and the smith Adam and his dead father have shown me many a kindness."

"Who means the smith any harm?"

"The receiver is as bad as the thief. If they catch him...."

"He'll be put in the stocks for a week. That's the worst that can befall him."

"No, no. Let me alone,--or I'll tell Adam what you're plotting...."

"Then I'll denounce you first, you gallows' fruit, you rogue, you poacher. They've suspected you a long time! Will you change your mind now, you blockhead?"

"Yes, yes; but Ulrich is here too, and the boy is as dear to me as my own child."

"I'll come here later, say that no vehicle can be had, and take him away with me. When it's all over, I'll let him go."

"Then I'll keep him. He already helps me as much, as if he were a grown man. Oh, dear, dear! The Jew, the gentle man, and the poor women, and the little girl, Ruth...."

"Big Jews and little Jews, nothing more. You've told me yourself, how the Hebrews were persecuted in your dead father's day. So we'll go shares. There's a light in the room still. You'll detain them. Count Frohlinger has been at his hunting-box since last evening....If they insist on moving forward, guide them to the village."

"And I've been an honest man all my life," whined the poacher, and then continued, threateningly: "If you harm a hair on Ulrich's head...."

"Fool that you are! I'll willingly leave the big feeder to you. Go in now, then I'll come and fetch the boy. There's money at stake--fifteen florins!" Fifteen minutes after, Jorg entered the but.

The smith and the doctor believed the charcoal-burner, when he told them that all the vehicles in the village were in use, but he would find one elsewhere. They must let the boy go with him, to enquire at the farm-houses in another village. Somebody would doubtless be found to risk his horses. The lad looked like a young nobleman, and the peasants would take earnest-money from him. If he, Jorg, should show them florins, it would get him into a fine scrape. The people knew he was as poor as a beggar.

The smith asked the poacher's opinion, and the latter growled:

"That will, doubtless, be a good plan."

He said no more, and when Adam held out his hand to the boy, and kissed him on the forehead, and the doctor bade him an affectionate farewell, Marx called himself a Judas, and would gladly have flung the tempting florins to the four winds, but it was too late.

The smith and Lopez heard him call anxiously to Jorg: "Take good care of the boy!" And when Adam patted him on the shoulder, saying: "You are a faithful fellow, Marx!" he could have howled like a mastiff and revealed all; but it seemed as if he again felt the rope around his neck, so he kept silence.

CHAPTER X.

THE grey dawn was already glimmering, yet neither the expected vehicle nor Jorg had come. Old Rahel, usually an early riser, was sleeping as soundly as if she had to make up the lost slumber of ten nights; but the smith's anxiety would no longer allow him to remain in the close room. Ruth followed him into the open air, and when she timidly touched him-- for there had always been something unapproachable to her in the silent man's gigantic figure--he looked at her from head to foot, with strange, questioning sympathy, and then asked suddenly, with a haste unusual to him.

"Has your father told you about Jesus Christ?"

"Often!" replied Ruth.

"And do you love Him?"

"Dearly. Father says He loved all children, and called them to Him."

"Of course, of course!" replied the smith, blushing with shame for his own distrust.

The doctor did not follow the others, and as soon as his wife saw that they were alone, she beckoned to him.

Lopez sat down on the couch beside her, and took her hand. The slender fingers trembled in his clasp, and when, with loving anxiety, he drew her towards him, he felt the tremor of her delicate limbs, while her eyes expressed bitter suffering and terrible dread.

"Are you afraid?" he asked, tenderly.

Elizabeth shuddered, threw her arms passionately around his neck, and nodded assent.

"The wagon will convey us to the Rhine Valley, please God, this very day, and there we shall be safe," he continued, soothingly. But she shook her head, her features assuming an expression of indifference and contempt. Lopez understood how to read their meaning, and asked: "So it is not the bailiffs you fear; something else is troubling you?"

She nodded again, this time still more eagerly, drew out the crucifix, which she had hitherto kept concealed under her coverlid, showed it to him, then pointed upward towards heaven, lastly to herself and him, and shrugged her shoulders with an air of deep, mournful renunciation.

"You are thinking of the other world," said Lopez; then, fixing his eyes on the ground, he continued, in a lower tone: "I know you are tortured by the fear of not meeting me there."

"Yes," she gasped, with a great effort, pressing her forehead against his shoulder.

A hot tear fell on the doctor's hand, and he felt as if his own heart was weeping with his beloved, anxious wife.

He knew that this thought had often poisoned her life and, full of tender sympathy, turned her beautiful face towards him and pressed a long kiss on her closed eyes, then said, tenderly:

"You are mine, I am yours, and if there is a life beyond the grave, and an eternal justice, the dumb will speak as they desire, and sing wondrous songs with the angels; the sorrowful will again be happy there. We will hope, we will both hope! Do you remember how I read Dante aloud to you, and tried to explain his divine creation, as we sat on the bench by the fig-tree. The sea roared below us, and our hearts swelled higher than its storm-lashed waves. How soft was the air, how bright the sunshine! This earth seemed doubly beautiful to you and me as, led by the hand of the divine seer and singer, we descended shuddering to the nether world. There the good and noble men of ancient times walked in a flowery meadow, and among them the poet beheld in solitary grandeur--do you still remember how the passage runs? 'E solo in parte vidi 'l Saladino.' Among them he also saw the Moslem Saladin, the conqueror of the Christians. If any one possessed the key of the mysteries of the other world, Elizabeth, it was Dante. He assigned a lofty place to the pagan, who was a true man--a man with a pure mind, a zeal for goodness and right, and I think I shall have a place there too. Courage, Elizabeth, courage!"

A beautiful smile had illumined the wife's features, while she was reminded of the happiest hours of her life, but when he paused, gazed into her eyes, and clasped her right hand in his, she was seized with an intense longing to pray once, only once, with him to the Saviour so, drawing her fingers from his, she pressed the image of the Crucified One to her breast with her left hand, pleading with mute motions of her lips, inteligible to him alone, and with ardent entreaty in her large, tearful eyes: "Pray, pray with me, pray to the saviour."

Lopez was greatly agitated; his heart beat faster, and a strong impulse urged him to start up, cry "no," and not allow himself to be moved, by an affectionate meakness, into bowing his manly soul before one, who, to him, was no more than human.

The noble figure of the crucified Saviour, carved by an artist's hand in ivory, hung from an ebony cross, and he thrust the image back, intending to turn proudly way, he gazed at the face and found there only pain, quiet endurance, and touching sorrow. Ah, his own heart had often bled, as the pure brow of this poor, persecuted, tortured saint bled beneath its crown of thorns. To defy this silent companion in suffering, was no manly deed-- to pay homage, out of love, to Him, who had brought love into the world, seemed to possess a sweet, ensnaring charm--so he clasped his slender hands closely round his dumb wife's fingers, pressed his dark curls gainst Elizabeth's fair hair, and both, for the first and last time, repeated together a mute, fervent prayer.

Before the hut, and surrounded by the forest, was a large clearing, where two roads crossed.

Adam, Marx and Ruth had gazed first down one and then the other, to look for the wagon, but nothing was to be seen or heard. As, with increasing anxiety, they turned back to the first path, the poacher grew restless. His crooked mouth twisted to and fro in strange contortions, not a muscle of his coarse face was till, and this looked so odd and yet so horrible, that Ruth could not help laughing, and the smith asked what ailed him.

Marx made no reply; his ear had caught the distant bay of a dog, and he knew what the sound meant. Work at the anvil impairs the hearing, and the smith did not notice the approaching peril, and repeated: "What ails you, man?"

"I am freezing," replied the charcoal-burner, cowering, with a piteous expression.

Ruth heard no more of the conversation, she had stopped and put her hand to her ear, listening with head bent forward, to the noises in the distance.

Suddenly she uttered a low cry, exclaiming: "There's a dog barking, Meister Adam, I hear it."

The smith turned pale and shook his head, but she cried earnestly: "Believe me; I hear it. Now it's barking again."

Adam too, now heard a strange noise in the forest. With lightning speed he loosened the hammer in his belt, took Ruth by the hand, and ran up the clearing with her.

Meantime, Lopez had compelled old Rahel to rise.

Everything must be ready, when Ulrich returned. In his impatience he had gone to the door, and when he saw Adam hurrying up the glade with the child, ran anxiously to meet them, thinking that some accident had happened to Ulrich.

"Back, back!" shouted the smith, and Ruth, releasing her hand from his, also motioned and shrieked "Back, back!"

The doctor obeyed the warning, and stopped; but he had scarcely turned, when several dogs appeared at the mouth of the ravine through which the party had come the day before, and directly after Count Frohlinger, on horseback, burst from the thicket.

The nobleman sat throned on his spirited charger, like the sun-god Siegfried. His fair locks floated dishevelled around his head, the steam rising from the dripping steed hovered about him in the fresh winter air like a light cloud. He had opened and raised his arms, and holding the reins in his left hand, swung his hunting spear with the right. On perceiving Lopez, a clear, joyous, exultant "Hallo, Halali!" rang from his bearded lips.

To-day Count Frohlinger was not hunting the stag, but special game, a Jew.

The chase led to the right cover, and how well the hounds had done, how stoutly Emir, his swift hunter, had followed.

This was a morning's work indeed!

"Hallo, Halali!" he shouted exultingly again, and ere the fugitives had escaped from the clearing, reached the doctor's side, exclaiming:

"Here is my game; to your knees, Jew!"

The count had far outstripped his attendants, and was entirely alone.

As Lopez stood still with folded arms, paying no heed to his command, he turned the spear, to strike him with the handle.

Then, for the first time in many years, the old fury awoke in Adam's heart; and rushing upon the count like a tiger, he threw his powerful arms around his waist, and ere he was aware of the attack, hurled him from his horse, set his knee on his breast, snatched the hammer from his belt, and with a mighty blow struck the dog that attacked him, to the earth. Then he again swung the iron, to crush the head of his hated foe. But Lopez would not accept deliverance at such a price, and cried in a tone of passionate entreaty:

"Let him go, Adam, spare him."

As he spoke, he clung to the smith's arm, and when the latter tried to release himself from his grasp, said earnestly:

"We will not follow their example!"

Again the hammer whizzed high in the air, and again the Jew clung to the smith's arm, this time exclaiming imperiously:

"Spare him, if you are my friend!"

What was his strength in comparison with Adam's? Yet as the hammer rose for the third time, he again strove to prevent the terrible deed, seizing the infuriated man's wrist, and gasping, as in the struggle he fell on his knees beside the count: "Think of Ulrich! This man's son was the only one, the only one in the whole monastery, who stood by Ulrich, your child--in the monastery--he was--his friend--among so many. Spare him--Ulrich! For Ulrich's sake, spare him!"

During this struggle the smith had held the count down with his left hand, and defended himself against Lopez with the right.

One jerk, and the hand upraised for murder was free again--but he did not use it. His friend's last words had paralyzed him.

"Take it," he said in a hollow tone, giving the hammer to the doctor.

The latter seized it, and rising joyously, laid his hand on the shoulder of the smith, who was still kneeling on the count's breast, and said beseechingly: "Let that suffice. The man is only...."

He went no farther--a gurgling, piercing cry of pain escaped his lips, and pressing one hand to his breast, and the other to his brow, he sank on the snow beside the stump of a giant pine.

A squire dashed from the forest--the archer, to whom this noble quarry had fallen a victim, appeared in the clearing, holding aloft the cross-bow from which he had sent the bolt. His arrow was fixed in the doctor's breast; alas, the man had only sent the shaft, to save his fallen master from the hammer in the Jew's hand.

Count Frohlinger rose, struggling for breath; his hand sought his hunting-knife, but in the fall it had slipped from its sheath and was lying in the snow.

Adam supported his dying friend in his arms, Ruth ran weeping to the hut, and before the nobleman had fully collected his thoughts, the squire reached his side, and young Count Lips, riding a swift bay-horse, dashed from the forest, closely followed by three mounted huntsmen.

When the attendants saw their master on foot, they too sprang from their saddles, Lips did the same, and an eager interchange of question and answer began among them.

The nobleman scarcely noticed his son, but greeted with angry words the man who had shot the Jew. Then, deeply excited, he hoarsely ordered his attendants to bind the smith, who made no resistance, but submitted to everything like a patient child.

Lopez no longer needed his arms.

The dumb wife sat on the stump, with her dying husband resting on her lap. She had thrown her arms around the bleeding form, and the feet hung limply down, touching the snow.

Ruth, sobbing bitterly, crouched on the ground by her mother's side, and old Rahel, who had entirely regained her self-control, pressed a cloth, wet with wine, on his forehead.

The young count approached the dying Jew. His father slowly followed, drew the boy to his side, and said in a low, sad tone:

"I am sorry for the man; he saved my life."

The wounded man opened his eyes, saw Count Frohlinger, his son and the fettered smith, felt his wife's tears on his brow, and heard Ruth's agonized weeping. A gentle smile hovered around his pale lips, and when he tried to raise his head Elizabeth helped him, pressing it gently to her breast.

The feeble lips moved and Lopez raised his eyes to her face, as if to thank her, saying in a low voice: "The arrow--don't touch it.... Elizabeth--Ruth, we have clung together faithfully, but now--I shall leave you alone, I must leave you." He paused, a shadow clouded his eyes, and the lids slowly fell. But he soon raised them again, and fixing his glance steadily on the count, said:

"Hear me, my Lord; a dying man should be heard, even if he is a Jew. See! This is my wife, and this my child. They are Christians. They will soon be alone in the world, deserted, orphaned. The smith is their only friend. Set him free; they--they, they will need a protector. My wife is dumb, dumb....alone in the world. She can neither beseech nor demand. Set

Adam free, for the sake of your Saviour, your son, free--yes, free. A wide, wide space must be between you; he must go away with them, far away. Set him free! I held his arm with the hammer.... You know--with the hammer. Set him free. My death--death atones for everything."

Again his voice failed, and the count, deeply moved, looked irresolutely now at him, now at the smith. Lips's eyes filled with tears; and as he saw his father delay in fulfilling the dying man's last wish, and a glance from the dim eyes met his, he pressed closer to the noble, who stood struggling with many contending emotions, and whispered, weeping:

"My Lord and Father, my Lord and Father, tomorrow will be Christmas. For Christ's sake, for love of me, grant his request: release Ulrich's father, set him free! Do so, my noble Father; I want no other Christmas gift."

Count Frohlinger's heart also overflowed, and when, raising his tear-dimmed eyes, he saw Elizabeth's deep grief stamped on her gentle features, and beheld reclining on her breast, the mild, beautiful face of the dying man, it seemed as if he saw before him the sorrowful Mother of God-- and to-morrow would be Christmas. Wounded pride was silent, he forgot the insult he had sustained, and cried in a voice as loud, as if he wished every word to reach the ear now growing dull in death:

"I thank you for your aid, man. Adam is free, and may go with your wife and child wherever he lists. My word upon it; you can close your eyes in peace!"

Lopez smiled again, raised his hand as if in gratitude, then let it fall upon his child's head, gazed lovingly at Ruth for the last time, and murmured in a low tone "Lift my head a little higher, Elizabeth." When she had obeyed his wish, he gazed earnestly into her face, whispered softly: "A dreamless sleep--reanimated to new forms in the endless circle. No!--Do you see, do you hear....Solo in parte'....with you ....with you....Oh, oh!--the arrow--draw the arrow from the wound. Elizabeth, Elizabeth--it aches. Well--well--how miserable we were, and yet, yet....You--you--I--we--we know, what happiness is. You--I.... Forgive me! I forgive, forgive...."

The dying man's hand fell from his child's head, his eyes closed, but the pleasant smile with which he had perished, hovered around his lips, even in death.

CHAPTER XI.

COUNT Frohlinger added a low "amen" to the last words of the dying man, then approached the widow, and in the kindly, cordial manner natural to him, strove to comfort her.

Finally he ordered his men, to loose the smith's bonds, and instantly guide him to the frontier with the woman and child. He also spoke to Adam, but said only a few words, not cheery ones as usual, but grave and harsh in purport.

They were a command to leave the country without delay, and never return to his home again.

The Jew's corpse was laid on a bier formed of pine, branches, and the bearers lifted it on their shoulders. Ruth clung closely to her mother, both trembling like leaves in the wind, while he who was dearest to them on earth was borne away, but only the child could weep.

The men, whom Count Frohlinger had left behind as a guard, waited patiently with the smith for his son's return until noon, then they urged departure, and the party moved forward.

Not a word was spoken, till the, travellers stopped before the charcoal-burner's house.

Jorg was in the city, but his wife said that the boy had been there, and had gone back to the forest an hour before. The tavern could accommodate a great many people, she added, and they could wait for him there.

The fugitives followed this advice, and after Adam had seen the women provided with shelter, he again sought the scene of the misfortune, and waited there for the boy until night.

Beside the stump on which his friend had died, he prayed long and earnestly, vowing to his dead preserver to live henceforth solely for his family. Unbroken stillness surrounded him, it seemed as if he were in church, and every tree in the forest was a witness of the oath he swore.

The next morning the smith again sought the charcoal-burner, and this time found him. Jorg laid the blame to Ulrich's impatience, but promised to go to Marx in search of him and bring him to the smith. The men composing the escort urged haste, so Adam went on without Ulrich towards the north-west, to the valley of the Rhine.

The charcoal-burner had lost the reward offered the informer, and could not even earn the money due a messenger.

He had lured Ulrich to the attic and locked him in there, but during his absence the boy escaped. He was a nimble fellow, for he had risked the leap from the window, and then swung himself over the fence into the road.

Jorg's conjecture did not deceive him, for as soon as Ulrich perceived that he had been betrayed into a trap, he had leaped into the open air.

He must warn his friends, and anxiety for them winged his feet.

Once and again he lost his way, but at last found the right path, though he had wasted many hours, first in the village, then behind the locked door, and finally in searching for the right road.

The sun had already passed the meridian, when he at last reached the clearing.

The but was deserted; no one answered his loud, anxious shouts.

Where had they gone?

He searched the wide, snow-covered expanse for traces, and found only too many. Here horses' hoofs, there large and small feet had pressed the snow, yonder hounds had run, and--Great Heaven!--here, by the tree-stump, red blood stained the glimmering white ground.

His breath failed, but he did not cease to search, look, examine.

Yonder, where for the length of a man the snow had vanished and grass and brown earth appeared, people had fought together, and there--Holy Virgin! What was this!--there lay his father's hammer. He knew it only too well; it was the smaller one, which to distinguish it from the two larger tools, Goliath and Samson, he called David-the boy had swung it a hundred times himself.

His heart stood still, and when he found some freshly-hewn pine-boughs, and a fir-trunk that had been rejected by one of the men, he said to himself: "The bier was made here," and his vivid imagination showed him his father fighting, struck down, and then a mournful funeral procession. Exulting bailiffs bore a tall strong-limbed corpse, and a slender, black-robed body, his father and his teacher. Then came the quiet, beautiful wife and Ruth in bonds, and behind them Marx and Rahel. He distinctly saw all this; it even seemed as if he heard the sobs of the women, and wailing bitterly, he thrust his hands in his floating locks and ran to and fro. Suddenly he thought that the troopers would return to seize him also. Away, away! anywhere--away! a voice roared and buzzed in his ears, and he set out on a run towards the south, always towards the south.

The boy had not eaten a mouthful, since the oatmeal porridge obtained at the charcoal-burner's, in the morning, but felt neither hunger nor thirst, and dashed on and on without heeding the way.

Long after his father had left the clearing for the second time, he still ran on--but gasping for breath while his steps grew slower and shorter. The moon rose, one star after another revealed its light, yet he still struggled forward.

The forest lay behind him; he had reached a broad road, which he followed southward, always southward, till his strength utterly failed. His head and hands were burning like fire, yet it was very, very cold; but little snow lay here in the valley, and in many places the moonlight showed patches of bare, dark turf.

Grief was forgotten. Fatigue, anxiety and hunger completely engrossed the boy's mind. He felt tempted to throw himself down in the road and sleep, but remembered the frozen people of whom he had heard, and dragged himself on to the nearest village. The lights had long been extinguished; as he approached, dogs barked in the yards, and the melancholy lowing of a cow echoed from many a stable. He was again among human beings; the thought exerted a soothing influence; he regained his self-control, and sought a shelter for the night.

At the end of the village stood a barn, and Ulrich noticed by the moonlight an open hatchway in the wall. If he could climb up to it! The framework offered some support for fingers and toes, so he resolved to try it.

Several times, when Half-way up, he slipped to the ground, but at last reached the top, and found a bed in the soft hay under a sheltering roof. Surrounded by the fragrance of the dried grasses, he soon fell asleep, and in a dream saw amidst various confused and repulsive shapes, first his father with a bleeding wound in his broad chest, and then the doctor, dancing with old Rahel. Last of all Ruth appeared; she led him into the forest to a juniper-bush, and showed him a nest full of young birds. But the half-naked creatures vexed him, and he trampled them under foot, over which the little girl lamented so loudly and bitterly, that he awoke.

Morning was already dawning, his head ached, and he was very cold and hungry, but he had no desire nor thought except to proceed; so he again went out into the open air, brushed off the hay that still clung to his hair and clothes, and walked on towards the south.

It had grown warmer and was beginning to snow heavily.

Walking became more and more difficult; his headache grew unendurable, yet his feet still moved, though it seemed as if he wore heavy leaden shoes.

Several freight-wagons with armed escorts, and a few peasants, with rosaries in their hands, who were on their way to church, met the lad, but no one had overtaken him.

On the hinge of noon he heard behind him the tramp of horses' hoofs and the rattle of wheels, approaching nearer and nearer with ominous haste.

If it should be the troopers!

Ulrich's heart stood still, and turning to look back, he saw several horse-men, who were trotting past a spur of the hill around which the road wound.

Through the falling flakes the boy perceived glittering weapons, gay doublets and scarfs, and now--now--all hope was over, they wore Count Frohlinger's colors!

Unless the earth should open before him, there was no escape. The road belonged to the horsemen; on the right lay a wide, snow-covered plain, on the left rose a cliff, kept from falling on the side towards the highway by a rude wall. It needed this support less on account of the road, than for the sake of a graveyard, for which the citizens of the neighboring borough used the gentle slope of the mountain.

The graves, the bare elder-bushes and bushy cypresses in the cemetery were covered with snow, and the brighter the white covering that rested on every surrounding object, the stronger was the relief in which the black crosses stood forth against it.

A small chapel in the rear of the graveyard caught Ulrich's eye. If it was possible to climb the wall, he might hide behind it. The horsemen were already close at his heels, when he summoned all his remaining strength, rushed to a stone projecting from the wall, and began to clamber up.

The day before it would have been a small matter for him to reach the cemetery; but now the exhausted boy only dragged himself upward, to slip on the smooth stones and lose the hold, that the dry, snow-covered plants growing in the wide crevices treacherously offered him.

The horsemen had noticed him, and a young man-at-arms exclaimed: "A runaway! See how the young vagabond acts. I'll seize him."

He set spurs to his horse as he spoke, and just as the boy succeeded in reaching his goal, grasped his foot; but Ulrich clung fast to a gravestone, so the shoe was left in the trooper's hand and his comrades burst into a loud laugh. It sounded merry, but it echoed in the ears of the tortured lad like a shriek from hell, and urged him onward. He leaped over two, five, ten graves--then he stumbled over a head-stone concealed by the snow.

With a great effort he rose again, but ere he reached the chapel fell once more, and now his will was paralyzed. In mortal terror he clung to a cross, and as his senses failed, thought of "the word." It seemed as if some one had called the right one, and from pure Weakness and fatigue, he could not remember it.

The young soldier was not willing to encounter the jeers of his comrades, by letting the vagabond escape. With a curt: "Stop, you rascal," he threw the shoe into the graveyard, gave his bridle to the next man in the line; and a few minutes after was kneeling by Ulrich's side. He shook and jerked him, but in vain; then growing anxious, called to the others that the boy was probably dead.

"People never die so quickly!" cried the greyhaired leader of the band: "Give him a blow."

The youth raised his arm, but did not strike the lad. He had looked into Ulrich's face, and found something there that touched his heart. "No, no," he shouted, "come up here, Peter; a handsome boy; but it's all over with him, I say."

During this delay, the traveller whom the men were escorting, and his old servant, approached the cemetery at a rapid trot. The former, a gentleman of middle age, protected from the cold by costly furs, saw with a single hasty glance the cause of the detention.

Instantly dismounting, he followed the leader of the troop to the end of the wall, where there was a flight of rude steps.

Ulrich's head now lay in the soldier's arms, and the traveller gazed at him with a look of deep sympathy. The steadfast glance of his bright eyes rested on the boy's features as if spellbound, then he raised his hand, beckoned to the elder soldier, and exclaimed: "Lift him; we'll take him with us; a corner can be found in the wagon."

The vehicle, of which the traveller spoke, was slow in coming. It was a long four-wheeled equipage, over which, as a protection against wind and storm, arched a round, sail-cloth cover. The driver crouched among the straw in a basket behind the horses, like a brooding hen.

Under the sheltering canopy, among the luggage of the fur-clad gentleman, sat and reclined four travellers, whom the owner of the vehicle had gradually picked up, and who formed a motley company.

The two Dominican friars, Magisters Sutor and Stubenrauch, had entered at Cologne, for the wagon came straight from Holland, and belonged to the artist Antonio Moor of Utrecht, who was going to King Philip's court. The beautiful fur border on the black cap and velvet cloak showed that he had no occasion to practise economy; he preferred the back of a good horse to a seat in a jolting vehicle.

The ecclesiastics had taken possession of the best places in the back of the wagon. They were inseparable brothers, and formed as it were one person, for they behaved like two bodies with one soul. In this double life, fat Magister Sutor represented the will, lean Stubenrauch reflection and execution. If the former proposed to be down or sit, eat or drink, sleep or talk, the latter instantly carried the suggestion into execution, rarely neglecting to establish, by wise words, for what reason the act in question should be performed precisely at that time.

Farther towards the front, with his back resting against a chest, lay a fine-looking young Lansquenet. He was undoubtedly a gay, active fellow, but now sat mute and melancholy, supporting with his right hand his wounded left arm, as if it were some brittle vessel.

Opposite to him rose a heap of loose straw, beneath which something stirred from time to time, and from which at short intervals a slight cough was heard.

As soon as the door in the back of the vehicle opened, and the cold snowy air entered the dark, damp space under the tilt, Magister Sutor's lips parted in a long-drawn "Ugh!" to which his lean companion instantly added a torrent of reproachful words about the delay, the draught, the danger of taking cold.

When the artist's head appeared in the opening, the priest paused, for Moor paid the travelling expenses; but when his companion Sutor drew his cloak around him with every token of discomfort and annoyance, he followed his example in a still more conspicuous way.

The artist paid no heed to these gestures, but quietly requested his guests to make room for the boy.

A muffled head was suddenly thrust out from under the straw, a voice cried: "A hospital on wheels!" then the head vanished again like that of a fish, which has risen to take a breath of air.

"Very true," replied the artist. "You need not draw up your limbs so far, my worthy Lansquenet, but I must request these reverend gentlemen to move a little farther apart, or closer together, and make room for the sick lad on the leather sack."

While these words were uttered, one of the escort laid the still senseless boy under the tilt.

Magister Sutor noticed the snow that clung to Ulrich's hair and clothing, and while struggling to rise, uttered a repellent "no," while Stubenrauch hastily added reproachfully: "There will be a perfect pool here, when that melts; you gave us these places, Meister Moor, but we hardly expected to receive also dripping limbs and rheumatic pains...."

Before he finished the sentence, the bandaged head again appeared from the straw, and the high, shrill voice of the man concealed under it, asked? "Was the blood of the wounded wayfarer, the good Samaritan picked up by the roadside, dry or wet?"

An encouraging glance from Sutor requested Stubenrauch to make an appropriate answer, and the latter in an unctuous tone, hastily replied: "It was the Lord, who caused the Samaritan to find the wounded man by the roadside--this did not happen in our case, for the wet boy is forced upon us, and though we are Samaritans....."

"You are not yet merciful," cried the voice from the straw.

The artist laughed, but the soldier, slapping his thigh with his sound hand, cried:

"In with the boy, you fellows outside; here, put him on my right--move farther apart, you gentlemen down below; the water will do us no harm, if you'll only give us some of the wine in your basket yonder."

The priests, willy-nilly, now permitted Ulrich to be laid on the leathern sack between them, and while first Sutor, and then Stubenrauch, shrunk away to mutter prayers over a rosary for the senseless lad's restoration to consciousness, and to avoid coming in contact with his wet clothes, the artist entered the vehicle, and without asking permission, took the wine from the priests' basket. The soldier helped him, and soon their united exertions, with the fiery liquor, revived the fainting boy.

Moor rode forward, and the wagon jolted on until the day's journey ended at Emmendingen. Count von Hochburg's retainers, who were to serve as escort from this point, would not ride on Christmas day. The artist made no objection, but when they also declared that no horse should leave the stable on the morrow, which was a second holiday, he shrugged his shoulders and answered, without any show of anger, but in a firm, haughty tone, that he should then probably be obliged--if necessary with their master's assistance,--to conduct them to Freiburg to-morrow.

The inns at Emmendingen were among the largest and best in the neighborhood of Freiburg, and on account of the changes of escort, which frequently took place here, there was no lack of accommodation for numerous horses and guests.

As soon as Ulrich was taken into the warm hostelry he fainted a second time, and the artist now cared for him as kindly as if he were the lad's own father.

Magister Sutor ordered the roast meats, and his companion Stubenrauch all the other requisites for a substantial meal, in which they had made considerable progress, while the artist was still engaged in ministering to the sick lad, in which kindly office the little man, who had been hidden under the straw in the wagon, stoutly assisted.

He had been a buffoon, and his dress still bore many tokens of his former profession. His big head swayed upon his thin neck; his droll, though emaciated features constantly changed their expression, and even when he was not coughing, his mouth was continually in motion.

As soon as Ulrich breathed calmly and regularly, he searched his clothing to find some clue to his residence, but everything he discovered in the lad's pockets only led to more and more amusing and startling conjectures, for nothing can contain a greater variety of objects than a school-boy's pockets, if we except a school-girl's.

There was a scrap of paper with a Latin exercise bristling with errors, a smooth stone, a shabby, notched knife, a bit of chalk for drawing, an iron arrow-head, a broken hobnail, and a falconer's glove, which Count Lips had given his comrade. The ring the doctor's wife had bestowed as a farewell token, was also discovered around his neck.

All these things led Pellicanus--so the jester was named--to make many a conjecture, and he left none untried.

As a mosaic picture is formed from stones, he by a hundred signs, conjured up a vision of the lad's character, home, and the school from which he had run away.

He called him the son of a noble of moderate property. In this he was of course mistaken, but in other respects perceived, with wonderful acuteness, how Ulrich had hitherto been circumstanced, nay even declared that he was a motherless child, a fact proved by many things he lacked. The boy had been sent to school too late--Pellicanus was a good Latin scholar--and perhaps had been too early initiated into the mysteries of riding, hunting, and woodcraft.

The artist, merely by the boy's appearance, gained a more accurate knowledge of his real nature, than the jester gathered from his investigations and inferences.

Ulrich pleased him, and when he saw the pen-and-ink sketch on the back of the exercise, which Pellicanus showed him, he smiled and felt strengthened in the resolve to interest himself still more in the handsome boy, whom fate had thrown in his way. He now only needed to discover who the lad's parents were, and what had driven him from the school.

The surgeon of the little town had bled Ulrich, and soon after he fell into a sound sleep, and breathed quietly. The artist and jester now dined together, for the monks had finished their meal long before, and were taking a noonday nap. Moor ordered roast meat and wine for the Lansquenet, who sat modestly in one corner of the large public room, gazing sadly at his wounded arm.

"Poor fellow!" said the jester, pointing to the handsome young man. "We are brothers in calamity; one just like the other; a cart with a broken wheel."

"His arm will soon heal," replied the artist, "but your tool"--here he pointed to his own lips--"is stirring briskly enough now. The monks and I have both made its acquaintance within the past few days."

"Well, well," replied Pellicanus, smiling bitterly, "yet they toss me into the rubbish heap."

"That would be . . . . ."

"Ah, you think the wise would then be fools with the fools," interrupted Pellicanus. "Not at all. Do you know what our masters expect of us?"

"You are to shorten the time for them with wit and jest."

"But when must we be real fools, my Lord? Have you considered? Least of all in happy hours. Then we are expected to play the wise man, warn against excess, point out shadows. In sorrow, in times of trouble, then, fool, be a fool! The madder pranks you play, the better. Make every effort, and if you understand your trade well, and know your master, you must compel him to laugh till he cries, when he would fain wail for grief, like a little girl. You know princes too, sir, but I know them better. They are gods on earth, and won't submit to the universal lot of mortals, to endure pain and anguish. When people are ill, the physician is summoned, and in trouble we are at hand. Things are as we take them--the gravest face may have a wart, upon which a jest can be made. When you have once laughed at a misfortune, its sting loses its point. We deaden it--we light up the darkness--even though it be with a will 'o the wisp--and if we understand our business, manage to hack the lumpy dough of heavy sorrow into little pieces, which even a princely stomach can digest."

"A coughing fool can do that too, so long as there is nothing wanting in his upper story."

"You are mistaken, indeed you are. Great lords only wish to see the velvet side of life--of death's doings, nothing at all. A man like me--do you hear--a cougher, whose marrow is being consumed--incarnate misery on two tottering legs--a piteous figure, whom one can no more imagine outside the grave, than a sportsman without a terrier, or hound--such a person calls into the ears of the ostrich, that shuts its eyes: 'Death is pointing at you! Affliction is coming!' It is my duty to draw a curtain between my lord and sorrow; instead of that, my own person brings incarnate suffering before his eyes. The elector was as wise as if he were his own fool, when he turned me out of the house."

"He graciously gave you leave of absence."

"And Gugelkopf is already installed in the palace as my successor! My gracious master knows that he won't have to pay the pension long. He would willingly have supported me up yonder till I died; but my wish to go to Genoa suited him exactly. The more distance there is between his healthy highness and the miserable invalid, the better."

"Why didn't you wait till spring, before taking your departure?"

"Because Genoa is a hot-house, that the poor consumptive does not need in summer. It is pleasant to be there in winter. I learned that three years ago, when we visited the duke. Even in January the sun in Liguria warms your back, and makes it easier to breathe. I'm going by way of Marseilles. Will you give me the corner in your carriage as far as Avignon?"

"With pleasure! Your health, Pellicanus! A good wish on Christmas day is apt to be fulfilled."

The artist's deep voice sounded full and cordial, as he uttered the words. The young soldier heard them, and as Moor and the jester touched glasses, he raised his own goblet, drained it to the dregs, and asked modestly: "Will you listen to a few lines of mine, kind sir?"

"Say them, say them!" cried the artist, filling his glass again, while the lansquenet, approaching the table, fixed his eyes steadily on the beaker, and in an embarrassed manner, repeated:

> "On Christmas-day, when Jesus Christ,
> To save us sinners came,
> A poor, sore-wounded soldier dared
> To call upon his name.

'Oh! hear,' he said, 'my earnest prayer,
For the kind, generous man,
Who gave the wounded soldier aid,
And bore him through the land.
So, in Thy shining chariot,
I pray, dear Jesus mine,
Thou'lt bear him through a happy life
To Paradise divine.'"

"Capital, capital!" cried the artist, pledging the lansquenet and insisting that he should sit down between him and the jester.

Pellicanus now gazed thoughtfully into vacancy, for what the wounded man could do, he too might surely accomplish. It was not only ambition, and the habit of answering every good saying he heard with a better one, but kindly feeling, that urged him to honor the generous benefactor with a speech.

After a few minutes, which Moor spent in talking with the soldier, Pellicanus raised his glass, coughed again, and said, first calmly, then in an agitated voice, whose sharp tones grew more and more subdued:

"A rogue a fool must be, 't is true,
Rog'ry sans folly will not do;
Where folly joins with roguery,
There's little harm, it seems to me.
The pope, the king, the youthful squire,
Each one the fool's cap doth attire;
He who the bauble will not wear,
The worst of fools doth soon appear.
Thee may the motley still adorn,
When, an old man, the laurel crown
Thy head doth deck, while gifts less vain,
Thine age to bless will still remain.
When fair grandchildren thee delight,
Mayst then recall this Christmas night.
When added years bring whitening hair,
The draught of wisdom then wilt share,
But it will lack the flavor due,
Without a drop of folly too.

And if the drop is not at hand,
Remember poor old Pellican,
Who, half a rogue and half a fool,
Yet has a faithful heart and whole."

"Thanks, thanks!" cried the artist, shaking the jester's hand. "Such a Christmas ought to be lauded! Wisdom, art, and courage at one table! Haven't I fared like the man, who picked up stones by the way side, and to- they were changed to pure gold in his knapsack."

"The stone was crumbling," replied the jester; "but as for the gold, it will stand the test with me, if you seek it in the heart, and not in the pocket. Holy Blasius! Would that my grave might lack filling, as long as my little strong-box here; I'd willingly allow it."

"And so would I!" laughed the soldier:

"Then travelling will be easy for you," said the artist. "There was a time, when my pouch was no fuller than yours. I know by the experience of those days how a poor man feels, and never wish to forget it. I still owe you my after-dinner speech, but you must let me off, for I can't speak your language fluently. In brief, I wish you the recovery of your health, Pellican, and you a joyous life of happiness and honor, my worthy comrade. What is your name?"

"Hans Eitelfritz von der Lucke, from Colln on the Spree," replied the soldier. "And, no offence, Herr Moor, God will care for the monks, but there were three poor invalid fellows in your cart. One goblet more to the pretty sick boy in there."

CHAPTER XII.

AFTER dinner the artist went with his old servant, who had attended to the horses and then enjoyed a delicious Christmas roast, to Count von Hochburg, to obtain an escort for the next day.

Pellicanus had undertaken to watch Ulrich, who was still sleeping quietly.

The jester would gladly have gone to bed himself, for he felt cold and tired, but, though the room could not be heated, he remained faithfully at his post for hours. With benumbed hands and feet, he watched by the light of the night-lamp every breath the boy drew, often gazing at him as anxiously and sympathizingly, as if he were his own child.

When Ulrich at last awoke, he timidly asked when he was, and when the jester had soothed him, begged for a bit of bread, he was so hungry.

How famished he felt, the contents of the dish that were speedily placed before him, soon discovered Pellicanus wanted to feed him like a baby, but the boy took the spoon out of his hand, and the former smilingly watched the sturdy eater, without disturbing, him, until he was perfectly satisfied; then he began to perplex the lad with questions, that seemed to him neither very intelligible, nor calculated to inspire confidence.

"Well, my little bird!" the jester began, joyously anticipating a confirmation of the clever inferences he had drawn, "I suppose it was a long flight to the churchyard, where we found you. On the grave is a better place than in it, and a bed at Emmendingen, with plenty of grits and veal, is preferable to being in the snow on the highway, with a grumbling stomach Speak freely, my lad! Where does your nest of robbers hang?"

"Nest of robbers?" repeated Ulrich in amazement.

"Well, castle or the like, for aught I care," continued Pellicanus inquiringly. "Everybody is at home somewhere, except Mr. Nobody; but as you are somebody, Nobody cannot possibly be your father. Tell me about the old fellow!"

"My father is dead," replied the boy, and as the events of the preceding day rushed back upon his memory, he drew the coverlet over his face and wept.

"Poor fellow!" murmured the jester, hastily drawing his sleeve across his eyes, and leaving the lad in peace, till he showed his face again. Then he continued: "But I suppose you have a mother at home?"

Ulrich shook his head mournfully, and Pellicanus, to conceal his own emotion, looked at him with a comical grimace, and then said very kindly, though not without a feeling of satisfaction at his own penetration:

"So you are an orphan! Yes, yes! So long as the mother's wings cover it, the young bird doesn't fly so thoughtlessly out of the warm nest into the wide world. I suppose the Latin school grew too narrow for the young nobleman?"

Ulrich raised himself, exclaiming in an eager, defiant tone:

"I won't go back to the monastery; that I will not."

"So that's the way the hare jumps!" cried the fool laughing. "You've been a bad Latin scholar, and the timber in the forest is dearer to you, than the wood in the school-room benches. To be sure, they send out no green shoots. Dear Lord, how his face is burning!" So saying, Pellicanus laid his hand on the boy's forehead and when he felt that It was hot, deemed it better to stop his examination for the day, and only asked his patient his name.

"Ulrich," was the reply.

"And what else?"

"Let me alone!" pleaded the boy, drawing the coverlet over his head again.

The jester obeyed his wish, and opened the door leading into the tap-room, for some one had knocked. The artist's servant entered, to fetch his master's portmanteau. Old Count von Hochburg had invited Moor to be his guest, and the painter intended to spend the night at the castle. Pellicanus was to take care of the boy, and if necessary send for the surgeon again.

An hour after, the sick jester lay shivering in his bed, coughing before sleeping and between naps. Ulrich too could obtain no slumber.

At first he wept softly, for he now clearly realized, for the first time, that he had lost his father and should never see Ruth, the doctor, nor the doctor's dumb wife Elizabeth again. Then he wondered how he had come to Einmendingen, what sort of a place it was, and who the queer little man could be, who had taken him for a young noble--the quaint little man with the cough, and a big head, whose eyes sparkled so through his tears. The jester's mistake made him laugh, and he remembered that Ruth had once advised him to command the "word," to transform him into a count.

Suppose he should say to-morrow, that his father had been a knight?

But the wicked thought only glided through his mind; even before he had reflected upon it, he felt ashamed of himself, for he was no liar.

Deny his father! That was very wrong, and when he stretched himself out to sleep, the image of the valiant smith stood with tangible distinctness before his soul. Gravely and sternly he floated upon clouds, and looked exactly like the pictures Ulrich had seen of God the Father, only he wore the smith's cap on his grey hair. Even in Paradise, the glorified spirit had not relinquished it.

Ulrich raised his hands as if praying, but hastily let them fall again, for there was a great stir outside of the inn. The tramp of steeds, the loud voices of men, the sound of drums and fifes were audible, then there was rattling, marching and shouting in the court-yard.

"A room for the clerk of the muster-roll and paymaster!" cried a voice.

"Gently, gently, children!" said the deep tones of the provost, who was the leader, counsellor and friend of the Lansquenets. "A devout servant must not bluster at the holy Christmas-tide; he's permitted to drink a glass, Heaven be praised. Your house is to be greatly honored, Landlord! The recruiting for our most gracious commander, Count von Oberstein, is--to be done here. Do you hear, man! Everything to be paid for in cash, and not a chicken will be lost; but the wine must be good! Do you understand? So this evening broach a cask of your best. Pardon me, children--the very best, I meant to say."

Ulrich now heard the door of the tap-room open, and fancied he could see the Lansquenets in gay costumes, each one different from the other, crowd into the apartment.

The jester coughed loudly, scolding and muttering to himself; but Ulrich listened with sparkling eyes to the sounds that came through the ill-fitting door, by which he could hear what was passing in the next room.

With the clerk of the muster-rolls, the paymaster and provost had appeared the drummers and fifers, who the day after to-morrow were to sound the license for recruiting, and besides these, twelve Lansquenets, who were evidently no novices.

Many an exclamation of surprise and pleasure was heard directly after their entrance into the tap-room, and amid the confusion of voices, the name of Hans Eitelfritz fell more than once upon Ulrich's ear.

The provost's voice sounded unusually cordial, as he greeted the brave fellow with the wounded hand--an honor of great value to the latter, for he had served five years in the same company with the provost, "Father Kanold," who read the very depths of his soldiers' hearts, and knew them all as if they were his own sons.

Ulrich could not understand much amid the medley of voices in the adjoining room, but when Hans Eitelfritz, from Colln on the Spree, asked to be the first one put down on the muster-roll, he distinctly heard the provost oppose the clerk's scruples, saying warmly "write, write; I'd rather have him with one hand, than ten peevish fellows with two. He has fun and life in him. Advance him some money too, he probably lacks many a piece of armor."

Meantime the wine-cask must have been opened, for the clink of glasses, and soon after loud singing was audible.

Just as the second song began, the boy fell asleep, but woke again two hours after, roused by the stillness that had suddenly succeeded the uproar.

Hans Eitelfritz had declared himself ready to give a new song in his best vein, and the provost commanded silence.

The singing now began; during its continuance Ulrich raised himself higher and higher in bed, not a word escaped him, either of the song itself, or the chorus, which was repeated by the whole party, with exuberant gayety, amid the loud clinking of goblets. Never before had the lad heard such bold, joyous voices; even at the second verse his heart bounded and it seemed as if he must join in the tune, which he had quickly caught. The song ran as follows:

> Who, who will venture to hold me back?
> Drums beat, fifes are playing a merry tune!
> Down hammer, down pen, what more need I, alack
> I go to seek fortune, good fortune!
>
> Oh father, mother, dear sister mine,
> Blue-eyed maid at the bridge-house, my fair one.
> Weep not, ye must not at parting repine,
> I go to seek fortune, good fortune!
>
> The cannon roar loud, the sword flashes bright,
> Who'll dare meet the stroke of my falchion?
> Close-ranked, horse and foot in battle unite,
> In war, war, dwells fortune, good fortune!
>
> The city is taken, the booty mine;
> With red gold, I'll deck--I know whom;
> Pair maids' cheeks burn red, red too glows the wine,
> Fortune, Paradise of good fortune!
>
> Deep, scarlet wounds, brave breasts adorn,
> Impoverished, crippled age I shun
> A death of honor, 'mid glory won,
> This too is good fortune, good fortune!
>
> A soldier-lad composed this ditty
> Hans Eitelfritz he, fair Colln's son,
> His kindred dwell in the goodly city,
> But he himself in fortune, good fortune!

"He himself in fortune, good fortune," sang Ulrich also, and while, amid loud shouts of joy, the glasses again clinked against each other, he repeated the glad "fortune, good fortune." Suddenly, it flashed upon him like a revelation, "Fortune," that might be the word!

Such exultant joy, such lark-like trilling, such inspiring promises of happiness had never echoed in any word, as they now did from the "fortune," the young lansquenet so gaily and exultantly uttered.

"Fortune, Fortune!" he exclaimed aloud, and the jester, who was lying sleepless in his bed and could not help smiling at the lad's singing, raised himself, saying:

"Do you like the word? Whoever understands how to seize it when it flits by, will always float on top of everything, like fat on the soup. Rods are cut from birches, willows, and knotted hazel-sticks-ho! ho! you know that, already;--but, for him who has good fortune, larded cakes, rolls and sausages grow. One bold turn of Fortune's wheel will bring him, who has stood at the bottom, up to the top with the speed of lightning. Brother Queer-fellow says: 'Up and down, like an avalanche.' But now turn over and go to sleep. To-morrow will also be a Christmas-day, which will perhaps bring you Fortune as a Christmas gift."

It seemed as if Ulrich had not called upon Fortune in vain, for as soon as he closed his eyes, a pleasant dream bore him with gentle hands to the forge on the market-place, and his mother stood beside the lighted Christmas-tree, pointing to the new sky-blue suit she had made him, and the apples, nuts, hobby-horse, and jumping jack, with a head as round as a ball, huge ears, and tiny flat legs. He felt far too old for such childish toys, and yet took a certain pleasure in them. Then the vision changed, and he again saw his mother; but this time she was walking among the angels in Paradise. A royal crown adorned her golden hair, and she told him she was permitted to wear it there, because she had been so reviled, and endured so much disgrace on earth.

When the artist returned from Count von Hochburg's the next morning, he was not a little surprised to see Ulrich standing before the recruiting-table bright and well.

The lad's cheeks were glowing with shame and anger, for the clerk of the muster-rolls and paymaster had laughed in his face, when he expressed his desire to become a Lansquenet.

The artist soon learned what was going on, and bade his protege accompany him out of doors. Kindly, and without either mockery or reproof, he represented to him that he was still far too young for military service, and after Ulrich had confirmed everything the painter had already heard from the jester, Moor asked who had given him instruction in drawing.

"My father, and afterwards Father Lukas in the monastery," replied the boy. "But don't question me as the little man did last night."

"No, no," said his protector. "But there are one or two more things I wish to know. Was your father an artist?"

"No," murmured the lad, blushing and hesitating. But when he met the stranger's clear gaze, he quickly regained his composure, and said:

"He only knew how to draw, because he understood how to forge beautiful, artistic things."

"And in what city did you live?"

"In no city. Outside in the woods."

"Oho!" said the artist, smiling significantly, for he knew that many knights practised a trade. "Answer only two questions more; then you shall be left in peace until you voluntarily open your heart to me. What is your name?"

"Ulrich."

"I know that; but your father's?"

"Adam."

"And what else?"

Ulrich gazed silently at the ground, for the smith had borne no other name.

"Well then," said Moor, "we will call you Ulrich for the present; that will suffice. But have you no relatives? Is no one waiting for you at home?"

"We have led such a solitary life--no one."

Moor looked fixedly into the boy's face, then nodded, and with a well-satisfied expression, laid his hand on Ulrich's curls, and said:

"Look at me. I am an artist, and if you have any love for my profession, I will teach you."

"Oh!" cried the boy, clasping his hands in glad surprise.

"Well then," Moor continued, "you can't learn much on the way, but we can work hard in Madrid. We are going now to King Philip of Spain."

"Spain, Portugal!" murmured Ulrich with sparkling eyes; all he had heard in the doctor's house about these countries returned to his mind.

"Fortune, good fortune!" cried an exultant voice in his heart. This was the "word," it must be, it was already exerting its spell, and the spell was to prove its inherent power in the near future.

That very day the party were to go to Count von Rappoltstein in the village of Rappolts, and this time Ulrich was not to plod along on foot, or he in a close baggage-wagon; no, he was to be allowed to ride a spirited horse. The escort would not consist of hired servants, but of picked men, and the count was going to join the train in person at the hill crowned by the castle, for Moor had promised to paint a portrait of the nobleman's daughter, who had married Count von Rappoltstein. It was to be a costly Christmas gift, which the old gentleman intended to make himself and his faithful wife.

The wagon was also made ready for the journey; but no one rode inside; the jester, closely muffled in wraps, had taken his seat beside the driver, and the monks were obliged to go on by way of Freiburg, and therefore could use the vehicle no longer.

They scolded and complained about it, as if they had been greatly wronged, and when Sutor refused to shake hands with the artist, Stubenrauch angrily turned his back upon the kind-hearted man.

The offended pair sullenly retired, but the Christmas sun shone none the less brightly from the clear sky, the party of travellers had a gay, spick and span, holiday aspect, and the world into which they now fared stoutly forth, was so wide and beautiful, that Ulrich forgot his grief, and joyously waved his new cap in answer to the Lansquenet's farewell gesture.

It was a merry ride, for on the way they met numerous travellers, who were going through the hamlet of Rappolts to the "three castles on the mountain" and saluted the old nobleman with lively songs. The Counts von Rappoltstein were the "piper-kings," the patrons of the brotherhood of musicians and singers on the Upper Rhine. Usually these joyous birds met at the castle of their "king" on the 8th of September, to pay him their little tax and be generously entertained in return; but this year, on account of the plague in the autumn, the festival had been deferred until the third day after Christmas, but Ulrich believed 'Fortune' had arranged it so for him.

There was plenty of singing, and the violins and rebecs, flutes, and reed-pipes were never silent. One serenade followed another, and even at the table a new song rang out at each new course.

The fiery wine, game and sweet cakes at the castle board undoubtedly pleased the palate of the artisan's son, but he enjoyed feasting his ears still more. He felt as if he were in Heaven, and thought less and less of the grief he had endured.

Day by day Fortune shook her horn of plenty, and flung new gifts down upon him.

He had told the stable-keepers of his power over refractory horses, and after proving what he could do, was permitted to tame wild stallions and ride them about the castle-yard, before the eyes of the old and young count and the beautiful young lady. This brought him praise and gifts of new clothes. Many a delicate hand stroked his curls, and it always seemed to him as if his mighty spell could bestow nothing better.

One day Moor took him aside, and told him that he had commenced a portrait of young Count Rappolstein too. The lad was obliged to be still, having broken his foot in a fall from his horse, and as Ulrich was of the same size and age, the artist wished him to put on the young count's clothes and serve as a model.

The smith's son now received the best clothes belonging to his aristocratic companion in age. The suit was entirely black, but each garment of a different material, the stockings silk, the breeches satin, the doublet soft Flanders velvet. Golden-yellow puffs and slashes stood forth in beautiful relief against the darker stuff. Even the knots of ribbon on the breeches and shoes were as yellow as a blackbird's beak. Delicate lace trimmed the neck and fell on the hands, and a clasp of real gems confined the black and yellow plumes in the velvet hat.

All this finery was wonderfully becoming to the smith's son, and he must have been blind, if he had not noticed how old and young nudged each other at sight of him. The spirit of vanity in his soul laughed in delight, and the lad soon knew the way to the large Venetian mirror, which was carefully kept in the hall of state. This wonderful glass showed Ulrich for the first time his whole figure and the image which looked back at him from the crystal, flattered and pleased him.

But, more than aught else, he enjoyed watching the artist's hand and eye during the sittings. Poor Father Lukas in the monastery must hide his head before this master. He seemed to actually grow while engaged in his work, his shoulders, which he usually liked to carry stooping forward, straightened, the broad, manly breast arched higher, and the kindly eyes grew stern, nay sometimes wore a terrible expression.

Although little was said during the sittings, they were always too short for the boy. He did not stir, for it always seemed to him as if any movement would destroy the sacred act he witnessed, and when, in the pauses, he looked at the canvas and saw how swiftly and steadily the work progressed, he felt as if before his own eyes, he was being born again to a nobler existence. In the wassail-hall hung the portrait of a young Prince of Navarre, whose life had been saved in the chase by a Rappoltstein. Ulrich, attired in the count's clothes, looked exactly like him. The jester had been the first to perceive this strange circumstance. Every one, even Moor, agreed with him, and so it happened that Pellicanus henceforth called his young friend the Navarrete. The name pleased the boy. Everything here pleased him, and he was full of happiness; only often at night he could not help grieving because, while his father was dead, he enjoyed such an overflowing abundance of good things, and because he had lost his mother, Ruth, and all who had loved him.

CHAPTER XIII.

ULRICH was obliged to share the jester's sleeping-room, and as Pellicanus shrank from getting out of bed, while suffering from night-sweats, and often needed something, he roused Ulrich from his sleep, and the latter was always ready to assist him. This happened more frequently as they continued their journey, and the poor little man's illness increased.

The count had furnished Ulrich with a spirited young horse, that shortened the road for him by its tricks and capers. But the jester, who became more and more attached to the boy, also did his utmost to keep the feeling of happiness alive in his heart. On warm days he nestled in the rack before the tilt with the driver, and when Ulrich rode beside him, opened his eyes to everything that passed before him.

The jester had a great deal to tell about the country and people, and he embellished the smallest trifle with tales invented by himself, or devised by others.

While passing a grove of birches, he asked the lad if he knew why the trunks of these trees were white, and then explained the cause, as follows:

"When Orpheus played so exquisitely on his lute, all the trees rushed forward to dance. The birches wanted to come too, but being vain, stopped to put on white dresses, to outdo the others. When they finally appeared on the dancing-ground, the singer had already gone--and now, summer and winter, year in and year out, they keep their white dresses on, to be prepared, when Orpheus returns and the lute sounds again."

A cross-bill was perched on a bough in a pine-wood, and the jester said that this bird was a very peculiar species. It had originally been grey, and its bill was as straight as a sparrow's, but when the Saviour hung upon the cross, it pitied him, and with its little bill strove to draw the nails from the wounded hands. In memory of this friendly act, the Lord had marked its beak with the cross, and painted a dark-red spot on its breast, where the bird hall been sprinkled with His Son's blood. Other rewards were bestowed upon it, for no other bird could hatch a brood of young ones in winter, and it also had the power of lessening the fever of those, who cherished it.

A flock of wild geese flew over the road and the hills, and Pellicanus cried: "Look there! They always fly in two straight lines, and form a letter of the alphabet. This time it is an A. Can you see it? When the Lord was writing the laws on the tablets, a flock of wild geese flew across Mt. Sinai, and in doing so, one effaced a letter with its wing. Since that time, they always fly in the shape of a letter, and their whole race, that is, all geese, are compelled to let those people who wish to write, pluck the feathers from their wings."

Pellicanus was fond of talking to the boy in their bedroom. He always called him Navarrete, and the artist, when in a cheerful mood, followed his example.

Ulrich felt great reverence for Moor; the jester, on the contrary, was only a good comrade, in whom he speedily reposed entire confidence.

Many an allusion and jesting word showed that Pellicanus still believed him to be the son of a knight, and this at last became unendurable to the lad.

One evening, when they were both in bed, he summoned up his courage and told him everything he knew about his past life.

The jester listened attentively, without interrupting him, until Ulrich finished his story with the words "And while I was gone, the bailiffs and dogs tracked them, but my father resisted, and they killed him and the doctor."

"Yes, yes," murmured the jester. "It's a pity about Costa. Many a Christian might feel honored at resembling some Jews. It is only a misfortune to be born a Hebrew, and be deprived of eating ham. The Jews are compelled to wear an offensive badge, but many a Christian child is born with one. For instance, in Sparta they would have hurled me into the gulf, on account of my big head, and deformed shoulder. Nowadays, people are less merciful, and let men like us drag the cripple's mark through life. God sees the heart; but men cannot forget their ancestor, the clod of earth--the outside is always more to them than the inside. If my head had only been smaller, and some angel had smoothed my shoulder, I might perhaps now be a cardinal, wear purple, and instead of riding under a grey tilt, drive in a golden coach, with well-fed black steeds. Your body was measured with a straight yard stick, but there's trouble in other places. So your father's name was Adam, and he really bore no other?"

"No, certainly not."

"That's too little by half. From this day we'll call you in earnest Navarrete: Ulrich Navarrete. That will be something complete. The name is only a dress, but if half of it is taken from your body, you are left half-bare and exposed to mockery. The garment must be becoming too, so we adorn it as we choose. My father was called Kurschner, but at the Latin school Olearius and Faber and Luscinius sat beside me, so I raised myself to the rank of a Roman citizen, and turned Kurschner into Pellicanus. . . ."

The jester coughed violently, and continued One thing more. To expect gratitude is folly, nine times out of ten none is reaped, and he who is wise thinks only of himself, and usually omits to seek thanks; but every one ought to be grateful, for it is burdensome to have enemies, and there is no one we learn to hate more easily, than the benefactor we repay with ingratitude. You ought and must tell the artist your history, for he has deserved your confidence.

The jester's worldly-wise sayings, in which selfishness was always praised as the highest virtue, often seemed very puzzling to the boy, yet many of them were impressed on his young soul. He followed the sick man's advice the very next morning, and he had no cause to regret it, for Moor treated him even more kindly than before.

Pellicanus intended to part from the travellers at Avignon, to go to Marseilles, and from there by ship to Savona, but before he reached the old city of the popes, he grew so feeble, that Moor scarcely hoped to bring him alive to the goal of his journey.

The little man's body seemed to continually grow smaller, and his head larger, while his hollow, livid cheeks looked as if a rose-leaf adorned the centre of each.

He often told his travelling-companions about his former life.

He had originally been destined for the ecclesiastical profession, but though he surpassed all the other pupils in the school, he was deprived of the hope of ever becoming a priest, for the Church wants no cripples. He was the child of poor people, and had been obliged to fight his way through his career as a student, with great difficulty.

"How shabby the broad top of my cap often was!" he said. "I was so much ashamed of it. I am so small. Dear me, anybody could see my head, and could not help noticing all the worn places in the velvet, if he cast his eyes down. How often have I sat beside the kitchen of a cook-shop, and seasoned dry bread with the smell of roast meat. Often too my poodledog went out and stole a sausage for me from the butcher."

At other times the little fellow had fared better; then, sitting in the taverns, he had given free-play to his wit, and imposed no constraint on his sharp tongue.

Once he had been invited by a former boon-companion, to accompany him to his ancestral castle, to cheer his sick father; and so it happened that he became a buffoon, wandered from one great lord to another, and finally entered the elector's service.

He liked to pretend that he despised the world and hated men, but this assertion could not be taken literally, and was to be regarded in a general, rather than a special sense, for every beautiful thing in the world kindled eager enthusiasm in his heart, and he remained kindly disposed towards individuals to the end.

When Moor once charged him with this, he said, smiling:

"What would you have? Whoever condemns, feels himself superior to the person upon whom he sits in judgment, and how many fools, like me, fancy themselves great, when they stand on tiptoe, and find fault even with the works of God! 'The world is evil,' says the philosopher, and whoever listens to him, probably thinks carelessly: 'Hear, hear! He would have made it better than our Father in heaven.' Let me have my pleasure. I'm only a little man, but I deal in great things. To criticise a single insignificant human creature, seems to me scarcely worth while, but when we pronounce judgment on all humanity and the boundless universe, we can open our mouths-wonderfully wide!"

Once his heart had been filled with love for a beautiful girl, but she had scornfully rejected his suit and married another. When she was widowed, and he found her in dire poverty, he helped her with a large share of his savings, and performed this kind service again, when the second worthless fellow she married had squandered her last penny.

His life was rich in similar incidents.

In his actions, the queer little man obeyed the dictates of his heart; in his speech, his head ruled his tongue, and this seemed to him the only sensible course. To practise unselfish generosity he regarded as a subtle, exquisite pleasure, which he ventured to allow himself, because he desired nothing more; others, to whom he did not grudge a prosperous career, he must warn against such folly.

There was a keen, bitter expression on his large, thin face, and whoever saw him for the first time might easily have supposed him to be a wicked, spiteful man. He knew this, and delighted in frightening the men and maid-servants at the taverns by hideous grimaces--he boasted of being able to make ninety-five different faces--until the artist's old valet at last dreaded him like the "Evil One."

He was particularly gay in Avignon, for he felt better than he had done for a long time, and ordered a seat to be engaged for him in a vehicle going to Marseilles.

The evening before their separation, he described with sparkling vivacity, the charms of the Ligurian coast, and spoke of the future as if he were sure of entire recovery and a long life.

In the night Ulrich heard him groaning louder than usual, and starting up, raised him, as he was in the habit of doing when the poor little man was tortured by difficulty of breathing. But this time Pellicanus did not swear and scold, but remained perfectly still, and when his heavy head fell like a pumpkin on the boy's breast, he was greatly terrified and ran to call the artist.

Moor was soon standing at the head of the sick-bed, holding a light, so that its rays could fall upon the face of the gasping man. The latter opened his eyes and made three grimaces in quick succession--very comical ones, yet tinged with sadness.

Pellicanus probably noticed the artist's troubled glance, for he tried to nod to him, but his head was too heavy and his strength too slight, so he only succeeded in moving it first to the right and then to the left, but his eyes expressed everything he desired to say. In this way several minutes elapsed, then Pellicanus smiled, and with a sorrowful gaze, though a mischievous expression hovered around his mouth, scanned:

"'Mox erit' quiet and mute, 'gui modo' jester 'erat'." Then he said as softly as if every tone came, not from his chest, but merely from his lips

"Is it agreed, Navarrete, Ulrich Navarrete? I've made the Latin easy for you, eh? Your hand, boy. Yours, too, dear, dear master.....Moor, Ethiopian--Blackskin...."

The words died away in a low, rattling sound, and the dying man's eyes became glazed, but it was several hours before he drew his last breath.

A priest gave him Extreme Unction, but consciousness did not return.

After the holy man had left him, his lips moved incessantly, but no one could understand what he said. Towards morning, the sun of Provence was shining warmly and brightly into the room and on his bed, when he suddenly threw his arm above his head, and half speaking, half singing to Hans Eitelfritz's melody, let fall from his lips the words: "In fortune, good fortune." A few minutes after he was dead.

Moor closed his eyes. Ulrich knelt weeping beside the bed, and kissed his poor friend's cold hand.

When he rose, the artist was gazing with silent reverence at the jester's features; Ulrich followed his eyes, and imagined he was standing in the presence of a miracle, for the harsh, bitter, troubled face had obtained a new expression, and was now the countenance of a peaceful, kindly man, who had fallen asleep with pleasant memories in his heart.

VOLUME 3

CHAPTER XIV.

FOR the first time in his life Ulrich had witnessed the death of a human being.

How often he had laughed at the fool, or thought his words absurd and wicked;--but the dead man inspired him with respect, and the thought of the old jester's corpse exerted a far deeper and more lasting influence upon him, than his father's supposed death. Hitherto he had only been able to imagine him as he had looked in life, but now the vision of him stretched at full length, stark and pale like the dead Pellicanus, often rose before his mind.

The artist was a silent man, and understood how to think and speak in lines and colors, better than in words. He only became eloquent and animated, when the conversation turned upon subjects connected with his art.

At Toulouse he purchased three new horses, and engaged the same number of French servants, then went to a jeweller and bought many articles. At the inn he put the chains and rings he had obtained, into pretty little boxes, and wrote on them in neat Gothic characters with special care: "Helena, Anna, Minerva, Europa and Lucia;" one name on each.

Ulrich watched him and remarked that those were not his children's names.

Moor looked up, and answered smiling: "These are only young artists, six sisters, each one of whom is as dear to me as if she were my own daughter. I hope we shall find them in Madrid, one of them, Sophonisba, at any rate."

"But there are only five boxes," observed the boy, "and you haven't written Sophonisba on any of them."

"She is to have something better," replied his patron smiling. "My portrait, which I began to paint yesterday, will be finished here. Hand me the mirror, the maul-stick, and the colors."

The picture was a superb likeness, absolutely faultless. The pure brow curved in lofty arches at the temples, the small eyes looked as clear and bright as they did in the mirror, the firm mouth shaded by a thin moustache, seemed as if it were just parting to utter a friendly word. The close-shaven beard on the cheeks and chin rested closely upon the white ruff, which seemed to have just come from under the laundresses' smoothing-iron.

How rapidly and firmly the master guided his brush! And Sophonisba, whom Moor distinguished by such a gift, how was he to imagine her? The other five sisters too! For their sakes he first anticipated with pleasure the arrival at Madrid.

In Bayonne the artist left the baggage-wagon behind. His luggage was put on mules, and when the party of travellers started, it formed an imposing caravan.

Ulrich expressed his surprise at such expenditure, and Moor answered kindly: "Pellicanus says: 'Among fools one must be a fool.' We enter Spain as the king's guests, and courtiers have weak eyes, and only notice people who give themselves airs."

At Fuenterrabia, the first Spanish city they reached, the artist received many honors, and a splendid troop of cavalry escorted him thence to Madrid.

Moor came as a guest to King Philip's capital for the third time, and was received there with all the tokens of respect usually paid only to great noblemen.

His old quarters in the treasury of the Alcazar, the palace of the kings of Castile, were again assigned to him. They consisted of a studio and suite of apartments, which by the monarch's special command, had been fitted up for him with royal magnificence.

Ulrich could not control his amazement. How poor and petty everything that a short time before, at Castle Rappolstein, had awakened his wonder and admiration now appeared.

During the first few days the artist's reception-room resembled a bee-hive; for aristocratic men and women, civil and ecclesiastical dignitaries passed in and out, pages and lackeys brought flowers, baskets of fruits, and other gifts. Every one attached to the court knew in what high favor the artist was held by His Majesty, and therefore hastened to win his good-will by attentions and presents. Every hour there was something new and astonishing to be seen, but the artist himself most awakened the boy's surprise.

The unassuming man, who on the journey had associated as familiarly with the poor invalids he had picked up by the wayside, the tavern-keepers, and soldiers of his escort, as if he were one of themselves, now seemed a very different person. True, he still dressed in black, but instead of cloth and silk, he wore velvet and satin, while two gold chains glittered beneath his ruff. He treated the greatest nobles as if he were doing them a favor by receiving them, and he himself were a person of unapproachable rank.

On the first day Philip and his queen Isabella of Valois, had sent for him and adorned him with a costly new chain.

On this occasion Ulrich saw the king. Dressed as a page he followed Moor, carrying the picture the latter intended for a gift to his royal host.

At the time of their entrance into the great reception-hall, the monarch was sitting motionless, gazing into vacancy, as if all the persons gathered around him had no existence for him. His head was thrown far back, pressing down the stiff ruff, on which it seemed to rest as if it were a platter. The fair-haired man's well-cut features wore the rigid, lifeless expression of a mask. The mouth and nostrils were slightly contracted, as if they shrank from breathing the same air with other human beings.

The monarch's face remained unmoved, while receiving the Pope's legates and the ambassadors from the republic of Venice. When Moor was led before him, a faint smile was visible beneath the soft, drooping moustache and close-shaven beard on the cheeks and chin; the prince's dull eyes also gained some little animation.

The day after the reception a bell rang in the studio, which was cleared of all present as quickly as possible, for it announced the approach of the king, who appeared entirely alone and spent two whole hours with Moor.

All these marks of distinction might have turned a weaker brain, but Moor received them calmly, and as soon as he was alone with Ulrich or Sophonisba, appeared no less unassuming and kindly, than at Emmendingen and on the journey through France.

A week after taking possession of the apartments in the treasury, the servants received orders to refuse admittance to every one, without distinction of rank or person, informing them that the artist was engaged in working for His Majesty.

Sophonisba Anguisciola was the only person whom Moor never refused to see. He had greeted the strange girl on his arrival, as a father meets his child.

Ulrich had been present when the artist gave her his portrait, and saw her, overwhelmed with joy and gratitude, cover her face with her hands and burst into loud sobs.

During Moor's first visit to Madrid, the young girl had come from Cremona to the king's court with her father and five sisters, and since then the task of supporting all six had rested on her shoulders.

Old Cavaliere Anguisciola was a nobleman of aristocratic family, who had squandered his large patrimony, and now, as he was fond of saying, lived day by day "by trusting God." A large portion of his oldest daughter's earnings he wasted at the gaming table with dissolute nobles, relying with happy confidence upon the talent displayed also by his younger children, and on what he called "trust in God." The gay, clever Italian was everywhere a welcome guest, and while Sophonisba toiled early and late, often without knowing how she was to obtain suitable food and clothing for her sisters and herself, his life was a series of banquets and festivals. Yet the noble girl retained the joyous courage inherited from her father, nay, more--even in necessity she did not cease to take a lofty view of art, and never permitted anything to leave her studio till she considered it finished.

At first Moor watched her silently, then he invited her to work in his studio, and avail herself of his advice and assistance.

So she had become his pupil, his friend.

Soon the young girl had no secrets from him, and the glimpses of her domestic life thus afforded touched him and brought her nearer and nearer to his heart.

The old Cavaliere praised the lucky accident, and was ready to show himself obliging, when Moor offered to let him and his daughters occupy a house he had purchased, that it might be kept in a habitable condition, and when the artist had induced the king to grant Sophonisba a larger annual salary, the father instantly bought a second horse.

The young girl, in return for so many benefits, was gratefully devoted to the artist, but she would have loved him even without them. His society was her greatest pleasure. To be allowed to stay and paint with him, become absorbed in conversation about art, its problems, means and purposes, afforded her the highest, purest happiness.

When she had discharged the duties imposed upon her by her attendance upon the queen, her heart drew her to the man she loved and honored. When she left him, it always seemed as if she had been in church, as if her soul had been steeped in purity and was effulgent. Moor had hoped to find her sisters with her in Madrid, but the old Cavaliere had taken them away with him to Italy. His "trust in God" was rewarded, for he had inherited a large fortune. What should he do longer in Madrid! To entertain the stiff, grave Spaniards and move them to laughter, was a far less pleasing occupation than to make merry with gay companions and be entertained himself at home.

Sophonisba was provided for, and the beautiful, gay, famous maid of honor would have no lack of suitors. Against his daughter's wish, he had given to the richest and most aristocratic among them, the Sicilian baron Don Fabrizio di Moncada, the hope of gaining her hand. "Conquer the fortress! When it yields--you can hold it," were his last words; but the citadel remained impregnable, though the besieger could bring into the field as allies a knightly, aristocratic bearing, an unsullied character, a handsome, manly figure, winning manners, and great wealth.

Ulrich felt a little disappointed not to find the five young girls, of whom he had dreamed, in Madrid; it would have been pleasant to have some pretty companions in the work now to begin.

Adjoining the studio was a smaller apartment, separated from the former room by a corridor, that could be closed, and by a heavy curtain. Here a table, at which the five girls might easily have found room, was placed in a favorable light for Ulrich. He was to draw from plastic models, and there was no lack of these in the Alcazar, for here rose a high, three-story wing, to which when wearied by the intrigues of statecraft and the restraints of court etiquette, King Philip gladly retired, yielding himself to the only genial impulse of his gloomy soul, and enjoyed the noble forms of art.

In the round hall on the lower floor countless plans, sketches, drawings and works of art were kept in walnut chests of excellent workmanship. Above this beautifully ornamented apartment--was the library, and in the third story the large hall containing the masterpieces of Titian.

The restless statesman, Philip, was no less eager to collect and obtain new and beautiful works by the great Venetian, than to defend and increase his own power and that of the Church. But these treasures were kept jealously guarded, accessible to no human being except himself and his artists.

Philip was all and all to himself; caring nothing for others, he did not deem it necessary, that they should share his pleasures. If anything outside the Church occupied a place in his regard, it was the artist, and therefore he did not grudge him what he denied to others.

Not only in the upper story, but in the lower ones also antique and modern busts and statues were arranged in appropriate places, and Moor was at liberty to choose from among them, for the king permitted him to do what was granted to no one else.

He often summoned him to the Titian Hall, and still more frequently rang the bell and entered the connecting corridor, accessible to himself alone, which led from the rooms devoted to art and science to the treasury and studio, where he spent hours with Moor. Ulrich eagerly devoted himself to the work, and his master watched his labor like an attentive, strict, and faithful teacher; meantime he carefully guarded against overtaxing the boy, allowed him to accompany him on many a ride, and advised him to look about the city. At first the lad liked to stroll through the streets and watch the long, brilliant processions, or timidly shrink back when closely-muffled men, their figures wholly invisible except the eyes and feet, bore a corpse along, or glided on mysterious missions through the streets. The bull-fights might have bewitched him, but be loved horses, and it grieved him to see the noble animal, wounded and killed.

He soon wearied of the civil and religious ceremonies, that might be witnessed nearly every day, and which always exerted the same power of attraction to the inhabitants of Madrid. Priests swarmed in the Alcazar, and soldiers belonging to every branch of military service, daily guarded or marched by the palace.

On the journey he had met plenty of mules with gay plumes and tassels, oddly-dressed peasants and citizens. Gentlemen in brilliant court uniforms, princes and princesses he saw daily in the court-yards, on the stairs, and in the park of the palace.

At Toulouse and in other cities, through which he had passed, life had been far more busy, active, and gay than in quiet Madrid, where everything went on as if people were on their way to church, where a cheerful face was rarely seen, and men and women knew of no sight more beautiful and attractive, than seeing poor Jews and heretics burned.

Ulrich did not need the city; the Alcazar was a world in itself, and offered him everything he desired.

He liked to linger in the stables, for there he could distinguish himself; but it was also delightful to work, for Moor chose models and designs that pleased the lad, and Sophonisba Anguisciola, who often painted for hours in the studio by the master's side, came to Ulrich in the intervals, looked at what he had finished, helped, praised, or scolded him, and never left him without a jest on her lips.

True, he was often left to himself; for the king sometimes summoned the artist and then quitted the palace with him for several days, to visit secluded country houses, and there--the old Hollander had told the lad-- painted under Moor's instructions.

On the whole, there were new, strange, and surprising things enough, to keep the sensation of "Fortune," alive in Ulrich's heart. Only it was vexatious that he found it so hard to make himself intelligible to people, but this too was soon to be remedied, for the pupil obtained two compa- nions.

CHAPTER XV.

ALONZO Sanchez Coello, a very distinguished Spanish artist, had his studio in the upper story of the treasury. The king was very friendly to him, and often took him also on his excursions. The gay, lively artist clung without envy, and with ardent reverence, to Moor, whose fellow-pupil he had been in Florence and Venice. During the Netherlander's first visit to Madrid, he had not disdained to seek counsel and instruction from his senior, and even now frequently visited his studio, bringing with him his children Sanchez and Isabella as pupils, and watched the Master closely while he painted.

At first Ulrich was not specially pleased with his new companions, for in the strangely visionary life he led, he had depended solely upon himself and "Fortune," and the figures living in his imagination were the most enjoyable society to him.

Formerly he had drawn eagerly in the morning, joyously anticipated Sophonisba's visit, and then gazed out over his paper and dreamed. How delightful it had been to let his thoughts wander to his heart's content. This could now be done no longer.

So it happened, that at first he could feel no real confidence in Sanchez, who was three years his senior, for the latter's thin limbs and close-cut dark hair made him look exactly like dark-browed Xaver. Therefore his relations with Isabella were all the more friendly.

She was scarcely fourteen, a dear little creature, with awkward limbs, and a face so wonderfully changeful in expression, that it could not fail to be by turns pretty and repellent. She always had beautiful eyes; all her other features were unformed, and might grow charming or exactly the reverse. When her work engrossed her attention, she bit her protruded tongue, and her raven-black hair, usually remarkably smooth, often became so oddly dishevelled, that she looked like a kobold; when, on the other hand, she talked pleasantly or jested, no one could help being pleased.

The child was rarely gifted, and her method of working was an exact contrast to that of the German lad. She progressed slowly, but finally accomplished something admirable; what Ulrich impetuously began had a showy, promising aspect, but in the execution the great idea shrivelled, and the work diminished in merit instead of increasing.

Sanchez Coello remained far behind the other two, but to make amends, he knew many things of which Ulrich's uncorrupted soul had no suspicion.

Little Isabella had been given by her mother, for a duenna, a watchful, ill-tempered widow, Senora Catalina, who never left the girl while she remained with Moor's pupils.

Receiving instruction with others urged Ulrich to rivalry, and also improved his knowledge of Spanish. But he soon became familiar with the language in another way, for one day, as he came out of the stables, a thin man in black, priestly robes, advanced towards him, looked searchingly into his face, then greeted him as a countryman, declaring that it made him happy to speak his dear native tongue again. Finally, he invited the "artist" to visit him. His name was Magister Kochel and he lodged with the king's almoner, for whom he was acting as clerk.

The pallid man with the withered face, deep-set eyes and peculiar grin, which always showed the bluish-red gums above the teeth, did not please the boy, but the thought of being able to talk in his native language attracted him, and he went to the German's.

He soon thought that by so doing he was accomplishing something good and useful, for the former offered to teach him to write and speak Spanish. Ulrich was glad to have escaped from school, and declined this proposal; but when the German suggested that he should content himself with speaking the language, assuring him that it could be accomplished without any difficulty, Ulrich consented and went daily at twilight to the Magister.

Instruction began at once and was pleasant enough, for Kochel let him translate merry tales and love stories from French and Italian books, which he read aloud in German, never scolded him, and after the first half-hour always laid the volume aside to talk with him.

Moor thought it commendable and right, for Ulrich to take upon himself the labor and constraint of studying a language, and promised, when the lessons were over, to give a fitting payment to the Magister, who seemed to have scanty means of livelihood.

The master ought to have been well disposed towards worthy Kochel, for the latter was an enthusiastic admirer of his works. He ranked the Netherlander above Titian and the other great Italian artists, called him the worthy friend of gods and kings, and encouraged his pupil to imitate him.

"Industry, industry!" cried the Magister. "Only by industry is the summit of wealth and fame gained. To be sure, such success demands sacrifices. How rarely is the good man permitted to enjoy the blessing of mass. When did he go to church last?"

Ulrich answered these and similar questions frankly and truthfully, and when Kochel praised the friendship uniting the artist to the king, calling them Orestes and Pylades, Ulrich, proud of the honor shown his master, told him how often Philip secretly visited the latter.

At every succeeding interview Kochel asked, as if by chance, in the midst of a conversation about other things: "Has the king honored you again?" or "You happy people, it is reported that the king has shown you his face again."

This "you" flattered Ulrich, for it allowed a ray of the royal favor to fall upon him also, so he soon informed his countryman, unasked, of every one of the monarch's visits to the treasury.

Weeks and months elapsed.

Towards the close of his first year's residence in Madrid, Ulrich spoke Spanish with tolerable fluency, and could easily understand his fellow-pupils; nay, be had even begun to study Italian.

Sophonisba Anguisciola still spent all her leisure hours in the studio, painting or conversing with Moor. Various dignitaries and grandees also went in and out of the studio, and among them frequently appeared, indeed usually when Sophonisba was present, her faithful admirer Don Fabrizio di Moncada.

Once Ulrich, without listening, heard Moor through the open door of the school-room, represent to her, that it was unwise to reject a suitor like the baron; he was a noble, high-minded gentleman and his love beyond question.

Her answer was long in coming; at last she rose, saying in an agitated voice: "We know each other, Master; I know your kind intentions. And yet, yet! Let me remain what I am, however insignificant that may be. I like the baron, but what better gifts can marriage bestow, than I already possess? My love belongs to Art, and you--you are my friend.... My sisters are my children. Have I not gained the right to call them so? I shall have no lack of duties towards them, when my father has squandered his inheritance. My noble queen will provide for my future, and I am necessary to her. My heart is filled--filled to the brim; I do what I can, and is it not a beautiful thought, that I am permitted to be something to those I love? Let me remain your Sophonisba, and a free artist."

"Yes, yes, yes! Remain what you are, girl!" Moor exclaimed, and then for a long time silence reigned in the studio.

Even before they could understand each other's language, a friendly intercourse had existed between Isabella and her German fellow-pupil, for in leisure moments they had sketched each other more than once.

These pictures caused much laughter and often occasional harmless scuffles between Ulrich and Sanchez, for the latter liked to lay hands on these portraits and turn them into hideous caricatures.

Isabella often earned the artist's unqualified praise, Ulrich sometimes received encouraging, sometimes reproving, and sometimes even harsh words. The latter Moor always addressed to him in German, but they deeply wounded the lad, haunting him for days.

The "word" still remained obedient to him. Only in matters relating to art, the power of "fortune" seemed to fail, and deny its service.

When the painter set him difficult tasks, which he could not readily accomplish, he called upon the "word;" but the more warmly and fervently he did so, the more surely he receded instead of advancing. When, on the contrary, he became angered against "fortune," reproached, rejected it, and relied wholly on himself, he accomplished the hardest things and won Moor's praise.

He often thought, that he would gladly resign his untroubled, luxurious life, and all the other gifts of Fortune, if he could only succeed in accomplishing what Moor desired him to attain in art. He knew and felt that this was the right goal; but one thing was certain, he could never attain it with pencil and charcoal. What his soul dreamed, what his mental vision beheld was colored. Drawing, perpetual drawing, became burdensome, repulsive, hateful; but with palette and brush in his hand he could not fail to become an artist, perhaps an artist like Titian.

He already used colors in secret; Sanchez Coello had been the cause of his making the first trial.

This precocious youth was suing for a fair girl's favor, and made Ulrich his confidant. One day, when Moor and Sanchez's father had gone with the king to Toledo, he took him to a balcony in the upper story of the treasury, directly opposite to the gate-keeper's lodgings, and only separated by a narrow court-yard from the window, where sat pretty Carmen, the porter's handsome daughter.

The girl was always to be found here, for her father's room was very dark, and she was compelled to embroider priestly robes from morning till night. This pursuit brought in money, which was put to an excellent use by the old man, who offered sacrifices to his own comfort at the cook-shop, and enjoyed fish fried in oil with his Zamora wine. The better her father's appetite was, the more industriously the daughter was obliged to embroider. Only on great festivals, or when an 'Auto-da-fe' was proclaimed, was Carmen permitted to leave the palace with her old aunt; yet she had already found suitors. Nineteen-year-old Sanchez did not indeed care for her hand, but merely for her love, and when it began to grow dusk, he stationed himself on the balcony which he had discovered, made signs to her, and flung flowers or bonbons on her table.

"She is still coy," said the young Spaniard, telling Ulrich to wait at the narrow door, which opened upon the balcony. "There sits the angel! Just look! I gave her the pomegranate blossom in her magnificent hair-- did you ever see more beautiful tresses? Take notice! She'll soon melt; I know women!"

Directly after a bouquet of roses fell into the embroiderer's lap. Carmen uttered a low cry, and perceiving Sanchez, motioned him away with her head and hand, finally turning her back upon him.

"She's in a bad humor to-day," said Sanchez; "but I beg you to notice that she'll keep my roses. She'll wear one to-morrow in her hair or on her bosom; what will you wager?"

"That may be," answered Ulrich. "She probably has no money to buy any for herself."

To be sure, the next day at twilight Carmen wore a rose in her hair.

Sanchez exulted, and drew Ulrich out upon the balcony. The beauty glanced at him, blushed, and returned the fair-haired boy's salutation with a slight bend of the head.

The gate-keeper's little daughter was a pretty child, and Ulrich had no fear of doing what Sanchez ventured.

On the third day he again accompanied him to the balcony, and this time, after silently calling upon the "word," pressed his hand upon his heart, just as Carmen looked at him.

The young girl blushed again, waved her fan, and then bent her little head so low, that it almost touched the embroidery.

The next evening she secretly kissed her fingers to Ulrich.

From this time the young lover preferred to seek the balcony without Sanchez. He would gladly have called a few tender words across, or sung to his lute, but that would not do, for people were constantly passing to and fro in the court-yard.

Then the thought occurred to him, that he could speak to the fair one by means of a picture.

A small panel was soon found, he had plenty of brushes and colors to choose from, and in a few minutes, a burning heart, transfixed by an arrow, was completed. But the thing looked horribly red and ugly, so he rejected it, and painted--imitating one of Titian's angels, which specially pleased him--a tiny Cupid, holding a heart in his hand.

He had learned many things from the master, and as the little figure rounded into shape, it afforded him so much pleasure, that he could not leave it, and finished it the third day.

It had not entered his mind to create a completed work of art, but the impetuosity of youth, revelling in good fortune, had guided his brush. The little Cupid bent joyously forward, drawing the right leg back, as if making a bow. Finally Ulrich draped about him a black and yellow scarf, such as he had often seen the young Austrian archduke wear, and besides the pierced heart, placed a rose in the tiny, ill-drawn hand.

He could not help laughing at his "masterpiece" and hurried out on the balcony with the wet painting, to show it to Carmen. She laughed heartily too, answered his salutations with tender greetings, then laid aside her embroidery and went back into the room, but only to immediately reappear at the window again, holding up a prayer-book and extending towards him the eight fingers of her industrious little hands.

He motioned that he understood her, and at eight o'clock the next morning was kneeling by her side at mass, where he took advantage of a favorable opportunity to whisper: "Beautiful Carmen!"

The young girl blushed, but he vainly awaited an answer. Carmen now rose, and when Ulrich also stood up to permit her to pass, she dropped her prayer-book, as if by accident. He stooped with her to pick it up, and when their heads nearly touched, she whispered hurriedly: "Nine o'clock this evening in the shell grotto; the garden will be open."

Carmen awaited him at the appointed place.

At first Ulrich's heart throbbed so loudly and passionately, that he could find no words; but the young girl helped him, by telling him that he was a handsome fellow, whom it would be easy to love.

Then he remembered the vows of tenderness he had translated at Kochel's, falteringly repeated them, and fell on one knee before her, like all the heroes in adventures and romances.

And behold! Carmen did exactly the same as the young ladies whose acquaintance he had made at his teacher's, begged him to rise, and when he willingly obeyed the command--for he wore thin silk stockings and the grotto was paved with sharp stones--drew him to her heart, and tenderly stroked his hair back from his face with her dainty fingers, while he gladly permitted her to press her soft young lips to his.

All this was delightful, and he had no occasion to speak at all; yet Ulrich felt timid and nervous. It seemed like a deliverance when the footsteps of the guard were heard, and Carmen drew him away through the gate with her into the court-yard.

Before the little door leading into her father's room she again pressed his hand, and then vanished as swiftly as a shadow.

Ulrich remained alone, pacing slowly up and down before the treasury, for he knew that he had done something very wrong, and did not venture to appear before the artist.

When he entered the dark garden, he had again summoned "fortune" to his aid; but now it would have pleased him better, if it had been less willing to come to his assistance.

Candles were burning in the studio, and Moor sat in his arm-chair, holding-- Ulrich would fain have bidden himself in the earth--the boy's Cupid in his hands.

The young culprit wanted to slip past his teacher with a low "good night," but the latter called him, and pointing to the picture, smilingly asked: "Did you paint this?"

Ulrich nodded, blushing furiously.

The artist eyed him from top to toe, saying: "Well, well, it is really very pretty. I suppose it is time now for us to begin to paint."

The lad did not know what had happened, for a few weeks before Moor had harshly refused, when he asked the same thing now voluntarily offered.

Scarcely able to control his surprise and joy, be bent over the artist's hand to kiss it, but the latter withdrew it, gazed steadily into his eyes with paternal affection, and said: "We will try, my boy, but we must not give up drawing, for that is the father of our art. Drawing keeps us within the bounds assigned to what is true and beautiful. The morning you must spend as before; after dinner you shall be rewarded by using colors." This plan was followed, and the pupil's first love affair bore still another fruit--it gave a different form to his relations with Sanchez. The feeling that he had stood in his way and abused his confidence sorely disturbed Ulrich, so he did everything in his power to please his companion.

He did not see the fair Carmen again, and in a few weeks the appointment was forgotten, for painting under Moor's instruction absorbed him as nothing in his life had ever done before, and few things did after.

CHAPTER XVI.

ULRICH was now seventeen, and had been allowed to paint for four months.

Sanchez Coello rarely appeared in the studio, for he had gone to study with the architect, Herrera; Isabella vied with Ulrich, but was speedily outstripped by the German.

It seemed as if he had been born with the power to use the brush, and the young girl watched his progress with unfeigned pleasure. When Moor harshly condemned his drawing, her kind eyes grew dim with tears; if the master looked at his studies with an approving smile, and showed them to Sophonisba with words of praise, she was as glad as if they had been bestowed upon herself.

The Italian came daily to the treasury as usual, to paint, talk or play chess with Moor; she rejoiced at Ulrich's progress, and gave him many a useful suggestion.

When the young artist once complained that he had no good models, she gaily offered to sit to him. This was a new and unexpected piece of good fortune. Day and night he thought only of Sophonisba. The sittings began.

The Italian wore a red dress, trimmed with gold embroidery, and a high white lace ruff, that almost touched her cheeks. Her wavy brown hair clung closely to the beautiful oval head, its heavy braids covering the back of the neck; tiny curls fluttered around her ears and harmonized admirably with the lovely, mischievous expression of the mouth, that won all hearts. To paint the intelligent brown eyes was no easy matter, and she requested Ulrich to be careful about her small, rather prominent chin, which was anything but beautiful, and not make her unusually high, broad forehead too conspicuous; she had only put on the pearl diadem to relieve it.

The young artist set about this task with fiery impetuosity, and the first sketch surpassed all expectations.

Don Fabrizio thought the picture "startlingly" like the original. Moor was not dissatisfied, but feared that in the execution his pupil's work would lose the bold freshness, which lent it a certain charm in his eyes, and was therefore glad when the bell rang, and soon after the king appeared, to whom he intended to show Ulrich's work.

Philip had not been in the studio for a long time, but the artist had reason to expect him; for yesterday the monarch must have received his letter, requesting that he would graciously grant him permission to leave Madrid.

Moor had remained in Spain long enough, and his wife and child were urging his return. Yet departure was hard for him on Sophonisba's account; but precisely because he felt that she was more to him than a beloved pupil and daughter, he had resolved to hasten his leave-taking.

All present were quickly dismissed, the bolts were drawn and Philip appeared.

He looked paler than usual, worn and weary.

Moor greeted him respectfully, saying: "It is long since Your Majesty has visited the treasury."

"Not 'Your Majesty;' to you I am Philip," replied the king. "And you wish to leave me, Antonio! Recall your letter! You must not go now."

The sovereign, without waiting for a reply, now burst into complaints about the tiresome, oppressive duties of his office, the incapacity of the magistrates, the selfishness, malice and baseness of men. He lamented that Moor was a Netherlander, and not a Spaniard, called him the only friend he possessed among the rebellious crew in Holland and Flanders, and stopped him when he tried to intercede for his countrymen, though repeatedly assuring him that he found in his society his best pleasure, his only real recreation; Moor must stay, out of friendship, compassion for him, a slave in the royal purple.

After the artist had promised not to speak of departure during the next few days, Philip began to paint a saint, which Moor had sketched, but at the end of half an hour he threw down his brush. He called himself negligent of duty, because he was following his inclination, instead of using his brain and hands in the service of the State and Church. Duty was his tyrant, his oppressor. When the day-laborer threw his hoe over his shoulder, the poor rascal was rid of toil and anxiety; but they pursued him everywhere, night and day. His son was a monster, his subjects were rebels or cringing hounds. Bands of heretics, like moles or senseless brutes, undermined and assailed the foundation of the throne and safeguard of society: the Church. To crush and vanquish was his profession, hatred his reward on earth. Then, after a moment's silence, he pointed towards heaven, exclaiming as if in ecstasy: "There, there! with Him, with Her, with the Saints, for whom I fight!"

The king had rarely come to the treasury in such a mood. He seemed to feel this too, and after recovering his self-control, said:

"It pursues me even here, I cannot succeed in getting the right coloring to-day. Have you finished anything new?"

Moor now pointed out to the king a picture by his own hand, and after Philip had gazed at it long and appreciatively, criticising it with excellent judgment, the artist led him to Ulrich's portrait of Sophonisba, and asked, not without anxiety: "What does Your Majesty say to this attempt?"

"Hm!" observed the monarch. "A little of Moor, something borrowed from Titian, yet a great deal that is original. The bluish-grey leaden tone comes from your shop. The thing is a wretched likeness! Sophonisba resembles a gardener's boy. Who made it?"

"My pupil, Ulrich Navarrete."

"How long has he been painting?"

"For several months, Sire."

"And you think he will be an artist of note?"

"Perhaps so. In many respects he surpasses my expectations, in others he falls below them. He is a strange fellow."

"He is ambitious, at any rate."

"No small matter for the future artist. What he eagerly begins has a very grand and promising aspect; but it shrinks in the execution. His mind seizes and appropriates what he desires to represent, at a single hasty grasp...."

"Rather too vehement, I should think."

"No fault at his age. What he possesses makes me less anxious, than what he lacks. I cannot yet discover the thoughtful artist-spirit in him."

"You mean the spirit, that refines what it has once taken, and in quiet meditation arranges lines, and assigns each color to its proper place, in short your own art-spirit."

"And yours also, Sire. If you had begun to paint early, you would have possessed what Ulrich lacks."

"Perhaps so. Besides, his defect is one of those which will vanish with years. In your school, with zeal and industry...."

"He will obtain, you think, what he lacks. I thought so too! But as I was saying: he is queerly constituted. What you have admitted to me more than once, the point we have started from in a hundred conversations--he cannot grasp: form is not the essence of art to him."

The king shrugged his shoulders and pointed to his forehead; but Moor continued: "Everything he creates must reflect anew, what he experienced at the first sight of the subject. Often the first sketch succeeds, but if it fails, he seeks without regard to truth and accuracy, by means of trivial, strange expedients, to accomplish his purpose. Sentiment, always sentiment! Line and tone are everything; that is our motto. Whoever masters them, can express the grandest things."

"Right, right! Keep him drawing constantly. Give him mouths, eyes, and hands to paint."

"That must be done in Antwerp."

"I'll hear nothing about Antwerp! You will stay, Antonio, you will stay. Your wife and child-all honor to them. I have seen your wife's portrait. Good, nourishing bread! Here you have ambrosia and manna. You know whom I mean; Sophonisba is attached to you; the queen says so."

"And I gratefully feel it. It is hard to leave your gracious Majesty and Sophonisba; but bread, Sire, bread--is necessary to life. I shall leave friends here, dear friends--it will be difficult, very difficult, to find new ones at my age."

"It is the same with me, and for that very reason you will stay, if you are my friend! No more! Farewell, Antonio, till we meet again, perhaps to-morrow, in spite of a chaos of business. Happy fellow that you are! In the twinkling of an eye you will be revelling in colors again, while the yoke, the iron yoke, weighs me down."

Moor thought he should be able to work undisturbed after the king had left him, and left the door unbolted. He was standing before the easel after dinner, engaged in painting, when the door of the corridor leading to the treasury was suddenly flung open, without the usual warning, and Philip again entered the studio. This time his cheeks wore a less pallid hue than in the morning, and his gait showed no traces of the solemn gravity, which had become a second nature to him,--on the contrary he was gay and animated.

But the expression did not suit him; it seemed as if he had donned a borrowed, foreign garb, in which he was ill at ease and could not move freely.

Waving a letter in his right hand, he pointed to it with his left, exclaiming:

"They are coming. This time two marvels at once. Our Saviour praying in the garden of Gethsemane, and Diana at the Bath. Look, look! Even this is a treasure. These lines are from Titian's own hand."

"A peerless old man," Moor began; but Philip impetuously interrupted: "Old man, old man? A youth, a man, a vigorous man. How soon he will be ninety, and yet--yet; who will equal him?"

As he uttered the last words, the monarch stopped before Sophonisba's portrait, and pointing to it with the scornful chuckle peculiar to him, continued gaily:

"There the answer meets me directly. That red! The Venetian's laurels seem to have turned your high flown pupil's head. A hideous picture!"

"It doesn't seem so bad to me," replied Moor. "There is even something about it I like."

"You, you?" cried Philip. "Poor Sophonisba!"

"Those carbuncle eyes! And a mouth, that looks as if she could eat nothing but sugar-plums. I don't know what tickles me to-day. Give me the palette. The outlines are tolerably good, the colors fairly shriek. But what boy can understand a woman, a woman like your friend! I'll paint over the monster, and if the picture isn't Sophonisba, it may serve for a naval battle."

The king had snatched the palette from the artist's hand, clipped his brush in the paint, and smiling pleasantly, was about to set to work; but Moor placed himself between the sovereign and the canvas; exclaiming gaily: "Paint me, Philip; but spare the portrait."

"No, no; it will do for the naval battle," chuckled the king, and while he pushed the artist back, the latter, carried away by the monarch's unusual freedom, struck him lightly on the shoulder with the maul-stick.

The sovereign started, his lips grew white, he drew his small but stately figure to its full height. His unconstrained bearing was instantly transformed into one of unapproachable, icy dignity.

Moor felt what was passing in the ruler's mind.

A slight shiver ran through his frame, but his calmness remained unshaken, and before the insulted monarch found time to give vent to his indignation in words, he said quickly, as if the offence he had committed was not worth mentioning:

"Queer things are done among comrades in art. The painter's war is over! Begin the naval battle, Sire, or still better, lend more charm and delicacy to the corners of the mouth. The pupil's worst failure is in the chin; more practised hands might be wrecked on that cliff. Those eyes! Perhaps they sparkled just in that way, but we are agreed in one thing: the portrait ought not to represent the original at a given moment, ruled by a certain feeling or engaged in a special act, but should express the sum of the spiritual, intellectual and personal attributes of the subject--his soul and person, mind and character-feelings and nature. King Philip, pondering over complicated political combinations, would be a fascinating historical painting, but no likeness...."

"Certainly not," said the king in a low voice; "the portrait must reveal the inmost spirit; mine must show how warmly Philip loves art and his artists. Take the palette, I beg. It is for you, the great Master, not for me, the overworked, bungling amateur, to correct the work of talented pupils."

There was a hypocritical sweetness in the tone of these words which had not escaped the artist.

Philip had long been a master in the school of dissimulation, but Moor knew him thoroughly, and understood the art of reading his heart.

This mode of expression from the king alarmed him more than a passionate outburst of rage. He only spoke in this way when concealing what was seething within. Besides, there was another token. The Netherlander had intentionally commenced a conversation on art, and it was almost unprecedented to find Philip disinclined to enter into one. The blow had been scarcely perceptible, but Majesty will not endure a touch.

Philip did not wish to quarrel with the artist now, but he would remember the incident, and woe betide him, if in some gloomy hour the sovereign should recall the insult offered him here. Even the lightest blow from the paw of this slinking tiger could inflict deep wounds--even death.

These thoughts had darted with the speed of lightning through the artist's mind, and still lingered there as, respectfully declining to take the palette, he replied "I beseech you, Sire, keep the brush and colors, and correct what you dislike."

"That would mean to repaint the whole picture, and my time is limited," answered Philip. "You are responsible for your pupils' faults, as well as for your own offences. Every one is granted, allowed, offered, what is his due; is it not so, dear master? Another time, then, you shall hear from me!" In the doorway the monarch kissed his hand to the artist, then disappeared.

CHAPTER XVII.

MOOR remained alone in the studio. How could he have played such a boyish prank!

He was gazing anxiously at the floor, for he had good reason to be troubled, though the reflection that he had been alone with the king, and the unprecedented act had occurred without witnesses, somewhat soothed him. He could not know that a third person, Ulrich, had beheld the reckless, fateful contest.

The boy had been drawing in the adjoining room, when loud voices were heard in the studio. He cherished a boundless reverence, bordering upon idolatry, for his first model, the beautiful Sophonisba, and supposing that it was she, discussing works of art with Moor, as often happened, he opened the door, pushed back the curtain, and saw the artist tap the chuckling king on the arm.

The scene was a merry one, yet a thrill of fear ran through his limbs, and he went back to his plaster model more rapidly than he had come.

At nightfall Moor sought Sophonisba. He had been invited to a ball given by the queen, and knew that he should find the maid of honor among Isabella's attendants.

The magnificent apartments were made as light as day by thousands of wax-candles in silver and bronze candelabra; costly Gobelin tapestry and purple Flanders hangings covered the walls, and the bright hues of the paintings were reflected from the polished floors, flooded with brilliant light.

No dancing had ever been permitted at the court before Philip's marriage with the French princess, who had been accustomed to greater freedom of manners; now a ball was sometimes given in the Alcazar. The first person who had ventured to dance the gaillarde before the eyes of the monarch and his horrified courtiers, was Sophonisba--her partner was Duke

Gonzaga. Strangely enough, the gayest lady at the court was the very person, who gave the gossips the least occasion for scandal.

A gavotte was just over, as Moor entered the superb rooms. In the first rank of the brilliant circle of distinguished ecclesiastics, ambassadors and grandees, who surrounded the queen, stood the Austrian archdukes, and the handsome, youthful figures of Alexander of Parma and of Don Juan, the half-brother of King Philip.

Don Carlos, the deformed heir to the throne, was annoying with his coarse jests some ladies of the court, who were holding their fans before their faces, yet did not venture to make the sovereign's son feel their displeasure.

Velvet, silk and jewels glittered, delicate laces rose and drooped around the necks and hands of the ladies and gentlemen. Floating curls, sparkling eyes, noble and attractive features enslaved the eye, but the necks, throats and arms of the court dames were closely concealed under high ruffs and lace frills, stiff bodices and puffed sleeves.

A subtile perfume filled the illuminated air of these festal halls; amidst the flirting of light fans, laughter, gay conversation, and slander reigned supreme. In an adjoining room golden zechins fell rattling and ringing on the gaming-table.

The morose, bigoted court, hampered by rigid formality, had been invaded by worldly pleasure, which disported itself unabashed by the presence of the distinguished prelates in violet and scarlet robes, who paced with dignified bearing through the apartments, greeting the more prominent ladies and grandees.

A flourish of trumpets was borne on the air, and Philip appeared. The cavaliers, bowing very low, suddenly stepped back from the fair dames, and the ladies curtsied to the floor. Perfect silence followed.

It seemed as if an icy wind had passed over the flower-beds and bent all the blossoms at once.

After a few minutes the gentlemen stood erect, and the ladies rose again, but even the oldest duchesses were not allowed the privilege of sitting in their sovereign's presence.

Gayety was stifled, conversation was carried on in whispers.

The young people vainly waited for the signal to dance.

It was long since Philip had been so proudly contemptuous, so morose as he was to-night. Experienced courtiers noticed that His Majesty held his head higher than usual, and kept out of his way. He walked as if engaged in scrutinizing the frescos on the ceiling, but nothing that he wished to see escaped his notice, and when he perceived Moor, he nodded graciously and smiled pleasantly upon him for a moment, but did not, as usual, beckon him to approach.

This did not escape the artist or Sophonisba, whom Moor had informed of what had occurred.

He trusted her as he did himself, and she deserved his confidence.

The clever Italian had shared his anxiety, and as soon as the king entered another apartment, she beckoned to Moor and held a long conversation with him in a window-recess. She advised him to keep everything in readiness for departure, and she undertook to watch and give him timely warning.

It was long after midnight, when Moor returned to his rooms. He sent the sleepy servant to rest, and paced anxiously to and fro for a short time; then he pushed Ulrich's portrait of Sophonisba nearer the mantel-piece, where countless candles were burning in lofty sconces.

This was his friend, and yet it was not. The thing lacking--yes, the king was right--was incomprehensible to a boy.

We cannot represent, what we are unable to feel. Yet Philip's censure had been too severe. With a few strokes of the brush Moor expected to make this picture a soul mirror of the beloved girl, from whom it was hard, unspeakably hard for him to part.

"More than fifty!" he thought, a melancholy smile hovering around his mouth.--"More than fifty, an old husband and father, and yet--yet--good nourishing bread at home--God bless it, Heaven preserve it! It only this girl were my daughter! How long the human heart retains its functional power! Perhaps love is the pith of life--when it dries, the tree withers too!"

Still absorbed in thought, Moor had seized his palette, and at intervals added a few short, almost imperceptible strokes to the mouth, eyes, and delicate nostrils of the portrait, before which he sat--but these few strokes lent charm and intellectual expression to his pupil's work.

When he at last rose and looked at what he had done, he could not help smiling, and asking himself how it was possible to imitate, with such trivial materials, the noblest possessions of man: mind and soul. Both now spoke to the spectator from these features. The right words were easy to the master, and with them he had given the clumsy sentence meaning and significance.

The next morning Ulrich found Moor before Sophonisba's portrait. The pupil's sleep had been no less restless than the master's, for the former had done something which lay heavy on his heart.

After being an involuntary witness of the scene in the studio the day before he had taken a ride with Sanchez and had afterwards gone to Kochel's to take a lesson. True, he now spoke Spanish with tolerable fluency and knew something of Italian, but Kochel entertained him so well, that he still visited him several times a week.

On this occasion, there was no translating. The German first kindly upbraided him for his long absence, and then, after the conversation had turned upon his painting and Moor, sympathizingly asked what truth there was in the rumor, that the king had not visited the artist for a long time and had withdrawn his favor from him.

"Withdrawn his favor!" Ulrich joyously exclaimed. "They are like two brothers! They wrestled together to-day, and the master, in all friendship, struck His Majesty a blow with the maul-stick....But--for Heaven's sake!--you will swear--fool, that I am--you will swear not to speak of it!"

"Of course I will!" Kochel exclaimed with a loud laugh. "My hand upon it Navarrete. I'll keep silence, but you! Don't gossip about that! Not on any account! The jesting blow might do the master harm. Excuse me for to-day; there is a great deal of writing to be done for the almoner."

Ulrich went directly back to the studio. The conviction that he had committed a folly, nay, a crime, had taken possession of him directly after the last word escaped his lips, and now tortured him more and more. If Kochel, who was a very ordinary man, should not keep the secret, what might not Moor suffer from his treachery! The lad was usually no prattler, yet now, merely to boast of his master's familiar intercourse with the king, he had forgotten all caution.

After a restless night, his first thought had been to look at his portrait of Sophonisba. The picture lured, bewitched, enthralled him with an irresistible spell.

Was this really his work?

He recognized every stroke of the brush. And yet! Those thoughtful eyes, the light on the lofty brow, the delicate lips, which seemed about parting to utter some wise or witty word--he had not painted them, never, never could he have accomplished such a masterpiece. He became very anxious. Had "Fortune," which usually left him in the lurch when creating, aided him on this occasion? Last evening, before he went to bed, the picture had been very different. Moor rarely painted by candlelight and he had heard him come home late, yet now--now.....

He was roused from these thoughts by the artist, who had been feasting his eyes a long time on the handsome lad, now rapidly developing into a youth, as he stood before the canvas as if spellbound. He felt what was passing in the awakening artist-soul, for a similar incident had happened to himself, when studying with his old master, Schorel.

"What is the matter?" asked Moor as quietly as usual, laying his hand upon the arm of his embarrassed pupil. "Your work seems to please you remarkably."

"It is-I don't know"--stammered Ulrich. "It seems as if in the night..."

"That often happens," interrupted the master. "If a man devotes himself earnestly to his profession, and says to himself: 'Art shall be everything to me, all else trivial interruptions,' invisible powers aid him, and when he sees in the morning what he has created the day before, he imagines a miracle has happened."

At these words Ulrich grew red and pale by turns. At last, shaking his head, he murmured in an undertone: "Yes, but those shadows at the corners of the mouth--do you see?--that light on the brow, and there--just look at the nostrils--I certainly did not paint those."

"I don't think them so much amiss," replied Moor. "Whatever friendly spirits now work for you at night, you must learn in Antwerp to paint in broad day at any hour."

"In Antwerp?"

"We shall prepare for departure this very day. It must be done with the utmost privacy. When Isabella has gone, pack your best clothes in the little knapsack. Perhaps we shall leave secretly; we have remained in Madrid long enough. Keep yourself always in readiness. No one, do you hear, no human being, not even the servants, must suspect what is going on. I know you; you are no babbler."

The artist suddenly paused and turned pale, for men's loud, angry voices were heard outside the door of the studio.

Ulrich too was startled.

The master's intention of leaving Madrid had pleased him, for it would withdraw the former from the danger that might result from his own imprudence. But as the strife in the anteroom grew louder, he already saw the alguazils forcing their way into the studio.

Moor went towards the door, but it was thrown wide open ere he reached it, and a bearded lansquenet crossed the threshold.

Laughing scornfully, he shouted a few derisive words at the French servants who had tried to stop him, then turning to the artist, and throwing back his broad chest, he held out his arms towards Moor, with passionate ardor, exclaiming: "These French flunkies--the varlets, tried to keep me from waiting upon my benefactor, my friend, the great Moor, to show my reverence for him. How you stare at me, Master! Have you forgotten Christmas-day at Emmendingen, and Hans Eitelfritz from Colln on the Spree?"

Every trace of anxiety instantly vanished from the face of the artist, who certainly had not recognized in this braggart the modest companion of those days.

Eitelfritz was strangely attired, so gaily and oddly dressed, that he could not fail to be conspicuous even among his comrades. One leg of his breeches, striped with red and blue, reached far below his knee, while the other, striped with yellow and green, enclosed the upper part of the limb, like a full muff. Then how many puffs, slashes and ribbons adorned his doublet! What gay plumes decked the pointed edge of his cap.

Moor gave the faithful fellow a friendly welcome, and expressed his pleasure at meeting him so handsomely equipped. He held his head higher now, than he used to do under the wagon-tilt and in quarters, and doubtless he had earned a right to do so.

"The fact is," replied Hans Eitelfritz, "I've received double pay for the past nine months, and take a different view of life from that of a poor devil of a man-at-arms who goes fighting through the country. You know the ditty:

> "'There is one misery on earth,
> Well, well for him, who knows it not!
> With beggar's staff to wander forth,
> Imploring alms from spot to spot.'

"And the last verse:

> "'And shall we never receive our due?
> Will our sore trials never end?
> Leader to victory, be true,
> Come quickly, death, beloved friend.'

"I often sang it in those days; but now: What does the world cost? A thousand zechins is not too much for me to pay for it!"

"Have you gained booty, Hans?"

"Better must come; but I'm faring tolerably well. Nothing but feasting! Three of us came here from Venice through Lombardy, by ship from Genoa to Barcelona, and thence through this barren, stony country here to Madrid."

"To take service?"

"No, indeed. I'm satisfied with my company and regiment. We brought some pictures here, painted by the great master, Titian, whose fame must surely have reached you. See this little purse! hear its jingle--it's all gold! If any one calls King Philip a niggard again, I'll knock his teeth down his throat."

"Good tidings, good reward!" laughed Moor. "Have you had board and lodging too?"

"A bed fit for the Roman Emperor,--and as for the rest?--I told you, nothing but feasting. Unluckily, the fun will be all over to-night, but to go without paying my respects to you.....Zounds! is that the little fellow--the Hop-o'my-Thumb-who pressed forward to the muster-table at Emmendingen?"

"Certainly, certainly."

"Zounds, he has grown. We'll gladly enlist you now, young sir. Can you remember me?"

"Of course I do," replied Ulrich. "You sang the song about 'good fortune'"

"Have you recollected that?" asked the lansquenet. "Foolish stuff! Believe it or not, I composed the merry little thing when in great sorrow and poverty, just to warm my heart. Now I'm prosperous, and can rarely succeed in writing a verse. Fires are not needed in summer."

"Where have you been lodged?"

"Here in the 'old cat.' That's a good name for this Goliath's palace."

When Eitelfritz had enquired about the jester and drunk a goblet of wine with Moor and Ulrich, he took leave of them both, and soon after the artist went to the city alone.

At the usual hour Isabella Coello came with her duenna to the studio, and instantly noticed the change Sophonisba's portrait had undergone.

Ulrich stood beside her before the easel, while she examined his work.

The young girl gazed at it a long, long time, without a word, only once pausing in her scrutiny to ask: "And you, you painted this--without the master?"

Ulrich shook his head, saying, in an undertone: "I suppose he thinks it is my own work; and yet--I can't understand it."

"But I can," she eagerly exclaimed, still gazing intently at the portrait.

At last, turning her round, pleasant flee towards him, she looked at him with tears in her eyes, saying so affectionately that the innermost depths of Ulrich's heart were stirred: "How glad I am! I could never accomplish such a work. You will become a great artist, a very distinguished one, like Moor. Take notice, you surely will. How beautiful that is!--I can find no words to express my admiration."

At these words the blood mounted to Ulrich's brain, and either the fiery wine he had drunk, or the delighted girl's prophetic words, or both, fairly intoxicated him. Scarcely knowing what he said or did, he seized Isabella's little hand, impetuously raised his curly head, and enthusiastically exclaimed: "Hear me! your prophecy shall be fulfilled, Belica; I will be an artist. Art, Art alone! The master said everything else is vain--trivial. Yes, I feel, I am certain, that the master is right."

"Yes, yes," cried Isabella; "you must become a great artist."

"And if I don't succeed, if I accomplish nothing more than this...."

Here Ulrich suddenly paused, for he remembered that he was going away, perhaps to-morrow, so he continued sadly, in a calmer tone: "Rely upon it;

I will do what I can, and whatever happens, you will rejoice, will you not, if I succeed-and if it should be otherwise...."

"No, no," she eagerly exclaimed. "You can accomplish everything, and I--I; you don't know how happy it makes me that you can do more than I!"

Again he held out his hand, and as Isabella warmly clasped it, the watchful duenna's harsh voice cried:

"What does this mean, Senorita? To work, I beg of you. Your father says time is precious."

CHAPTER XVIII.

TIME is precious! Magister Kochel had also doubtless said this to himself, as soon as Ulrich left him the day before. He had been hired by a secret power, with which however he was well ac-quainted, to watch the Netherland artist and collect evidence for a charge--a gravamen--against him.

The spying and informing, which he had zealously pursued for years in the service of the Holy Inquisition, he called "serving the Church," and hoped, sooner or later, to be rewarded with a benefice; but even if this escaped him, informing brought him as large an income as he required, and had become the greatest pleasure, indeed, a necessity of life to him.

He had commenced his career in Cologne as a Dominican friar, and remained in communication with some of his old brethren of the Order.

The monks, Sutor and Stubenrauch, whom Moor had hospitably received in his wagon at the last Advent season but one, sometimes answered Kochel's letters of enquiry.

The latter had long known that the unusual favor the king showed the artist was an abomination, not only to the heads of the Holy Inquisition, but also to the ambassadors and court dignitaries, yet Moor's quiet, stainless life afforded no handle for attack. Soon, however, unexpected aid came to him from a distance.

A letter arrived, dictated by Sutor, and written by Stubenrauch in the fluent bad Latin used by him and those of his ilk. Among other things it contained an account of a journey, in which much was said about Moor, whom the noble pair accused of having a heretical and evil mind. Instead of taking them to the goal of the journey, as he had promised, he had deserted them in a miserable tavern by the way-side, among rough, godless lansquenets, as the mother of Moses abandoned her babe. And such a man as this, they had heard with amazement at Cologne, was permitted to boast of the favor of His Most Catholic Majesty, King Philip. Kochel must take heed, that this leprous soul did not infect the whole flock, like a mangy sheep, or even turn the shepherd from the true pasture.

This letter had induced Kochel to lure Ulrich into the snare. The monstrous thing learned from the lad that day, capped the climax of all he had heard, and might serve as a foundation for the charge, that the heretical Netherlander--and people were disposed to regard all Netherlanders as heretics--had deluded the king's mind with magic arts, enslaved his soul and bound him with fetters forged by the Prince of Evil.

His pen was swift, and that very evening he went to the palace of the Inquisition, with the documents and indictment, but was detained there a long time the following day, to have his verbal deposition recorded. When he left the gloomy building, he was animated with the joyous conviction that he had not toiled in vain, and that the Netherlander was a lost man.

Preparations for departure were secretly made in the painter's rooms in the Alcazar during the afternoon. Moor was full of anxiety, for one of the royal lackeys, who was greatly devoted to him, had told him that a disguised emissary of the Dominicans--he knew him well--had come to the door of the studio, and talked there with one of the French servants. This meant as imminent peril as fire under the roof, water rising in the hold of a ship, or the plague in the house.

Sophonisba had told him that he would hear from her that day, but the sun was already low In the heavens, and neither she herself nor any message had arrived.

He tried to paint, and finding the attempt useless, gazed into the garden and at the distant chain of the Guadarrama mountains; but to-day he remained unmoved by the delicate violet-blue mist that floated around the bare, naked peaks of the chain.

It was wrath and impatience, mingled with bitter disappointment, that roused the tumult in his soul, not merely the dread of torture and death.

There had been hours when his heart had throbbed with gratitude to Philip, and he had believed in his friendship. And now? The king cared for nothing about him, except his brush.

He was still standing at the window, lost in gloomy thoughts, when Sophonisba was finally announced.

She did not come alone, but leaning on the arm of Don Fabrizio di Moncada. During the last hours of the ball the night before she had voluntarily given the Sicilian her hand, and rewarded his faithful wooing by accepting his suit.

Moor was rejoiced--yes, really glad at heart, and expressed his pleasure; nevertheless he felt a sharp pang, and when the baron, in his simple, aristocratic manner, thanked him for the faithful friendship he had always shown Sophonisba and her sisters, and then related how graciously the queen had joined their hands, he only listened with partial attention, for many doubts and suspicions beset him.

Had Sophonisba's heart uttered the "yes," or had she made a heavy sacrifice for him and his safety? Perhaps she would find true happiness by the side of this worthy noble, but why had she given herself to him now, just now? Then the thought darted through his mind, that the widowed Marquesa Romero, the all-powerful friend of the Grand Inquisitor was Don Fabrizio's sister.

Sophonisba had left the conversation to her betrothed husband; but when the doors of the brightly-lighted reception-room were opened, and the candles in the studio lighted, the girl could no longer endure the restraint she had hitherto imposed upon herself, and whispered hurriedly, in broken accents:

"Dismiss the servants, lock the studio, and follow us."

Moor did as he was requested, and, with the baron, obeyed her request to search the anterooms, to see that no unbidden visitor remained. She herself raised the curtains and looked up the chimney.

Moor had rarely seen her so pale. Unable to control the muscles of her face, shoulders and hands, she went into the middle of the room, beckoned the men to come close to her, raised her fan to her face, and whispered:

"Don Fabrizio and I are now one. God hears me! You, Master, are in great peril and surrounded by spies. Some one witnessed yesterday's incident, and it is now the talk of the town. Don Fabrizio has made inquiries. There is an accusation against you, and the Inquisition will act upon it. The informers call you a heretic, a sorcerer, who has bewitched the king. They will seize you to-morrow, or the day after. The king is in a terrible mood. The Nuncio openly asked him whether it was true, that he had been offered an atrocious insult in your studio. Is everything ready? Can you fly?"

Moor bent his head in assent.

"Well then," said the baron, interrupting Sophonisba; "I beg you to listen to me. I have obtained leave of absence, to go to Sicily to ask my father's blessing. It will be no easy matter for me to leave my happiness, at the moment my most ardent wish is fulfilled--but Sophonisba commands and I obey. I obey gladly too, for if I succeed in saving you, a new and beautiful star will adorn the heaven of my memory."

"Quick, quick!" pleaded Sophonisba, clenching the back of a chair firmly with her hand. "You will yield, Master; I beseech you, I command you!"

Moor bowed, and Don Fabrizio continued: "We will start at four o'clock in the morning. Instead of exchanging vows of love, we held a council of war. Everything is arranged. In an hour my servants will come and ask for the portrait of my betrothed bride; instead of the picture, you will put your baggage in the chest. Before midnight you will come to my apartments. I have passports for myself, six servants, the equerry, and a chaplain. Father Clement will remain safely concealed at my sister's, and you will accompany me in priestly costume. May we rely upon your consent?"

"With all the gratitude of a thankful heart, but...."

"But?"

"There is my old servant--and my pupil Ulrich Navarrete."

"The old man is taciturn, Don Fabrizio!" said Sophonisba. "If he is forbidden to speak at all.... He is necessary to the Master."

"Then he can accompany you," said the baron. "As for your pupil, he must help us secure your flight, and lead the pursuers on a false trail. The king has honored you with a travelling-carriage.--At half-past eleven order horses to be put to it and leave the Alcazar. When you arrive before our palace, stop it, alight, and remain with me. Ulrich, whom everybody knows--who has not noticed the handsome, fair-haired lad in his gay clothes--will stay with the carriage and accompany it along the road towards Burgos, as far as it goes. A better decoy than he cannot be imagined, and besides he is nimble and an excellent horseman. Give him your own steed, the white Andalusian. If the blood-hounds should overtake him...."

Here Moor interrupted the baron, saying gravely and firmly: "My grey head will be too dearly purchased at the cost of this young life. Change this part of your plan, I entreat you."

"Impossible!" exclaimed the Sicilian. "We have few hours at our command, and if they don't follow him, they will pursue us, and you will be lost."

"Yet...." Moor began; but Sophonisba, scarcely able to command her voice, interrupted: "He owes everything to--you. I know him. Where is he?"

"Let us maintain our self-control!" cried the Netherlander. "I do not rely upon the king's mercy, but perhaps in the decisive hour, he will remember what we have been to each other; if Ulrich, on the contrary, robs the irritated lion of his prey and is seized...."

"My sister shall watch over him," said the baron but Sophonisba tore open the door, rushed into the studio, and called as loudly as she could: "Ulrich, Ulrich! Ulrich!"

The men followed her, but scarcely had they crossed the threshold, when they heard her rap violently at the door of the school-room, and Ulrich asking: "What is it?"

"Open the door!"

Soon after, with pallid face and throbbing heart, he was standing before the others, asking: "What am I to do?"

"Save your master!" cried Sophonisba. "Are you a contemptible Wight, or does a true artist's heart beat in your breast? Would you fear to go, perhaps to your death, for this imperilled man?"

"No, no!" cried the youth as joyously as if a hundred-pound weight had been lifted from his breast. "If it costs my life, so much the better! Here I am! Post me where you please, do with me as you will! He has given me everything, and I--I have betrayed him. I must confess, even if you kill me! I gossiped, babbled--like a fool, a child--about what I accidentally saw here yesterday. It is my fault, mine, if they pursue him. Forgive me, master, forgive me! Do with me what you will. Beat me, slay me, and I will bless you."

As he uttered the last words, the young artist, raising his clasped hands imploringly, fell on his knees before his beloved teacher. Moor bent towards him, saying with grave kindness:

"Rise, poor lad. I am not angry with you."

When Ulrich again stood before him, he kissed his forehead and continued:

"I have not been mistaken in you. Do you, Don Fabrizio, recommend Navarrete to the Marquesa's protection, and tell him what we desire. It would scarcely redound to his happiness, if the deed, for which my imprudence and his thoughtlessness are to blame, should be revenged on me. It comforts us to atone for a wrong. Whether you save me, Ulrich, or I perish--no matter; you are and always will be, my dear, faithful friend."

Ulrich threw himself sobbing on the artist's breast, and when he learned what was required of him, fairly glowed with delight and eagerness for action; he thought no greater joy could befall him than to die for the Master.

As the bell of the palace-chapel was ringing for evening service, Sophonisba was obliged to leave her friend; for it was her duty to attend the nocturnus with the queen.

Don Fabrizio turned away, while she bade Moor farewell.

"If you desire my happiness, make him happy," the artist whispered; but she could find no words to reply, and only nodded silently.

He drew her gently towards him, kissed her brow, and said: "There is a hard and yet a consoling word Love is divine; but still more divine is sacrifice. To-day I am both your friend and father. Remember me to your sisters. God bless you, child!"

"And you, you!" sobbed the girl.

Never had any human being prayed so fervently for another's welfare in the magnificent chapel of the Alcazar, as did Sophonisba Anguisciola on this evening. Don Fabrizio's betrothed bride also pleaded for peace and calmness in her own heart, for power to forget and to do her duty.

CHAPTER XIX.

HALF an hour before midnight Moor entered the calash, and Ulrich Navarrete mounted the white Andalusian.

The artist, deeply agitated, had already taken leave of his protege in the studio, had given him a purse of gold for his travelling-expenses and any other wants, and told him that he would always find with him in Flanders a home, a father, love, and instruction in his art.

The painter alighted before Don Fabrizio's palace; a short time after Ulrich noisily drew the leather curtain before the partition of the calash, and then called to the coachman, who had often driven Moor when he was unexpectedly summoned to one of the king's pleasure-palaces at night: "Go ahead!"

They were stopped at the gate, but the guards knew the favorite's calash and fair-haired pupil, and granted the latter the escort he asked for his master. So they went forward; at first rapidly, then at a pace easy for the horses. He told the coachman that Moor had alighted at the second station, and would ride with His Majesty to Avila, where he wished to find the carriage.

During the whole way, Ulrich thought little of himself, and all the more of the master. If the pursuers had set out the morning after the departure, and followed him instead of Don Fabrizio's party, Moor might now be safe. He knew the names of the towns on the road to Valencia and thought: "Now he may be here, now he may be there, now he must be approaching Tarancon."

In the evening the calash reached the famous stronghold of Avila where, according to the agreement, Ulrich was to leave the carriage and try to make his own escape. The road led through the town, which was surrounded by high walls and deep ditches. There was no possibility of going round it, yet the drawbridges were already raised and the gates locked, so he boldly called the warder and showed his passport.

An officer asked to see the artist. Ulrich said that he would follow him; but the soldier was not satisfied, and ordered him to alight and accompany him to the commandant.

Ulrich struck his spurs into the Andalusian's flanks and tried to go back over the road by which he had come; but the horse had scarcely begun to gallop, when a shot was fired, that stretched it on the ground. The rider was dragged into the guard-house as a prisoner, and subjected to a severe examination.

He was suspected of having murdered Moor and of having stolen his money, for a purse filled with ducats was found on his person. While he was being fettered, the pursuers reached Avila.

A new examination began, and now trial followed trial, torture, torture.

Even at Avila a sack was thrown over his head, and only opened, when to keep him alive, he was fed with bread and water. Firmly bound in a two-wheeled cart, drawn by mules, he was dragged over stock and stones to Madrid.

Often, in the darkness, oppressed for breath, jolted, bruised, unable to control his thoughts, or even his voice, he expected to perish; yet no fainting-fit, no moment of utter unconsciousness pityingly came to his relief, far less did any human heart have compassion on his suffering.

At last, at last he was unbound, and led, still with his head covered, into a small, dark room.

Here he was released from the sack, but again loaded with chains.

When he was left alone and had regained the capacity to think, he felt convinced that he was in one of the dungeons of the Inquisition. Here were the damp walls, the wooden bench, the window in the ceiling, of which he had heard. He was soon to learn that he had judged correctly.

His body was granted a week's rest, but during this horrible week he did not cease to upbraid himself as a traitor, and execrate the fate which had used him a second time to hurl a friend and benefactor into ruin. He cursed himself, and when he thought of the "word" "fortune, fortune!" he gnashed his teeth scornfully and clenched his fist.

His young soul was darkened, embittered, thrown off its balance. He saw no deliverance, no hope, no consolation. He tried to pray, to God, to Jesus Christ, to the Virgin, to the Saints; but they all stood before him, in a vision, with lifeless features and paralyzed arms. For him, who had relied on "Fortune," and behaved like a fool, they felt no pity, no compassion, they would not lend their aid.

But soon his former energy returned and with it the power to lift his soul in prayer. He regained them during the torture, on the rack.

Weeks, months elapsed. Ulrich still remained in the gloomy cell, loaded with chains, scantily fed on bread and water, constantly looking death in the face; but a fresh, beautiful spirit of defiance and firm determination to live animated the youth, who was now at peace with himself. On the rack he had regained the right to respect himself, and striven to win the master's praise, the approval of the living and his beloved dead.

The wounds on his poor, crushed, mangled hands and feet still burned. The physician had seen them, and when they healed, shook his head in amazement.

Ulrich rejoiced in his scars, for on the rack and in the Spanish boot, on nails, and the pointed bench, in the iron necklace and with the stifling helmet on his head, he had resolutely refused to betray through whom and whither the master had escaped.

They might come back, burn and spear him; but through him they should surely learn nothing, nothing at all. He was scarcely aware that he had a right to forgiveness; yet he felt he had atoned.

Now he could think of the past again. The Holy Virgin once more wore his lost mother's features; his father, Ruth, Pellicanus, Moor looked kindly at him. But the brightest light shone into his soul through the darkness of the dungeon, when he thought of art and his last work. It stood before him distinctly in brilliant hues, feature for feature, as on the canvas; he esteemed himself happy in having painted it, and would willingly have gone to the rack once, twice, thrice, if he could merely have obtained the certainty of creating other pictures like this, and perhaps still nobler, more beautiful ones.

Art! Art! Perhaps this was the "word," and if not, it was the highest, most exquisite, most precious thing in life, beside which everything else seemed small, pitiful and insipid. With what other word could God have created the world, human beings, animals, and plants? The doctor had often called every flower, every beetle, a work of art, and Ulrich now understood his meaning, and could imagine how the Almighty, with the thirst for creation and plastic hand of the greatest of all artists had formed the gigantic bodies of the stars, had given the sky its glittering blue, had indented and rounded the mountains, had bestowed form and color on everything that runs, creeps, flies, buds and blossoms, and had fashioned man--created in His own image--in the most majestic form of all.

How wonderful the works of God appeared to him in the solitude of the dark dungeon--and if the world was beautiful, was it not the work of His Divine Art!

Heaven and earth knew no word greater, more powerful, more mighty in creating beauty than: Art. What, compared with its gifts, were the miserable, delusive ones of Fortune: gay clothes, spiced dishes, magnificent rooms, and friendly glances from beautiful eyes, that smile on every one who pleases them! He would blow them all into the air, for the assistance of Art in joyous creating. Rather, a thousand times rather, would he beg his bread, and attain great things in Art, than riot and revel in good-fortune.

Colors, colors, canvas, a model like Sophonisba, and success in the realm of Art! It was for these things he longed, these things made him yearn with such passionate eagerness for deliverance, liberty.

Months glided by, maturing Ulrich's mind as rapidly as if they had been years; but his inclination to retire within himself deepened into intense reserve.

At last the day arrived on which, through the influence of the Marquesa Romero, the doors of his dungeon opened.

It was soon after receiving a sharp warning to renounce his obstinacy at the next examination, that the youth was suddenly informed that he was free.

The jailer took off his fetters, and helped him exchange his prison garb for the dress he had worn when captured; then disguised men threw a sack over his head and led him up and down stairs and across pavements, through dust and grass, into the little court-yard of a deserted house in the suburbs. There they left him, and he soon released his head from its covering.

How delicious God's free air seemed, as his chest heaved with grateful joy! He threw out his arms like a bird stretching its wings to fly, then he clasped his hands over his brow, and at last, as if a second time pursued, rushed out of the court-yard into the street. The passers-by looked after him, shaking their heads, and he certainly presented a singular spectacle, for the dress in which he had fled many months before, had sustained severe injuries on the journey from Avila; his hat was lost on the way, and had not been replaced by a new one. The cuffs and collar, which belonged to his doublet, were missing, and his thick, fair hair hung in dishevelled locks over his neck and temples; his full, rosy cheeks had grown thin, his eyes seemed to have enlarged, and during his imprisonment a soft down had grown on his cheeks and chin.

He was now eighteen, but looked older, and the grave expression on his brow and in his eyes, gave him the appearance of a man.

He had rushed straight forward, without asking himself whither; now he reached a busy street and checked his career. Was he in Madrid? Yes, for there rose the blue peaks of the Guadarrama chain, which he knew well. There were the little trees at which the denizen of the Black Forest had often smiled, but which to-day looked large and stately. Now a toreador, whom he had seen more than once in the arena, strutted past. This was the gate, through which he had ridden out of the city beside the master's calash.

He must go into the town, but what should he do there?

Had they restored the master's gold with the clothes?

He searched the pockets, but instead of the purse, found only a few large silver coins, which he knew he had not possessed at the time of his capture.

In a cook-shop behind the gate he enjoyed some meat and wine after his long deprivation, and after reflecting upon his situation he decided to call on Don Fabrizio.

The porter refused him admittance, but after he had mentioned his name, kindly invited him into the porch, and told him that the baron and his wife were in the country with the Marquesa Romero. They were expected back on Tuesday, and would doubtless receive him then, for they had already asked about him several times. The young gentleman probably came from some foreign country; it was the custom to wear hats in Madrid.

Ulrich now noticed what he lacked, but before leaving, to supply the want, asked the porter, if he knew what had become of Master Moor.

Safe! He was safe! Several weeks before Donna Sophonisba had received a letter sent from Flanders, and Ulrich's companion was well informed, for his wife served the baroness as 'doncella'.

Joyously, almost beside himself with pure, heart-cheering delight, the released prisoner hurried away, bought himself a new cap, and then sought the Alcazar.

Before the treasury, in the place of old Santo, Carmen's father, stood a tall, broad portero, still a young man, who rudely refused him admittance.

"Master Moor has not been here for a long time," said the gate-keeper angrily: "Artists don't wear ragged clothes, and if you don't wish to see the inside of a guard-house--a place you are doubtless familiar with--you had better leave at once."

Ulrich answered the gate-keeper's insulting taunts indignantly and proudly, for he was no longer the yielding boy of former days, and the quarrel soon became serious.

Just then a dainty little woman, neatly dressed for the evening promenade, with the mantilla on her curls, a pomegranate blossom in her hair, and another on her bosom, came out of the Alcazar. Waving her fan, and tripping over the pavement like a wag-tail, she came directly towards the disputants.

Ulrich recognized her instantly; it was Carmen, the pretty embroiderer of the shell-grotto in the park, now the wife of the new porter, who had obtained his dead predecessor's office, as well as his daughter.

"Carmen!" exclaimed Ulrich, as soon as he saw the pretty little woman, then added confidently. "This young lady knows me."

"I?" asked the young wife, turning up her pretty little nose, and looking at the tall youth's shabby costume. "Who are you?"

"Master Moor's pupil, Ulrich Navarrete; don't you remember me?"

"I? You must be mistaken!"

With these words she shut her fan so abruptly, that it snapped loudly, and tripped on.

Ulrich shrugged his shoulders, then turned to the porter more courteously, and this time succeeded in his purpose; for the artist Coello's body-servant came out of the treasury, and willingly announced him to his master, who now, as court-artist, occupied Moor's quarters.

Ulrich followed the friendly Pablo into the palace, where every step he mounted reminded him of his old master and former days.

When he at last stood in the anteroom, and the odor of the fresh oil-colors, which were being ground in an adjoining room, reached his nostrils, he inhaled it no less eagerly than, an hour before, he had breathed the fresh air, of which he had been so long deprived.

What reception could he expect? The court-artist might easily shrink from coming in contact with the pupil of Moor, who had now lost the sovereign's favor. Coello was a very different man from the Master, a child of the moment, varying every day. Sometimes haughty and repellent, on other occasions a gay, merry companion, who had jested with his own children and Ulrich also, as if all were on the same footing. If today ....But Ulrich did not have much time for such reflections; a few minutes after Pablo left, the door was torn open, and the whole Coello family rushed joyously to meet him; Isabella first. Sanchez followed close behind her, then came the artist, next his stout, clumsy wife, whom Ulrich had rarely seen, because she usually spent the whole day lying on a couch with her lap-dog. Last of all appeared the duenna Catalina, a would-be sweet smile hovering around her lips.

The reception given him by the others was all the more joyous and cordial.

Isabella laid her hands on his arm, as if she wanted to feel that it was really he; and yet, when she looked at him more closely, she shook her head as if there was something strange in his appearance. Sanchez embraced him, whirling him round and round, Coello shook hands, murmuring many kind words, and the mother turned to the duenna, exclaiming:

"Holy Virgin! what has happened to the pretty boy? How famished he looks! Go to the kitchen instantly, Catalina, and tell Diego to bring him food--food and drink."

At last they all pulled and pushed him into the sitting-room, where the mother immediately threw herself on the couch again; then the others questioned him, making him tell them how he had fared, whence he came, and many other particulars.

He was no longer hungry, but Senora Petra insisted upon his seating himself near her couch and eating a capon, while he told his story.

Every face expressed sympathy, approval, pity, and at last Coello said:

"Remain here, Navarrete. The king longs for Moor, and you will be as safe with us, as if you were in Abraham's lap. We have plenty for you to do. You come to me as opportunely, as if you had dropped from the skies. I was just going to write to Venice for an assistant. Holy Jacob! You can't stay so, but thanks to the Madonna and Moor, you are not poor. We have ample means, my young sir. Donna Sophonisba gave me a hundred zechins for you; they are lying in yonder chest, and thank Heaven, haven't grown impatient by waiting. They are at your disposal. Your master, my master, the noble master of all portrait-painters, our beloved Moor arranged it. You won't go about the streets in this way any longer. Look, Isabella; this sleeve is hanging by two strings, and the elbow is peering out of the window. Such a dress is airy enough, certainly. Take him to the tailor's at once, Sanchez, Oliverio, or..... but no, no; we'll all stay together to-day. Herrera is coming from the Escurial. You will endure the dress for the sake of the wearer, won't you, ladies? Besides, who is to choose the velvet and cut for this young dandy? He always wore something unusual. I can still see the master's smile, provoked by some of the lad's new contrivances in puffs and slashes. It is pleasant to have you here, my boy! I ought to slay a calf, as the father did for the prodigal son; but we live in miniature. Instead of neat-cattle, only a capon!...."

"But you're not drinking, you're not drinking! Isabella, fill his glass. Look! only see these scars on his hands and neck. It will need a great deal of lace to conceal them. No, no, they are marks of honor, you must show them. Come here, I will kiss this great scar, on your neck, my brave, faithful fellow, and some day a fair one will follow my example. If Antonio were only here! There's a kiss for him, and another, there, there. Art bestows it, Art, for whom you have saved Moor!"

A master's kiss in the name of Art! It was sweeter than the beautiful Carmen's lips!

Coello was himself an artist, a great painter! Where could his peers be found--or those of Moor, and the architect Herrera, who entered soon after. Only those, who consecrated their lives to Art, the word of words, could be so noble, cheerful, kind.

How happy he was when he went to bed! how gratefully he told his beloved dead, in spirit, what had fallen to his lot, and how joyously he could pray!

The next morning he went with a full purse into the city, returning elegantly dressed, and with neatly-arranged locks. The peinador had given his budding moustache a bold twist upward.

He still looked thin and somewhat awkward, but the tall youth promised to become a stately man.

CHAPTER XX.

TOWARDS noon Coello called Ulrich into Moor's former studio; the youth could not fail to observe its altered appearance.

Long cartoons, containing sketches of figures, large paintings, just commenced or half-finished, leaned against the easels; mannikins, movable wooden horse's heads, and plaster-models stood on the floor, the tables, and in the windows. Stuffs, garments, tapestries, weapons hung over the backs of the chairs, or lay on chests, tables and the stone-floor. Withered laurel-wreaths, tied with long ribbons, fluttered over the mantel-piece; one had fallen, dropped over the bald head of Julius Caesar, and rested on the breast.

The artist's six cats glided about among the easels, or stretched their limbs on costly velvet and Arabian carpets.

In one corner stood a small bed with silk curtains--the nursery of the master's pets. A magnificent white cat was suckling her kittens in it.

Two blue and yellow cockatoos and several parrots swung screaming in brass hoops before the open window, and Coello's coal-black negro crept about, cleaning the floor of the spacious apartment, though it was already noon. While engaged in this occupation, he constantly shook his woolly head, displaying his teeth, for his master was singing loudly at his work, and the gaily-clad African loved music.

What a transformation bad taken place in the Netherlander's quiet, orderly, scrupulously neat studio! But, even amid this confusion, admirable works were created; nay, the Spaniard possessed a much more vivid imagination, and painted pictures, containing a larger number of figures and far more spirited than Moor's, though they certainly were not pervaded by the depth and earnestness, the marvellous fidelity to nature, that characterized those of Ulrich's beloved master.

Coello called the youth to the easel, and pointing to the sketches in color, containing numerous figures, on which he was painting, said:

"Look here, my son. This is to be a battle of the Centaurs, these are Parthian horsemen;--Saint George and the Dragon, and the Crusaders are not yet finished. The king wants the Apocalyptic riders too. Deuce take it! But it must be done. I shall commence them to-morrow. They are intended for the walls and ceiling of the new winter riding-school. One person gets along slowly with all this stuff, and I--I.....The orders oppress me. If a man could only double, quadruple himself! Diana of Ephesus had many breasts, and Cerberus three heads, but only two hands have grown on my wrists. I need help, and you are just the person to give it. You have had nothing to do with horses yet, Isabella tells me; but you are half a Centaur yourself. Set to work on the steeds now, and when you have progressed far enough, you shall transfer these sketches to the ceiling and walls of the riding-school. I will help you perfect the thing, and give it the finishing touch."

This invitation aroused more perplexity than pleasure in Ulrich's mind, for it was not in accordance with Moor's opinions. Fear of his fellow-men no longer restrained him, so he frankly said that he would rather sketch industriously from nature, and perhaps would do well to seek Moor in Flanders. Besides, he was afraid that Coello greatly overrated his powers.

But the Spaniard eagerly cut him short:

"I have seen your portrait of Sophonisba. You are no longer a pupil, but a rising artist. Moor is a peerless portrait-painter, and you have profited greatly by his teaching. But Art has still higher aims. Every living thing belongs to her. The Venus, the horse....which of those two pictures won Apelles the greater fame? Not only copying, but creating original ideas, leads to the pinnacle of art. Moor praised your vivid imagination. We must use what we possess. Remember Buonarotti, Raphael! Their compositions and frescos, have raised their names above all others. Antonio has tormented you sufficiently with drawing lifeless things. When you transfer these sketches, many times enlarged, to a broad surface, you will learn more than in years of copying plaster-casts. A man must have talent, courage and industry; everything else comes of its own accord, and thank Heaven, you're a lucky fellow! Look at my horses--they are not so bad, yet I never sketched a living one in my life till I was commissioned to paint His Majesty on horseback. You shall have a better chance. Go to the stables and the old riding-school to-morrow. First try noble animals, then visit the market and shambles, and see how the knackers look. If you make good speed, you shall soon see the first ducats you yourself have earned." The golden reward possessed little temptation for Ulrich, but he allowed himself to be persuaded by his senior, and drew and painted horses and mares with pleasure and success, working with Isabella and Coello's pupil, Felice de Liano, when they sketched and painted from living models. When the scaffolding was erected in the winter riding-school, he went there under the court-artist's direction, to measure, arrange and finally transfer the painter's sketches to the wide surfaces.

He did this with increasing satisfaction, for though Coello's sketches possessed a certain hardness, they were boldly devised and pleased him.

The farther he progressed, the more passionately interested he became in his work. To create on a grand scale delighted him, and the fully occupied life, as well as the slight fatigue after his work was done, which was sweetened by the joy of labor accomplished, were all beautiful, enjoyable things; yet Ulrich felt that this was not exactly the right course, that a steeper, more toilsome path must lead to the height he desired to attain.

He lacked the sharp spurring to do better and better, the censure of a master, who was greatly his superior. Praise for things, which did not satisfy himself, vexed him and roused his distrust.

Isabella, and--after his return--Sophonisba, were his confidantes.

The former had long felt what he now expressed. Her young heart clung to him, but she loved in him the future great artist as much as the man. It was certainly no light matter for her to be deprived of Ulrich's society, yet she unselfishly admitted that her father, in the vast works he had undertaken, could not be a teacher like Moor, and it would probably be best for him to seek his old master in Flanders, as soon as his task in the riding-school was completed.

She said this, because she believed it to be her duty, though sadly and anxiously; but he joyously agreed with her, for Sophonisba had handed him a letter from the master, in which the latter cordially invited him to come to Antwerp.

Don Fabrizio's wife summoned him to her palace, and Ulrich found her as kind and sympathizing as when she had been a girl, but her gay, playful manner had given place to a more quiet dignity.

She wished to be told in detail all he had suffered for Moor, how he employed himself, what he intended to do in the future; and she even sought him more than once in the riding-school, watched him at his work, and examined his drawings and sketches.

Once she induced him to tell her the story of his youth.

This was a boon to Ulrich; for, although we keep our best treasures most closely concealed, yet our happiest hours are those in which, with the certainty of being understood, we are permitted to display them.

The youth could show this noble woman, this favorite of the Master, this artist, what he would not have confided to any man, so he permuted her to behold his childhood, and gaze deep into his soul.

He did not even hide what he knew about the "word"--that he believed he had found the right one in the dungeon, and that Art would remain his guiding star, as long as he lived.

Sophonisba's cheeks flushed deeper and deeper, and never had he seen her so passionately excited, so earnest and enthusiastic, as now when she exclaimed:

"Yes, Ulrich, yes! You have found the right word!

"It is Art, and no other. Whoever knows it, whoever serves it, whoever impresses it deeply on his soul and only breathes and moves in it, no longer has any taint of baseness; he soars high above the earth, and knows nothing of misery and death. It is with Art the Divinity bridges space and descends to man, to draw him up ward to brighter worlds. This word transfigures everything, and brings fresh green shoots even from the dry wood of souls defrauded of love and hope. Life is a thorny rose-bush, and Art its flower. Here Mirth is melancholy--Joy is sorrowful and Liberty is dead. Here Art withers and--like an exotic--is prevented perishing outright only by artificial culture. But there is a land, I know it well, for it is my home--where Art buds and blossoms and throws its shade over all the highways. Favorite of Antonio, knight of the Word--you must go to Italy!"

Sophonisba had spoken. He must go to Italy. The home of Titian! Raphael! Buonarotti! where also the Master went to school.

"Oh, Word, Word!" he cried exultingly in his heart. "What other can disclose, even on earth, such a glimpse of the joys of Paradise."

When he left Sophonisba, he felt as if he were intoxicated.

What still detained him in Madrid?

Moor's zechins were not yet exhausted, and he was sure of the assistance of the "word" upon the sacred soil of Italy.

He unfolded his plan to Coello without delay, at first modestly, then firmly and defiantly. But the court-artist would not let him go. He knew how to maintain his composure, and even admitted that Ulrich must travel, but said it was still too soon. He must first finish the work he had undertaken in the riding-school, then he himself would smooth the way to Italy for him. To leave him, so heavily burdened, in the lurch now, would be treating him ungratefully and basely.

Ulrich was forced to acknowledge this, and continued to paint on the scaffold, but his pleasure in creating was spoiled. He thought of nothing but Italy.

Every hour in Madrid seemed lost. His lofty purposes were unsettled, and he began to seek diversion for his mind, especially at the fencing-school with Sanchez Coello.

His eye was keen, his wrist pliant, and his arm was gaining more and more of his father's strength, so he soon performed extraordinary feats.

His remarkable skill, his reserved nature, and the natural charm of his manner soon awakened esteem and regard among the young Spaniards, with whom he associated.

He was invited to the banquets given by the wealthier ones, and to join the wild pranks, in which they sometimes indulged, but spite of persuasions and entreaties, always in vain.

Ulrich needed no comrades, and his zechins were sacred to him; he was keeping them for Italy.

The others soon thought him an odd, arrogant fellow, with whom no friendly ties could be formed, and left him to his own resources. He wandered about the streets at night alone, serenaded fair ladies, and compelled many gentlemen, who offended him, to meet him in single combat.

No one, not even Sanchez Coello, was permitted to know of these nocturnal adventures; they were his chief pleasure, stirred his blood, and gave him the blissful consciousness of superior strength.

This mode of life increased his self-confidence, and expressed itself in his bearing, which gained a touch of the Spanish air. He was now fully grown, and when he entered his twentieth year, was taller than most Castilians, and carried his head as high as a grandee.

Yet he was dissatisfied with himself, for he made slow progress in his art, and cherished the firm conviction that there was nothing more for him to learn in Madrid; Coello's commissions were robbing him of the most precious tIme.

The work in the riding-school was at last approaching completion. It had occupied far more than the year in which it was to have been finished, and His Majesty's impatience had become so great, that Coello was compelled to leave everything else, to paint only there, and put his improving touches to Ulrich's labor.

The time for departure was drawing near. The hanging-scaffold, on which he had lain for months, working on the master's pictures, had been removed, but there was still something to be done to the walls.

Suddenly the court-artist was ordered to suspend the work, and have the beams, ladders and boards, which narrowed the space in the picadero,-- [Riding School]--removed.

The large enclosure was wanted during the next few days for a special purpose, and there were new things for Coello to do.

Don Juan of Austria, the king's chivalrous half-brother, had commenced his heroic career, and vanquished the rebellious Moors in Granada. A magnificent reception was to be prepared for the young conqueror, and Coello received the commission to adorn a triumphal arch with hastily- sketched, effective pictures.

The designs were speedily completed, and the triumphal arch erected in a court-yard of the Alcazar, for here, within the narrow circle of the court, not publicly, before the whole population, had the suspicious monarch resolved to receive and honor the victor.

Ulrich had again assisted Coello in the execution of his sketches. Everything was finished at the right time, and Don Juan's reception brilliantly carried out with great pomp and dignity, through the whole programme of a Te Deum and three services, processions, bull-fights, a grand 'Auto-da-fe', and a tournament.

After this festival, the king again resigned the riding-school to the artists, who instantly set to work. Everything was finished except the small figures at the bottom of the larger pictures, and these could be executed without scaffolding.

Ulrich was again standing on the ladder, for the first time after this interruption, and Coello had just followed him into the picadero, when a great bustle was heard outside.

The broad doors flew open, and the manege was soon filled with knights and ladies on foot and horseback.

The most brilliant figures in all the stately throng were Don Juan himself, and his youthful nephew, Alexander Farnese, Prince of Parma.

Ulrich feasted his eyes on the splendid train, and the majestic, haughty, yet vivacious manner of the conqueror.

Never in his life, he thought, had he seen a more superb youthful figure. Don Juan stopped directly opposite to him, and bared his head. The thick, fair hair brushed back behind his ears, hung in wonderfully soft, waving locks down to his neck, and his features blended feminine grace with manly vigor.

As, hat in hand, he swung himself from the saddle, unassisted, to greet the fair duchess of Medina Celi, there was such a charm in his movements, that the young artist felt inclined to believe all the tales related of the successful love affairs of this favorite of fortune, who was the son of the Emperor Charles, by a German washerwoman.

Don Juan graciously requested his companion to retire to the back of the manege, assisted the ladies from their saddles and, offering his hand to the duchess, led her to the dais, then returning to the ring, he issued some orders to the mounted officers in his train, and stood conversing with the ladies, Alexander Farnese, and the grandees near him.

Loud shouts and the tramp of horses hoofs were now heard outside of the picadero, and directly after nine bare-backed horses were led into the ring, all selected animals of the best blood of the Andalusian breed, the pearls of all the horses Don Juan had captured.

Exclamations and cries of delight echoed through the building, growing louder and warmer, when the tenth and last prize, a coal-black young stallion, dragged the sinewy Moors that led him, into the ring, and rearing lifted them into the air with him.

The brown-skinned young fellows resisted bravely; but Don Juan turning to Alexander Farnese, said: "What a superb animal! but alas, alas, he has a devilish temper, so we have called him Satan. He will bear neither saddle nor rider. How dare I venture....there he rears again....It is quite impossible to offer him to His Majesty. Just look at those eyes, those crimson nostrils. A perfect monster!"

"But there cannot be a more beautiful creature! "cried the prince, warmly. "That shining black coat, the small head, the neck, the croup, the carriage of his tail, the fetlocks and hoofs. Oh, oh, that was serious!" The vicious stallion had reared for the third time, pawing wildly with his fore-legs, and in so doing struck one of the Moors. Shrieking and wailing, the latter fell on the ground, and directly after the animal released itself from the second groom, and now dashed freely, with mighty leaps, around the course, rushing hither and thither as if mad, kicking furiously, and hurling sand and dust into the faces of the ladies on the dais. The latter shrieked loudly, and their screams increased the animal's furious excitement. Several gentlemen drew back, and the master of the horse loudly ordered the other barebacked steeds to be led away.

Don Juan and Alexander Farnese stood still; but the former drew his sword, exclaiming, vehemently:

"Santiago! I'll kill the brute!"

He was not satisfied with words, but instantly rushed upon the stallion; the latter avoiding him, bounded now backward, now sideways, at every fresh leap throwing sand upon the dais.

Ulrich could remain on the ladder no longer.

Fully aware of his power over refractory horses, he boldly entered the ring and walked quietly towards the snorting, foaming steed. Driving the animal back, and following him, he watched his opportunity, and as Satan turned, reached his side and boldly seized his nostrils firmly with his hand.

Satan plunged more and more furiously, but the smith's son held him as firmly as if in a vise, breathed into his nostrils, and stroked his head and muzzle, whispering soothing words.

The animal gradually became quieter, tried once more to release himself from his tamer's iron hand, and when he again failed, began to tremble and meekly stood still with his fore legs stretched far apart.

"Bravo! Bravamente!" cried the duchess, and praise from such lips intoxicated Ulrich. The impulse to make a display, inherited from his mother, urged him to take still greater risks. Carefully winding his left hand in the stallion's mane, he released his nostrils and swung himself on his back. Taken by surprise Satan tried to rid himself of his burden, but the rider sat firm, leaned far over the steed's neck, stroked--his head again, pressed his flanks and, after the lapse of a few minutes, guided him merely by the pressure of his thighs first at a walk, then at a trot over the track. At last springing off, he patted Satan, who pranced peacefully beside him, and led him by the bridle to Don Juan.

The latter measured the tall, brave fellow with a hasty glance, and turning, half to him, half to Alexander Farnese, said:

"An enviable trick, and admirable performance, by my love!"

Then he approached the stallion, stroked and patted his shining neck, and continued:

"I thank you, young man. You have saved my best horse. But for you I should have stabbed him. You are an artist?"

"At your service, Your Highness."

"Your art is beautiful, and you alone know how it suits you. But much honor, perhaps also wealth and fame, can be gained among my troopers. Will you enlist?"

"No, Your Highness," replied Ulrich, with a low bow. "If I were not an artist, I should like best to be a soldier; but I cannot give up my art."

"Right, right! Yet....do you think your cure of Satan will be lasting; or will the dance begin again to-morrow?"

"Perhaps so; but grant me a week, Your Highness, and the swarthy fellows can easily manage him. An hour's training like this every morning, and the work will be accomplished. Satan will scarcely be transformed into an angel, but probably will become a perfectly steady horse."

"If you succeed," replied Don Juan, joyously, "you will greatly oblige me. Come to me next week. If you bring good tidings.... consider meantime, how I can serve you."

Ulrich did not need to consider long. A week would pass swiftly, and then-- then the king's brother should send him to Italy. Even his enemies knew that he was liberal and magnanimous.

The week passed away, the horse was tamed and bore the saddle quietly. Don Juan received Ulrich's petition kindly, and invited him to make the journey on the admiral's galley, with the king's ambassador and his secretary, de Soto.

The very same day the happy artist obtained a bill of exchange on a house on the Rialto, and now it was settled, he was going to Italy.

Coello was obliged to submit, and his kind heart again showed itself; for he wrote letters of introduction for Ulrich to his old artist friends in Venice, and induced the king to send the great Titian a present--which the ambassador was to deliver. The court-artist obtained from the latter a promise to present his pupil Navarrete to the grey-Haired prince of artists.

Everything was now ready for departure; Ulrich again packed his belongings in the studio, but with very different feelings from the first time.

He was a man, he now knew what the right "word" was, life lay open before him, and the paradise of Art was about to unclose its gates.

The studies he had finished in Madrid aroused his compassion; in Italy he would first really begin to become an artist: there work must bring him what it had here denied: satisfaction, success! Gay as a boy, half frantic with joy, happiness and expectation, he crushed the sketches, which seemed to him too miserable, into the waste-paper basket with a maul-stick.

During this work of destruction, Isabella entered the room.

She was now sixteen. Her figure had developed early, but remained petite. Large, deep, earnest eyes looked forth from the little round face, and the fresh, tiny mouth could not help pleasing everyone. Her head now reached only to Ulrich's breast, and if he had always treated her like a dear, sensible, clever child, her small stature had certainly been somewhat to blame for it. To-day she was paler than usual and her features were so grave, that the young man asked her in surprise, yet full of sympathy:

"What is the matter, little one? Are you not well?"

"Yes, yes," she answered, quickly, "only I must talk with you once more alone."

"Do you wish to hear my confession, Belita?"

"Cease jesting now. I am no longer a child. My heart aches, and I must not conceal the cause."

"Speak, speak! How you look! One might really be alarmed."

"If I only can! No one here tells you the truth; but I--I love you; so I will do it, ere it is too late. Don't interrupt me now, or I shall lose courage, and I will, I must speak."

"My studies lately have not pleased you; nor me either. Your father...."

"He has led you in false paths, and now you are going to Italy, and when you see what the greatest artists have created, you will wish to imitate them immediately and forget Meister Moor's lessons. I know you, Ulrich, I know it! But I also know something else, and it must now be said frankly. If you allow yourself to be led on to paint pictures, if you do not submit to again become a modest pupil, and honestly torment yourself with studying, you will make no progress, you will never again accomplish a portrait like the one in the old days, like your Sophonisba. You will then be no great artist and you can, you must become one."

"I will, Belita, I will!"

"Well, well; but first be a pupil! If I were in your place, I would, for aught I care, go to Venice and look about me, but from there I would ride to Flanders, to Moor, to the master."

"Give up Italy? Can you be in earnest? Your father, himself, told me, that I.....well, yes....in portrait-painting, he too thinks I am no blunderer. Where do the Netherlanders go to learn anything new? To Italy, always to Italy! What do they create in Flanders? Portraits, portraits, nothing more. Moor is great, very great in this department, but I take a very different view of art; it has higher aims. My head is full of plans. Wait, only wait! In Italy I shall learn to fly, and when I have finished my Holy Family and my Temple of Art, with all the skill I intend to attain...."

"Then, then, what will happen then?"

"Then you will perhaps change your opinion and cease your tutoring, once for all. This fault-finding, this warning vexes me. It spoils my pleasure, it clouds my fancy. You are poisoning my happiness, you--you....the croaker's voice is disagreeable to me."

Isabella sadly bent her head in silence. Ulrich approached her, saying:

"I do not wish to wound you, Belita; indeed, I do not. You mean well, and you love me, a poor forsaken fellow; do you not, little girl?"

"Yes, Ulrich, and that is just why I have told you what I think. You are rejoicing now in the thought of Italy...."

"Very, very much, unspeakably! There, too, I will remember you, and what a dear, faithful, wise little creature you are. Let us part in friendship, Isabella. Come with me; that would be the best way!"

The young girl flushed deeply, and made no answer except: "How gladly I would!"

The words sounded so affectionate and came so tenderly from the inmost depths of the heart, that they entered his soul. And while she spoke, her eyes gazed so faithfully, lovingly, and yearningly into his, that he saw nothing else. He read in them love, true, self-sacrificing love; not like pretty Carmen's or that given by the ladies, who had thrown flowers to him from their balconies. His heart swelled, and when he saw how the flush on Isabella's dear face deepened under his answering glance, unspeakable gratitude and joy seized upon him, and he could not help clasping her in his arms and drawing her into his embrace.

She permitted it, and when she looked up at him and her soft scarlet lips, from which gleamed two rows of dazzling white teeth, bloomed temptingly near him, he bent his, he knew not how, towards them. They kissed each other again and again, and Isabella flung her little hands around his neck, for she could not reach him with her arms, and said she had always loved him; he assured her in an agitated voice that he believed it, and that there was no better, sweeter, brighter creature on earth than she; only he forgot to say that he loved her. She gave, he received, and it seemed to him natural.

She saw and felt nothing except him and her happiness; he was wholly absorbed by the bliss of being loved and the sweetness of her kiss; so neither noticed that Coello had opened the door and watched them for a minute, with mingled wrath and pleasure, irresolutely shaking his head.

When the court-artist's deep voice exclaimed loudly:

"Why, why, these are strange doings!" they hastily started back.

Startled, sobered, confused, Ulrich sought for words, and at last stammered:

"We have, we wanted....the farewell.... Coello found no time to interrupt him, for his daughter had thrown herself on his breast, exclaiming amid tears:

"Forgive us, father-forgive us; he loves me, and I, I love him so dearly, and now that we belong to each other, I am no longer anxious about him, he will not rest, and when he returns...."

"Enough, enough!" interrupted Coello, pressing his hand upon her mouth. "That is why a duenna is kept for the child; and this is my sensible Belita! It is of no importance, that yonder youth has nothing, I myself courted your mother with only three reales in my pocket, but he cannot yet do any really good work, and that alters the case. It is not my way to dun debtors, I have been in debt too often myself for that; but you, Navarrete, have received many favors from me, when you were badly off, and if you are not a scamp, leave the girl in peace and do not see her again before your departure. When you have studied in Italy and become a real artist, the rest will take care of itself. You are already a handsome, well-formed fellow, and my race will not degenerate in you. There are very different women in Italy, from this dear little creature here. Shut your eyes, and beware of breaking her heart. Your promise! Your hand upon it! In a year and a half from to-day come here again, show what you can do, and stand the test. If you have become what I hope, I'll give her to you; if not, you can quietly go your way. You will make no objection to this, you silly little, love-sick thing. Go to your room now, Belita, and you, Navarrete, come with me."

Ulrich followed the artist to his chamber, where the latter opened a chest, in which lay the gold he had earned. He did not know himself, how much it was, for it was neither counted, nor entered in books. Grasping the ducats, he gave Ulrich two handfuls, exclaiming:

"This one is for your work here, the other to relieve you from any care concerning means of living, while pursuing your studies in Venice and Florence. Don't make the child wretched, my lad; if you do, you will be a contemptible, dishonorable rascal, a scoundrel, a.... but you don't look like a rogue!"

There was a great deal of bustle in Coello's house that evening. The artist's indolent wife was unusually animated. She could not control her surprise and wrath. Isabella had been from childhood a great favorite of Herrera, the first architect in Spain, who had already expressed his love for the young girl, and now this vagabond pauper, this immature boy, had come to destroy the prosperity of her child's life.

She upbraided Coello with being faithless to his paternal duty, and called him a thoughtless booby. Instead of turning the ungrateful rascal out of the house, he, the dunce, had given him hopes of becoming her poor, dazzled, innocent daughter's husband. During the ensuing weeks, Senora Petra prepared Coello many bad days and still worse nights; but the painter persisted in his resolution to give Isabella to Ulrich, if in a year and a half he returned from Italy a skilful artist.

VOLUME 4

CHAPTER XXI.

THE admiral's ship, which bore King Philip's ambassador to Venice, reached its destination safely, though it had encountered many severe storms on the voyage, during which Ulrich was the only passenger, who amid the rolling and pitching of the vessel, remained as well as an old sailor.

But, on the other hand his peace of mind was greatly impaired, and any one who had watched him leaning over the ship's bulwark, gazing into the sea, or pacing up and down with restless bearing and gloomy eyes, would scarcely have suspected that this reserved, irritable youth, who was only too often under the dominion of melancholy moods, had won only a short time before a noble human heart, and was on the way to the realization of his boldest dreams, the fulfilment of his most ardent wishes.

How differently he had hoped to enter "the Paradise of Art!"

Never had he been so free, so vigorous, so rich, as in the dawn of the day, at whose close he was to unite Isabella's life with his own--and now--now!

He had expected to wander through Italy from place to place as untrammelled, gay, and free as the birds in the air; he had desired to see, admire, en joy, and after becoming familiar with all the great artists, choose a new master among them. Sophonisba's home was to have become his, and it had never entered his mind to limit the period of his enjoyment and study on the sacred soil.

How differently his life must now be ordered! Until he went on board of the ship in Valencia, the thought of calling a girl so good, sensible and loving as Isabella his own, rejoiced and inspired him, but during the solitary hours a sea-voyage so lavishly bestows, a strange transformation in his feelings occurred.

The wider became the watery expanse between him and Spain, the farther receded Isabella's memory, the less alluring and delightful grew the thought of possessing her hand.

He now told himself that, before the fatal hour, he had rejoiced at the anticipation of escaping her pedantic criticism, and when he looked forward to the future and saw himself, handsome Ulrich Navarrete, whose superior height filled the smaller Castilians with envy, walking through the streets with his tiny wife, and perceived the smiles of the people they met, he was seized with fierce indignation against himself and his hard fate.

He felt fettered like the galley-slaves, whose chains rattled and clanked, as they pulled at the oars in the ship's waist. At other times he could not help recalling her large, beautiful, love-beaming eyes, her soft, red lips, and yearningly confess that it would have been sweet to hold her in his arms and kiss her, and, since he had forever lost his Ruth, he could find no more faithful, sensible, tender wife than she.

But what should he, the student, the wandering disciple of Art, do with a bride, a wife? The best and fairest of her sex would now have seemed to him an impediment, a wearisome clog. The thought of being obliged to accomplish some fixed task within a certain time, and then be subjected to an examination, curbed his enjoyment, oppressed, angered him.

Grey mists gathered more and more densely over the sunny land, for which he had longed with such passionate ardor, and it seemed as if in that luckless hour, he had been faithless to the "word,"--had deprived himself of its assistance forever.

He often felt tempted to send Coello his ducats and tell him he had been hasty, and cherished no desire to wed his daughter; but perhaps that would break the heart of the poor, dear little thing, who loved him so tenderly! He would be no dishonorable ingrate, but bear the consequences of his own recklessness.

Perhaps some miracle would happen in Italy, Art's own domain. Perhaps the sublime goddess would again take him to her heart, and exert on him also the power Sophonisba had so fervently praised.

The ambassador and his secretary, de Soto, thought Ulrich an unsocial dreamer; but nevertheless, after they reached Venice, the latter invited him to share his lodgings, for Don Juan had requested him to interest himself in the young artist.

What could be the matter with the handsome fellow? The secretary tried to question him, but Ulrich did not betray what troubled him, only alluding in general terms to a great anxiety that burdened his mind.

"But the time is now coming when the poorest of the poor, the most miserable of all forsaken mortals, cast aside their griefs!" cried de Soto. "Day after to morrow the joyous Carnival season will begin! Hold up your head, young man! Cast your sorrows into the Grand Canal, and until Ash-Wednesday, imagine that heaven has fallen upon earth!"

Oh! blue sea, that washes the lagunes, oh! mast-thronged Lido, oh! palace of the Doges, that chains the eye, as well as the backward gazing, mind, oh! dome of St. Mark, in thy incomparable garb of gold and paintings, oh! ye steeds and other divine works of bronze, ye noble palaces, for which the still surface of the placid water serves as a mirror, thou square of St. Mark, where, clad in velvet, silk and gold, the richest and freest of all races display their magnificence, with just pride! Thou harbor, thou forest of masts, thou countless fleet of stately galleys, which bind one quarter of the globe to another, inspiring terror, compelling obedience, and gaining boundless treasures by peaceful voyages and with shining blades. Oh! thou Rialto, where gold is stored, as wheat and rye are elsewhere;--ye proud nobles, ye fair dames with luxuriant tresses, whose raven hue pleases ye not, and which ye dye as bright golden as the glittering zechins ye squander with such small, yet lavish hands! Oh! Venice, Queen of the sea, mother of riches, throne of power, hall of fame, temple of art, who could escape thy spell!

What wanton Spring is to the earth, thy carnival season is to thee! It transforms the magnificence of color of the lagune-city into a dazzling radiance, the smiles to Olympic laughter, the love-whispers to exultant songs, the noisy, busy life of the mighty commercial city into a mad whirlpool, which draws everything into its circle, and releases nothing it has once seized.

De Soto urged and pushed the youth, who had already lost his mental equipoise, into the midst of the gulf, ere he had found the right current.

On the barges, amid the throngs in the streets, at banquets, in ball-rooms, at the gaming-table, everywhere, the young, golden-haired, superbly-dressed artist, who was on intimate terms with the Spanish king's ambassador, attracted the attention of men, and the eyes, curiosity and admiration of the women; though people as yet knew not whence he came.

He chose the tallest and most stately of the slender dames of Venice to lead in the dance, or through the throng of masks and citizens intoxicated with the mirth of the carnival. Whithersoever he led the fairest followed.

He wished to enjoy the respite before execution. To forget--to forget--to indemnify himself for future seasons of sacrifice, dulness, self- conquest, torment.

Poor little Isabella! Your lover sought to enjoy the sensation of showing himself to the crowd with the stateliest woman in the company on his arm! And you, Ulrich, how did you feel when people exclaimed behind you: "A splendid pair! Look at that couple!"

Amid this ecstasy, he needed no helping word, neither "fortune" nor "art; "without any magic spell he flew from pleasure to pleasure, through every changing scene, thinking only of the present and asking no questions about the future.

Like one possessed he plunged into passion's wild whirl. From the embrace of beautiful arms he rushed to the gaming-table, where the ducats he flung down soon became a pile of gold; the zechins filled his purse to overflowing.

The quickly-won treasure melted like snow in the sun, and returned again like stray doves to their open cote.

The works of art were only enjoyed with drunken eyes--yet, once more the gracious word exerted its wondrous power on the misguided youth.

On Shrove-Tuesday, the ambassador took Ulrich to the great Titian.

He stood face to face with the mighty monarch of colors, listened to gracious words from his lips, and saw the nonogenarian, whose tall figure was scarcely bowed, receive the king's gifts.

Never, never, to the close of his existence could he forget that face!

The features were as delicately and as clearly outlined, as if cut with an engraver's chisel from hard metal; but pallid, bloodless, untinged by the faintest trace of color. The long, silver-white beard of the tall venerable painter flowed in thick waves over his breast, and the eyes, with which he scanned Ulrich, were those of a vigorous, keen-sighted man. His voice did not sound harsh, but sad and melancholy; deep sorrow shadowed his glance, and stamped itself upon the mouth of him, whose thin, aged hand still ensnared the senses easily and surely with gay symphonies of color!

The youth answered the distinguished Master's questions with trembling lips, and when Titian invited him to share his meal, and Ulrich, seated at the lower end of the table in the brilliant banqueting-hall, was told by his neighbors with what great men he was permitted to eat, he felt so timid, small, and insignificant, that he scarcely ventured to touch the goblets and delicious viands the servants offered.

He looked and listened; distinguishing his old master's name, and hearing him praised without stint as a portrait-painter. He was questioned about him, and gave confused answers.

Then the guests rose.

The February sun was shining into the lofty window, where Titian seated himself to talk more gaily than before with Paolo Cagliari, Veronese, and other great artists and nobles.

Again Ulrich heard Moor mentioned. Then the old man, from whom the youth had not averted his eyes for an instant, beckoned, and Cagliari called him, saying that he, the gallant Antonio Moor's pupil, must now show what he could do; the Master, Titian, would give him a task.

A shudder ran through his frame; cold drops of perspiration, extorted by fear, stood on his brow.

The old man now invited him to accompany his nephew to the studio. Daylight would last an hour longer. He might paint a Jew; no usurer nor dealer in clothes, but one of the noble race of prophets, disciples, apostles.

Ulrich stood before the easel.

For the first time after a long period he again called upon the "word," and did so fervently, with all his heart. His beloved dead, who in the tumult of carnival mirth had vanished from his memory, again rose before his mind, among them the doctor, who gazed rebukingly at him with his clear, thoughtful eyes.

Like an inspiration a thought darted through the youth's brain. He could and would paint Costa, his friend and teacher, Ruth's father.

The portrait he had drawn when a boy appeared before his memory, feature for feature. A red pencil lay close at hand.

Sketching the outlines with a few hasty strokes, he seized the brush, and while hurriedly guiding it and mixing the colors, he saw in fancy Costa standing before him, asking him to paint his portrait.

Ulrich had never forgotten the mild expression of the eyes, the smile hovering about the delicate lips, and now delineated them as well as he could. The moments slipped by, and the portrait gained roundness and life. The youth stepped back to see what it still needed, and once more called upon the "word" from the inmost depths of his heart; at the same instant the door opened, and leaning on a younger painter, Titian, with several other artists, entered the studio.

He looked at the picture, then at Ulrich, and said with an approving smile: "See, see! Not too much of the Jew, and a perfect apostle! A Paul, or with longer hair and a little more youthful aspect, an admirable St. John. Well done, well done! my son!"

Well done, well done! These words from Titian had ennobled his work; they echoed loudly in his soul, and the measure of his bliss threatened to overflow, when no less a personage than the famous Paolo Veronese, invited him to come to his studio as a pupil on Saturday.

Enraptured, animated by fresh hope, he threw himself into his gondola.

Everyone had left the palace, where he lodged with de Soto. Who would remain at home on the evening of Shrove-Tuesday?

The lonely rooms grew too confined for him.

Quiet days would begin early the next morning, and on Saturday a new, fruitful life in the service of the only true word, Art, divine Art, would commence for him. He would enjoy this one more evening of pleasure, this night of joy; drain it to the dregs. He fancied he had won a right that day to taste every bliss earth could give.

Torches, pitch-pans and lamps made the square of St. Mark's as bright as day, and the maskers crowded upon its smooth pavement as if it were the floor of an immense ball-room.

Intoxicating music, loud laughter, low, tender whispers, sweet odors from the floating tresses of fair women bewildered Ulrich's senses, already confused by success and joy. He boldly accosted every one, and if he suspected that a fair face was concealed under a mask, drew nearer, touched the strings of a lute, that hung by a purple ribbon round his neck, and in the notes of a tender song besought love.

Many a wave of the fan rewarded, many an angry glance from men's dark eyes rebuked the bold wooer. A magnificent woman of queenly height now passed, leaning on the arm of a richly-dressed cavalier.

Was not that the fair Claudia, who a short time before had lost enormous sums at the gaming-table in the name of the rich Grimani, and who had invited Ulrich to visit her later, during Lent?

It was, he could not be mistaken, and now followed the pair like a shadow, growing bolder and bolder the more angrily the cavalier rebuffed him with wrathful glances and harsh words; for the lady did not cease to signify that she recognized him and enjoyed his playing. But the nobleman was not disposed to endure this offensive sport. Pausing in the middle of the square, he released his arm with a contemptuous gesture, saying: "The lute-player, or I, my fair one; you can decide----"

The Venetian laughed loudly, laid her hand on Ulrich's arm and said: "The rest of the Shrove-Tuesday night shall be yours, my merry singer."

Ulrich joined in her gayety, and taking the lute from his neck, offered it to the cavalier, with a defiant gesture, exclaiming:

"It's at your disposal, Mask; we have changed parts. But please hold it firmer than you held your lady." High play went on in the gaming hall; Claudia was lucky with the artist's gold.

At midnight the banker laid down the cards. It was Ash-Wednesday, the hall must be cleared; the quiet Lenten season had begun.

The players withdrew into the adjoining rooms, among them the much-envied couple.

Claudia threw herself upon a couch; Ulrich left her to procure a gondola.

As soon as he was gone, she was surrounded by a motley throng of suitors.

How the beautiful woman's dark eyes sparkled, how the gems on her full neck and dazzling arms glittered, how readily she uttered a witty repartee to each gay sally.

"Claudia unaccompanied!" cried a young noble. "The strangest sight at this remarkable carnival!"

"I am fasting," she answered gaily; "and now that I long for meagre food, you come! What a lucky chance!"

"Heavy Grimani has also become a very light man, with your assistance."

"That's why he flew away. Suppose you follow him?"

"Gladly, gladly, if you will accompany me."

"Excuse me to-day; there comes my knight."

Ulrich had remained absent a long time, but Claudia had not noticed it. Now he bowed to the gentlemen, offered her his arm, and as they descended the staircase, whispered: "The mask who escorted you just now detained me;--and there....see, they are picking him up down there in the court- yard.--He attacked me...."

"You have--you...."

"'They came to his assistance immediately. He barred my way with his unsheathed blade."

Claudia hastily drew her hand from the artist's arm, exclaiming in a low, anxious tone: "Go, go, unhappy man, whoever you may be! It was Luigi Grimani; it was a Grimani! You are lost, if they find you. Go, if you love your life, go at once!"

So ended the Shrove-Tuesday, which had begun so gloriously for the young artist. Titian's "well done" no longer sounded cheerfully in his ears, the "go, go," of the venal woman echoed all the more loudly.

De Soto was waiting for him, to repeat to him the high praise he had heard bestowed upon his art-test at Titian's; but Ulrich heard nothing, for he gave the secretary no time to speak, and the latter could only echo the beautiful Claudia's "go, go!" and then smooth the way for his flight.

When the morning of Ash-Wednesday dawned cool and misty, Venice lay behind the young artist. Unpursued, but without finding rest or satisfaction, he went to Parma, Bologna, Pisa, Florence.

Grimani's death burdened his conscience but lightly. Duelling was a battle in miniature, to kill one's foe no crime, but a victory. Far different anxieties tortured him.

Venice, whither the "word" had led him, from which he had hoped and expected everything, was lost to him, and with it Titian's favor and Cagliari's instruction.

He began to doubt himself, his future, the sublime word and its magic spell. The greater the works which the traveller's eyes beheld, the more insignificant he felt, the more pitiful his own powers, his own skill appeared.

"Draw, draw!" advised every master to whom he applied, as soon as he had seen his work. The great men, to whom he offered himself as a pupil, required years of persevering study. But his time was limited, for the misguided youth's faithful German heart held firmly to one resolve; he must present himself to Coello at the end of the appointed time. The happiness of his life was forfeited, but no one should obtain the right to call him faithless to his word, or a scoundrel.

In Florence he heard Sebastiano Filippi--who had been a pupil of Michael Angelo-praised as a good drawer; so he sought him in Ferrara and found him ready to teach him what he still lacked. But the works of the new master did not please him. The youth, accustomed to Moor's wonderful clearness, Titian's brilliant hues, found Filippi's pictures indistinct, as if veiled by grey mists. Yet he forced himself to remain with him for months, for he was really remarkably skilful in drawing, and his studio never lacked nude models; he needed them for the preliminary studies for his "Day of Judgment."

Without satisfaction, without pleasure in the wearisome work, without love for the sickly master, who held aloof from any social intercourse with him when the hours of labor were over, he felt discontented, bored, disenchanted.

In the evening he sought diversion at the gaming-table, and fortune favored him here as it had done in Venice. His purse overflowed with zechins; but with the red gold, Art withdrew from him her powerful ally, necessity, the pressing need of gaining a livelihood by the exertion of his own strength.

He spent the hours appointed for study like a careless lover, and worked without inclination, without pleasure, without ardor, yet with visible increase of skill.

In gambling he forgot what tortured him, it stirred his blood, dispelled weariness; the gold was nothing to him.

The lion's share of his gains he loaned to broken gamblers, without expectation of return, gave to starving artists, or flung with lavish hand to beggars.

So the months in Ferrara glided by, and when the allotted time was over, he took leave of Sebastiano Filippi without regret. He returned by sea to Spain, and arrived in Madrid richer than he had gone away, but with impoverished confidence in his own powers, and doubting the omnipotence of Art.

CHAPTER XXII.

ULRICH again stood before the Alcazar, and recalled the hour when, a poor lad, just escaped from prison, he had been harshly rebuffed by the same porter, who now humbly saluted the young gentleman attired in costly velvet.

And yet how gladly he would have crossed this threshold poor as in those days, but free and with a soul full of enthusiasm and hope; how joyfully he would have effaced from his life the years that lay between that time and the present.

He dreaded meeting the Coellos; nothing but honor urged him to present himself to them.

Yes--and if the old man rejected him?--so much the better!

The old cheerful confusion reigned in the studio. He had a long time to wait there, and then heard through several doors Senora Petra's scolding voice and her husband's angry replies.

At last Coello came to him and after greeting him, first formally, then cordially, and enquiring about his health and experiences, he shrugged his shoulders, saying:

"My wife does not wish you to see Isabella again before the trial. You must show what you can do, of course; but I..... you look well and apparently have collected reales. Or is it true," and he moved his hand as if shaking a dice-box. "He who wins is a good fellow, but we want no more to do with such people here! You find me the same as of old, and you have returned at the right time, that is something. De Soto has told me about your quarrel in Venice. The great masters were pleased with you and this, you Hotspur, you forfeited! Ferrara for Venice! A poor exchange. Filippi-- understands drawing; but otherwise.... Michael Angelo's pupil! Does he still write on his back? Every monk is God's servant, but in how few does the Lord dwell! What have you drawn with Sebastiano?"

Ulrich answered these questions in a subdued tone; and Coello listened with only partial attention, for he heard his wife telling the duenna Catalina in an adjoining room what she thought of her husband's conduct. She did so very loudly, for she wished to be overheard by him and Ulrich. But she was not to obtain her purpose, for Coello suddenly interrupted the returned travellers story, saying:

"This is getting beyond endurance. If she does her utmost, you shall see Isabella. A welcome, a grasp of the hand, nothing more. Poor young lovers! If only it did not require such a confounded number of things to live....Well, we will see!"

As soon as the artist had entered the adjoining room, a new and more violent quarrel arose there, but, though Senora Petra finally called a fainting-fit to her aid, her husband remained firm, and at last returned to the studio with Isabella.

Ulrich had awaited her, as a criminal expects his sentence. Now she stood before him led by her father's hand-and he, he struck his forehead with his fist, closed his eyes and opened them again to look at her--to gaze as if he beheld a wondrous apparition. Then feeling as if he should die of shame, grief, and joyful surprise, he stood spellbound, and knew not what to do, save to extend both hands to her, or what to say, save I....I--I," then with a sudden change of tone exclaimed like a madman:

"You don't know! I am not.... Give me time, master. Here, here, girl, you must, you shall, all must not be over!"

He had opened his arms wide, and now hastily approached her with the eager look of the gambler, who has staked his last penny on a card.

Coello's daughter did not obey.

She was no longer little, unassuming Belita; here stood no child, but a beautiful, blooming maiden. In eighteen months her figure had gained height; anxious yearning and constant contention with her mother had wasted her superabundance of flesh; her face had become oval, her bearing self-possessed. Her large, clear eyes now showed their full beauty, her half-developed features had acquired exquisite symmetry, and her raven-black hair floated, like a shining ornament, around her pale, charming face.

"Happy will be the man, who is permitted to call this woman his own!" cried a voice in the youth's breast, but another voice whispered "Lost, lost, forfeited, trifled away!"

Why did she not obey his call? Why did she not rush into his open arms? Why, why?

He clenched his fists, bit his lips, for she did not stir, except to press closely to her father's side.

This handsome, splendidly-dressed gentleman, with the pointed beard, deep-set eyes, and stern, gloomy gaze, was an entirely different person from the gay enthusiastic follower of art, for whom her awakening heart had first throbbed more quickly; this was not the future master, who stood before her mind as a glorious favorite of fortune and the muse, transfigured by joyous creation and lofty success--this defiant giant did not look like an artist. No, no; yonder man no longer resembled the Ulrich, to whom, in the happiest hour of her life, she had so willingly, almost too willingly, offered her pure lips.

Isabella's young heart contracted with a chill, yet she saw that he longed for her; she knew, could not deny, that she had bound herself to him body and soul, and yet--yet, she would so gladly have loved him.

She strove to speak, but could find no words, save "Ulrich, Ulrich," and these did not sound gay and joyous, but confused and questioning.

Coello felt her fingers press his shoulder closer and closer. She was surely seeking protection and aid from him, to keep her promise and resist her lover's passionate appeal.

Now his darling's eyes filled with tears, and he felt the tremor of her limbs.

Softened by affectionate weakness and no longer able to resist the impulse to see his little Belita happy, he whispered:

"Poor thing, poor young lovers! Do as you choose, I won't look."

But Isabella did not leave him; she only drew herself up higher, summoned all her courage and looking the returned traveller more steadily in the face, said:

"You are so changed, so entirely changed, Ulrich I cannot tell what has come over me. I have anticipated this hour day and night, and now it is here;--what is this? What has placed itself between us?"

"What, indeed!" he indignantly exclaimed, advancing towards her with a threatening air. "What? Surely you must know! Your mother has destroyed your regard for the poor bungler. Here I stand! Have I kept my promise, yes or no? Have I become a monster, a venomous serpent? Do not look at me so again, do not! It will do no good; to you or me. I will not allow myself to be trifled with!"

Ulrich had shouted these words, as if some great injustice had been done him, and he believed himself in the right.

Coello tried to release himself from his daughter, to confront the passionately excited man, but she held him back, and with a pale face and trembling voice, but proud and resolute manner, answered:

"No one has trifled with you, I least of all; my love has been earnest, sacred earnest."

"Earnest!" interrupted Ulrich, with cutting irony.

"Yes, yes, sacred earnest;--and when my mother told me you had killed a man and left Venice for a worthless woman's sake, when it was rumored, that in Ferrara you had become a gambler, I thought: 'I know him better, they are slandering him to destroy the love you bear in your heart.' I did not believe it; but now I do. I believe it, and shall do so, till you have withstood your trial. For the gambler I am too good, to the artist Navarrete I will joyfully keep my promise. Not a word, I will hear no more. Come, father! If he loves me, he will understand how to win me. I am afraid of this man."

Ulrich now knew who was in fault, and who in the right. Strong impulse urged him away from the studio, away from Art and his betrothed bride; for he had forfeited all the best things in life.

But Coello barred his way. He was not the man, for the sake of a brawl and luck at play, to break friendship with the faithful companion, who had shown distinctly enough how fondly he loved his darling. He had hidden behind these bushes himself in his youth, and yet become a skilful artist and good husband.

He willingly yielded to his wife in small matters, in important ones he meant to remain master of the house. Herrera was a great scholar and artist, but an insignificant man; and he allowed himself to be paid like a bungler. Ulrich's manly beauty had pleased him, and under his, Coello's teaching, he would make his mark. He, the father knew better what suited Isabella than she herself. Girls do not sob so bitterly as she had done, as soon as the door of the studio closed behind her, unless they are in love.

Whence did she obtain this cool judgment? Certainly not from him, far less from her mother.

Perhaps she only wished to arouse Navarrete to do his best at the trial. Coello smiled; it was in his power to judge mildly.

So he detained Ulrich with cheering words, and gave him a task in which he could probably succeed. He was to paint a Madonna and Child, and two months were allowed him for the work. There was a studio in the Casa del Campo, he could paint there and need only promise never to visit the Alcazar before the completion of the work.

Ulrich consented. Isabella must be his. Scorn for scorn!

She should learn which was the stronger.

He knew not whether he loved or hated her, but her resistance had passionately inflamed his longing to call her his. He was determined, by summoning all his powers, to create a masterpiece. What Titian had approved must satisfy a Coello! so he began the task.

A strong impulse urged him to sketch boldly and without long consideration, the picture of the Madonna, as it had once lived in his soul, but he restrained himself, repeating the warning words which had so often been dinned into his ears: Draw, draw!

A female model was soon found; but instead of trusting his eyes and boldly reproducing what he beheld, he measured again and again, and effaced what the red pencil had finished. While painting his courage rose, for the hair, flesh, and dress seemed to him to become true to nature and effective. But he, who in better times had bound himself heart and soul to Art and served her with his whole soul, in this picture forced himself to a method of work, against which his inmost heart rebelled. His model was beautiful, but he could read nothing in the regular features, except that they were fair, and the lifeless countenance became distasteful to him. The boy too caused him great trouble, for he lacked appreciation of the charm of childish innocence, the spell of childish character.

Meantime he felt great secret anxiety. The impulse that moved his brush was no longer the divine pleasure in creation of former days, but dread of failure, and ardent, daily increasing love for Isabella.

Weeks elapsed.

Ulrich lived in the lonely little palace to which he had retired, avoiding all society, toiling early and late with restless, joyless industry, at a work which pleased him less with every new day.

Don Juan of Austria sometimes met him in the park. Once the Emperor's son called to him:

"Well, Navarrete, how goes the enlisting?"

But Ulrich would not abandon his art, though he had long doubted its omnipotence. The nearer the second month approached its close, the more frequently, the more fervently he called upon the "word," but it did not hear.

When it grew dark, a strong impulse urged him to go to the city, seek brawls, and forget himself at the gaming-table; but he did not yield, and to escape the temptation, fled to the church, where he spent whole hours, till the sacristan put out the lights.

He was not striving for communion with the highest things, he felt no humble desire for inward purification; far different motives influenced him.

Inhaling the atmosphere laden with the soft music of the organ and the fragrant incense, he could converse with his beloved dead, as if they were actually present; the wayward man became a child, and felt all the gentle, tender emotions of his early youth again stir his heart.

One night during the last week before the expiration of the allotted time, a thought which could not fail to lead him to his goal, darted into his brain like a revelation.

A beautiful woman, with a child standing in her lap, adorned the canvas.

What efforts he had made to lend these features the right expression.

Memory should aid him to gain his purpose. What woman had ever been fairer, more tender and loving than his own mother?

He distinctly recalled her eyes and lips, and during the last few days remaining to him, his Madonna obtained Florette's joyous expression, while the sensual, alluring charm, that had been peculiar to the mouth of the musician's daughter, soon hovered around the Virgin's lips.

Ay, this was a mother, this must be a true mother, for the picture resembled his own!

The gloomier the mood that pervaded his own soul, the more sunny and bright the painting seemed. He could not weary of gazing at it, for it transported him to the happiest hours of his childhood, and when the Madonna looked down upon him, it seemed as if he beheld the balsams behind the window of the smithy in the market-place, and again saw the Handsome nobles, who lifted him from his laughing mother's lap to set him on their shoulders.

Yes! In this picture he had been aided by the "joyous art," in whose honor Paolo Veronese, had at one of Titian's banquets, started up, drained a glass of wine to the dregs, and hurled it through the window into the canal.

He believed himself sure of success, and could no longer cherish anger against Isabella. She had led him back into the right path, and it would be sweet, rapturously sweet, to bear the beloved maiden tenderly and gently in his strong arms over the rough places of life.

One morning, according to the agreement, he notified Coello that the Madonna was completed.

The Spanish artist appeared at noon, but did not come alone, and the man, who preceded him, was no less important a personage than the king himself.

With throbbing heart, unable to utter a single word, Ulrich opened the door of the studio, bowing low before the monarch, who without vouchsafing him a single glance, walked solemnly to the painting.

Coello drew aside the cloth that covered it, and the sarcastic chuckle Ulrich had so often heard instantly echoed from the king's lips; then turning to Coello he angrily exclaimed, loud enough to be heard by the young artist:

"Scandalous! Insulting, offensive botchwork! A Bacchante in the garb of a Madonna! And the child! Look at those legs! When he grows up, he may become a dancing-master. He who paints such Madonnas should drop his colors! His place is the stable--among refractory horses."

Coello could make no reply, but the king, glancing at the picture again, cried wrathfully:

"A Christian's work, a Christian's! What does the reptile who painted this know of the mother, the Virgin, the stainless lily, the thornless rose, the path by which God came to men, the mother of sorrow, who bought the world with her tears, as Christ did with His sacred blood. I have seen enough, more than enough! Escovedo is waiting for me outside! We will discuss the triumphal arch to-morrow!"

Philip left the studio, the court-artist accompanying him to the door.

When he returned, the unhappy youth was still standing in the same place, gazing, panting for breath, at his condemned work.

"Poor fellow!" said Coello, compassionately, approaching him; but Ulrich interrupted, gasping in broken accents:

"And you, you? Your verdict!"

The other shrugged his shoulders and answered with sincere pity:

"His Majesty is not indulgent; but come here and look yourself. I will not speak of the child, though it.... In God's name, let us leave it as it is. The picture impresses me as it did the king, and the Madonna--I grieve to say it, she belongs anywhere rather than in Heaven. How often this subject is painted! If Meister Antonio, if Moor should see this...."

"Then, then?" asked Ulrich, his eyes glowing with a gloomy fire.

"He would compel you to begin at the beginning once more. I am sincerely sorry for you, and not less so for poor Belita. My wife will triumph! You know I have always upheld your cause; but this luckless work..."

"Enough!" interrupted the youth. Rushing to the picture, he thrust his maul-stick through it, then kicked easel and painting to the floor.

Coello, shaking his head, watched him, and tried to soothe him with kindly words, but Ulrich paid no heed, exclaiming:

"It is all over with art, all over. A Dios, Master! Your daughter does not care for love without art, and art and I have nothing more to do with each other."

At the door he paused, strove to regain his self-control, and at last held out his hand to Coello, who was gazing sorrowfully after him.

The artist gladly extended his, and Ulrich, pressing it warmly, murmured in an agitated, trembling voice:

"Forgive this raving....It is only....I only feel, as if I was bearing all that had been dear to me to the grave. Thanks, Master, thanks for many kind-nesses. I am, I have--my heart--my brain, everything is confused. I only know that you, that Isabella, have been kind to me. and I, I have--it will kill me yet! Good fortune gone! Art gone! A Dios, treacherous world! A Dios, divine art!"

As he uttered the last sentence he drew his hand from the artist's grasp, rushed back into the studio, and with streaming eyes pressed his lips to the palette, the handle of the brush, and his ruined picture; then he dashed past Coello into the street.

The artist longed to go to his child; but the king detained him in the park. At last he was permitted to return to the Alcazar.

Isabella was waiting on the steps, before the door of their apartments. She had stood there a long, long time.

"Father!" she called.

Coello looked up sadly and gave an answer in the negative by compassionately waving his hand.

The young girl shivered, as if a chill breeze had struck her, and when the artist stood beside her, she gazed enquiringly at him with her dark eyes, which looked larger than ever in the pallid, emaciated face, and said in a low, firm tone:

"I want to speak to him. You will take me to the picture. I must see it."

"He has thrust his maul-stick through it. Believe me, child, you would have condemned it yourself."

"And yet, yet! I must see it," she answered earnestly, "see it with these eyes. I feel, I know--he is an artist. Walt, I'll get my mantilla."

Isabella hurried back with flying feet, and when a short time after, wearing the black lace kerchief on her head, she descended the staircase by her father's side, the private secretary de Soto came towards them, exclaiming:

"Do you want to hear the latest news, Coello? Your pupil Navarrete has become faithless to you and the noble art of painting. Don Juan gave him the enlistment money fifteen minutes ago. Better be a good trooper, than a mediocre artist! What is the matter, Senorita?"

"Nothing, nothing," Isabella murmured gently, and fell fainting on her father's breast.

CHAPTER XXIII.

TWO years had passed. A beautiful October day was dawning; no cloud dimmed the azure sky, and the sun's disk rose, glowing crimson, behind the narrow strait, that afforded ingress to the Gulf of Corinth.

The rippling waves of the placid sea, which here washed the sunny shores of Hellas, yonder the shady coasts of the Peloponnesus, glittered like fresh blooming blue-bottles.

Bare, parched rocks rise in naked beauty at the north of the bay, and the rays of the young day-star shot golden threads through the light white mists, that floated around them.

The coast of Morea faces the north; so dense shadows still rested on the stony olive-groves and the dark foliage of the pink laurel and oleander bushes, whose dense clumps followed the course of the stream and filled the ravines.

How still, how pleasant it usually was here in the early morning!

White sea-gulls hovered peacefully over the waves, a fishing-boat or galley glided gently along, making shining furrows in the blue mirror of the water; but today the waves curled under the burden of countless ships, to-day thousands of long oars lashed the sea, till the surges splashed high in the air with a wailing, clashing sound. To-day there was a loud clanking, rattling, roaring on both sides of the water-gate, which afforded admittance to the Bay of Lepanto.

The roaring and shouting reverberated in mighty echoes from the bare northern cliffs, but were subdued by the densely wooded southern shore.

Two vast bodies of furious foes confronted each other like wrestlers, who stretch their sinewy arms to grasp and hurl their opponents to the ground.

Pope Pius the Fifth had summoned Christianity to resist the land-devouring power of the Ottomans. Cyprus, Christian Cyprus, the last province Venice possessed in the Levant, had fallen into the hands of the Moslems. Spain and Venice had formed an alliance with Christ's vicegerent; Genoese, other Italians, and the Knights of St. John were assembling in Messina to aid the league.

The finest and largest Christian armada, which had left a Christian port for a long time, put forth to sea from this harbor. In spite of all intrigues, King Philip had entrusted the chief command to his young half-brother, Don Juan of Austria.

The Ottomans too had not been idle, and with twelve myriads of soldiers on three hundred ships, awaited the foe in the Gulf of Lepanto.

Don Juan made no delay. The Moslems had recently murdered thousands of Christians at Cyprus, an outrage the fiery hero could not endure, so he cast to the winds the warnings and letters of counsel from Madrid, which sought to curb his impetuous energy, his troops, especially the Venetians, were longing for vengeance.

But the Moslems were no less eager for the fray, and at the close of his council-of-war, and contrary to its decision, Kapudan Pacha sailed to meet the enemy.

On the morning of October 7th every ship, every man was ready for battle.

The sun appeared, and from the Spanish ships musical bell-notes rose towards heaven, blending with the echoing chant: "Allahu akbar, allahu akbar, allahu akbar," and the devout words: "There is no God save Allah, and Mohammed is the prophet of Allah; to prayer!"

"To prayer!" The iron tongue of the bell uttered the summons, as well as the resonant voice of the Muezzin, who to-day did not call the worshippers to devotion from the top of a minaret, but from the masthead of a ship. On both sides of the narrow seagate, thousands of Moslems and Christians thought, hoped and believed, that the Omnipotent One heard them.

The bells and chanting died away, and a swift galley with Don Juan on board, moved from ship to ship. The young hero, holding a crucifix in his hand, shouted encouraging words to the Christian soldiers.

The blare of trumpets, roll of drums, and shouts of command echoed from the rocky shores.

The armada moved forward, the admiral's galley, with Don Juan, at its head.

The Turkish fleet advanced to meet it.

The young lion no longer asked the wise counsel of the experienced admiral. He desired nothing, thought of nothing, issued no orders, except "forward," "attack," "board," "kill," "sink," "destroy!"

The hostile fleets clashed into the fight as bulls, bellowing sullenly, rush upon each other with lowered heads and bloodshot eyes.

Who, on this day of vengeance, thought of Marco Antonio Colonna's plan of battle, or the wise counsels of Doria, Venieri, Giustiniani?

Not the clear brain and keen eye--but manly courage and strength would turn the scale to-day. Alexander Farnese, Prince of Parma, had joined his young uncle a short time before, and now commanded a squadron of Genoese ships in the front. He was to keep back till Doria ordered him to enter the battle. But Don Juan had already boarded the vessel commanded by the Turkish admiral, scaled the deck, and with a heavy sword-stroke felled Kapudan Pacha. Alexander witnessed the scene, his impetuous, heroic courage bore him on, and he too ordered: "Forward!"

What was the huge ship he was approaching? The silver crescent decked its scarlet pennon, rows of cannon poured destruction from its sides, and its lofty deck was doubly defended by bearded wearers of the turban.

It was the treasure-galley of the Ottoman fleet. It would be a gallant achievement could the prince vanquish this bulwark, this stronghold of the foe; which was three times greater in size, strength, and number of its crew, than Farnese's vessel. What did he care, what recked he of the shower of bullets and tar-hoops that awaited him?

Up and at them.

Doria made warning signals, but the prince paid no heed, he would neither see nor hear them.

Brave soldiers fell bleeding and gasping on the deck beside him, his mast was split and came crashing down. "Who'll follow me?" he shouted, resting his hand on the bulwark.

The tried Spanish warriors, with whom Don Juan had manned his vessel, hesitated. Only one stepped mutely and resolutely to his side, flinging over his shoulder the two-handed sword, whose hilt nearly reached to the tall youth's eyes.

Every one on board knew the fair-haired giant. It was the favorite of the commander in chief--it was Navarrete, who in the war against the Moors of Cadiz and Baza had performed many an envied deed of valor. His arm seemed made of steel; he valued his life no more than one of the plumes in his helmet, and risked it in battle as recklessly as he did his zechins at the gaming-table.

Here, as well as there, he remained the winner.

No one knew exactly whence he came as he never mentioned his family, for he was a reserved, unsocial man; but on the voyage to Lepanto he had formed a friendship with a sick soldier, Don Miguel Cervantes. The latter could tell marvellous tales, and had his own peculiar opinions about everything between heaven and earth.

Navarrete, who carried his head as high as the proudest grandee, devoted every leisure hour to his suffering comrade, uniting the affection of a brother, with the duties of a servant.

It was known that Navarrete had once been an artist, and he seemed one of the most fervent of the devout Castilians, for he entered every church and chapel the army passed, and remained standing a long, long time before many a Madonna and altar-painting as if spellbound.

Even the boldest dared not attack him, for death hovered over his sword, yet his heart had not hardened. He gave winnings and booty with lavish hand, and every beggar was sure of assistance.

He avoided women, but sought the society of the sick and wounded, often watching all night beside the couch of some sorely-injured comrade, and this led to the rumor that he liked to witness death.

Ah, no! The heart of the proud, lonely man only sought a place where it might be permitted to soften; the soldier, bereft of love, needed some nook where he could exercise on others what was denied to himself: "devoted affection."

Alexander Farnese recognized in Navarrete the horse-tamer of the picadero in Madrid; he nodded approvingly to him, and mounted the bulwark. But the other did not follow instantly, for his friend Don Miguel had joined him, and asked to share the adventure. Navarrete and the captain strove to dissuade the sick man, but the latter suddenly felt cured of his fever, and with flashing eyes insisted on having his own way.

Ulrich did not wait for the end of the dispute, for Farnese was now springing into the hostile ship, and the former, with a bold leap, followed.

Alexander, like himself, carried a two-Banded sword, and both swung them as mowers do their scythes. They attacked, struck, felled, and the foremost foes shrank from the grim destroyers. Mustapha Pacha, the treasurer and captain of the galley, advanced in person to confront the terrible Christians, and a sword-stroke from Alexander shattered the hand that held the curved sabre, a second stretched the Moslem on the deck.

But the Turks' numbers were greatly superior and threatened to crush the heroes, when Don Miguel Cervantes, Ulrich's friend, appeared with twelve fresh soldiers on the scene of battle, and cut their way to the hard-pressed champions. Other Spanish and Genoese warriors followed and the fray became still more furious.

Ulrich had been forced far away from his royal companion-in-arms, and was now swinging his blade beside his invalid friend. Don Miguel's breast was already bleeding from two wounds, and he now fell by Ulrich's side; a bullet had broken his left arm.

Ulrich stooped and raised him; his men surrounded him, and the Turks were scattered, as the tempest sweeps clouds from the mountain.

Don Miguel tried to lift the sword, which had dropped from his grasp, but he only clutched the empty air, and raising his large eyes as if in ecstasy, pressed his hand upon his bleeding breast, exclaiming enthusiastically: "Wounds are stars; they point the way to the heaven of fame-of-fame...."

His senses failed, and Ulrich bore him in his strong aims to a part of the treasure-ship, which was held by Genoese soldiers. Then he rushed into the fight again, while in his ears still rang his friend's fervid words:

"The heaven of fame!"

That was the last, the highest aim of man! Fame, yes surely fame was the "word"; it should henceforth be his word!

It seemed as if a gloomy multitude of heavy thunderclouds had gathered over the still, blue arm of the sea. The stifling smoke of powder darkened the clear sky like black vapors, while flashes of lightning and peals of thunder constantly illumined and shook the dusky atmosphere.

Here a magazine flew through the air, there one ascended with a fierce crash towards the sky. Wails of pain and shouts of victory, the blare of trumpets, the crash of shattered ships and falling masts blended in hellish uproar.

The sun's light was obscured, but the gigantic frames of huge burning galleys served for torches to light the combatants.

When twilight closed in, the Christians had gained a decisive victory. Don Juan had killed the commander-in-chief of the Ottoman force, Ali Pacha, as Farnese hewed down the treasurer. Uncle and nephew emerged from the battle as heroes worthy of renown, but the glory of this victory clung to Don Juan's name.

Farnese's bold assault was kindly rebuked by the commander-in-chief, and when the former praised Navarrete's heroic aid before Don Juan, the general gave the bold warrior and gallant trooper, the honorable commission of bearing tidings of the victory to tile king. Two galleys stood out to sea in a westerly direction at the same time: a Spanish one, bearing Don Juan's messenger, and a Venetian ship, conveying the courier of the Republic.

The rowers of both vessels had much difficulty in forcing a way through the wreckage, broken masts and planks, the multitude of dead bodies and net work of cordage, which covered the surface of the water; but even amid these obstacles the race began.

The wind and sea were equally favorable to both galleys; but the Venetians outstripped the Spaniards and dropped anchor at Alicante twenty-four hours before the latter.

It was the rider's task, to make up for the time lost by the sailors. The messenger of the Republic was far in advance of the general's. Everywhere that Ulrich changed horses, displaying at short intervals the prophet's banner, which he was to deliver to the king as the fairest trophy of victory-- it was inscribed with Allah's name twenty-eight thousand nine hundred times--he met rejoicing throngs, processions, and festal decorations.

Don Juan's name echoed from the lips of men and women, girls and children. This was fame, this was the omnipresence of a god; there could be no higher aspiration for him, who had obtained such honor.

Fame, fame! again echoed in Ulrich's soul; if there is a word, which raises a man above himself and implants his own being in that of millions of fellow-creatures, it is this.

And now he urged one steed after another until it broke down, giving himself no rest even at night; half an hour's ride outside of Madrid he overtook the Venetian, and passed by him with a courteous greeting.

The king was not in the capital, and he went on without delay to the Escurial.

Covered with dust, splashed from head to foot with mud, bruised, tortured as if on the rack, he clung to the saddle, yet never ceased to use whip and spur, and would trust his message to no other horseman.

Now the barren peaks of the Guadarrama mountains lay close before him, now he reached the first workshops, where iron was being forged for the gigantic palace in process of building. How many chimneys smoked, how many hands were toiling for this edifice, which was to comprise a royal residence, a temple, a peerless library, a museum and a tomb.

Numerous carts and sledges, on which blocks of light grey granite had been drawn hither, barred his way. He rode around them at the peril of falling with his horse over a precipice, and now found himself before a labyrinth of scaffolds and free-stone, in the midst of a wild, grey, treeless mountain valley. What kind of a man was this, who had chosen this desert for his home, in life as well as in death! The Escurial suited King Philip, as King Philip suited the Escurial. Here he felt most at ease, from here the royal spider ceaselessly entangled the world in his skilful nets.

His majesty was attending vespers in the scarcely completed chapel. The chief officer of the palace, Fray Antonio de Villacastin, seeing Ulrich slip from his horse, hastened to receive the tottering soldier's tidings, and led him to the church.

The 'confiteor' had just commenced, but Fray Antonio motioned to the priests, who interrupted the Mass, and Ulrich, holding the prophet's standard high aloft, exclaimed: "An unparalleled victory!--Don Juan.... October 7th....! at Lepanto--the Ottoman navy totally destroyed....!"

Philip heard this great news and saw the standard, but seemed to have neither eyes nor ears; not a muscle in his face stirred, no movement betrayed that anything was passing in his mind. Murmuring in a sarcastic, rather than a joyous tone: "Don Juan has dared much," he gave a sign, without opening the letter, to continue the Mass, remaining on his knees as if nothing had disturbed the sacred rite.

The exhausted messenger sank into a pew and did not wake from his stupor, until the communion was over and the king had ordered a Te Deum for the victory of Lepanto.

Then he rose, and as he came out of the pew a newly-married couple passed him, the architect, Herrera, and Isabella Coello, radiant in beauty.

Ulrich clenched his fist, and the thought passed through his mind, that he would cast away good-fortune, art and fame as carelessly as soap-bubbles, if he could be in Herrera's place.

CHAPTER XXIV.

WHAT fame is--Ulrich was to learn!

He saw in Messina the hero of Lepanto revered as a god. Wherever the victor appeared, fair hands strewed flowers in his path, balconies and windows were decked with hangings, and exulting women and girls, joyous children and grave men enthusiastically shouted his name and flung laurel-wreaths and branches to him. Messages, congratulations and gifts arrived from all the monarchs and great men of the world.

When he saw the wonderful youth dash by, Ulrich marvelled that his steed did not put forth wings and soar away with him into the clouds. But he too, Navarrete, had done his duty, and was to enjoy the sweetness of renown. When he appeared on Don Juan's most refractory steed, among the last of the victor's train, he felt that he was not overlooked, and often heard people tell each other of his deeds.

This made him raise his head, swelled his heart, urged him into new paths of fame.

The commander-in-chief also longed to press forward, but found himself condemned to inactivity, while he saw the league dissolve, and the fruit of his victory wither. King Philip's petty jealousy opposed his wishes, poisoned his hopes, and barred the realization of his dreams.

Don Juan was satiated with fame. "Power" was the food for which he longed. The busy spider in the Escurial could not deprive him of the laurel, but his own "word," his highest ambition in life, his power, he would consent to share with no mortal man, not even his brother.

"Laurels are withering leaves, power is arable land," said Don Juan to Escovedo.

It befits an emperor's son, thought Ulrich, to cherish such lofty wishes; to men of lower rank fame can remain the guiding star on life's pathway.

The elite of the army was in the Netherlands; there he could find what he desired.

Don Juan let him go, and when fame was the word, Ulrich had no cause to complain of its ill-will.

He bore the standard of the proud "Castilian" regiment, and when strange troops met him as he entered a city, one man whispered to another: "That is Navarrete, who was in the van at every assault on Haarlem, who, when all fell back before Alkmaar, assailed the walls again, it was not his fault that they were forced to retreat....he turned the scale with his men on Mook-Heath....have you heard the story? How, when struck by two bullets, he wrapped the banner around him, and fell with, and on it, upon the grass."

And now, when with the rebellious army he had left the island of Schouwen behind him and was marching through Brabant, it was said:

"Navarrete! It was he, who led the way for the Spaniards with the standard on his head, when they waded through the sea that stormy night, to surprise Zierikzee."

Whoever bore arms in the Netherlands knew his name; but the citizens also knew who he was, and clenched their fists when they spoke of him.

On the battle-field, in the water, on the ice, in the breaches of their firm walls, in burning cities, in streets and alleys, in council-chambers and plundered homes, he had confronted them as a murderer and destroyer. Yet, though the word fame had long been embittered to him, the inhumanity which clung to his deeds had the least share in it.

He was the servant of his monarch, nothing more. All who bore the name of Netherlander were to him rebels and heretics, condemned by God, sentenced by his king; not worthy peasants, skilful, industrious citizens, noble men, who were risking property and life for religion and liberty.

This impish crew disdained to pray to the merciful mother of God and the saints, these temple violaters had robbed the churches of their statues, driven the pious monks and nuns from their cloisters! They called the Pope the Anti-Christ, and in every conquered city he found satirical songs and jeering verses about his lord, the king, his generals and all Spaniards.

He had kept the faith of his childhood, which was shared by every one who bore arms with him, and had easily obtained absolution, nay, encouragement and praise, for the most terrible deeds of blood.

In battle, in slaughter, when his wounds burned, in plundering, at the gaming-table, everywhere he called upon the Holy Virgin, and also, but very rarely, on the "word," fame.

He no longer believed in it, for it did not realize what he had anticipated. The laurel now rustled on his curls like withered leaves. Fame would not fill the void in his heart, failed to satisfy his discontented mind; power offered the lonely man no companionship of the soul, it could not even silence the voice which upbraided him--the unapproachable champion, him at whom no mortal dared to look askance--with being a miserable fool, defrauded of true happiness and the right ambition.

This voice tortured him on the soft down beds in the town, on the straw in the camp, over his wine and on the march.

Yet how many envied him. Ay! when he bore the standard at the head of the regiment he marched like a victorious demi-god! No one else could support so well as he the heavy pole, plated with gold, and the large embroidered silken banner, which might have served as a sail for a stately ship; but he held the staff with his right hand, as if the burden intrusted to him was an easily-managed toy. Meantime, with inimitable solemnity, he threw back the upper portion of the body and his curly head, placing his left hand on his hip. The arch of the broad chest stood forth in fine relief, and with it the breast-plate and points of his armor. He seemed like a proud ship under swelling sails, and even in hostile cities, read admiration in the glances of the gaping crowd. Yet he was a miserable, discontented man, and could not help thinking more and more frequently of Don Juan's "word."

He no longer trusted to the magic power of a word, as in former times. Still, he told himself that the "arable field" of the emperor's son, "power," was some thing lofty and great-ay, the loftiest aim a man could hope to attain.

Is not omnipotence God's first attribute? And now, on the march from Schouwen through Brabant, power beckoned to him. He had already tasted it, when the mutinous army to which he belonged attempted to pillage a smithy. He had stepped before the spoilers and saved the artisan's life and property. Whoever swung the hammer before the bellows was sacred to him; he had formerly shared gains and booty with many a plundered member of his father's craft.

He now carried a captain's staff, but this was mere mummery, child's play, nothing more. A merry soldier's-cook wore a captain's plume on the side of his tall hat. The field-officer, most of the captains and the lieutenants, had retired after the great mutiny on the island of Schouwen was accomplished, and their places were now occupied by ensigns, sergeants and quartermasters. The higher officers had gone to Brussels, and the mutinous army marched without any chief through Brabant.

They had not received their well-earned pay for twenty-two months, and the starving regiments now sought means of support wherever they could find them.

Two years since, after the battle of Mook-Heath, the army had helped itself, and at that time, as often happened on similar occasions, an Eletto-- [The chosen one. The Italian form is used, instead of the Spanish 'electo'.]-- had been chosen from among the rebellious subaltern officers. Ulrich had then been lying seriously wounded, but after the end of the mutiny was told by many, that no other would have been made Eletto had he only been well and present. Now an Eletto was again to be chosen, and whoever was elected would have command of at least three thousand men, and possibly more, as it was expected that other regiments would join the insurrection. To command an army! This was power, this was the highest attainment; it was worth risking life to obtain it.

The regiments pitched their camp at Herenthals, and here the election was to be held.

In the arrangement of the tents, the distribution of the wagons which surrounded the camp like a wall, the stationing of field-pieces at the least protected places, Ulrich had the most authority, and while exercising it forced himself, for the first time in his life, to appear gentle and yielding, when he would far rather have uttered words of command. He lived in a state of feverish excitement; sleep deserted his couch, he imagined that every word he heard referred to himself and his election.

During these days he learned to smile when he was angry, to speak pleasantly while curses were burning on his lips. He was careful not to betray by look, word, or deed what was passing in his mind, as he feared the ridicule that would ensue should he fail to achieve his purpose.

One more day, one more night, and perhaps he would be commander-in-chief, able to conquer a kingdom and keep the world in terror. Perhaps, only perhaps; for another was seeking with dangerous means to obtain control of the army.

This was Sergeant-Major and Quartermaster Zorrillo, an excellent and popular soldier, who had been chosen Eletto after the battle of Mook-Heath, but voluntarily resigned his office at the first serious opposition he encountered.

It was said that he had done this by his wife's counsel, and this woman was Ulrich's most dangerous foe.

Zorrillo belonged to another regiment, but Ulrich had long known him and his companion, the "campsibyl."

Wine was sold in the quartermaster's tent, which, before the outbreak of the mutiny, had been the rendezvous of the officers and chaplains.

The sibyl entertained the officers with her gay conversation, while they drank or sat at the gaining-table; she probably owed her name to the skill she displayed in telling fortunes by cards. The common soldiers liked her too, because she took care of their sick wives and children.

Navarrete preferred to spend his time in his own regiment, so he did not meet the Zorrillos often until the mutiny at Schouwen and on the march through Brabant. He had never sought, and now avoided them; for he knew the sibyl was leaving no means untried to secure her partner's election. Therefore he disliked them; yet he could not help occasionally entering their tent, for the leaders of the mutiny held their counsels there. Zorrillo always received him courteously; but his companion gazed at him so intently and searchingly, that an anxious feeling, very unusual to the bold fellow, stole over him.

He could not help asking himself whether he had seen her before, and when the thought that she perhaps resembled his mother, once entered his mind, he angrily rejected it.

The day before she had offered to tell his fortune; but he refused point-blank, for surely no good tidings could come to him from those lips.

To-day she had asked what his Christian name was, and for the first time in years he remembered that he was also called "Ulrich." Now he was nothing but "Navarrete," to himself and others. He lived solely for himself, and the more reserved a man is, the more easily his Christian name is lost to him.

As, years before, he had told the master that he was called nothing but Ulrich, he now gave the harsh answer: "I am Navarrete, that's enough!"

CHAPTER XXV.

TOWARDS evening, the members of the mutiny met at the Zorrillos to hold a council.

The weather outside was hot and sultry, and the more people assembled, the heavier and more oppressive became the air within the spacious tent, the interior of which looked plain enough, for its whole furniture consisted of some small roughly-made tables, some benches and chairs, and one large table, and a superb ebony chest with ivory ornaments, evidently stolen property. On this work of art lay the pillows used at night, booty obtained at Haarlem; they were covered with bright but worn-out silk, which had long shown the need of the thrifty touch of a woman's hand. Pictures of the saints were pasted on the walls, and a crucifix hung over the door.

Behind the great table, between a basket and the wine cask, from which the sibyl replenished the mugs, stood a high-backed chair. A coarse barmaid, who had grown up in the camp, served the assembled men, but she had no occasion to hurry, for the Spaniards were slow drinkers.

The guests sat, closely crowded together, in a circle, and seemed grave and taciturn; but their words sounded passionate, imperious, defiant, and the speakers often struck their coats of mail with their clenched fists, or pounded on the floor with their swords.

If there was any difference of opinion, the disputants flew into a furious rage, and then a chorus of fierce, blustering voices rose like a tenfold echo. It often seemed as if the next instant swords must fly from their sheaths and a bloody brawl begin; but Zorrillo, who had been chosen to preside over the meeting, only needed to raise his baton and command order, to transform the roar into a low muttering; the weather-beaten, scarred, pitiless soldiers, even when mutineers, yielded willing obedience to the word of command and the iron constraint of discipline.

On the sea and at Schouwen their splendid costumes had obtained a beggarly appearance. The velvet and brocade extorted from the rich citizens of Antwerp, now hung tattered and faded around their sinewy limbs. They looked like foot-pads, vagabonds, pirates, yet sat, as military custom required, exactly in the order of their rank; on the march and in the camp, every insurgent willingly obeyed the orders of the new leader, who by the fortune of war had thrown pairs-royal on the drumhead.

One thing was certain: some decisive action must be taken. Every one needed doublets and shoes, money and good lodgings. But in what way could these be most easily procured? By parleying and submitting on acceptable conditions, said some; by remaining free and capturing a city, roared others; first wealthy Mechlin, which could be speedily reached. There they could get what they wanted without money. Zorrillo counselled prudent conduct; Navarrete impetuously advised bold action. They, the insurgents, he cried, were stronger than any other military force in the Netherlands, and need fear no one. If they begged and entreated they would be dismissed with copper coins; but if they enforced their demands they would become rich and prosperous.

With flashing eyes he extolled what the troops, and he himself had done; he enlarged upon the hardships they had borne, the victories won for the king. He asked nothing but good pay for blood and toil, good pay, not coppers and worthless promises.

Loud shouts of approval followed his speech, and a gunner, who now held the rank of captain, exclaimed enthusiastically:

"Navarrete, the hero of Lepanto and Haarlem, is right! I know whom I will choose."

"Victor, victor Navarrete!" echoed from many a bearded lilt.

But Zorrillo interrupted these declarations, exclaiming, not without dignity, while raising his baton still higher. "The election will take place to-morrow, gentlemen; we are holding a council to-day. It is very warm in here; I feel it as much as you do. But before we separate, listen a few minutes to a man, who means well." Zorrillo now explained all the reasons, which induced him to counsel negotiations and a friendly agreement with the command-er-in-chief. There was sound, statesmanlike logic in his words, yet his language did not lack warmth and charm. The men perceived that he was in earnest, and while he spoke the sibyl went behind him, laid her hand on his shoulder, and wiped the perspiration from his brow with her handkerchief. Zorrillo permitted it, and without interrupting himself, gave her a grateful, affectionate glance.

The bronzed warriors liked to look at her, and even permitted her to utter a word of advice or warning during their discussions, for she was a wise woman, not one of the ordinary stamp. Her blue eyes sparkled with intelligence and mirth, her full lips seemed formed for quick, gay repartee, she was always kind and cheer ful in her manner even to the most insignificant. But whence came the deep lines about her red mouth and the outer corners of her eyes? She covered them with rouge every day, to conceal the evidence of the sorrowful hours she spent when alone? The lines were well disguised, yet they increased, and year by year grew deeper.

No wrinkle had yet dared to appear on the narrow forehead; and the delicate features, dazzlingly-white teeth, girlish figure, and winning smile lent this woman a youthful aspect. She might be thirty, or perhaps even past forty.

A pleasure made her younger by ten summers, a vexation transformed her into a matron. The snow white hair, carefully arranged on her forehead, seemed to indicate somewhat advanced age; but it was known that it had turned grey in a few days and nights, eight years before, when a discontented blackguard stabbed the quartermaster, and he lay for weeks at the point of death.

This white hair harmonized admirably with the red cheeks of the campsibyl, who appreciating the fact, did not dye it.

During Zorrillo's speech her eyes more than once rested on Ulrich with a strangely intense expression. As soon as he paused, she went back again behind the table to the crying child, to cradle it in her arms.

Zorrillo--perceiving that a new and violent argument was about to break forth among the men--closed the meeting. Before adjourning, however, it was unanimously decided that the election should be held on the morrow.

While the soldiers noisily rose, some shaking hands with Zorrillo, some with Navarrete, the stately sergeant-major of a German lansquenet troop, which was stationed in Antwerp, and did not belong to the insurgents, entered the wide open door of the tent. His dress was gay and in good order; a fine Dalmatian dog followed him.

A thunder-storm had begun, and it was raining violently. Some of the Spaniards were twisting their rosaries, and repeating prayers, but neither thunder, lightning, nor water seemed to have destroyed the German's good temper, for he shook the drops from his plumed hat with a merry "phew," gaily introducing himself to his comrades as an envoy from the Pollviller regiment.

His companions, he said, were not disinclined to join the "free army"-- he had come to ask how the masters of Schouwen fared.

Zorrillo offered the sergeant-major a chair, and after the latter had raised and emptied two beakers from the barmaid's pewter waiter in quick succession, he glanced around the circle of his rebel comrades. Some he had met before in various countries, and shook hands with them. Then he fixed his eyes on Ulrich, pondering where and under what standard he had seen this magnificent, fair-haired warrior.

Navarrete recognizing the merry lansquenet, Hans Eitelfritz of Colln on the Spree, held out his hand, and cried in the Spanish language, which the lansquenet had also used:

"You are Hans Eitelfritz! Do you remember Christmas in the Black Forest, Master Moor, and the Alcazar in Madrid?"

"Ulrich, young Master Ulrich! Heavens and earth!" cried Eitelfritz;--but suddenly interrupted himself; for the sibyl, who had risen from the table to bring the envoy, with her own hands, a larger goblet of wine, dropped the beaker close beside him.

Zorrillo and he hastily sprung to support the tottering woman, who was almost fainting. But she recovered herself, waving them back with a mute gesture.

All eyes were fixed upon her, and every one was startled; for she stood as if benumbed, her bright, youthful face had suddenly become aged and haggard. "What is the matter?" asked Zorrillo anxiously. Recovering her self-control, she answered hastily "The thunder, the storm...."

Then, with short, light steps, she went back to the table, and as she resumed her seat the bell for evening prayers was heard outside.

Most of the company rose to obey the summons.

"Good-bye till to-morrow morning, Sergeant! The election will take place early to-morrow."

"A Dios, a Dios, hasta mas ver, Sibila, a Dios!" was loudly shouted, and soon most of the guests had left the tent.

Those who remained behind were scattered among the different tables. Ulrich sat at one alone with Hans Eitelfritz.

The lansquenet had declined Zorrillo's invitation to join him; an old friend from Madrid was present, with whom he wished to talk over happier days. The other willingly assented; for what he had intended to say to his companions was against Ulrich and his views. The longer the sergeant-major detained him the better. Everything that recalled Master Moor was dear to Ulrich, and as soon as he was alone with Hans Eitelfritz, he again greeted him in a strange mixture of Spanish and German. He had forgotten his home, but still retained a partial recollection of his native language. Every one supposed him to be a Spaniard, and he himself felt as if he were one.

Hans Eitelfritz had much to tell Ulrich; he had often met Moor in Antwerp, and been kindly received in his studio.

What pleasure it afforded Navarrete to hear from the noble artist, how he enjoyed being able to speak German again after so many years, difficult as it was. It seemed as if a crust melted away from his heart, and none of those present had ever seen him so gay, so full of youthful vivacity. Only one person knew that he could laugh and play noisily, and this one was the beautiful woman at the long table, who knew not whether she should die of joy, or sink into the earth with shame.

She had taken the year old infant from the basket. It was a pale, puny little creature, whose father had fallen in battle, and whose mother had deserted it.

The handsome standard-bearer yonder was called Ulrich! He must be her son! Alas, and she could only cast stolen glances at him, listen by stealth to the German words that fell from the beloved lips. Nothing escaped her notice, yet while looking and listening, her thoughts wandered to a far distant country, long vanished days; beside the bearded giant she saw a beautiful, curly-haired child; besides the man's deep voice she heard clear, sweet childish tones, that called her "mother" and rang out in joyous, silvery laughter.

The pale child in her arms often raised its little hand to its cheek, which was wet with the tears of the woman; who tended it. How hard, how unspeakably, terribly hard it was for this woman, with the youthful face and white locks, to remain quiet! How she longed to start up and call joyously to the child, the man, her lover's enemy, but her own, own Ulrich:

"Look at me, look at me! I am your mother. You are mine! Come, come to my heart! I will never leave you more!"

Ulrich now laughed heartily again, not suspecting what was passing in a mother's heart, close beside him; he had no eyes for her, and only listened to the jests of the German lansquenet, with whom he drained beaker after beaker.

The strange child served as a shield to protect the camp-sibyl from her son's eyes, and also to conceal from him that she was watching, listening, weeping. Eitelfritz talked most and made one joke after another; but she did not laugh, and only wished he would stop and let Ulrich speak, that she might be permitted to hear his voice again.

"Give the dog Lelaps a little corner of the settle," cried Hans Eitelfritz. "He'll get his feet wet on the damp floor--for the rain is trickling in--and take cold. This choice fellow isn't like ordinary dogs."

"Do you call the tiger Lelaps?" asked Ulrich. "An odd name."

"I got him from a student at Tubingen, dainty Junker Fritz of Hallberg, in exchange for an elephant's tusk I obtained in the Levant, and he owes his name to the merry rogue. I tell you, he's wiser than many learned men; he ought to be called Doctor Lelaps."

"He's a pretty creature."

"Pretty! More, far more! For instance, at Naples we had the famous Mortadella sausage for breakfast, and being engaged in eager conversation, I forgot him. What did my Lelaps do? He slipped quietly into the garden, returned with a bunch of forget-me-nots in his mouth, and offered it to me, as a gallant presents a bouquet to his fair one. That meant: dogs liked sausage too, and it was not seemly to forget him. What do you say to that show of sense?"

"I think your imagination more remarkable than the dog's sagacity."

"You believed in my good fortune in the old days, do you now doubt this true story?"

"To be sure, that is rather preposterous, for whoever loyally and faithfully trusts good-fortune--your good fortune--is ill-advised. Have you composed any new songs?"

"'That is all over now!" sighed the trooper. "See this scar! Since an infidel dog cleft my skull before Tunis, I can write no more verses; yet it hasn't grown quiet in my upper story on that account. I lie now, instead of composing. My boon companions enjoy the nonsensical trash, when I pour it forth at the tavern."

"And the broken skull: is that a forget-me-not story too, or was it...."

"Look here! It's the actual truth. It was a bad blow, but there's a grain of good in everything evil. For instance, we were in the African desert just dying of thirst, for that belongs to the desert as much as the dot does to the letter i. Lelaps yonder was with me, and scented a spring. Then it was necessary to dig, but I had neither spade nor hatchet, so I took out the loose part of the skull, it was a hard piece of bone, and dug with it till the water gushed out of the sand, then I drank out of my brain-pan as if it were a goblet."

"Man, man!" exclaimed Ulrich, striking his clenched fist on the table.

"Do you suppose a dog can't scent a spring?" asked Eitelfritz, with comical wrath. "Lelaps here was born in Africa, the native land of tigers, and his mother...."

"I thought you got him in Tubingen?"

"I said just now that I tell lies. I imposed upon you, when I made you think Lelaps came from Swabia; he was really born in the desert, where the tigers live.

"No offence, Herr Ulrich! We'll keep our jests for another evening. As soon as I'm knocked down, I stop my nonsense. Now tell me, where shall I find Navarrete, the standard-bearer, the hero of Lepanto and Schouwen? He must be a bold fellow; they say Zorrillo and he...."

The lansquenet had spoken loudly; the quartermaster, who caught the name Navarrete, turned, and his eyes met Ulrich's.

He must be on his guard against this man.

The instant Zorrillo recognized him as a German, he would hold a powerful weapon. The Spaniards would give the command only to a Spaniard.

This thought now occurred to him for the first time. It had needed the meeting with Hans Eitelfritz, to remind him that he belonged to a different nation from his comrades. Here was a danger to be encountered, so with the rapid decision, acquired in the school of war, he laid his hand heavily on his countryman's, saying in a low, impressive tone: "You are my friend, Hans Eitelfritz, and have no wish to injure me."

"Zounds, no! What's up?"

"Well then, keep to yourself where and how we first met each other. Don't interrupt me. I'll tell you later in my tent, where you must take up your quarters, how I gained my name, and what I have experienced in life. Don't show your surprise, and keep calm. I, Ulrich, the boy from the Black Forest, am the man you seek, I am Navarrete."

"You?" asked the lansquenet, opening his eyes in amazement. "Nonsense! You're paying me off for the yarns I told you just now."

No, Hans Eitelfritz, no! I am not jesting, I mean it. I am Navarrete! Nay more! If you keep your mouth shut, and the devil doesn't put his finger into the pie, I think, spite of all the Zorrillos, I shall be Eletto to-morrow.

"You know the Spanish temper! The German Ulrich will be a very different person to them from the Castilian Navarrete. It is in your power to spoil my chance."

The other interrupted him by a peal of loud, joyous laughter, then shouted to the dog: "Up, Lelaps! My respects to Caballero Navarrete."

The Spaniards frowned, for they thought the German was drunk, but Hans Eitelfritz needed more liquor than that to upset his sobriety.

Flashing a mischievous glance at Ulrich from his bright eyes, he whispered: "If necessary, I too can be silent. You man without a country! You soldier of fortune! A Swabian the commander of these stiffnecked braggarts. Now see how I'll help you."

"What do you mean to do?" asked Ulrich; but Hans Eitelfritz had already raised the huge goblet, banging it down again so violently that the table shook. Then he struck the top with his clenched fist, and when the Spaniards fixed their eyes on him, shouted in their language: "Yes, indeed, it was delightful in those days, Caballero Navarrete. Your uncle, the noble Conde in what's its name, that place in Castile, you know, and the Condesa and Condesilla. Splendid people! Do you remember the coal-black horses with snow-white tails in your father's stable, and the old servant Enrique. There wasn't a longer nose than his in all Castile! Once, when I was in Burgos, I saw a queer, longish shadow coming round a street corner, and two minutes after, first a nose and then old Enrique appeared."

"Yes, yes," replied Ulrich, guessing the lansquenet's purpose. "But it has grown late while we've been gossiping; let us go!"

The woman at the table had not heard the whispers exchanged between the two men; but she guessed the object of the lansquenet's loud words. As the latter slowly rose, she laid the child in the basket, drew a long breath, pressed her fingers tightly upon her eyes for a short time, and then went directly up to her son.

Florette did not know herself, whether she owed the name of sibyl to her skill in telling fortunes by cards, or to her wise counsel. Twelve years before, while still sharing the tent of the Walloon captain Grandgagnage, it had been given her, she could not say how or by whom. The fortune-telling she had learned from a sea-captain's widow, with whom she had lodged a long time.

When her voice grew sharp and weaker, in order to retain consideration and make herself important, she devoted herself to predicting the future; her versatile mind, her ambition, and the knowledge of human-nature gained in the camp and during her wanderings from land to land, aided her to acquire remarkable skill in this strange pursuit.

Officers of the highest rank had sat opposite to her cards, listening to her oracular sayings, and Zorrillo, the man who had now been her lover for ten years, owed it to her influence, that he did not lose his position as quartermaster after the last mutiny.

Hans Eitelfritz had heard of her skill and when, as he was leaving, she approached and offered to question the cards for him, he would not allow Ulrich to prevent him from casting a glance into the future.

On the whole, what was predicted to him sounded favorable, but the prophetess did not keep entirely to the point, for in turning the cards she found much to say to Ulrich, and once, pointing to the red and green knaves, remarked thoughtfully: "That is you, Navarrete; that is this gentleman. You must have met each other on some Christmas day, and not here, but in Germany; if I see rightly, in Swabia."

She had just overheard all this.

But a shudder ran through Ulrich's frame when he heard it, and this woman, whose questioning glance had always disturbed him, now inspired him with a mysterious dread, which he could not control. He rose to withdraw; but she detained him, saying: "Now it is your turn, Captain."

"Some other time," replied Ulrich, repellently. Good fortune always comes in good time, and to know ill-luck in advance, is a misfortune I should think."

"I can read the past, too."

Ulrich started. He must learn what his rival's companion knew of his former life, so he answered quickly, "Well, for aught I care, begin."

"Gladly, gladly, but when I look into the past, I must be alone with the questioner. Be kind enough to give Zorrillo your company for quarter of an hour, Sergeant."

"Don't believe everything she tells you, and don't look too deep into her eyes. Come, Lelaps, my son!" cried the lansquenet, and did as he was requested.

The woman dealt the cards silently, with trembling hands, but Ulrich thought: "Now she will try to sound me, and a thousand to one will do everything in her power to disgust me with desiring the Eletto's baton. That's the way blockheads are caught. We will keep to the past."

His companion met this resolution halfway; for before she had dealt the last two rows, she rested her chin on the cards in her hands and, trying to meet his glance, asked:

"How shall we begin? Do you still remember your childhood?"

"Certainly."

"Your father?"

"I have not seen him for a long time. Don't the cards tell you, that he is dead?"

"Dead, dead:--of course he's dead. You had a mother too?"

"Yes, yes," he answered impatiently; for he was unwilling to talk with this woman about his mother.

She shrank back a little, and said sadly: "That sounds very harsh. Do you no longer like to think of your mother?"

"What is that to you?"

"I must know."

"No, what concerns my mother is....I will--is too good for juggling."

"Oh," she said, looking at him with a glance from which he shrank. Then she silently laid down the last cards, and asked: "Do you want to hear anything about a sweetheart?"

"I have none. But how you look at me! Have you grown tired of Zorrillo? I am ill-suited for a gallant."

She shuddered slightly. Her bright face had again grown old, so old and weary that he pitied her. But she soon regained her composure, and continued:

"What are you saying? Ask the questions yourself now, if you please."

"Where is my native place?"

"A wooded, mountainous region in Germany."

"Ah, ha! and what do you know of my father?"

"You look like him, there is an astonishing resemblance in the forehead and eyes; his voice, too, was exactly like yours."

"A chip of the old block."

"Well, well. I see Adam before me...."

"Adam?" asked Ulrich, and the blood left his cheeks.

"Yes, his name was Adam," she continued more boldly, with increasing vivacity: "there he stands. He wears a smith's apron, a small leather cap rests on his fair hair. Auriculas and balsams stand in the bow-window. A roan horse is being shod in the market-place below."

The soldier's head swam, the happiest period of his childhood, which he had not recalled for a long time, again rose before his memory; he saw his father stand before him, and the woman, the sibyl yonder, had the eyes and mouth, not of his mother, but of the Madonna he had destroyed with his maul-stick. Scarcely able to control himself, he grasped her hand, pressing it violently, and asked in German:

"What is my name? And what did my mother call me?"

She lowered her eyes as if in shame, and whispered softly in German: "Ulrich, Ulrich, my darling, my little boy, my lamb, Ulrich--my child! Condemn me, desert me, curse me, but call me once more "my mother."

"My mother," he said gently, covering his face with his hands--but she started up, hurried back to the pale baby in the cradle, and pressing her face upon the little one's breast, moaned and wept bitterly.

Meantime, Zorrillo had not averted his eyes from Navarrete and his companion. What could have passed between the two, what ailed the man?

Rising slowly, he approached the basket before which the sibyl was kneeling, and asked anxiously: "What was it, Flora?"

She pressed her face closer to the weeping child, that he might not see her tears, and answered quickly "I predicted things, things....go, I will tell you about it later."

He was satisfied with this answer, but she was now obliged to join the Spaniards, and Ulrich took leave of her with a silent salutation.

VOLUME 5

CHAPTER XXVI.

THE Spanish nature is contagious, thought Hans Eitelfritz, tossing on his couch in Ulrich's tent. What a queer fellow the gay young lad has become! Sighs are cheap with him, and every word costs a ducat. He is worthy all honor as a soldier. If they make him Eletto, it will be worth while to join the free army.

Ulrich had briefly told the lansquenet, how he had obtained the name of Navarrete and how he had come from Madrid and Lepanto to the Netherlands. Then he went to rest, but he could not sleep.

He had found his mother again. He now possessed the best gift Ruth had asked him to beseech of the "word." The soldier's sweetheart, the faithless wife, the companion of his rival, whom only yesterday he had avoided, the fortune-teller, the camp-sibyl, was the woman who had given him birth. He, who thought he had preserved his honor stainless, whose hand grasped the sword if another looked askance at him, was the child of one, at whom every respectable woman had the right to point her finger. All these thoughts darted through his brain; but strangely enough, they melted like morning mists when the sun rises, before the feeling of joy that he had his mother again.

Her image did not rise before his memory in Zorrillo's tent, but framed by balsams and wall-flowers. His vivid imagination made her twenty years younger, and how beautiful she still was, how winningly she could glance and smile. Every appreciative word, all the praises of the sibyl's beauty, good sense and kindness, which he had heard in the camp, came back freshly to his mind, and he would fain have started up to throw himself on her bosom, call her his mother, hear her give him all the sweet, pet names, which sounded so tender from her lips, and feel the caress of her soft hands. How rich the solitary man felt, how surpassingly rich! He had been entirely alone, deserted even by his mother! Now he was so no longer, and pleasant dreams blended with his ambitious plans, like golden threads in dark cloth.

When power was once his, he would build her a beautiful, cosy nest with his share of the booty. She must leave Zorrillo, leave him to-morrow. The little nest should belong to her and him alone, entirely alone, and when his soul longed for peace, love, and quiet, he would rest there with her, recall with her the days of his childhood, cherish and care for her, make her forget all her sins and sufferings, and enjoy to the full the happiness of having her again, calling a loving mother's heart his own.

At every breath he drew he felt freer and gayer. Suddenly there was a rustling at the tent-door. He seized his two-handed sword, but did not raise it, for a beloved voice he recognized, called softly: "Ulrich, Ulrich, it is I!"

He started up, hastily threw on his doublet, rushed towards her, clasped her in his arms, and let her stroke his curls, kiss his cheeks and eyes, as in the old happy days. Then he drew her into the tent, whispering "Softly, softly, the snorer yonder is the German."

She followed him, leaned against him, and raised his hand to her lips; he felt them grow wet with tears. They had not yet said anything to each other, except how happy, how glad, how thankful they were to have each other again; then a sentinel passed, and she started up, exclaiming anxiously: "So late, so late; Zorrillo will be waiting!"

"Zorrillo!" cried Ulrich scornfully, "you have been a long time with him. If they give me the power...."

"They will choose you, child, they shall choose you," she hastily interrupted. "Oh, God! oh, God! perhaps this will bring you misfortune instead of blessing; but you desire it! Count Mannsfeld is coming tomorrow; Zorrillo knows it. He will bring a pardon for all; promotions too, but no money yet."

"Oh, ho!" cried Ulrich, "that may decide the matter."

"Perhaps so, you deserve to command them. You were born for some special purpose, and your card always turns up so strangely. Eletto! It sounds proud and grand, but many have been ruined by it...."

"Because power was too hard for them."

"It must serve you. You are strong. A child of good fortune. Folly! I will not fear. You have probably fared well in life. Ah, my lamb, I have done little for you, but one thing I did unceasingly: I prayed for you, poor boy, morning and night; have you noticed, have you felt it?"

He drew her to his heart again, but she released herself from his embrace, saying: "To-morrow, Ulrich; Zorrillo...."

"Zorrillo, always Zorrillo," he repeated, his blood boiling angrily. "You are mine and, if you love me, you will leave him."

"I cannot, Ulrich, it will not do. He is kind, you will yet be friends."

"We, we? On the day of judgment, nay, not even then! Are you more firmly bound to yon smooth fellow, than to my honest father? There stands something in the darkness, it is good steel, and if needful will cut the tie asunder."

"Ulrich, Ulrich!" wailed Flora, raising her hands beseechingly. "Not that, not that; it must not be. He is kind and sensible, and loves me fondly. Oh, Heaven! Oh, Ulrich! The mother has glided to her son at night, as if she were following forbidden paths. Oh, this is indeed a punishment. I know how heavily I have sinned, I deserve whatever may befall me; but you, you must not make me more wretched, than I already am. Your father, he ....if he were still alive, for your sake I would crawl to him on my knees, and say: "Here I am, forgive me--but he is dead. Pasquale, Zorrillo lives; do not think me a vain, deluded woman; Zorrillo cannot bear to have me leave him...."

"And my father? He bore it. But do you know how? Shall I describe his life to you?"

"No, no! Oh, child, how you torture me! I know how I sinned against your father, the thought does not cease to torture me, for he truly loved me, and I loved him, too, loved him tenderly. But I cannot keep quiet a long time, and cast down my eyes, like the women there, it is not in my blood; and Adam shut me up in a cage and for many years let me see nothing except himself, and the cold, stupid city in the ravine by the forest. One day a fierce longing came upon me, I could not help going forth--forth into the wide world, no matter with whom or whither. The soldier only needed to hint and I fell.--I did not stay with him long, he was a windy braggart; but

I was faithful to Captain Grandgagnage and accompanied the wild fellow with the Walloons through every land, until he was shot. Then ten years ago, I joined Zorrillo; he is my friend, he shares my feelings, I am necessary to his existence. Do not laugh, Ulrich; I well know that youth lies behind me, that I am old, yet Pasquale loves me; since I have had him, I have been more content and, Holy Virgin! now--I love him in return. Oh, Heaven! Oh, Heaven! Why is it so? This heart, this miserable heart, still throbs as fast as it did twenty years ago."

"You will not leave him?"

"No, no, I love him, and I know why. Every one calls him a brave man, yet they only half know him; no one knows him wholly as I do. No one else is so good, so generous. You must let me speak! Do you suppose I ever forgot you? Never, never! But you have always been to me the dear little boy; I never thought of you as a man, and since I could not have you and longed so greatly for you, for a child, I opened my heart to the soldiers' orphans, the little creature you saw in the tent is one of these poor things, I have often had two or three such babies at the same time. It would have been an abomination to Grandgagnage, but Zorrillo rejoices in my love for children, and I have given what the Walloon bequeathed me and his own booty to the soldiers' widows and the little naked babies in the camp. He was satisfied, for whatever I do pleases him. I will not, cannot leave him!"

She paused, hiding her face in her hands, but Ulrich paced to and fro, violently agitated. At last he said firmly: "Yet you must part from him. He or I! I will have nothing to do with the lover of my father's wife. I am Adam's son, and will be constant to him. Ah, mother, I have been deprived of you so long. You can tend strangers' orphaned children, yet you make your own son an orphan. Will you do this? No, a thousand times, no, you cannot! Do not weep so, you must not weep! Hear me, hear me! For my sake, leave this Spaniard! You will not repent it. I have just been dreaming of the nest I will build for you. There I will cherish and care for you, and you shall keep as many orphan children as you choose. Leave him, mother, you must leave him for the sake of your child, your Ulrich!"

"Oh, God! oh, God!" she sobbed. "I will try, yes, I will try.... My child, my dear child!"

Ulrich clasped her closely in his arms, kissed her hair, and said, softly: "I know, I know, you need love, and you shall find it with me."

"With you!" she repeated, sobbing. Then releasing herself from his embrace she hurried to the feverish woman, at whose summons she had left her tent.

As morning dawned, she returned home and found Zorrillo still awake. He enquired about her patient, and told her he had given the child something to drink while she was away.

Flora could not help weeping bitterly again, and Zorrillo, noticing it, exclaimed chidingly: "Each has his own griefs to bear, it is not wise to take strangers' troubles so deeply to heart."

"Strangers' troubles," she repeated, mournfully, and went to rest.

White-haired woman, why have you remained so young? All the cares and sorrows of youth and age are torturing you at the same time! One love is fighting a mortal battle with another in your breast. Which will conquer?

She knows, she knew it ere she entered the tent. The mother fled from the child, but she cannot abandon her new-found son. Oh, maternal love, thou dost hover in radiant bliss far above the clouds, and amid choirs of angels! Oh, maternal heart, thou dost bleed pierced with swords, more full of sorrows than any other!

Poor, poor Florette! On this July morning she was enduring superhuman tortures, all the sins she had committed arrayed themselves against her, shrieking into her ear that she was a lost woman, and there could be no pardon for her either in this world or the next. Yet!--the clouds drift by, birds of passage migrate, the musician wanders singing from land to land, finds love, and remorselessly strips off light fetters to seek others. His child imitates the father, who had followed the example of his, the same thing occurring back to their remotest ancestors! But eternal justice? Will it measure the fluttering leaf by the same standard as the firmly-rooted plant?

When Zorrillo saw Flora by the daylight, he said, kindly: "You have been weeping?"

"Yes," she answered, fixing her eyes on the ground. He thought she was anxious, as on a former occasion, lest his election to the office of Eletto might prove his ruin, so he drew her towards him, exclaiming "Have no fear, Bonita. If they choose me, and Mannsfeld comes, as he promised, the play will end this very day. I hope, even at the twelfth hour, they will listen to reason, and allow themselves to be guided into the right course. If they make the young madcap Eletto--his head will be at stake, not mine. Are you ill? How you look, child! Surely, surely you must be suffering; you shall not go out at night to nurse sick people again!"

The words came from an anxious heart, and sounded warm and gentle. They penetrated Florette's inmost soul, and overwhelmed with passionate emotion she clasped his hands, kissed them, and exclaimed, softly "Thanks, thanks, Pasquale, for your love, for all. I will never, never forget it, whatever happens! Go, go; the drum is beating again."

Zorrillo fancied she was uttering mere feverish ravings, and begged her to calm herself; then he left the tent, and went to the place where the election was to be held.

As soon as Flora was alone, she threw herself on her knees before the Madonna's picture, but knew not whether it would be right to pray that her son might obtain an office, which had proved the ruin of so many; and when she besought the Virgin to give her strength to leave her lover, it seemed to her like treason to Pasquale.

Her thoughts grew confused, and she could not pray. Her mobile mind wandered swiftly from lofty to petty things; she seized the cards to see whether fate would unite her to Zorrillo or to Ulrich, and the red ten, which represented herself, lay close beside the green knave, Pasquale. She angrily threw them down, determined, in spite of the oracle, to follow her son.

Meantime in the camp drums beat, fifes screamed shrilly, trumpets blared, and the shouts and voices of the assembled soldiers sounded like the distant roar of the surf.

A fresh burst of military music rang out, and now Florette started to her feet and listened. It seemed as if she heard Ulrich's voice, and the rapid throbbing of her heart almost stopped her breath. She must go out, she must see and hear what was passing. Hastily pushing the white hair back from her brow, she threw a veil over it, and hurried through the camp to the spot where the election was taking place.

The soldiers all knew her and made way for her. The leaders of the mutineers were standing on the wall of earth between the field-pieces, and amid the foremost rank, nay, in front of them all, her son was addressing the crowd.

The choice wavered between him and Zorrillo. Ulrich had already been speaking a long time. His cheeks were glowing and he looked so handsome, so noble, in his golden helmet, from beneath which floated his thick, fair locks, that her heart swelled with joy, and as the night grows brighter when the black clouds are torn asunder and the moon victoriously appears, grief and pain were suddenly irradiated by maternal love and pride.

Now he drew his tall figure up still higher, exclaiming: "Others are readier and bolder with the tongue than I, but I can speak with the sword as well as any one."

Then raising the heavy two-handed sword, which others laboriously managed with both hands, he swung it around his head, using only his right hand, in swift circles, until it fairly whistled through the air.

The soldiers shouted exultingly as they beheld the feat, and when he had lowered the weapon and silence was restored, he continued, defiantly, while his breath came quick and short: "And where do the talkers, the parleyers seek to lead us? To cringe like dogs, who lick their masters' feet, before the men who cheat us. Count Mannsfeld will come to-day; I know it, and I have also learned that he will bring everything except what is our due, what we need, what we intend to demand, what we require for our bare feet, our ragged bodies; money, money he has not to offer! This is so, I swear it; if not, stand forth, you parleyers, and give me the lie! Have you inclination or courage to give the lie to Navarrete?--You are silent!--But we will speak! We will not suffer ourselves to be mocked and put off! What we demand is fair pay for good work. Whoever has patience, can wait. Mine is exhausted.

"We are His Majesty's obedient servants and wish to remain so. As soon as he keeps his bargain, he can rely upon us; but when he breaks it, we are bound to no one but ourselves, and Santiago! we are not the weaker party.

We need money, and if His Majesty lacks ducats, a city where we can find what we want. Money or a city, a city or money! The demand is just, and if you elect me, I will stand by it, and not shrink if it rouses murmuring behind me or against me. Whoever has a brave heart under his armor, let him follow me; whoever wishes to creep after Zorrillo, can do so. Elect me, friends, and I will get you more than we need, with honor and fame to boot. Saint Jacob and the Madonna will aid us. Long live the king!"

"Long live the king! Long live Navarrete! Navarrete! Hurrah for Navarrete!" echoed loudly, impetuously from a thousand bearded lips.

Zorrillo had no opportunity to speak again. The election was made.

Ulrich was chosen Eletto.

As if on wings, he went from man to man, shaking hands with his comrades. Power, power, the highest prize on earth, was attained, was his! The whole throng, soldiers, tyros, women, girls and children, crowded around him, shouting his name; whoever wore a hat or cap, tossed it in the air, whoever had a kerchief, waved it. Drums beat, trumpets sounded, and the gunner ordered all the field-pieces to be discharged, for the choice pleased him.

Ulrich stood, as if intoxicated, amid the shouts, shrieks of joy, military music, and thunder of the cannon. He raised his helmet, waved salutations to the crowd, and strove to speak, but the uproar drowned his words.

After the election Florette slipped quietly away; first to the empty tent then to the sick woman who needed her care.

The Eletto had no time to think of his mother; for scarcely had he given a solemn oath of loyalty to his comrades and received theirs, when Count Mannsfeld appeared.

The general was received with every honor. He knew Navarrete, and the latter entered into negotiations with the manly dignity natural to him; but the count really had nothing but promises to offer, and the insurgents would not give up their demand: "Money or a city!"

The nobleman reminded them of their oath of allegiance, made lavish use of kind words, threats and warnings, but the Eletto remained firm. Mannsfeld perceived that he had come in vain; the only concession he could obtain from Navarrete was, that some prudent man among the leaders should accompany him to Brussels, to explain the condition of the regiments to the council of state there, and receive fresh proposals. Then the count suggested that Zorrillo should be entrusted with the mission, and the Eletto ordered the quartermaster to prepare for departure at once. An hour after the general left the camp with Flora's lover in his train.

CHAPTER XXVII.

THE fifth night after the Eletto's election was closing in, a light rain was falling, and no sound was heard in the deserted streets of the encampment except now and then the footsteps of a sentinel, or the cries of a child. In Zorrillo's tent, which was usually brightly lighted until a late hour of the night, only one miserable brand was burning, beside which sat the sleepy bar-maid, darning a hole in her frieze-jacket. The girl did not expect any one, and started when the door of the tent was violently torn open, and her master, followed by two newly-appointed captains, came straight up to her.

Zorrillo held his hat in his hand, his hair, slightly tinged with grey, hung in a tangled mass over his forehead, but he carried himself as erect as ever. His body did not move, but his eyes wandered from one corner of the tent to another, and the girl crossed herself and held up two fingers towards him, for his dark glance fell upon her, as he at last exclaimed, in a hollow tone:

"Where is the mistress?"

"Gone, I could not help it" replied the girl.

"Where?"

"To the Eletto, to Navarrete."

"When?"

"He came and took her and the child, directly after you had left the camp."

"And she has not returned?"

"She has just sent a roast chicken, which I was to keep for you when you came home. There it is." Zorrillo laughed. Then he turned to his companions, saying:

"I thank you. You have now.... Is she still with the Eletto?"

"Why, of course."

"And who--who saw her the night before the election--let me sit down--who saw her with him then?"

"My brother," replied one of the captains. "She was just coming out of the tent, as he passed with the guard."

"Don't take the matter to heart," said the other. "There are plenty of women! We are growing old, and can no longer cope with a handsome fellow like Navarrete."

"I thought the sibyl was more sensible," added the younger captain. "I saw her in Naples sixteen years ago. Zounds, she was a beautiful woman then! A pretty creature even now; but Navarrete might almost be her son. And you always treated her kindly, Pasquale. Well, whoever expects gratitude from women...."

Suddenly the quartermaster remembered the hour just before the election, when Florette had thrown herself upon his breast, and thanked him for his kindness; clenching his teeth, he groaned aloud.

The others were about to leave him, but he regained his self-control, and said:

"Take him the count's letter, Renalo. What I have to say to him, I will determine later."

Zorrillo was a long time unlacing his jerkin and taking out the paper. Both of his companions noticed how his fingers trembled, and looked at each other compassionately; but the older one said, as he received the letter:

"Man, man, this will do no good. Women are like good fortune."

"Take the thing as a thousand others have taken it, and don't come to blows. You wield a good blade, but to attack Navarrete is suicide. I'll take him the letter. Be wise, Zorrillo, and look for another love at once."

"Directly, directly, of course," replied the quartermaster; but as soon as he had sent the maid-servant away, and was entirely alone, he bowed his forehead upon the table and his shoulders heaved convulsively. He remained in this attitude a long time, then paced to and fro with forced calmness. Morning dawned long ere he sought his couch.

Early the next day he made his report to the Eletto before the assembled council of war, and when it broke up, approached Navarrete, saying, in so loud a tone that no one could fail to hear:

"I congratulate you on your new sweetheart."

"With good reason," replied the Eletto. "Wait a little while, and I'll wager that you'll congratulate me more sincerely than you do to-day."

The offers from Brussels had again proved unacceptable. It was necessary now to act, and the insurgent commander profited by the time at his disposal. It seemed as if "power" doubled his elasticity and energy. It was so delightful, after the march, the council of war, and the day's work were over, to rest with his mother, listen to her, and open his own heart. How had she preserved--yes, he might call it so--her aristocratic bearing, amid the turmoil, perils, and mire of camp-life, in spite of all, all! How cleverly and entertainingly she could talk about men and things, how comical the ideas, with which she understood how to spice the conversation, and how well versed he found her in everything that related to the situation of the regiments and his own position. She had not been the confidante of army leaders in vain.

By her advice he relinquished his plan of capturing Mechlin, after learning from spies that it was prepared and expecting the attack of the insurgents.

He could not enter upon a long siege with the means at his command; his first blow must not miss the mark. So he only showed himself near Brussels, sent Captain Montesdocca, who tried to parley again, back with his mission unaccomplished, marched in a new direction to mislead his foes, and then unexpectedly assailed wealthy Aalst in Flanders.

The surprised inhabitants tried to defend their well-fortified city, but the citizens' strength could not withstand the furious assault of the well-drilled, booty-seeking army.

The conquered city belonged to the king. It was the pledge of what the rebels required, and they indemnified themselves in it for the pay that had been with held. All who attempted to offer resistance fell by the sword, all the citizens' possessions were seized by the soldiers, as the wages that belonged to them.

In the shops under the Belfry, the great tower from whence the bell summoned the inhabitants when danger threatened, lay plenty of cloth for new doublets. Nor was there any lack of gold or silver in the treasury of the guild-hall, the strong boxes of the merchants, the chests of the citizens. The silver table-utensils, the gold ornaments of the women, the children's gifts from godparents fell into the hands of the conquerors, while a hundred and seventy rich villages near Aalst were compelled to furnish food for the mutineers.

Navarrete did not forbid the plundering. According to his opinion, what soldiers took by assault was well-earned booty. To him the occupation of Aalst was an act of righteous self-defence, and the regiments shared his belief, and were pleased with their Eletto.

The rebels sought and found quarters in the citizens' houses, slept in their beds, eat from their dishes, and drank their wine-cellars empty. Pillage was permitted for three days. On the fifth discipline was restored, the quartermaster's department organized, and the citizens were permitted to assemble at the guild-hall, pursue their trades and business, follow the pursuits to which they had been accustomed. The property they had saved was declared unassailable; besides, robbery had ceased to be very remunerative.

The Eletto was at liberty to choose his own quarters, and there was no lack of stately dwellings in Aalst. Ulrich might have been tempted to occupy the palace of Baron de Hierges, but passed it by, selecting as a home for his mother and himself a pretty little house on the market-place, which reminded him of his father's smithy. The bow-windowed room, with the view of the belfry and the stately guildhall, was pleasantly fitted up for his mother, and the city gardeners received orders to send the finest house-plants to his residence. Soon the sitting-room, adorned with flowers and enlivened by singing-birds, looked far handsomer and more cosy than the nest of which he had dreamed. A little white dog, exactly like the one Florette had possessed in the smithy, was also procured, and when in the evening the warm summer air floated into the open windows, and Ulrich sat alone with Florette, recalling memories of the past, or making plans for the future, it seemed as if a new spring had come to his soul. The citizens' distress did not trouble him. They were the losing party in the grim game of war, enemies--rebels. Among his own men he saw nothing but joyous faces; he exercised the power--they obeyed.

Zorrillo bore him ill-will, Ulrich read it in his eyes; but he made him a captain, and the man performed his duty as quartermaster in the most exemplary manner. Florette wished to tell him that the Eletto was her son, but the latter begged her to wait till his power was more firmly established, and how could she refuse her darling anything? She had grieved deeply, very deeply, but this mood soon passed away, and now she could be happy in Ulrich's society, and forget sorrow and heartache.

What joy it was to have him back, to be loved by him! Where was there a more affectionate son, a pleasanter home than hers? The velvet and brocade dresses belonging to the Baroness de Hierges had fallen to the Eletto. How young Florette looked in them! When she glanced into the mirror, she was astonished at herself.

Two beautiful riding-horses for ladies' use and elegant trappings had been found in the baron's stable. Ulrich had told her of it, and the desire to ride with him instantly arose in her mind. She had always accompanied Grandgagnage, and when she now went out, attired in a long velvet riding-habit, with floating plumes in her dainty little hat, beside her son, she soon noticed how admiringly even the hostile citizens and their wives looked after them. It was a pretty sight to behold the handsome soldier, full of pride and power, galloping on the most spirited stallion, beside the beautiful, white-haired woman, whose eyes sparkled with vivacious light.

Zorrillo often met them, when they passed the guildhall, and Florette always gave him a friendly greeting with her whip, but he intentionally averted his eyes or if he could not avoid it, coldly returned her recognition.

This wounded her deeply, and when alone, it often happened that she sunk into gloomy reverie and, with an aged, weary face, gazed fixedly at the floor. But Ulrich's approach quickly cheered and rejuvenated her.

Florette now knew what her son had experienced in life, what had moved his heart, his soul, and could not contradict him, when he told her that power was the highest prize of existence.

The Eletto's ambitious mind could not be satisfied with little Aalst. The mutineers had been outlawed by an edict from Brussels, but the king had nothing to do with this measure; the shameful proclamation was only intended to stop the wailing of the Netherlanders. They would have to pay dearly for it! There was a great scheme in view.

The Antwerp of those days was called "as rich as the Indies;" the project under consideration was the possibility of manoeuvring this abode of wealth into the hands of the mutineers; the whole Spanish army in the Netherlands being about to follow the example of the regiments in Aalst.

The mother was the friend and counsellor of the son. At every step he took he heard her opinion, and often yielded his own in its favor. This interest in the direction of great events occupied the sibyl's versatile mind. When, on many occasions, pros and tons were equal in weight, she brought out the cards, and this oracle generally turned the scale.

No high aim, no desire to accomplish good and great things in wider spheres, influenced the thoughts and actions of this couple.

What cared they, that the weal and woe of thousands depended on their decision? The deadly weapon in their bands was to them only a valuable utensil in which they delighted, and with which fruits were plucked from the trees.

Ulrich now saw the fulfilment of Don Juan's words, that power was an arable field; for there were many full ears in Aalst for them both to harvest.

Florette still nursed, with maternal care, the soldier's orphan which she had taken to her son's house; the child, born on a bed of straw--was now clothed in dainty linen, laces and other beautiful finery. It was necessary to her, for she occupied herself with the helpless little creature when, during the long morning hours of Ulrich's absence, sorrowful thought troubled her too deeply.

Ulrich often remained absent a long time, far longer than the service required. What was he doing? Visiting a sweetheart? Why not? She only marvelled that the fair women did not come from far and near to see the handsome man.

Yes, the Eletto had found an old love. Art, which he had sullenly forsaken. News had reached his ears, that an artist had fallen in the defence of the city. He went to the dead man's house to see his works, and how did he find the painter's dwelling! Windows, furniture were shattered, the broken doors of the cupboards hung into the rooms on their bent hinges. The widow and her children were lying in the studio on a heap of straw. This touched his heart, and he gave alms with an open hand to the sorrowing woman. A few pictures of the saints, which the Spaniards had spared, hung on the walls; the easel, paints and brushes had been left untouched.

A thought, which he instantly carried into execution, entered his mind. He would paint a new standard! How his heart beat, when he again stood before the easel!

He regarded the heretics as heathens. The Spaniards were shortly going to fight against them and for the faith. So be painted the Saviour on one side of the standard, the Virgin on the other. The artist's widow sat to him for the Madonna, a young soldier for the Christ.

No scruples, no consideration for the criticisms of teachers now checked his creating hand; the power was his, and whatever he did must be right.

He placed upon the Saviour's bowed figure, Costa's head, as he had painted it in Titian's studio, and the Madonna, in defiance of the stern judges in Madrid, received the sibyl's face, to please himself and do honor to his mother. He made her younger, transformed her white hair to gleaming golden tresses. One day he asked Flora to sit still and think of something very serious; he wanted to sketch her.

She gaily placed herself in position, saying:

"Be quick, for serious thoughts don't last long with me."

A few days later both pictures were finished, and possessed no mean degree of merit; he rejoiced that after the long interval he could still accomplish something. His mother was delighted with her son's master-pieces, especially the Madonna, for she instantly recognized herself, and was touched by this proof of his faithful remembrance. She had looked exactly like it when a young girl, she said; it was strange how precisely he had hit the color of her hair; but she was afraid it was blaspheming to paint a Madonna with her face; she was a poor sinner, nothing more.

Florette was glad that the work was finished, for restlessness again began to torture her, and the mornings had been so lonely. Zorrillo--it caused her bitter pain--had not cast even a single glance at her, and she began to miss the society of men, to which she had been accustomed. But she never complained, and always showed Ulrich the same cheerful face, until the latter told her one day that he must leave her for some time.

He had already defeated in little skirmishes small bodies of peasants and citizens, who had taken the field against the mutineers; now Colonel Romero called upon him to help oppose a large army of patriots, who had assembled between Lowen and Tirlemont, under the command of the noble Sieur de Floyon. It was said to consist Of students and other rebellious brawlers, and so it proved; but the "rebels" were the flower of the youth of the shamefully-oppressed nation, noble souls, who found it unbearable to see their native land enslaved by mutinous hordes.

Ulrich's parting with his mother was not a hard one. He felt sure of victory and of returning home, but the excitable woman burst into tears as she bade him farewell.

The Eletto took the field with a large body of troops; the majority of the mutineers, with them. Captain and Quartermaster Zorrillo, remained behind to hold the citizens in check.

CHAPTER XXVIII.

A considerable, but hastily-collected army of patriots had been utterly routed at Tisnacq by a small force of disciplined Spaniards.

Ulrich had assisted his countrymen to gain the speedy victory, and had been greeted by his old colonel, the brave Romero, the bold cavalry-commander, Mendoza, and other distinguished officers as one of themselves. Since these aristocrats had become mutineers, the Eletto was a brother, and they did not disdain to secure his cooperation in the attack they were planning upon Antwerp.

He had shown great courage under fire, and wherever he appeared, his countrymen held out their hands to him, vowing obedience and loyalty unto death.

Ulrich felt as if he were walking on air, mere existence was a joy to him. No prince could revel in the blissful consciousness of increasing power, more fully than he. The evening after the decision he had attended a splendid banquet with Romero, Vargas, Mendoza, Tassis, and the next morning the prisoners, who had fallen into the hands of his men, were brought before him.

He had left the examination of the students, citizens' sons, and peasants to his lieutenant; but there were also three noblemen, from whom large ransoms could be obtained. The two older ones had granted what he asked and been led away; the third, a tall man in knightly armor, was left last.

Ulrich had personally encountered the latter. The prisoner, mounted upon a tall steed, had pressed him very closely; nay, the Eletto's victory was not decided, until a musket-shot had stretched the other's horse on the ground.

The knight now carried his arm in a sling. In the centre of his coat of mail and on the shoulder-pieces of his armor, the ensigns armorial of a noble family were embossed.

"You were dragged out from under your horse," said the Eletto to the knight. "You wield an excellent blade."

He had spoken in Spanish, but the other shrugged his shoulders, and answered in the German language "I don't understand Spanish."

"Are you a German?" Ulrich now asked in his native tongue. "How do you happen to be among the Netherland rebels?"

The nobleman looked at the Eletto in surprise. But the latter, giving him no time for reflection, continued "I understand German; your answer?"

"I had business in Antwerp?"

"What business?"

"That is my affair."

"Very well. Then we will drop courtesy and adopt a different tone."

"Nay, I am the vanquished party, and will answer you."

"Well then?"

"I had stuffs to buy."

"Are you a merchant?"

The knight shook his head and answered, smiling: "We have rebuilt our castle since the fire."

"And now you need hangings and artistic stuff. Did you expect to capture them from us?"

"Scarcely, sir."

"Then what brought you among our enemies?"

"Baron Floyon belongs to my mother's family. He marched against you, and as I approved his cause...."

"And pillage pleases you, you felt disposed to break a lance."

"Quite right."

"And you have done your cause no harm. Where do you live?"

"Surely you know: in Germany."

"Germany is a very large country."

"In the Black Forest in Swabia."

"And your name?"

The prisoner made no reply; but Ulrich fixed his eyes upon the coat of arms on the knight's armor, looked at him more steadily, and a strange smile hovered around his lips as he approached him, saying in an altered tone: "You think the Navarrete will demand from Count von Frohlinger a ransom as large as his fields and forests?"

"You know me?"

"Perhaps so, Count Lips."

"By Heavens!"

"Ah, ha, you went from the monastery to the field."

"From the monastery? How do you know that, sir?"

"We are old acquaintances, Count Lips. Look me in the eyes."

The other gazed keenly at the Eletto, shook his head, and said: "You have not seemed a total stranger to me from the first; but I never was in Spain."

"But I have been in Swabia, and at that time you did me a kindness. Would your ransom be large enough to cover the cost of a broken church window?"

The count opened his eyes in amazement and a bright smile flashed over his face as, clapping his hands, he exclaimed with sincere delight:

"You, you--you are Ulrich! I'll be damned, if I'm mistaken! But who the devil would discover a child of the Black Forest in the Spanish Eletto?"

"That I am one, must remain a secret between us for the present," exclaimed Ulrich, extending his hand to the count. "Keep silence, and you will be free--the window will cover the ransom!"

"Holy Virgin! If all the windows in the monastery were as dear, the monks might grow fat!" cried the count. "A Swabian heart remains half Swabian, even when it beats under a Spanish doublet. Its luck, Turk's luck, that I followed Floyon;--and your old father, Adam? And Ruth--what a pleasure!"

"You ought to know....my father is dead, died long, long ago!" said Ulrich, lowering his eyes.

"Dead!" exclaimed the other. "And long ago? I saw him at the anvil three weeks since."

"My father? At the anvil? And Ruth?...." stammered Ulrich, gazing at the other with a pallid, questioning face.

"They are alive, certainly they are alive! I met him again in Antwerp. No one else can make you such armor. The devil is in it, if you hav'nt heard of the Swabian armorer."

"The Swabian--the Swabian--is he my father?"

"Your own father. How long ago is it? Thirteen years, for I was then sixteen. That was the last time I saw him, and yet I recognized him at the first glance. True, I shall never forget the hour, when the dumb woman drew the arrow from the Jew's breast. The scene I witnessed that day in the forest still rises before my eyes, as if it were happening now."

"He lives, they did not kill him!" exclaimed the Eletto, now first beginning to rejoice over the surprising news. "Lips, man--Philipp! I have found my mother again, and now my father too. Wait, wait! I'll speak to the lieutenant, he must take my place, and you and I will ride to Lier; there you will tell me the whole story. Holy Virgin! thanks, a thousand thanks! I shall see my father again, my father!"

It was past midnight, but the schoolmates were still sitting over their wine in a private room in the Lion at Lier. The Eletto had not grown weary of questioning, and Count Philipp willingly answered.

Ulrich now knew what death the doctor had met, and that his father had gone to Antwerp and lived there as an armorer for twelve years. The Jew's dumb wife had died of grief on the journey, but Ruth was living with the old man and kept house for him. Navarrete had often heard the Swabian and his work praised, and wore a corselet from his workshop.

The count could tell him a great deal about Ruth. He acknowledged that he had not sought Adam the Swabian for weapons, but on account of his beautiful daughter. The girl was slender as a fir-tree! And her face! once seen could never be forgotten. So might have looked the beautiful Judith, who slew Holophernes, or Queen Zenobia, or chaste Lucretia of Rome! She was now past twenty and in the bloom of her beauty, but cold as glass; and though she liked him on account of his old friendship for Ulrich and the affair in the forest, he was only permitted to look at, not touch her. She would rejoice when she heard that Ulrich was still alive, and what he had become. And the smith, the smith! Nay, he would not go home now, but back to Antwerp to be Ulrich's messenger! But now he too would like to relate his own experiences.

He did so, but in a rapid, superficial way, for the Eletto constantly reverted to old days and his father. Every person whom they had both known was enquired for.

Old Count Frohlinger was still alive, but suffered a great deal from gout and the capricious young wife he had married in his old age. Hangemarx had grown melancholy and, after all, ended his life by the rope, though by his own hand. Dark-skinned Xaver had entered the priesthood and was living in Rome in high esteem, as a member of a Spanish order. The abbot still presided over the monastery and had a great deal of time for his studies; for the school had been broken up and, as part of the property of the monastery had been confiscated, the number of monks had diminished. The magistrate had been falsely accused of embezzling minors' money, remained in prison for a year and, after his liberation, died of a liver complaint.

Morning was dawning when the friends separated. Count Philipp undertook to tell Ruth that Ulrich had found his mother again. She was to persuade the smith to forgive his wife, with whose praises her son's lips were overflowing.

At his departure Philipp tried to induce the Eletto to change his course betimes, for he was following a dangerous path; but Ulrich laughed in his face, exclaiming: "You know I have found the right word, and shall use it to the end. You were born to power in a small way; I have won mine myself, and shall not rest until I am permitted to exercise it on a great scale, nay, the grandest. If aught on earth affords a taste of heavenly joy, it is power!"

In the camp the Eletto found the troops from Aalst prepared for departure, and as he rode along the road saw in imagination, sometimes his parents, his parents in a new and happy union, sometimes Ruth in the full splendor of her majestic beauty. He remembered how proudly he had watched his father and mother, when they went to church together on Sunday, how he had carried Ruth in his arms on their flight; and now he was to see and experience all this again.

He gave his men only a short rest, for he longed to reach his mother. It was a glorious return home, to bring such tidings! How beautiful and charming he found life; how greatly he praised his destiny!

The sun was setting behind pleasant Aalst as he approached, and the sky looked as if it was strewn with roses.

"Beautiful, beautiful!" he murmured, pointing out to his lieutenant the brilliant hues in the western horizon.

A messenger hastened on in advance, the thunder of artillery and fanfare of music greeted the victors, as they marched through the gate. Ulrich sprang from his horse in front of the guildhall and was received by the captain, who had commanded during his absence.

The Eletto hastily described the course of the brilliant, victorious march, and then asked what had happened.

The captain lowered his eyes in embarrassment, saying, in a low tone: "Nothing of great importance; but day before yesterday a wicked deed was committed, which will vex you. The woman you love, the camp sibyl...."

"Who? What? What do you mean?"

"She went to Zorrillo, and he--you must not be startled--he stabbed her."

Ulrich staggered back, repeating, in a hollow tone "Stabbed!" Then seizing the other by the shoulder, he shrieked: "Stabbed! That means murdered-killed!"

"He thrust his dagger into her heart, she must have died as quickly as if struck by lightning. Then Zorrillo went away, God knows where. Who could suspect, that the quiet man...."

"You let him escape, helped the murderer get off, you dogs!" raved the wretched man. "We will speak of this again. Where is she, where is her body?"

The captain shrugged his shoulders, saying, in a soothing tone: "Calm yourself, Navarrete! We too grieve for the sibyl; many in the camp will miss her. As for Zorrillo, he had the password, and could go through the gate at any hour. The body is still lying in his quarters."

"Indeed!" faltered the Eletto. Then calming himself, he said, mournfully: "I wish to see her."

The captain walked silently by his side and opened the murderer's dwelling.

There, on a bed of pine-shavings, in a rude coffin made of rough planks, lay the woman who had given him birth, deserted him, and yet who so tenderly loved him. A poor soldier's wife, to whom she had been kind, was watching beside the corpse, at whose head a singly brand burned with a smoky, yellow light. The little white dog had found its way to her, and was snuffing the floor, still red with its mistress's blood.

Ulrich snatched the brand from the bracket, and threw the light on the dead woman's face. His tear-dimmed eyes sought his mother's features, but only rested on them a moment--then he shuddered, turned away, and giving the torch to his companion, said, softly: "Cover her head."

The soldier's wife spread her coarse apron over the face, which-had smiled so sweetly: but Ulrich threw himself on his knees beside the coffin, buried his face, and remained in this attitude for many minutes.

At last he slowly rose, rubbed his eyes as if waking from some confused dream, drew himself up proudly, and scanned the place with searching eyes.

He was the Eletto, and thus men honored the woman who was dear to him!

His mother lay in a wretched pauper's coffin, a ragged camp-follower watched beside her--no candles burned at her head, no priest prayed for the salvation of her soul!

Grief was raging madly in his breast, now indignation joined this gloomy guest; giving vent to his passionate emotion, Ulrich wildly exclaimed:

"Look here, captain! This corpse, this woman--proclaim it to every one-- the sibyl was my mother yes, yes, my own mother! I demand respect for her, the same respect that is shown myself! Must I compel men to render her fitting honor? Here, bring torches. Prepare the catafalque in St. Martin's church, and place it before the altar! Put candles around it, as many as can be found! It is still early! Lieutenant! I am glad you are there! Rouse the cathedral priests and go to the bishop. I command a solemn requiem for my mother! Everything is to be arranged precisely as it was at the funeral of the Duchess of Aerschot! Let trumpets give the signal for assembling. Order the bells to be rung! In an hour all must be ready at St. Martin's cathedral! Bring torches here, I say! Have I the right to command-- yes or no? A large oak coffin was standing at the joiner's close by. Bring it here, here; I need a better death- couch for my mother. You poor, dear woman, how you loved flowers, and no one has brought you even one! Captain Ortis, I have issued my commands! Everything must be done, when I return;--Lieutenant, you have your orders!"

He rushed from the death-chamber to the sitting-room in his own house, and hastily tore stalks and blossoms from the plants. The maid-servants watched him timidly, and he harshly ordered them to collect what he had gathered and take them to the house of death.

His orders were obeyed, and when he next appeared at Zorrillo's quarters, the soldiers, who had assembled there in throngs, parted to make way for him.

He beckoned to them, and while he went from one to another, saying: "The sibyl was my mother--Zorrillo has murdered my mother," the coffin was borne into the house.

In the vestibule, he leaned his head against the wall, moaning and sighing, until Florette was laid in her last bed, and a soldier put his hand on his shoulder. Then Ulrich strewed flowers over the corpse, and the joiner came to nail up the coffin. The blows of the hammer actually hurt him, it seemed as if each one fell upon his own heart.

The funeral procession passed through the ranks of soldiers, who filled the street. Several officers came to meet it, and Captain Ortis, approaching close to the Eletto, said: "The bishop refuses the catafalque and the solemn requiem you requested. Your mother died in sin, without the sacrament. He will grant as many masses for the repose of her soul as you desire, but such high honors...."

"He refuses them to us?"

"Not to us, to the sibyl."

"She was my mother, your Eletto's mother. To the cathedral, forward!"

"It is closed, and will remain so to-day, for the bishop...."

"Then burst the doors! We'll show them who has the power here."

"Are you out of your senses? The Holy Church!"

"Forward, I say! Let him who is no cowardly wight, follow me!"

Ulrich drew the commander's baton from his belt and rushed forward, as if he were leading a storming-party; but Ortis cried: "We will not fight against St. Martin!" and a murmur of applause greeted him.

Ulrich checked his pace, and gnashing his teeth, exclaimed: "Will not? Will not?" Then gazing around the circle of comrades, who surrounded him on all sides, he asked: "Has no one courage to help me to my rights? Ortis, de Vego, Diego, will you follow me, yes or no?"

"No, not against the Church!"

"Then I command you," shouted the Eletto, furiously. "Obey, Lieutenant de Vega, forward with your company, and burst the cathedral doors."

But no one obeyed, and Ortis ordered: "Back, every man of you! Saint Martin is my patron saint; let all who value their souls refuse to attack the church and defend it with me."

The blood rushed to Ulrich's brain, and incapable of longer self-control, he threw his baton into the ranks of the mutineers, shrieking: "I hurl it at your feet; whoever picks it up can keep it!"

The soldiers hesitated; but Ortis repeated his "Back!" Other officers gave the same order, and their men obeyed. The street grew empty, and the Eletto's mother was only followed by a few of her son's friends; no priest led the procession. In the cemetery Ulrich threw three handfuls of earth into the open grave, then with drooping head returned home.

How dreary, how desolate the bright, flower-decked room seemed now, for the first time the Eletto felt really deserted. No tears came to relieve his grief, for the insult offered him that day aroused his wrath, and he cherished it as if it were a consolation.

He had thrown power aside with the staff of command. Power! It too was potter's trash, which a stone might shatter, a flower in full bloom, whose leaves drop apart if touched by the finger! It was no noble metal, only yellow mica!

The knocker on the door never stopped rapping. One officer after another came to soothe him, but he would not even admit his lieutenant.

He rejoiced over his hasty deed. Fortune, he thought, cannot be escaped, art cannot be thrown aside; fame may be trampled under foot, yet still pursue us.

Power has this advantage over all three, it can be flung off like a worn-out doublet. Let it fly! Had he owed it the happiness of the last few weeks? No, no! He would have been happy with his mother in a poor, plain house, without the office of Eletto, without flowers, horses or servants. It was to her, not to power, that he was indebted for every blissful hour, and now that she had gone, how desolate was the void in his heart!

Suddenly the recollection of his father and Ruth illumined his misery like a sunbeam. The game of Eletto was now over, he would go to Antwerp the next day.

Why had fate snatched his mother from him just now, why did it deny him the happiness of seeing his parents united? His father--she had sorely wronged him, but for what will not death atone? He must take him some remembrance of her, and went to her room to look through her chest. But it no longer stood in the old place--the owner of the house, a rich matron, who had been compelled to occupy an attic-room, while strangers were quartered in her residence, had taken charge of the pale orphan and the boxes after Florette's death.

The good Netherland dame provided for the adopted child and the property of her enemy, the man whose soldiers had pillaged her brothers and cousins. The death of the woman below had moved her deeply, for the wonderful charm of Florette's manner had won her also.

Towards midnight Ulrich took the lamp and went upstairs. He had long since forgotten to spare others, by denying himself a wish.

The knocking at the door and the passing to and fro in the entry had kept Frau Geel awake. When she heard the Eletto's heavy step, she sprang up from her spinning-wheel in alarm, and the maid-servant, half roused from sleep, threw herself on her knees.

"Frau Geel!" called a voice outside.

She recognized Navarrete's tones, opened the door, and asked what he desired.

"It was his mother," thought the old lady as he threw clothes, linen and many a trifle on the floor. "It was his mother. Perhaps he wants her rosary or prayer book. He is her son! They looked like a happy couple when they were together. A wild soldier, but he isn't a wicked man yet."

While he searched she held the light for him, shaking her head over the disorder among the articles where he rummaged.

Ulrich had now reached the bottom of the chest. Here he found a valuable necklace, booty which Zorrillo had given his companion for use in case of need. This should be Ruth's. Close beside it lay a small package, tied with rose-pink ribbon, containing a tiny infant's shirt, a gay doll, and a slender gold circlet; her wedding-ring! The date showed that it had been given to her by his father, and the shirt and doll were mementos of him, her darling--of himself.

He gazed at them, changing them from one hand to the other, till suddenly his heart overflowed, and without heeding Frau Geel, who was watching him, he wept softly, exclaiming: "Mother, dear mother!"

A light hand touched his shoulder, and a woman's kind voice said: "Poor fellow, poor fellow! Yes, she was a dear little thing, and a mother, a mother--that is enough!"

The Eletto nodded assent with tearful eyes, and when she again gently repeated in a tone of sincere sympathy, her "poor fellow!" it sounded sweeter, than the loudest homage that had ever been offered to his fame and power.

CHAPTER XXIX.

THE next morning while Ulrich was packing his luggage, assisted by his servant, the sound of drums and fifes, bursts of military music and loud cheers were heard in the street, and going to the window, he saw the whole body of mutineers drawn up in the best order.

The companies stood in close ranks before his house, impetuous shouts and bursts of music made the windows rattle, and now the officers pressed into his room, holding out their swords, vowing fealty unto death, and entreating him to remain their commander.

He now perceived, that power cannot be thrown aside like a worthless thing. His tortured heart was stirred with deep emotion, and the drooping wings of ambition unfolded with fresh energy. He reproached, raged, but yielded; and when Ortis on his knees, offered him the commander's baton, he accepted it.

Ulrich was again Eletto, but this need not prevent his seeing his father and Ruth once more, so he declared that he would retain his office, but should be obliged to ride to Antwerp that day, secretly inform the officers of the conspiracy against the city, and the necessity of negotiating with the commandant, that their share of the rich prize might not be lost.

What many had suspected and hoped was now to become reality. Their Eletto was no idle man! When Navarrete appeared at noon in front of the troops with his own work, the standard, in his hand, he was received with shouts of joy, and no one murmured, though many recognized in the Madonna's countenance the features of the murdered sibyl.

Two days later Ulrich, full of eager expectation, rode into Antwerp, carrying in his portmanteau the mementos he had taken from his mother's chest, while in imagination he beheld his father's face, the smithy at Richtberg, the green forest, the mountains of his home, the Costas' house, and his little playfellow. Would he really be permitted to lean on his father's broad breast once more?

And Ruth, Ruth! Did she still care for him, had Philipp described her correctly?

He went to the count without delay, and found him at home. Philipp received him cordially, yet with evident timidity and embarrassment. Ulrich too was grave, for he had to inform his companion of his mother's death.

"So that is settled," said the count. "Your father is a gnarled old tree, a real obstinate Swabian. It's not his way to forgive and forget."

"And did he know that my mother was so near to him, that she was in Aalst."

"All, all!"

"He will forgive the dead. Surely, surely he will, if I beseech him, when we are united, if I tell him...."

"Poor fellow! You think all this is so easy.--It is long since I have had so hard a task, yet I must speak plainly. He will have nothing to do with you, either."

"Nothing to do with me?" cried Ulrich.

"Is he out of his senses? What sin have I committed, what does he...."

"He knows that you are Navarrete, the Eletto of Herenthals, the conqueror of Aalst, and therefore...."

"Therefore?"

"Why of course. You see, Ulrich, when a man becomes famous like you, he is known for a long distance, everything he does makes a great hue and cry, and echo repeats it in every alley."

"To my honor before God and man."

"Before God? Perhaps so; certainly before the Spaniards. As for me--I was with the squadron myself, I call you a brave soldier; but--no offence--you have behaved ill in this country. The Netherlanders are human beings too."

"They are rebels, recreant heretics."

"Take care, or you will revile your own father. His faith has been shaken. A preacher, whom he met on his flight here, in some tavern, led him astray by inducing him to read the bible. Many things the Church condemns are sacred to him. He thinks the Netherlanders a free, noble nation. Your King Philip he considers a tyrant, oppressor, and ruthless destroyer. You who have served him and Alba--are in his eyes; but I will not wound you...."

"What are we, I will hear."

"No, no, it would do no good. In short, to Adam the Spanish army is a bloody pest, nothing more."

"There never were braver soldiers."

"Very true; but every defeat, all the blood you have shed, has angered him and this nation, and wrath, which daily receives fresh food and to which men become accustomed, at last turns to hate. All great crimes committed in this war are associated with Alba's name, many smaller ones with yours, and so your father...."

"Then we will teach him a better opinion! I return to him an honest soldier, the commander of thousands of men! To see him once more, only to see him! A son remains a son! I learned that from my mother. We were rivals and enemies, when I met her! And then, then--alas, that is all over! Now I wish to find in my father what I have lost; will you go to the smithy with me?"

"No, Ulrich, no. I have said everything to your father that can be urged in your defence, but he is so devoured with rage...."

"Santiago!" exclaimed the Eletto, bursting into sudden fury, "I need no advocate! If the old man knows what share I have taken in this war, so much the better. I'll fill up the gaps myself. I have been wherever the fight raged hottest! 'Sdeath! that is my pride! I am no longer a boy and have fought my way through life without father or mother. What I am, I have made myself, and can defend with honor, even to the old man. He carries heavy guns, I know; but I am not accustomed to shoot with feather balls!"

"Ulrich, Ulrich! He is an old man, and your father!"

"I will remember that, as soon as he calls me his son."

One of the count's servants showed Ulrich the way to the smith's house.

Adam had entirely given up the business of horseshoeing, for nothing was to be seen in the ground floor of the high, narrow house, except the large door, and a window on each side. Behind the closed one at the right were several pieces of armor, beautifully embossed, and some artistically-wrought iron articles. The left-hand one was partly open, granting entrance to the autumn sunshine. Ulrich dismissed the servant, took the mementos of his mother in his hand, and listened to the hammer-strokes, that echoed from within.

The familiar sound recalled pleasant memories of his childhood and cooled his hot blood. Count Philipp was right. His father was an old man, and entitled to demand respect from his son. He must endure from him what he would tolerate from no one else. Nay, he again felt that it was a great happiness to be near the beloved one, from whom he had so long been parted; whatever separated him from his old father, must surely vanish into nothing, as soon as they looked into each other's eyes.

What a master in his trade, his father still was! No one else would have found it so easy to forge the steel coat of mail with the Medusa head in the centre. He was not working alone here as he did at Richtberg; for Ulrich heard more than one hammer striking iron in the workshop.

Before touching the knocker, he looked into the open window.

A woman's tall figure was standing at the desk. Her back was turned, and he saw only the round outline of the head, the long black braids, the plain dress, bordered with velvet, and the lace in the neck. An elderly man in the costume of a merchant was just holding out his hand in farewell, and he heard him say: "You've bought too cheap again, far too cheap, Jungfer Ruth."

"Just a fair price," she answered quietly. "You will have a good profit, and we can afford to pay it. I shall expect the iron day after to-morrow."

"It will be delivered before noon. Master Adam has a treasure in you, dear Jungfer. If my son were alive, I know where he would seek a wife. Wilhelm Ykens has told me of his troubles; he is a skilful goldsmith. Why do you give the poor fellow no hope? Consider! You are past twenty, and every year it grows harder to say yes to a lover."

"Nothing suits me better, than to stay with father," she answered gaily. "He can't do without me, you know, nor I without him. I have no dislike to Wilhelm, but it seems very easy to live without him. Farewell, Father Keulitz."

Ulrich withdrew from the window, until the merchant had vanished down a side street; then he again glanced into the narrow room. Ruth was now seated at the desk, but instead of looking over the open account book, her eyes were gazing dreamily into vacancy, and the Eletto now saw her beautiful, calm, noble face. He did not disturb her, for it seemed as if he could never weary of comparing her features with the fadeless image his memory had treasured during all the vicissitudes of life.

Never, not even in Italy, had he beheld a nobler countenance. Philipp was right. There was something royal in her bearing. This was the wife of his dreams, the proud woman, with whom the Eletto desired to share power and grandeur. And he had already held her once in his arms! It seemed as if it were only yesterday. His heart throbbed higher and higher. As she now rose and thoughtfully approached the window, he could no longer contain himself, and exclaimed in a low tone: "Ruth, Ruth! Do you know me, girl? It is I--Ulrich!"

She shrank back, putting out her hands with a repellent gesture; but only for a moment. Then, struggling to maintain her composure, she joyously uttered his name, and as he rushed into the room, cried "Ulrich!" "Ulrich!" and no longer able to control her feelings, suffered him to clasp her to his heart.

She had daily expected him with ardent longing, yet secret dread: for he was the fierce Eletto, the commander of the insurgents, the bloody foe of the brave nation she loved. But at sight of his face all, all was forgotten, and she felt nothing but the bliss of being reunited to him whom she had never, never forgotten, the joy of seeing, feeling that he loved her.

His heart too was overflowing with passionate delight. Faltering tender words, he drew her head to his breast, then raised it to press his mouth to her pure lips. But her intoxication of joy passed away--and before he could prevent it, she had escaped from his arms, saying sternly: "Not that, not that.... Many a crime lies between us and you."

"No, no!" he eagerly exclaimed. "Are you not near me? Your heart and mine have belonged to each other since that day in the snow. If my father is angry because I serve other masters than his, you, yes you, must reconcile us again. I could stay in Aalst no longer."

"With the mutineers?" she asked sadly. "Ulrich, Ulrich, that you should return to us thus!"

He again seized her hand, and when she tried to withdraw it, only smiled, saying with the confidence of a man, who is sure of his cause:

"Cast aside this foolish reserve. To-morrow you will freely give me, not only one hand, but both. I am not so bad as you think. The fortune of war flung me under the Spanish flag, and 'whose bread I eat, his song I sing,' says the soldier. What would you have? I served with honor, and have done some doughty deeds; let that content you."

This angered Ruth, who resolutely exclaimed:

"No, a thousand times no! You are the Eletto of Aalst, the pillager of cities, and this cannot be swept aside as easily as the dust from the floor. I.... I am only a feeble girl;--but father, he will never give his hand to the blood-stained man in Spanish garb! I know him, I know it."

Ulrich's breath came quicker; but he repressed the angry emotion and replied, first reproachfully, then beseechingly:

"You are the old man's echo. What does he know of military honor and warlike fame; but you, Ruth, must understand me. Do you still remember our sport with the "word," the great word that accomplished everything? I have found it; and you shall enjoy with me what it procures. First help me appease my father; I shall succeed, if you aid me. It will doubtless be a hard task. He could not bring himself to forgive his poor wife--Count

Philipp says so;--but now! You see, Ruth, my mother died a few days ago; she was a dear, loving woman and might have deserved a better fate.

"I am alone again now, and long for love--so ardently, so sincerely, more than I can tell you. Where shall I find it, if not with you and my own father? You have always cared for me; you betray it, and after all you know I am not a bad man, do you not? Be content with my love and take me to my father, yourself. Help me persuade him to listen to me. I have something here which you can give him from me; you will see that it will soften his heart!"

"Then give it to me," replied Ruth, "but whatever it may be--believe me, Ulrich, so long as you command the Spanish mutineers, he will remain hard, hard as his own iron!"

"Spaniards! Mutineers! Nonsense! Whoever wishes to love, can love; the rest may be settled afterwards. You don't know how high my heart throbs, now that I am near you, now that I see and hear you. You are my good angel and must remain so, now look here. This is my mother's legacy. This little shirt I once wore, when I was a tiny thing, the gay doll was my plaything, and this gold hoop is the wedding-ring my father gave his bride at the altar--she kept all these things to the last, and carried them like holy relics from land to land, from camp to camp. Will you take these mementos to him?"

She nodded silently.

"Now comes the best thing. Have you ever seen more beautiful workmanship? You must wear this necklace, Ruth, as my first gift."

He held up the costly ornament, but she shrank back, asking bitterly

"Captured booty?"

"In honorable war, he answered, proudly, approaching to fasten the jewels round her neck with his own hands; but she pushed him back, snatched the ornament, and hurled it on the floor, exclaiming angrily:

"I loathe the stolen thing. Pick it up. It may suit the camp-followers."

This destroyed his self-control, and seizing both her arms in an iron grasp, he muttered through his clenched teeth:

"That is an insult to my mother; take it back." But Ruth heard and saw nothing; full of indignation she only felt that violence was being done her, and vainly struggled against the irresistible strength, which held her fast.

Meantime the door had opened wide, but neither noticed it until a man's deep voice loudly and wrathfully exclaimed:

"Back, you scoundrel! Come here, Ruth. This is the way the assassin greets his family; begone, begone! you disgrace of my house!"

Adam had uttered the words, and now drew the hammer from the belt of his leather apron.

Ulrich gazed mutely into his face. There stood his father, strong, gigantic, as he had looked thirteen years before. His head was a little bowed, his beard longer and whiter, his eyebrows were more bushy and his expression had grown more gloomy; otherwise he was wholly unchanged in every feature.

The son's eyes rested on the smith as if spellbound. It seemed as if some malicious fate had drawn him into a snare.

He could say nothing except, "father, father," and the smith found no other answer than the harsh "begone!"

Ruth approached the armorer, clung to his side, and pleaded:

"Hear him, don't send him away so; he is your child, and if anger just now overpowered him...."

"Spanish custom--to abuse women!" cried Adam. "I have no son Navarrete, or whatever the murderous monster calls himself. I am a burgher, and have no son, who struts about in the stolen clothes of noblemen; as to this man and his assassins, I hate them, hate them all. Your foot defiles my house. Out with you, knave, or I will use my hammer."

Ulrich again exclaimed, "father, father!" Then, regaining his self-control by a violent effort, he gasped:

"Father, I came to you in good will, in love. I am an honest soldier and if any one but you--'Sdeath--if any other had dared to offer me this...."

"Murder the dog, you would have said," interrupted the smith. "We know the Spanish blessing: a sandre, a carne!--[Blood, murder.]--Thanks for your forbearance. There is the door. Another word, and I can restrain myself no longer."

Ruth had clung firmly to the smith, and motioned Ulrich to go. The Eletto groaned aloud, struck his forehead with his clenched fist, and rushed into the open air.

As soon as Adam was alone with Ruth she caught his hand, exclaiming beseechingly:

"Father, father, he is your own son! Love your enemies, the Saviour commanded; and you...."

"And I hate him," said the smith, curtly and resolutely. "Did he hurt you?"

"Your hate hurts me ten times as much! You judge without examining; yes, father, you do! When he assaulted me, he was in the right. He thought I had insulted his mother."

Adam shrugged his shoulders, and she continued "The poor woman is dead. Ulrich brought you yonder ring; she never parted with it."

The armorer started, seized the golden hoop, looked for the date inside, and when he had found it, clasped the ring in his hands and pressed them silently to his temples. He stood in this attitude a short time, then let his arms fall, and said softly:

"The dead must be forgiven...."

"And the living, father? You have punished him terribly, and he is not a wicked man, no, indeed he is not! If he comes back again, father?"

"My apprentices shall show the Spanish mutineer the door," cried the old man in a harsh, stern tone; "to the burgher's repentant son my house will be always open."

Meantime the Eletto wandered from one street to another. He felt bewildered, disgraced.

It was not grief--no quiet heartache that disturbed--but a confused blending of wrath and sorrow. He did not wish to appear before the friend of his youth, and even avoided Hans Eitelfritz, who came towards him. He was blind to the gay, joyous bustle of the capital; life seemed grey and hollow. His intention of communicating with the commandant of the citadel remained unexecuted; for he thought of nothing but his father's anger, of Ruth, his own shame and misery.

He could not leave so.

His father must, yes, he must hear him, and when it grew dusk, he again sought the house to which he belonged, and from which he had been so cruelly expelled.

The door was locked. In reply to his knock, a man's unfamiliar voice asked who he was, and what he wanted.

He asked to speak with Adam, and called himself Ulrich.

After waiting a long time he heard a door torn open, and the smith angrily exclaim:

"To your spinning-wheel! Whoever clings to him so long as he wears the Spanish dress, means evil to him as well as to me."

"But hear him! You must hear him, father!" cried Ruth.

The door closed, heavy steps approached the door of the house; it opened, and again Adam confronted his son.

"What do you want?" he asked harshly.

"To speak to you, to tell you that you did wrong to insult me unheard."

"Are you still the Eletto? Answer!"

"I am!"

"And intend to remain so?"

"Que como--puede ser--" faltered Ulrich, who confused by the question, had strayed into the language in which he had been long accustomed to think. But scarcely had the smith distinguished the foreign words, when fresh anger seized him.

"Then go to perdition with your Spaniards!" was the furious answer.

The door slammed so that the house shook, and by degrees the smith's heavy tread died away in the vestibule.

"All over, all over!" murmured the rejected son. Then calming himself, he clenched his fist and muttered through his set teeth: "There shall be no lack of ruin; whoever it befalls, can bear it."

While walking through the streets and across the squares, he devised plan after plan, imagining what must come. Sword in hand he would burst the old man's door, and the only booty he asked for himself should be Ruth, for whom he longed, who in spite of everything loved him, who had belonged to him from her childhood.

The next morning he negotiated cleverly and boldly with the commandant of the Spanish forces in the citadel. The fate of the city was sealed! and when he again crossed the great square and saw the city-hall with its proud, gable-crowned central building, and the shops in the lower floor crammed with wares, he laughed savagely.

Hans Eitelfritz had seen him in the distance, and shouted:

"A pretty little house, three stories high. And how the broad windows, between the pillars in the side wings, glitter!"

Then he lowered his voice, for the square was swarming with men, carts and horses, and continued:

"Look closer and choose your quarters. Come with me! I'll show you where the best things we need can be found. Haven't we bled often enough for the pepper-sacks? Now it will be our turn to fleece them. The castles here, with the gingerbread work on the gables, are the guildhalls. There is gold enough in each one, to make the company rich. Now this way! Directly behind the city-hall lies the Zucker Canal. There live stiff-necked people, who dine off of silver every day. Notice the street!"

Then he led him back to the square, and continued "The streets here all lead to the quay. Do you know it? Have you seen the warehouses? Filled to the very roof! The malmsey, dry canary and Indian allspice, might transform the Scheldt and Baltic Sea into a huge vat of hippocras."

Ulrich followed his guide from street to street. Wherever he looked, he saw vast wealth in barns and magazines; in houses, palaces and churches.

Hans Eitelfritz stopped before a jeweller's shop, saying:

"Look here! I particularly admire these things, these toys: the little dog, the sled, the lady with the hoopskirt, all these things are pure silver. When the pillage begins, I shall grasp these and take them to my sister's little children in Colln; they will be delighted, and if it should ever be necessary, their mother can sell them."

What a throng crowded the most aristocratic streets! English, Spanish, Italian and Hanseatic merchants tried to ouldo the Netherland traders in magnificent clothes and golden ornaments. Ulrich saw them all assembled in the Gothic exchange on the Mere, the handsomest square in the city. There they stood in the vast open hall, on the checkered marble floor, not by hundreds, but by thousands, dealing in goods which came from all quarters of the globe--from the most distant lands. Their offers and bids mingled in a noise audible at a long distance, which was borne across the square like the echo of ocean surges.

Sums were discussed, which even the winged imagination of the lansque-net could scarcely grasp. This city was a remarkable treasure, a thousand-fold richer booty than had been garnered from the Ottoman treasure-ship on the sea at Lepanto.

Here was the fortune the Eletto needed, to build the palace in which he intended to place Ruth. To whom else would fall the lion's share of the enormous prize!

His future happiness was to arise from the destruction of this proud city, stifling in its gold.

These were ambitious brilliant plans, but he devised them with gloomy eyes, in a darkened mind. He intended to win by force what was denied him, so long as the power belonged to him.

There could be no lack of flames and carnage; but that was part of his trade, as shavings belong to flames, hammer-strokes to smiths.

Count Philipp had no suspicion of the assault, was not permitted to suspect anything. He attributed Ulrich's agitated manner to the rejection he had encountered in his father's house, and when he took leave of him on his departure to Swabia, talked kindly with his former schoolmate and advised him to leave the Spanish flag and try once more to be reconciled to the old man.

Before the Eletto quitted the city, he gave Hans Eitelfritz, whose regiment had secretly joined the mutiny, letters of safeguard for his family and the artist, Moor.

He had not forgotten the latter, but well-founded timidity withheld him from appearing before the honored man, while cherishing the gloomy thoughts that now filled his soul.

In Aalst the mutineers received him with eager joy, harsh and repellent as he appeared, they cheerfully obeyed him; for he could hold out to them a prospect, which lured a bright smile to the bearded lips of the grimmest warrior.

If power was the word, he scarcely understood how to use it aright, for wholly absorbed in himself, he led a joyless life of dissatisfied longing and gloomy reverie.

It seemed to him as if he had lost one half of himself, and needed Ruth to become the whole man. Hours grew to days, days to weeks, and not until

Roda's messenger appeared from the citadel in Antwerp to summon him to action, did he revive and regain his old vivacity.

CHAPTER XXX.

ON the twentieth of October Mastricht fell into the Spaniards' hands, and was cruelly pillaged. The garrison of Antwerp rose and began to make common cause with the friends of the mutineers in the citadel.

Foreign merchants fled from the imperilled city. Governor Champagny saw his own person and the cause of order seriously threatened by the despots in the fortress, which dominated the town. A Netherland army, composed principally of Walloons, under the command of the incapable Marquis Havre, the reckless de Heze and other nobles appeared before the capital, to prevent the worst.

Champagny feared that the German regiments would feel insulted and scent treason, if he admitted the government troops--but the majority of the lansquenets were already in league with the insurgents, the danger hourly increased, everywhere loyalty wavered, the citizens urgently pressed the matter, and the gates were opened to the Netherlanders.

Count Oberstein, the German commander of the lansquenets, who while intoxicated had pledged himself to make common cause with the mutineers in the citadel, remembered his duty and remained faithful to the end. The regiment in which Hans Eitelfritz served, and the other companies of lansquenets, had succumbed to the temptation, and only waited the signal for revolt. The inhabitants felt just like a man, who keeps powder and firebrands in the cellar, or a traveller, who recognizes robbers and murderers in his own escort.

Champagny called upon the citizens to help themselves, and used their labor in throwing up a wall of defence in the open part of the city, which was most dangerously threatened by the citadel. Among the men and women who voluntarily flocked to the work by thousands, were Adam, the smith, his apprentices, and Ruth. The former, with his journeymen, wielded the spade under the direction of a skilful engineer, the girl, with other women, braided gabions from willow-rods.

She had lived through sorrowful days. Self-reproach, for having by her hasty fit of temper caused the father's outburst of anger to his son, constantly tortured her.

She had learned to hate the Spaniards as bitterly as Adam; she knew that Ulrich was following a wicked, criminal course, yet she loved him, his image had been treasured from childhood, unassailed and unsullied, in the most sacred depths of her heart. He was all in all to her, the one person destined for her, the man to whom she belonged as the eye does to the face, the heart to the breast.

She believed in his love, and when she strove to condemn and forget him, it seemed as if she were alienating, rejecting the best part of-herself.

A thousand voices told her that she lived in his soul, as much as he did in hers, that his existence without her must be barren and imperfect. She did not ask when and how, she only prayed that she might become his, expecting it as confidently as light in the morning, spring after winter. Nothing appeared so irrefutable as this faith; it was the belief of her loving soul. Then, when the inevitable had happened they would be one in their aspirations for virtue, and the son could no longer close his heart against the father, nor the father shut his against the son.

The child's vivid imagination was still alive in the maiden. Every leisure hour she had thought of her lost playfellow, every day she had talked to his father about him, asking whether he would rather see him return as a famous artist, a skilful smith, or commander of a splendid ship.

Handsome, strong, superior to other men, he had always appeared. Now she found him following evil courses, on the path to ruin; yet even here he was peerless among his comrades; whatever stain rested upon him, he certainly was not base and mean.

As a child, she always had transformed him into a splendid fairy-prince, but she now divested him of all magnificence, seeing him attired in plain burgher dress, appear humbly before his father and stand beside him at the forge. She dreamed that she was by his side, and before her stood the table she covered with food for him, and the water she gave him after his work. She heard the house shake under the mighty blows of his hammer, and in imagination beheld him lay his curly head in her lap, and say he had found love and peace with her.

The cannonade from the citadel stopped the citizens' work. Open hostilities had begun.

On the morning of November 4th, under the cover of a thick fog, the treacherous Spaniards, commanded by Romero, Vargas and Valdez entered the fortress. The citizens, among them Adam, learned this fact with rage and terror, but the mutineers of Aalst had not yet collie.

"He is keeping them back," Ruth had said the day before. "Antwerp, our home, is sacred to him!"

The cannon roared, culverins crashed, muskets and arquebuses rattled; the boding notes of the alarm-bells and the fierce shouts of soldiers and citizens hurrying to battle mingled with the deafening thunder of the artillery.

Every hand seized a weapon, every shop was closed; hearts stood still with fear, or throbbed wildly with rage and emotion. Ruth remained calm. She detained the smith in the house, repeating her former words: "The men from Aalst are not coming; he is keeping diem back." Just at that moment the young apprentice, whose parents lived on the Scheldt, rushed with dishevelled hair into the workshop, gasping:

"The men from Aalst are here. They crossed in peatboats and a galley. They wear green twigs in their helmets, and the Eletto is marching in the van, bearing the standard. I saw them; terrible--horrible--sheathed in iron from top to toe."

He said no more, for Adam, with a savage imprecation, interrupted him, seized his huge hammer, and rushed out of the house.

Ruth staggered back into the workshop.

Adam hurried straight to the rampart. Here stood six thousand Walloons, to defend the half-finished wall, and behind them large bodies of armed citizens.

"The men from Aalst have come!" echoed from lip to lip.

Curses, wails of grief, yells of savage fury, blended with the thunder of the artillery and the ringing of the alarm bells.

A fugitive now dashed from the counterscarp towards the Walloons, shouting:

"They are here, they are here! The blood-hound, Navarrete, is leading them. They will neither eat nor drink, they say, till they dine in Paradise or Antwerp. Hark, hark! there they are!"

And they were there, coming nearer and nearer; foremost of all marched the Eletto, holding the standard in his upraised hand.

Behind him, from a thousand bearded lips, echoed furious, greedy, terrible cries; "Santiago, Espana, a sangre, a carne, a fuego, a saco!"--[St. Jago; Spain, blood, murder, fire, pillage]--but Navarrete was silent, striding onward, erect and haughty, as if he were proof against the bullets, that whistled around him on all sides. Consciousness of power and the fierce joy of battle sparkled in his eyes. Woe betide him, who received a blow from the two-handed sword the Eletto still held over his shoulder, now with his left hand.

Adam stood with upraised hammer beside the front ranks of the Walloons! his eyes rested as if spellbound on his approaching son and the standard in his hand. The face of the guilty woman, who had defrauded him of the happiness of his life, gazed at him from the banner. He knew not whether he was awake, or the sport of some bewildering dream.

Now, now his glance met the Eletto's, and unable to restrain himself longer, he raised his hammer and tried to rush forward, but the Walloons forced him back.

Yes, yes, he hated his own child, and trembling with rage, burning to rush upon him, he saw the Eletto spring on the lowest projection of the wall, to climb up. For a short time he was concealed from his eyes, then he saw the top of the standard, then the banner itself, and now his son stood on the highest part of the rampart, shouting: "Espana, Espana!"

At this moment, with a deafening din, a hundred arquebuses were discharged close beside the smith, a dense cloud of smoke darkened the air, and when the wind dispersed it, Adam no longer beheld the standard. It lay on the ground; beside it the Eletto, with his face turned upward, mute and motionless.

The father groaned aloud and closed his eyes; when he opened them, hundreds of iron-mailed mutineers had scaled the rampart. Beneath their feet lay his bleeding child.

Corpse after corpse sank on the stone wall beside the fallen man, but the iron wedge of the Spaniards pressed farther and farther forward.

"Espana, a sangre, a carne!"

Now they had reached the Walloons, steel clashed against steel, but only for a moment, then the defenders of the city wavered, the furious wedge entered their ranks, they parted, yielded, and with loud shrieks took to flight. The Spanish swords raged among them, and overpowered by the general terror, the officers followed the example of the soldiers, the flying army, like a resistless torrent, carrying everything with it, even the smith.

An unparalleled massacre began. Adam seeing a frantic horde rush into the houses, remembered Ruth, and half mad with terror hastened back to the smithy, where he told those left behind what he had witnessed. Then, arming himself and his journeymen with weapons forged by his own hand, he hurried out with them to renew the fight.

Hours elapsed; the noise, the firing, the ringing of the alarm bells still continued; smoke and the smell of fire penetrated through the doors and windows.

Evening came, and the richest, most flourishing commercial capital in the world was here a heap of ashes, there a ruin, everywhere a plundered treasury.

Once the occupants of the smith's shop heard a band of murderers raging and shouting outside of the smithy; but they passed by, and all day long no others entered the quiet street, which was inhabited only by workers in metal.

Ruth and old Rahel had remained behind, under the protection of the brave foreman. Adam had told them to fly to the cellar, if any uproar arose outside the door. Ruth wore a dagger, determined in the worst extremity to turn it against her own breast. What did she care for life, since Ulrich had perished!

Old Rahel, an aged dame of eighty, paced restlessly, with bowed figure, through the large room, saying compassionately, whenever her eyes met the girl's: "Ulrich, our Ulrich!" then, straightening herself and looking upward. She no longer knew what had happened a few hours before, yet her memory faithfully retained the incidents that occurred many years previous. The maidservant, a native of Antwerp, had rushed home to her parents when the tumult began.

As the day drew towards a close, the panes were less frequently shaken by the thunder of the artillery, the noise in the streets diminished, but the house became more and more filled with suffocating smoke.

Night came, the lamp was lighted, the women started at every new sound, but anxiety for Adam now overpowered every other feeling in Ruth's mind. Just then the door opened, and the smith's deep voice called in the vestibule: "It is I! Don't be frightened, it is I!"

He had gone out with five journeymen: he returned with two. The others lay slain in the streets, and with them Count Oberstein's soldiers, the only ones who had stoutly resisted the Spanish mutineers and their allies to the last man.

Adam had swung his hammer on the Mere and by the Zucker Canal among the citizens, who fought desperately for the property and lives of their families;--but all was vain. Vargas's troopers had stifled even the last breath of resistance.

The streets ran blood, corpses lay in heaps before the doors and on the pavement--among them the bodies of the Margrave of Antwerp, Verreyck, Burgomaster van der Mere, and many senators and nobles. Conflagration after conflagration crimsoned the heavens, the superb city-hall was blazing, and from a thousand windows echoed the screams of the assailed, plundered, bleeding citizens, women and children.

The smith hastily ate a few mouthfuls to restore his strength, then raised his head, saying: "No one has touched our house. The door and shutters of neighbor Ykens' are shattered."

"A miracle!" cried old Rahel, raising her staff. "The generation of vipers scent richer booty than iron at the silversmith's."

Just at that moment the knocker sounded. Adam started up, put on his coat of mail again, motioned to his journeymen and went to the door.

Rahel shrieked loudly: "To the cellar, Ruth. Oh, God, oh, God, have mercy upon us! Quick--where's my shawl?--They are attacking us!--Come, come! Oh, I am caught, I can go no farther!"

Mortal terror had seized the old woman; she did not want to die. To the girl death was welcome, and she did not stir.

Voices were now audible in the vestibule, but they sounded neither noisy nor threatening; yet Rahel shrieked in despair as a lansquenet, fully armed, entered the workshop with the armorer.

Hans Eitelfritz had come to look for Ulrich's father. In his arms lay the dog Lelaps, which, bleeding from the wound made by a bullet, that grazed its neck, nestled trembling against its master.

Bowing courteously to Ruth, the soldier said:

"Take pity on this poor creature, fair maiden, and wash its wound with a little wine. It deserves it. I could tell you such tales of its cleverness! It came from distant India, where a pirate.... But you shall hear the story some other time. Thanks, thanks! As to your son, Meister, it's a thousand pities about him. He was a splendid fellow, and we were like two brothers. He himself gave me the safeguard for you and the artist, Moor. I fastened them on the doors with my own hands, as soon as the fray began. My swordbearer got the paste, and now may the writing stick there as an honorable memento till the end of the world. Navarrete was a faithful fellow, who never forgot his friends! How much good that does Lelaps! See, see! He is licking your hands, that means, 'I thank you.'"

While Ruth had been washing the dog's wound, and the lansquenet talked of Ulrich, her tearful eyes met the father's.

"They say he cut down twenty-one Walloons before he fell," continued Hans.

"No, sir," interrupted Adam. "I saw him. He was shot before he raised his guilty sword."

"Ah, ah!--but it happened on the rampart."

"They rushed over him to the assault."

"And there he still lies; not a soul has cared for the dead and wounded."

The girl started, and laid the dog in the old man's lap, exclaiming: "Suppose Ulrich should be alive! Perhaps he was not mortally wounded, perhaps...."

"Yes, everything is possible," interrupted the lansquenet. "I could tell you things.... for instance, there was a countryman of mine whom, when we were in Africa, a Moorish Pacha struck....no lies now....perhaps! In earnest; it might happen that Ulrich....wait.... at midnight I shall keep guard on the rampart with my company, then I'll look...."

"We, we will seek him!" cried Ruth, seizing the smith's arm.

"I will," replied the smith; "you must stay here."

"No, father, I will go with you."

The lansquenet also shook his head, saying "Jungfer, Jungfer, you don't know what a day this is. Thank Our Heavenly Father that you have hitherto escaped so well. The fierce lion has tasted blood. You are a pretty child, and if they should see you to-day...."

"No matter," interrupted the girl. "I know what I am asking. You will take me with you, father! Do so, if you love me! I will find him, if any one can!

"Oh, sir, sir, you look kind and friendly! You have the guard. Escort us; let me seek Ulrich. I shall find him, I know; I must seek him--I must."

The girl's cheeks were glowing; for before her she saw her playfellow, her lover, gasping for breath, with staring eyes, her name upon his dying lips.

Adam sadly shook his head, but Hans Eitelfritz was touched by the girl's eager longing to help the man who was dear to him, so he hastily taxed his inventive brain, saying:

"Perhaps it might be risked....listen to me, Meister! You won't be particularly safe in the streets, yourself, and could hardly reach the rampart without me. I shall lose precious time; but you are his father, and this girl-- is she his sister?--No?--So much the better for him, if he lives! It isn't an easy matter, but it can be done. Yonder good dame will take care of Lelaps for me. Poor dog! That feels good, doesn't it? Well then....I can be here again at midnight. Have you a handcart in the house?"

For coal and iron."

"That will answer. Let the woman make a kettle of soup, and if you have a few hams...."

"There are four in the store-room," cried Ruth.

"Take some bread, a few jugs of wine, and a keg of beer, too, and then follow me quietly. I have the password, my servant will accompany me, and I'll make the Spaniards believe you belong to us, and are bringing my men their supper. Blacken your pretty face a little, my dear girl, wrap yourself up well, and if we find Ulrich we will put him in the empty cart, and I will accompany you home again. Take yonder spicesack, and if we find the poor fellow, dead or alive, hide him with it. The sack was intended for other things, but I shall be well content with this booty. Take care of these silver toys. What pretty things they are! How the little horse rears, and see the bird in the cage! Don't look so fierce, Meister! In catching fish we must be content even with smelts; if I hadn't taken these, others would have done so; they are for my sister's children, and there is something else hidden here in my doublet; it shall help me to pass my leisure hours. One man's meat is another man's poison."

When Hans Eitelfritz returned at midnight, the cart with the food and liquor was ready. Adam's warnings were unavailing. Ruth resolutely insisted upon accompanying him, and he well knew what urged her to risk safety and life as freely as he did himself.

Old Rahel had done her best to conceal Ruth's beauty.

The dangerous nocturnal pilgrimage began.

The smith pulled the cart, and Ruth pushed, Hans Eitelfritz, with his sword-bearer, walking by her side. From time to time Spanish soldiers met and accosted them; but Hans skilfully satisfied their curiosity and dispelled their suspicions.

Pillage and murder had not yet ceased, and Ruth saw, heard, and mistrusted scenes of horror, that congealed her blood. But she bore up until they reached the rampart.

Here Eitelfritz was among his own men.

He delivered the meat and drink to them, told them to take it out of the cart, and invited them to fall to boldly. Then, seizing a lantern, he guided Ruth and the smith, who drew the light cart after them, through the intense darkness of the November night to the rampart.

Hans Eitelfritz lighted the way, and all three searched. Corpse lay beside corpse. Wherever Ruth set her foot, it touched some fallen soldier. Dread, horror and loathing threatened to deprive her of consciousness; but the ardent longing, the one last hope of her soul sustained her, steeled her energy, sharpened her sight.

They had reached the centre of the rampart, when she saw in the distance a tall figure stretched at full length.

That, yes, that was he!

Snatching the lantern from the lansquenet's hand, she rushed to the prostrate form, threw herself on her knees beside it, and cast the light upon the face.

What had she seen?

Why did the shriek she uttered sound so agonized? The men were approaching, but Ruth knew that there was something else to be done, besides weeping and wailing.

She pressed her ear close to the mailed breast to listen, and when she heard no breath, hurriedly unfastened the clasps and buckles that confined the armor.

The cuirass fell rattling on the ground, and now--no, there was no deception, the wounded man's chest rose under her ear, she heard the faint throbbing of his heart, the feeble flutter of a gasping breach.

Bursting into loud, convulsive weeping, she raised his head and pressed it to her bosom.

"He is dead; I thought so!" said the lansquenet, and Adam sank on his knees before his wounded son. But Ruth's sobs now changed to low, joyous, musical laughter, which echoed in her voice as she exclaimed: "Ulrich breathes, he lives! Oh, God! oh, God! how we thank Thee!"

Then--was she deceived, could it be? She heard the inflexible man beside her sob, saw him bend over Ulrich, listen to the beating of his heart, and press his bearded lips first to his temples, then on the hand he had so harshly rejected.

Hans Eitelfritz warned them to hasten, carried the senseless man, with Adam's assistance, to the cart, and half an hour later the dangerously wounded, outcast son was lying in the most comfortable bed in the best room in his father's house. His couch was in the upper story; down in the kitchen old Rahel was moving about the hearth, preparing her "good salve" herself. While thus engaged she often chuckled aloud, murmuring "Ulrich," and while mixing and stirring the mixture could not keep her old feet still; it almost seemed as if she wanted to dance.

Hans Eitelfritz promised Adam to tell no one what had become of his son, and then returned to his men. The next morning the mutineers from Aalst sought their fallen leader; but he had disappeared, and the legend now became wide-spread among them, that the Prince of Evil had carried Navarrete to his own abode. The dog Lelaps died of his wound, and scarcely a week after the pillage of flourishing Antwerp by the "Spanish

Furies," Hans Eitelfritz's regiment was ordered to Ghent. He came with drooping head to the smithy, to take his leave. He had sold his costly booty, and, like so many other pillagers, gambled away the stolen property at the exchange. Nothing was left him of the great day in Antwerp, except the silver toys for his sister's children in Colln on the Spree.

CHAPTER XXXI.

THE fire in the smithy was extinguished, no hammer fell on the anvil; for the wounded man lay in a burning fever; every loud noise disturbed him. Adam had noticed this himself, and gave no time to his work, for he had to assist in nursing his son, when it was necessary to raise his heavy body, and to relieve Ruth, when, after long night-watches, her vigorous strength was exhausted.

The old man saw that the girl's bands were more deft than his own toil-hardened ones, and let her take the principal charge-but the hours when she was resting in her room were the dearest to him, for then he was alone with Ulrich, could read his countenance undisturbed and rejoice in gazing at every feature, which reminded him of his child's boyhood and of Flora.

He often pressed his bearded lips to the invalid's burning forehead or limp hand, and when the physician with an anxious face had left the house, he knelt beside Ulrich's couch, buried his forehead among the pillows, and fervently prayed the Heavenly Father, to spare his child and take in exchange his own life and all that he possessed.

He often thought the end had come, and gave himself up without resistance to his grief; Ruth, on the contrary, never lost hope, not even in the darkest hours. God had not let her find Ulrich, merely to take him from her again. The end of danger was to her the beginning of deliverance. When he recognized her the first time, she already saw him, leaning on her shoulder, walk through the room; when he could raise himself, she thought him cured.

Her heart was overflowing with joy, yet her mind remained watchful and thoughtful during the long, toilsome nursing. She did not forget the smallest trifle, for before she undertook anything she saw in her mind every detail involved, as if it were already completed. Ulrich took no food which she had not prepared with her own hand, no drink which she had not herself brought from the cellar or the well. She perceived in advance what disturbed him, what pleased him, what he needed. If she opened or closed the curtain, she gave or withheld no more light than was agreeable to him; if she arranged the pillows behind him, she placed them neither too high nor too low, and bound up his wounds with a gentle yet firm hand, like an experienced physician. Whatever he felt--pain or comfort--she experienced with him.

By degrees the fever vanished; consciousness returned, his pain lessened, he could move himself again, and began to feel stronger. At first he did not know where he was; then he recognized Ruth, and then his father.

How still, how dusky, how clean everything that surrounded him was! Delightful repose stole over him, pleasant weariness soothed every stormy emotion of his heart. Whenever he opened his eyes, tender, anxious glances met him. Even when the pain returned he enjoyed peaceful, consoling mental happiness. Ruth felt this also, and regarded it as a peerless reward.

When she entered the sick-room with fresh linen, and the odor of lavender her dead mother had liked floated softly to him from the clean sheets, he thought his boyhood had returned, and with it the wise, friendly doctor's house. Elizabeth, the shady pine-woods of his home, its murmuring brooks and luxuriant meadows, again rose before his mind; he saw Ruth and himself listening to the birds, picking berries, gathering flowers, and beseeching beautiful gifts from the "word." His father appeared even more kind, affectionate, and careful than in those days. The man became the boy again, and all his former good traits of character now sprang up freshly under the bright light and vivifying dew of love.

He received Ruth's unwearied attentions with ardent gratitude, and when he gazed into her faithful eyes, when her hand touched him, her soft, deep voice penetrated the depths of his soul, an unexampled sense of happiness filled his breast.

Everything, from the least to the greatest, embraced his soul with the arms of love. It seemed as if the ardent yearning of his heart extended far beyond the earth, and rose to God, who fills the universe with His infinite paternal love. His every breath, Ulrich thought, must henceforth be a prayer, a prayer of gratitude to Him, who is love itself, the Love, through and in which he lived.

He had sought love, to enjoy its gifts; now he was glad to make sacrifices for its sake. He saw how Ruth's beautiful face saddened when he was suffering, and with manly strength of will concealed inexpressible agony under a grateful smile. He feigned sleep, to permit her and his father to rest, and when tortured by feverish restlessness, lay still to give his beloved nurses pleasure and repay their solicitude. Love urged him to goodness, gave him strength for all that is good. His convalescence advanced and, when he was permitted to leave his bed, his father was the first one to support him through the room and down the steps into the court-yard. He often felt with quiet emotion the old man stroke the hand that rested on his arm, and when, exhausted, he returned to the sick-room, he sank with a grateful heart into his comfortable seat, casting a look of pleasure at the flowers, which Ruth had taken from her chamber window and placed on the table beside him.

His family now knew what he had endured and experienced, and the smith found a kind, soothing word for all that, a few months before, he had considered criminal and unpardonable.

During such a conversation, Ulrich once exclaimed "War! You know not how it bears one along with it; it is a game whose stake is life. That of others is of as little value as your own; to do your worst to every one, is the watchword; but now--every thing has grown so calm in my soul, and I have a horror of the turmoil in the field. I was talking with Ruth yesterday about her father, and she reminded me of his favorite saying, which I had forgotten long ago. Do you know what it is? 'Do unto others, as ye would that others should do unto you.' I have not been cruel, and never drew the sword out of pleasure in slaying; but now I grieve for having brought woe to so many!

"What things were done in Haarlem! If you had moved there instead of to Antwerp, and you and Ruth....I dare not think of it! Memories of those days torture me in many a sleepless hour, and there is much that fills me with bitter remorse. But I am permitted to live, and it seems as if I were new-born, and henceforth existence and doing good must be synonymous to me. You were right to be angry...."

"That is all forgiven and forgotten," interrupted the smith in a resonant voice, pressing his son's fingers with his hard right hand.

These words affected the convalescent like a strengthening potion, and when the hammers again moved in the smithy, Ulrich was no longer satisfied with his idle life, and began with Ruth to look forward to and discuss the future.

The words: 'fortune,' 'fame,' 'power,'" he said once, "have deceived me; but art! You don't know, Ruth, what art is! It does not bestow everything, but a great deal, a great deal. Meister Moor was indeed a teacher! I am too old to begin at the beginning once more. If it were not for that...."

"Well, Ulrich?"

"I should like to try painting again."

The girl exhorted him to take courage, and told his father of their conversation. The smith put on his Sunday clothes and went to the artist's house. The latter was in Brussels, but was expected home soon.

From this time, every third day, Adam donned his best clothes, which he disliked to wear, and went to the artist's; but always in vain.

In the month of February the invalid was playing chess with Ruth,-- she had learned the game from the smith and Ulrich from her,--when Adam entered the room, saying: "when the game is over, I wish to speak to you, my son."

The young girl had the advantage, but instantly pushed the pieces together and left the two alone.

She well knew what was passing in the father's mind, for the day before he had brought all sorts of artist's materials, and told her to arrange the little gable-room, with the large window facing towards the north, and put the easel and colors there. They had only smiled at each other, but they had long since learned to understand each other, even without words.

"What is it?" asked Ulrich in surprise.

The smith then told him what he had provided and arranged, adding: "the picture on the standard--you say you painted it yourself."

"Yes, father."

"It was your mother, exactly as she looked when....She did not treat either of us rightly--but she!--the Christian must forgive;--and as she was your mother--why--I should like.... perhaps it is not possible; but if you could paint her picture, not as a Madonna, only as she looked when a young wife...."

"I can, I will!" cried Ulrich, in joyous excitement. "Take me upstairs, is the canvas ready?"

"In the frame, firmly in the frame! I am an old man, and you see, child, I remember how wonderfully sweet your mother was; but I can never succeed in recalling just how she looked then. I have tried, tried thousands and thousands of times; at--Richtberg, here, everywhere--deep as was my wrath!"

"You shall see her again surely--surely!" interrupted Ulrich. "I see her before me, and what I see in my mind, I can paint!"

The work was commenced the very same day. Ulrich now succeeded wonderfully, and lavished on the portrait all the wealth of love, with which his heart was filled.

Never had he guided the brush so joyously; in painting this picture he only wished to give, to give--give his beloved father the best he could accomplish, so he succeeded.

The young wife, attired in a burgher dress, stood with her bewitching eyes and a melancholy, half-tender, half-mournful smile on her lips.

Adam was not permitted to enter the studio again until the portrait was completed. When Ulrich at last unveiled the picture, the old man--unable longer to control himself--burst into loud sobs and fell upon his son's breast. It seemed to Adam that the pretty creature in the golden frame -- far from needing his forgiveness--was entitled to his gratitude for many blissful hours.

Soon after, Adam found Moor at home, and a few hours later took Ulrich to him. It was a happy and a quiet meeting, which was soon followed by a second interview in the smith's house.

Moor gazed long and searchingly at Ulrich's work. When he had examined it sufficiently, he held out his hand to his pupil, saying warmly:

"I always said so; you are an artist! From to-morrow we will work together again, daily, and you will win more glorious victories with the brush than with the sword."

Ulrich's cheeks glowed with happiness and pride.

Ruth had never before seen him look so, and as she gazed joyfully into his eyes, he held out his hands to her, exclaiming: "An artist, an artist again! Oh, would that I had always remained one! Now I lack only one thing more--yourself!"

She rushed to his embrace, exclaiming joyously "Yours, yours! I have always been so, and always shall be, to-day, to-morrow, unto death, forever and ever!"

"Yes, yes," he answered gravely. "Our hearts are one and ever will be, nothing can separate them; but your fate shall not be linked to mine till, Moor himself calls me a master. Love imposes no condition--I am yours and you are mine--but I impose the trial on myself, and this time I know it will be passed."

A new spirit animated the pupil. He rushed to his work with tireless energy, and even the hardest task became easy, when he thought of the prize he sought. At the end of a year, Moor ceased to instruct him, and Ruth became the wife of Meister Ulrich Schwab.

The famous artist-guild of Antwerp soon proudly numbered him among them, and even at the present day his pictures are highly esteemed by connoisseurs, though they are attributed to other painters, for he never signed his name to his works.

Of the four words, which illumined his life-path as guiding-stars, he had learned to value fame and power least; fortune and art remained faithful to him, but as the earth does not shine by its own might, but receives its light from the sun, so they obtained brilliancy, charm and endearing power through love.

The fierce Eletto, whose sword raged in war, following the teachings of his noble Master, became a truly Christian philanthropist.

Many have gazed with quiet delight at the magnificent picture, which represents a beautiful mother, with a bright, intelligent face, leading her three blooming children towards a pleasant old man, who holds out his arms to them. The old man is Adam, the mother Ruth, the children are the armorer's grandchildren; Ulrich Schwab was the artist.

Meister Moor died soon after Ulrich's marriage, and a few years after, Sophonisba di Moncada came to Antwerp to seek the grave of him she had loved. She knew from the dead man that he had met his dear Madrid pupil, and her first visit was to the latter.

After looking at his works, she exclaimed:

"The word! Do you remember, Meister? I told you then, that you had found the right one. You are greatly altered, and it is a pity that you have lost your flowing locks; but you look like a happy man, and to what do you owe it? To the word, the only right word: 'Art!'"

He let her finish the sentence, then answered gravely "There is still a loftier word, noble lady! Whoever owns it--is rich indeed. He will no longer wander--seek in doubt.

"And this is?" she asked incredulously, with a smile of superior knowledge.

"I have found it," he answered firmly. "It is 'Love.'"

Sophonisba bent her head, saying softly and sadly: "yes, yes--love."